Mollie's Quest

Havoc in Wyoming

Part 3: Mollie's Quest

Millie Copper

Copyright © 2019 CU Publishing
ISBN-13: 978-1-7327482-4-8

Written by Millie Copper

Edited by Ameryn Tucker

Proofread by Light Hand Proofreading

Cover design by Kesandra Adams

Also by Millie Copper

Now Available

Havoc in Wyoming: Part 1, Caldwell's Homestead

Havoc in Wyoming: Part 2, Katie's Journey

Havoc in Wyoming: Part 4, Shields and Ramparts

Havoc Begins: A Havoc in Wyoming Story

Stock the Real Food Pantry: A Handbook for Making the Most of Your Pantry

Design a Dish: Save Your Food Dollars

Real Food Hits the Road: Budget Friendly Tips, Ideas, and Recipes for Enjoying Real Food Away from Home

Coming Soon

Havoc in Wyoming: Part 5, Fowler's Snare

Join my reader's club! Receive a complimentary copy of *Wyoming Refuge: A Havoc in Wyoming Prequel*. As part of my reader's club, you'll be the first to know about new releases and specials. I also share info on books I'm reading, preparedness tips, and more. Please sign up on my website:

MillieCopper.com

Who's Who

Mollie Caldwell: Wife to Jake and mom to daughters Sarah, Angela, Calley, and Katie plus ten-year-old son Malcolm. With a full-time, work-from-home job, homeschooling Malcolm, and their small farm—she keeps busy. Mollie and Jake have been working to repair their once broken marriage. Things are better, but a closely guarded secret may change things.

Jake Caldwell: Single until age thirty-seven, he married Mollie and suddenly became a dad to four girls. A couple years later, they added their son. Jake juggles work, a farm, and family life—sometimes it's a struggle.

Malcolm Caldwell: Jake and Mollie's youngest child. He's *almost* eleven and is Jake's right-hand man. He's the only child still living at home.

Sarah Garrett: Mollie's oldest daughter, wife to Tate. They recently moved less than two hours away from Mollie and Jake, neighbors by Wyoming standards. Tate's parents, Keith and Lois, along with his older sister, Karen, are visiting from Oklahoma.

Katrina "Katie" Andrews: Mollie's youngest daughter, a twenty-one-year-old college student working toward a graphic design degree at K-State.

Leo Burnett: Katie's boyfriend. A business major at K-State, construction worker, and Marine.

Calista "Calley" Curtis: Mollie's second to the youngest daughter. Calley and her husband, Mike, make their home in Casper, Wyoming. Mike's parents, Roy and Deanne, live next door. Mike's recently single sister, Sheila Stapleton, also lives in Casper. They're a tight-knit family, at least it seems so on the surface.

Angela Carpenter: Mollie's second to oldest daughter, wife to Tim and mom to two-year-old Gavin, living in Casper, Wyoming.

Alvin and Dodie Caldwell: Jake's parents. They're both in their seventies and fiercely independent. They live nearby Mollie and Jake in Prospect, Wyoming. As things progress, they worry about Jake's brother, Robert, and his wife and children living in California. Have they been severely affected by these tragedies?

Doris and Evan Snyder: Neighbor and good friends of Mollie and Jake. Evan is a retired deputy sheriff, having been part of the Specialized Services Division. Doris is retired from both the Navy and a government job. She insists she wasn't a spy or anything, but she doesn't talk about the work she used to do.

Dan Morse: The community bully. He tends to make a show of knowing it all. Evan calls Dan "an imbecile who lacks a shred of common sense."

Belinda and TJ Bosco: Community members. Belinda, a nurse practitioner, is fourth generation Bakerville and related to the founders of the community. TJ is friends with Malcolm. Belinda's mom, Tammy, a retired labor and delivery nurse, and dad, Tom, a retired hunting and fishing guide, also live in the community.

Phil and Kelley Hudson: Community members. Mollie considers Kelley one of her closest friends. Phil, retired Coast Guard, is a leader of the community. Kelley is a psychiatric nurse practitioner, retired from Commissioned Corps.

Olivia Hatch: Nearby neighbor of Mollie and Jake. Katie and Olivia become fast friends. Olivia's son, Tony, is friends with Malcolm, and her young daughter, Lily, loves everyone. Olivia's husband, Jason, is away for work.

Chapter 1

Sunday

The roar of the engine makes it difficult to hear anything, except the person sitting next to me. His rather strong coffee breath, combined with the stench of the toilet, has my olfactory system wanting to shut down.

This small plane sports twelve double seats on the right and thirteen on the left. My seat, 13B, is at the very back, right next to the lavatory. I chose this seat on purpose. Most people don't want to sit back here, and I often have the entire row to myself. Unfortunately, on this full flight, we're packed in like sardines in a can.

My coffee breath is likely not much better. I take out a breath strip, then offer one to my seatmate. I'm grateful when he accepts.

"Some beautiful country here," he gushes. "I was up here visiting a friend. He took me to Yellowstone and up in the Big Horns where we did some fishing outside of Saddlestring. Amazing. Just amazing. You live here?"

I nod as he asks, "Vacationing in Salt Lake?"

"No, just connecting on to PDX. I work about an hour and half from Portland."

"You live in Cody and work in Oregon?"

"Not exactly. I live outside of Prospect, not too far from Cody, and usually work from home. A few times a year I need to work on-site. Been doing it for a while. It works real well for my family."

"Your husband doesn't mind you being gone?"

"He's a good sport about it," I answer, thinking of this morning's argument in which he really wasn't a good sport.

It started simply enough when I asked Jake, "Do you have the to-do list and a plan for your week?" Things went downhill from there. We ended up in a bit of a tiff—never a good way to start the morning. Especially not good when I'll be gone for five days.

1

It ended up okay, though, when Jake said, "Okay, Mollie. I'm sorry to be such a bear this morning. I'm feeling overwhelmed, and I do hate it when you're gone."

A few months ago, he wanted me gone permanently, so I kind of enjoy hearing this. Like most marriages, there was a time we couldn't get enough of each other. Yes, the new eventually wears off, but for us, it was more. Our trouble started with a phone call. The kind of phone call no one wants to receive.

With my woolgathering, I realize I missed my seatmate talking to me. "I'm sorry, what was that?"

"I said, I've been to Portland a few times. Pretty, but it rained each time I was there."

"Yeah, rain is one of the reasons I no longer live in Oregon. June usually isn't too terrible, so it should be fairly nice this week."

"Mm-hmm, I think I was there in February. I live outside Salt Lake City. I love it there. Of course, I thought Cody was real nice too. There are some similarities. You able to garden?"

"We do have a decent garden, but it takes some work. Our annual precipitation is only around ten inches, and with the wind and heat, the moisture easily evaporates. Some crops do better than others."

He nods in understanding. "Yeah. I guess that's why Wyoming is cattle country. You raise beef?"

"No. We only have thirty acres. We raise goats, chickens, sheep, and pigs along with having the garden, a small orchard, plus assorted vines," I answer.

"Sounds like you folks are kind of self-sufficient. Smart."

"Well… I wouldn't go that far. We do what we can."

"You know anything about Mormons?" he asks.

"Some," I don't want to tell him I have used the LDS storehouse many times.

"I'm Mormon, and we're encouraged to have basic food and water along with savings. We used to be commanded to keep a year supply of food, but that was too hard, so now it's three months, plus more if you can. 'Course, some people take it to an extreme and have the old one-year amount, plus do more beyond. I don't know… I kind of feel like anything beyond what's expected of us is excessive, and maybe even borders on hoarding."

I stifle a laugh. No doubt he'd think Jake and I are hoarders.

Our home is full of long-term food storage goods, clothing in assorted sizes, and more. He'd be really amazed if I told him we subscribe to the old-school LDS guidelines in our own life and store a year of food per family member—and not just for the three of us living at home.

We store for my husband's parents, our adult children, their spouses, our grandchild, and even some members of the children's spouses' immediate family. Our basement resembles a warehouse.

Our little farm isn't just a farm, but a retreat for our loved ones. With our home, a studio apartment, a bunkhouse, and a cabin, we can comfortably house twenty-eight people, including my husband, ten-year-old son, and myself—even more if we squeeze.

He'd probably really think I'm nuts if I told him about our combination safe room and fallout shelter. But, of course, I say nothing. Admitting to being a prepper and sharing the extent of preps just isn't done while chatting with a stranger on an airplane.

Chapter 2

I'm at the Salt Lake City Airport waiting for my next flight, watching the people and somewhat paying attention to the news channel.

"Grover, Wyoming, home of last month's tragic school shooting, is once again in the news. Sheriff Deputy Ray Sandoval was shot in the line of duty. His killer is still at large and there are no suspects…"

What? Grover again? Now a deputy killed? And the school shooting, in Wyoming… people said it could never happen here.

While it was terrible, and three adults lost their lives, the shooters were taken down before anyone else was killed. Credit for this was given to a husband and wife visiting their child's classroom.

The stories out after the shooting were interesting. Dr. and Dr. Mitchell—the husband a physician, and the wife a chiropractor—were interviewed and stated the school was "attacked by two men." However, there was a third man, barely out of boyhood, already dead when they found him.

The men were dressed in all black and wearing what was referred to as combat clothes. The boy was in jeans and T-shirt. The school's secretary backed up this information, saying she was sure the boy was dead before the others and she knew the Mitchells didn't do it. The gym teacher, also quick to come to the Mitchells' aid, collaborated the boy being nowhere near the men or the Mitchells.

The boy's mom was found dead in her house down the road. The boy was known by friends and family to be somewhat of a loner. There was very little information about the two men the Mitchells killed. A report was leaked saying they carried no ID and their fingerprints weren't in any databases.

A few days after the shooting, the gym teacher died in a car accident. Then the secretary disappeared; her body was soon found, and the cause of death was declared a suicide by carbon monoxide poisoning. Then the Mitchell family disappeared. They've yet to be located.

To say the conspiracy theorists' tongues were wagging would be an understatement. Jake and I had discussed this a few times, and we both

4

felt it sounded a little fishy. We've been waiting for the Mitchell family to be found dead, following some sort of tragic accident.

Grover has certainly had its share of tragedy lately. Could the deputy's death be related to the school shooting? I don't think of myself as a conspiracy theorist—not really, anyway. I believe events many called hoaxes actually happened. Perhaps not the same way we're led to believe they happened.

Truth is, I may be more of a conspiracist than the average person, but I just don't take the time to pursue all the rabbit trails. I tend to go with my gut and exercise a healthy dose of skepticism in most cases. One thing I definitely avoid is trusting the bulk of what's being touted on mainstream media. Yeah, I guess it makes me one of "those people."

Chapter 3

The SLC to PDX leg of my trip is uneventful. Since I only have a carry-on, I quickly get my rental car and hit the road. In less than two hours, I'm at the shop. I've worked for father and son, Bart and Ben, for twelve years now. When Jake and I decided to move from Oregon to Wyoming, they offered to keep me on as a telecommuter. Working from home over the internet was pretty rare back then, but it was an answer to our prayers.

At first, I was only part time, doing the bookkeeping, payroll, and whatever else they needed. But as the business has grown, so have my responsibilities, to include online marketing, managing our quality system, and more.

I now work full time from home, except for two one-week trips each year when I come back for meetings and an audit of our quality management system.

Even though I'm full time, my hours are somewhat flexible, making sure I'm available whenever the shop is functioning. It's working well, for the most part, and the pay is quite nice. In addition to a generous base, I receive a commission on work I bring in from my online efforts, plus quarterly bonuses.

The pay has been great for helping Jake and I achieve our personal goals. We try to live carefully and stretch our money as best we can, but we do add in a few fun things when I make a great sale.

The shop is a half hour east of Alto and the nearest hotel. Because of the distance, I usually stay with Ben and his family. I cram a lot into the week I work on-site—appointments with the CPA and attorney, plus an audit of our quality management system are all happening.

When my daughters were younger, they, along with my son, Malcolm, would sometimes join me on my work trips. Then we'd get a hotel and make an event out of it.

When Malcolm alone joins me, we still stay with Ben's family. Malcolm and Liam, Ben's son, are friends. There's probably a slight hero worship going on over thirteen-year-old Liam. Liam is a very good sport about it, but I know he's always happy when our visit ends.

Clarice, Ben's wife, always tries to make my stay as restful as possible, doing little things to spoil me. Their hospitality takes a lot of the discomfort out of traveling. My biggest trouble when staying with Ben and Clarice is the terrible cell phone reception I get.

Jake and I try to talk when I'm in the office during the week, and we can usually text when I'm at Ben's house. Sometimes I can even get a phone signal if I hold my phone up in the air, stand on one leg, and do a jig. Just kidding about the jig. I've tried; it didn't help.

Chapter 4

Thursday, Day 1

My week has gone well, and Jake and I do the best we can to keep in touch during the week. We take a few minutes to talk each morning and again at the end of my day, using the office landline. Then we text our goodnights before bed.

Jake is a ten-month employee with the school district, meaning he doesn't have work when school isn't in session. He usually takes a summer job with the custodial or grounds crew, going from school to school to do deep cleaning or yard work.

This year, the school district had huge budget cuts and decided to forgo extra help on the grounds. The custodians will start two weeks before school begins and just do what they can. So, Jake's working on our small farm.

It's not really what he wanted to be doing, but it seems to be going well. We made a to-do list so he could catch up on things we've been neglecting and get the place back in shape. We're talking about liquidating the farm—selling all the livestock, shrinking the garden, and letting things go.

We've had trouble in our marriage the last couple years. We're better, but we're discovering neither of us really want to be farmers any longer.

The main event of my on-site work, the audit of our quality management system, is happening today.

Shortly before we wrap up, the secretary calls me to the reception area.

"Mollie, there's a call for you. I told him you were in the middle of something, but he insisted it was important and would only take a minute."

"Sure, I can take it. Jim's doing his paperwork, so I'll take it in the production room. Which line?"

"Parked on line one."

Even though I usually work from home, with today's technology, I'm still well-connected to the office, with my phone from home tying into the office phones so I can make and receive calls under the company umbrella. It's a pretty slick setup and really makes things easy. As such, I'm used to receiving many calls in a day, so this is nothing unusual.

"Good afternoon, Mollie Caldwell. How may I help you?"

"It's Brad. Don't hang up."

I suck in my breath. I want nothing more than to slam the phone down, just like I've done the last four times he's called. Instead, I say, "I've asked you not to contact me."

"I know you think you can put me off, but you can't. I'm not going away."

"You are going away. I want nothing to do with you," I hiss.

"We have unfinished business."

"We have no business. Goodbye."

"I want the truth. Tell me now or I'll show up on your doorstep."

"I've told you, you're wasting your time. What you think you know is... it's wrong. You're mistaken."

"I've seen pictures! I know what I've seen."

"We are done. Do not contact me again."

"I wasn't lying about showing up on your doorstep. I have business in Wyoming. It's not even out of my way to show up in Bakerville."

He knows I live in Bakerville?

"Leave me alone or I'll contact the authorities."

Now I slam the phone down. My mouth is dry, and tears are threatening to spill over. I can't believe Brad is contacting me. And, if he's still the Brad I used to know, he wasn't lying about showing up on my doorstep.

"Mollie?" Jill hollers from the reception area. "Jim's ready to finish the audit."

I shake my head and straighten my shoulders. I'll deal with this when I get home. I'll finally talk with Jake about it, and we'll make a plan together.

9

Chapter 5

We cut out of work early today. Bart, Ben, Clarice, and Liam are treating me to dinner at an upscale restaurant in Alto.

Even though I pack light for these trips, I include a semi-nice outfit since dinner is a tradition when I visit. While I have the nice outfit, I left my jewelry bag at home, so I'm completely without accessories. Not a big deal at all but slightly annoying.

My "nice" outfit is a knee-length sleeveless dress in midnight blue with white birds and leaves. The wrinkle-resistant jersey material makes it a wonderful item for travel. This basic dress can easily go from casual to semi-dressy by changing out the shoes and accessories.

Of course, my lack of accessories means I'm somewhat limited in how dressy I can be. My traveling outfit included gold, small-hooped earrings and an oversized scarf in off-white with a gold thread. I've found, even in summer, airplanes are often chilly when inflight, and a large scarf makes me much more comfortable. With the scarf tied loosely around my shoulders as a shrug, gold earrings, and ballet flats, I decide I don't look too bad.

I wear my dark brown hair in a pixie cut and give it a little extra styling gel to add some height on top. The brown has a nice sheen to it since I'm only a week past my last color job. Without the color, I sport patches of gray. Sometimes I'll try to go without dying and let the natural color grow in, but the gray, while not terrible, seems to have a mind of its own and grows in oddly. For now, I'll stick with the fake color.

I've often been told I don't look my age and was still being ID'd into my midthirties. Now, two months into my fiftieth year, I think I definitely do look my age but work hard to stay active and defy the aging process as best I can. It's not that I'm in denial; it's more that I plan to keep my health as long as I can.

God gave me a physical body, wonderfully made. I realized I owed it to him to care for it. Plus, I was getting the dreaded middle-age spread. Yikes.

At only five foot two, I'm short. I try to focus on my health and aim to be strong, as opposed to skinny. I make a point of having movement and physical activity as part of my day—aiming for forty-five minutes to an hour of dedicated movement each day. It's not always easy!

At home, caring for our small farm is a workout in itself. In addition, I shoot for a daily form of exercise, preferring yoga, walking, and kickboxing. I'll also add in Zumba and yoga classes at our community center when my schedule permits. We like family fitness through hiking and backpacking during the summers and skiing and snowshoeing in the winters.

Last fall Jake, Malcolm, and I started taking a self-defense martial art called Yongmudo. What a workout! I like how it uses some of the kickboxing moves but takes it all a step further.

We started learning Yongmudo specifically for the self-defense aspect of it. We had no idea the workouts would be so intense, or that there was a smaller community within the greater martial arts community.

We have two classes a week and also practice at home—noncontact sparring with each other to sharpen our skills. Noncontact is the key. Sometimes we'll accidentally connect… never a good thing. We've even had a few private classes with our Master, specifically to hone in on the defender skills. Yongmudo is a great close-in style and uses technique rather than strength, making it very effective for smaller, slighter framed individuals like Malcolm and me.

This week, while working away from home, I've still managed to get in some form of exercise each day. I'm not what people refer to as a "natural athlete," and if I'm honest, I'd rather skip exercise all together. But I've found daily physical activity helps me in many ways—not just combatting the effects of age on my body; I sleep better and think more clearly. Plus, I'm preparing for my first 5K over the Fourth of July, so I can't afford to take the week off.

Even though I don't look too bad for our dinner out, Clarice looks amazing. She's tall, at five-ten, with the body of a dancer: very lean and willowy. Ten years younger than me, she's able to maintain her physique without effort. Yes, I'm jealous regular workouts and paying attention to my diet are necessary to keep me from ballooning up.

Tonight, she's wearing the quintessential little black dress. It's a beautifully fitted wrap style with three-quarter length sleeves and a tying sash belt. The lightly flared skirt falls to a flirty hem ending just above the knee, showing off her shapely, long legs. Four-inch stiletto, black suede, open-toe heels with a single toe band and an ankle strap complete the look. Yeah, I'm suddenly feeling a little on the frumpy side.

We try a new restaurant in town, which is quite nice. The wait staff is attentive, and the food is wonderful. They each order steak. We eat a lot of steak at home, usually elk or venison, so I order the oysters. Amazing.

Chapter 6

After dinner, Ben, Clarice, and I are relaxing in their living room. Since I'm heading home tomorrow, we're getting the last of our visiting in and planning for my next visit. I'm returning in October for a marketing event at the Portland Convention Center. The TV is on, as background only, while we make our plans.

"So, I think we should order embroidered shirts this time to help with marketing our company," Clarice says.

"You really think we need that?" Ben, ever mindful of our bottom dollar, asks.

"I think it'd make us look more professional. Remember the last thing like this we went to, most of the companies had matching shirts."

"I thought we looked fine. Mollie had us all wear black shirts. It was close enough," Ben shrugs.

I'm making notes on my computer and look up when the conversation halts. Clarice is staring at the television, a look of horror on her face. Ben, oblivious, is looking at his phone. I turn to the TV screen and see the ticker across the bottom of the screen.

BREAKING NEWS
PLANES CRASH WHILE LANDING AT LAX, JFK AND ORD
TERRORISTS EXPECTED

"Ben," Clarice says, nudging his arm.

"What?"

"Hand me the remote. I want to change to the news station."

"Oh no," I say.

Ben stares at the TV for a moment before grabbing the remote and switching the channel.

We're quiet, dumbfounded, until Ben asks, "Where's ORD?"

"Chicago, I think. I think he said Chicago," Clarice answers.

"Was Jim flying into LAX?" I ask Ben.

"Uh… I don't know. I know he lives out of LA but not sure if he was flying into there. Man, I hope it wasn't his plane that went down."

Jim was here today, auditing our procedures. He's been our auditor since we started this quality system almost ten years ago. To think he might be on one of the flights that crashed... I struggle to keep from crying.

As the male newscaster continues, the female sitting next to him breaks in. *"Paul, we're receiving reports of a fourth crash. This crash is at Dallas/Fort Worth. Again, within the last few minutes, planes have crashed while attempting to land at Los Angeles, John F. Kennedy, Chicago O'Hare, and just minutes ago, Dallas/Fort Worth International Airports. We're still confirming the DFW crash but believe this information to be accurate."*

"It certainly sounds like a planned attack," Ben says. Clarice and I nod in agreement.

"Mom, Dad, I think there was some kind of plane crash," Liam yells down from his room.

"We're watching it on TV," Clarice answers. He comes into the living room and sits down near his mom, and she hugs him close. There's no word of survivors from any of the crashes. It's likely each plane had at least two hundred people on board. I'm still thinking of Jim and praying he's okay.

My text indicator goes off. It's Jake. He's trying to call me but can't get through. I run upstairs to try connecting from my bedroom—no success. We settle on texting so I can watch the news at the same time.

Clarice switches around to a different station and sees a ticker indicating all planes are being grounded. With an average of over three thousand flights in the US per hour, it will take some time to get everyone on the ground.

Unfortunately, there's another crash as a plane is coming into Miami. We watch the news for a bit longer before finding out the LAX crash originated in Atlanta. I breathe a sigh of relief it wasn't Jim's plane.

Five plane crashes in just over half an hour. The crashes were at five of the busiest airports in the US. All flights originating and landing in the US have been grounded. I pull out my computer to check my flight. I'm sure it's canceled for tomorrow but check anyway. Right now, it's showing as delayed.

Clarice turns to me. "I'm sure you won't be able to fly home tomorrow. You know you can stay as long as needed."

"Do you remember how long air travel was grounded after 9/11?" Ben asks.

"Only a couple days," Clarice says.

"Yeah, but this could be different," Liam offers. "How are they crashing the planes? Are they using rockets? It kind of sounds like they think it's rockets. They'd have a hard time preventing rockets from crashing planes."

He's right. There isn't anything I can do about this mess. I'm going to get ready for bed and then try to reach Jake. I'm dressing when Clarice knocks on my door and says, "Mollie, there's more trouble."

I open the door a crack, poking my head out, as she says, "We were watching the news in our room. There's been an explosion at the airport in New York, separate from the crash. They think it was a bomb, possibly more than one. Do you want to come down to watch?"

I definitely do. My phone rings, causing me to jump. Jake. I'm surprised he got through.

"Give me just a minute, then I'll be down."

At my hello, Jake says, "There's been an explosion, or maybe even multiple explosions, in New York."

"Clarice just told me. I was going to go down and watch the TV. Is anyone claiming responsibility? Surely everyone knows this is related."

"It seems they do. Oh, they're saying the president is going to speak in a few minutes."

"With my plane canceled, I wonder how long they'll remain grounded if it's missiles being shot. How do you defend against that?"

"I have no idea. I think you should keep the rental car and drive home tomorrow. I don't like you being there with all of this going on. I'm glad you took the suitcase, the get-home bag, with you before. You may need it. I'm calling Doris after we hang up to see if Malcolm can stay with her while I run into town. I'm going with *Plan A*."

"It's a good idea," I agree. "What about the children? Katie is so far from home."

"I think we should encourage them to do their own *Plan A*. I feel like these are simply terrorist attacks as opposed to our country being under attack, you know? What do you think?"

"That's how I feel. But with Katie being so far away, she'd have a super hard time getting home if things went bad quick. That scares me. I'm so glad Sarah and Tate live nearby now. Angela, Tim, and Gavin would have a long trip if they had to walk, but they could do it. I know Calley says she'll stay at her home and band together with Mike's family. You know how I feel about that... I just wish she was still a little girl and I could tell her what to do. Suggest they enact *Plan A*, yeah... I guess that's all we can do."

"Yes, uh, can you do the thing where you text them all at the same time? Just suggest to implement *Plan A*. Don't push them too much. Tread easy, Mollie."

Oh no he didn't. Did he just imply I don't know how not to overreact to this with my girls?

"Jake. I'm well aware of the need to tread easy. I think I know them pretty well. And, yes, I know they aren't fully onboard with all our... plans... especially Calley. I can handle this."

"Sorry, honey. I know you can handle it. And, honestly, it's better for you to be the one sending the text. Besides, I can never remember how to do that group thing you do."

Jake gives a weak laugh before rushing on with, "I know what you mean about Calley. You raised her to be an independent person. She'll do what she feels is best, with Mike's input. You can't blame her husband for wanting to stay with his folks. He knows they're all welcome here, but this will be a last resort for them."

I'm thinking about what Jake has said, but apparently my pause was longer than intended.

"Are you still there?" he says.

"Yes. I'm here. Just thinking. It's just so... cliché."

"What is?"

"You know, this... I can't even tell you how many end-of-the-world books I've read where the husband and wife are apart when the trouble happens. It's such a tired story line."

"Uh-huh, only this isn't one of those books. This is really happening."

"Uh... right. I know that. It's just so beyond my belief it *is* happening. And I know we discussed it could, and we made provisions and plans for it, but... I never really thought... I mean, seriously, Jake. I'm gone so rarely the odds should've been I'd be at home."

"We can't control things like this. Sure, the timing is terrible, but it has happened."

I have tears running down my cheeks. I know he's right, and as strange as the timing is, it's happened.

"Mollie, honey, let's pray," Jake says softly.

Just his suggesting we pray fills me with hope. There was a time, not long ago, when he wouldn't have even thought to petition God with our concerns. Neither of us would have. In fact, I didn't even think of it tonight. Even though I'm saved by Christ, I tend to want to do things on my own instead of relying on God's strength through the difficult times.

"Yes, let's pray."

"Our Heavenly Father, we come to you tonight with heavy hearts. We are... shocked over these events—the planes, which have been purposefully crashed, and now the explosions. Please be with the families who have experienced loss tonight. Let them feel your comfort. I ask you be with Mollie and bring her home to us quickly and safely. And be with our daughters, to keep them away from harm. If it's your will, Lord, please use this tragedy to fully open their hearts to you. Please give Malcolm and me strength while we wait for Mollie to return. It's hard for me to agree to sit idly by and not rush to her rescue. I'll need your help with this, Lord. We pray these things in Jesus' holy name, amen."

I sniff. "Thank you. I love you, Jake. I'm going to go watch the news for a bit. Stay in touch as best you can. And kiss Malcolm for me."

As we hang up, I think about his words. I love that he remembered to include our girls. My four daughters are grown adults with lives of their own. Some people would classify them as Prodigal Daughters. While none are off doing wild and crazy things, only my youngest, Katie, has a close relationship with God... to the point of even talking about doing mission work.

At one point, all four of the girls had something similar to Katie's ardor. Then Jamie, my first husband, died. I ended up in a bad place and stopped going to his church. I'd take the girls, dropping them off and going for a coffee, then pick them up when they were done. I know this has a lot to do with where my children are with their own spiritual walk. The guilt doesn't do me any good.

Chapter 7

I let out a large sigh and compose a group text to my four adult daughters. *"Jake and I are enacting Plan A. You should think about doing this also. We don't know what tomorrow will bring. We included information on Plan A in your backpack on the sheet: Smart Practices. I love you."*

Plan A is something we've discussed and perfected over time. Our homestead is our home base, a retreat, and where we want to be in an emergency situation. If an emergency hits and we're away, we make our way back home. If the emergency is immediate, say an EMP, then we go straight home—likely on foot.

I read the book *One Second After*, and it scared the daylights out of me. I shared the highlights with Jake. We've both read *Alas, Babylon*, one of my favorites, and felt the warning Mark gave Randy in the book, so he had time to get things together, made sense. If we're in what we feel is a warning time, we call it *Plan A*.

Since we moved up to our thirty-acre farm in Bakerville, we've been preparing a retreat for our children to join us if the need were to arise. Over the last few months, we started talking about how they'd get there. So, we created bug-out bags for each of them.

Even though all of the children know about the retreat we've been creating, it wasn't until after we sent the bags they realized we were serious. When we visited at Easter, Angela and Tim sent us home with a carload of food storage items to add to our collection. Katie started having food shipped to us, and Sarah and Tate sent cash while in Oregon and have brought food over twice since moving nearby.

And then there's Calley… Last summer Calley married Mike. He was "the boy next door." They were friends in middle school, started dating in high school, and waited until they were both twenty-two to get married.

Their beautiful wedding was an elaborate outdoor event. Calley put a lot of time and effort into the perfect decorations; white fabric and white lights, along with plenty of candles, lined the reception area, giving it almost a fairyland feel. The outdoor wedding site overlooked Casper Mountain. The weather cooperated and the famous Wyoming wind stayed away. Calley said it was exactly the wedding she envisioned.

Calley and Mike are buying our previous home in Casper. They love the location, right next door to Mike's parents, and we were able to give them a good deal. Plus, with the shop and small acreage, it's a great place for Mike to be able to do backyard mechanic work. It's a nice pastime for him, and he brings in a little extra money buying cheap cars, fixing them up, and selling them for a small profit.

Out of all of the girls, Calley has always been the least receptive to our preparedness ways. While Calley and Mike did thank us for the backpacks, they let us know, in no uncertain terms, they had no intentions of leaving their place.

First, they can't imagine any event that would make them to need to leave. And second, if something did happen, they'd just band together with Mike's folks and ride it out. They also figure their next-door neighbors Sue and Adam, our good friends from when we lived there, would be an asset.

Sue and Adam have an amazing garden and greenhouse area along with several fruit trees, chickens, and pigeons. The things they're able to do on their two-acre parcel is inspiring. I suspect they also have a very full pantry and several other secrets, which leads me to believe they're preppers to some degree.

I love that Calley has her own mind, but my mama heart hurts to think she wouldn't want to come up with us. We've even made it very clear Mike's family is also welcome.

To put our money where our mouth is, we've included their numbers in our plans, adding extra bulk foods to accommodate four adults—Mike's mom, dad, sister, and brother-in-law. Nothing fancy, just many pounds of beans and grains, but it will keep them from starving.

Of course, our greatest hope and prayer is we're never faced with a situation where Casper is so dangerous, they need to come to our place. My second hope is, if there was an imminent danger, Calley and Mike would recognize it and hotfoot it to our place.

Chapter 8

The limited news coming out of New York is bad. The explosions happened in and around JFK. It's suspected there was an ambulance loaded with explosives. There were several other smaller detonations around the airport. The president makes a very brief announcement detailing what is known, and indicating we will prevail. He's on for only a few minutes, his speech reminding me of President Bush's speech after 9/11.

I've seen enough. I'm going to take action and enact my own *Plan A*. I run upstairs and change back into street clothes.

Last year, on one of my trips out here, I brought a large suitcase with me. This checked bag contains a backpack and supplies to create a "get-home bag." Even though this bag gives me a good start, there are several additional items I'd like to add. The nearby gas station and convenience store will provide many of these things.

On my way to the gas station, the news reports bombings in each of the plane crash cities. It's believed the first responders were targeted, along with people in and around the airport.

Once again, I think of my friend Jim—not about him being on one of the crashed planes, since we now know the flight didn't originate in Portland, but about him living in the Los Angeles area. Did he fly into LAX? Was he at the airport when the crash and follow-up destruction occurred? As soon as I complete my errand, I'll call Jake about this latest news. While these new explosions are terrible, they seem isolated to the chosen cities.

The convenience store is quiet. I fill the gas tank on my rental car and run inside to pull money out of the ATM. I hate paying the four-dollar ATM fee, and I know my bank charges an additional three-dollar fee for not using one of their ATMs. Seven dollars to get out my own money. Argh. My paranoia comes at a cost.

Besides for cash, I'm collecting traveling food. I have some very basic, noncook food in the suitcase Ben's been storing for me, nothing even remotely exciting, but sustenance. Things like high-calorie energy bars. The kind you break into thirds and eat one bar per day, giving you a measly 1,200 calories per day—which is fine, if you're lying on the couch all day.

I grab a hand basket and start filling it with an obscene amount of jerky, granola bars, cookies, crackers, a couple bags of tortilla chips, trail mix, nuts, and candy bars. I like Snickers and Pay Day. I rarely eat candy bars, but when I do, I convince myself these have nutrition in the nuts, and I fully enjoy them. Now I'm thinking there really is nutrition in the nuts and I may need it. That's my story…

This convenience store has an aisle with canned goods. I pick up a few cans each of tuna, chicken, salmon, and sardines. There are also tuna and salmon in foil packs, so I grab several of these. I spy a small bottle of malt vinegar and add this to my rather heavy basket, then toss in three cans of ready-to-heat soup with pop-top lids. I have one of those little P-38 can openers as part of my get-home bag, but pop-top is easier. I always struggle with the can opener. I decide I have enough. I sit it on the counter and grab a case of water and a six-pack of Gatorade. I don't particularly care for Gatorade, but the small number of electrolytes it replaces may be helpful.

The clerk gives me an odd look. I smile weakly. I know I'm being a little bit ridiculous. Our *Plan A* isn't something normal, nonprepping people would likely even think about. Part of me wishes I thought like the bulk of the general population, instead of constantly feeling the need to tighten my tinfoil hat. As a result of my folly, I pay more than any other convenience store stop ever, coming close to rivaling a full-on grocery store run. It takes me two trips to get everything out to my car.

The store closes behind me. My tank is full, and I have cash and food. I shake my head at the ridiculousness.

Chapter 9

Back in the car, I try calling Jake. The call goes straight to voicemail. It's a few minutes after 11:00 in Wyoming. I text Jake, letting him know I've filled my gas tank and have cash and some food. I haven't heard from any of the girls and wonder if they received my *Plan A* text.

Jake and I, while we do text, both really dislike it and tend to keep things short. Unlike probably 97 percent of the rest of the US, we both use flip phones. When we put the kids' backpacks together, we included a cheap prepaid flip phone in each of them. These tend to hold their batteries better and, with less bells and whistles, have less to go wrong with them. It's unlikely they'd ever need them, but adding these gave us a little extra security and a bit of a chuckle since they make fun of us for our cheap phones.

My phone rings. I don't even look, assuming it's Jake. "Hey, babe. You okay?"

"Mom? It's Sarah."

"Sarah! I'm glad you've called. I was just thinking of you. All of you kids."

"I got your text. You're supposed to come home tomorrow, right? What will you do?"

"I've decided to drive. I've just filled up my fuel tank and picked up a few things. I'm going to drive back to Ben's place and get my things."

"You have a car?"

"I got a rental this time. I'm supposed to return it to PDX tomorrow. I'll call them and tell them I'm keeping it and will return it in Prospect. It will cost me, but I'll feel better being home as soon as I can, rather than waiting until they unground the flights. I can't even imagine how long that can be with everything happening tonight."

"I think you're right, Mom. Tate and I are talking about how we would know when it's time to go to your place. You remember his parents are on their way here? They're in Nebraska tonight."

22

"I remember about his folks. It will be good for Tate to have them with you with the craziness happening right now. They plan to stay a week and a half? Maybe things will be back to normal before they go home."

Tate's parents live in Tulsa, Oklahoma. They have been talking of moving near all of us since Tate and Sarah made the move to Billings. Tate's mom, recently retired from her teaching job, and his dad will be visiting Billings for the first time.

They're also going to spend a couple days with us to check out our area. They've looked at our area online and it interests them, especially the fact Wyoming doesn't have state taxes, so Lois's retirement wouldn't be taxed. Keith, Tate's dad, is semi-retired. He's a charter bus driver and still works several days per week. I think he hopes to find similar work once they move.

"Yeah. I hope things will be okay. Mom, do you think they will be? Or do you think this is something really big?"

"It's definitely something big. I suspect there will be many changes, something like what we saw after 9/11 with TSA and the Patriot Act. But I'm not sure how TSA could help with something like this. If they were shooting the planes down during landing, from a location off the airport property, how can this be prevented?"

"You think there could be a problem with the banks and food shortages from this? Is that why you texted about *Plan A*?"

"Ah, Sarah, I don't know. Things were precarious before this. At the moment, I think we wait and watch, plus be ready. If this is the end of the attacks, then we should know more within time. If the attacks continue, then... I really don't know. Jake took Malcolm to the neighbor's house. He's making a run into SuperMart to pick up a few things."

"Okay... for your *Plan A*?"

"Yes, exactly. We keep a list, and when we think of things, we add it to the list. Plus he'll buy a few more food items. The things you and Tate sent, plus the food Angela and Katie have sent, have really beefed up our stores. With the way Malcolm and Gavin are growing, more can never hurt. Plus, you and Tate will be parents someday. More food makes sense."

I know I may have touched on a sore subject. Sarah has suffered many disappointing months since they've been trying to conceive.

One month was full of joy with a positive pregnancy test; unfortunately, she miscarried.

I quickly continue, "So what do you think of *Plan A*?"

"We thought it was smart and we're driving now. We've already stopped at the bank and are now going to SuperMart. Can you believe I'm going to SuperMart? You know how I feel about that place, but it's open and will have more of what we need. At least, Tate says it will. I can't remember the last time I was in one of *those* stores."

My call waiting beeps, and I can see Jake's name pop up.

"I have to go, Sarah. Jake's calling. I love you."

As I switch the call over to Jake, I quickly think about how I hope we're overreacting. "Hey, babe. Where are you?"

"Just pulled into SuperMart. Did you hear all the cities with plane crashes have now had explosions?"

"Yeah, I heard. I'm going to gather my stuff and leave tonight."

"You think it wouldn't be best to wait until morning? You can get some sleep and leave when you're fresh."

"I'm not sure what morning will bring. Will the attacks stop? Will they escalate overnight? I'm thinking I should at least try to get out of the I-5 corridor area. It seems Seattle and Portland would be good targets if they wanted to stop commerce. Whoever 'they' may be. Is Malcolm with Doris? Was she still up?"

"He is. She was. Evan had gone to bed, but Doris woke him up when she found out about what was happening. He's with me. He's stocking up too. After this we're stopping at the ATMs to get out cash."

"You can also get more cash when you check out. I think they'll let you have a hundred."

"Yep, I'll do that and still go to the ATM. That way I can get money out of both the checking and savings."

"Good thinking. If I leave tonight, I'll stop by one of the bank branches and pull out more money. Did you bring our saved cash with you?"

"No. I left it at home. I figured there would be no problem using the debit card tonight."

"Perfect. I think we should use the credit card, then we'll just settle it up when the bill comes in. We have a good amount of cash at home, but I'd like to save it and get more as we can. I have paychecks ready, and I'm going to ask Ben if he's okay with distributing them to everyone tomorrow. I'll have Jill, from my office, drop my check in the bank for me. I think it's best to get as much cash out of the bank as possible tonight and hold on to it. Who knows what the daylight will bring?"

"Yeah... you know, everything will probably be okay, and we'll have egg on our face."

"I'm okay with that—"

"Me too. Still, this is a good idea."

"It is. I bought several things at the mini-mart when I filled up. It just seemed smart."

"I grabbed the list you had started," Jake says, "I thought of a few more things while driving in. Is there anything you want me to make sure and grab?"

"Canning jars, we can always use more of those... flats too. Even though we have the reusable ones, I'd like more flats and a few rings. First aid items, dried and canned food... gosh, Jake. Everything. I know you know what we usually get, so follow your gut. Even if this turns out to be nothing, we can always use the basic items."

"Uh-huh. Also, I heard from Katie," Jake says. "She must have tried you after she got your text, but it wouldn't connect. She's upset, of course, and following through with *Plan A*."

"I talked with Sarah. Tate's folks are on their way for their planned visit. They're somewhere in Nebraska tonight and will be at their place tomorrow. It will be good for Tate to have them there."

"I'm going to head into the store. Let me know if you decide to leave tonight. I'll trust you to know what feels best to you. I just want you to be safe."

"Okay," I say, not really wanting to disconnect, "I'll make a decision when I get back and check the latest news."

"I love you. Be safe."

The beep of an incoming text went off a few times while I was talking to Jake. I have a message from Angela, saying she tried to call me, but it wouldn't connect. She'd just hung up with Sarah and thought it was good I was driving home instead of waiting until the flights were going again. She received the message on *Plan A*, and Tim headed out to take care of it. Tim works on an oil rig and is usually out of town. She makes a point of saying how fortunate it is his rig is out of commission due to repairs, so he's working out of the shop this week instead of on the road.

I send a quick message back, letting her know I'll be leaving either tonight or tomorrow and I can't wait to get home.

The second message is from Calley, asking what I'm going to do and if I really thought she should drive into town and get money from the ATM.

I tell her I'm driving the rental car home and will let her know when I'm on my way. And, YES, she should get as much money out as she can plus some food and fill up her gas… then hit send.

I know she keeps quite a bit of money on hand. She works as a barista at a coffee shop and much of her income is in tips. When she was younger and we all lived together, Malcolm would joke that her bedroom was like a bank.

I really dislike texting but am very happy the group text reached everyone and they're either taking action or, in Calley's case, *thinking* of taking action. It does make sense they'd have trouble reaching me by phone. The service is so bad here to begin with, and I imagine many people all over the US are on their phones tonight. When we had our big storm all those years ago, texts would go through when voice calls wouldn't. Maybe that's what's happening now?

Chapter 10

At Ben's, they're crowded together on the sofa watching the television. Clarice and Liam's eyes are rimmed red, while Ben is looking very stoic. Clarice announces school has been canceled for tomorrow and she's called in sick to work.

"I'm not surprised," I answer. "I'm going to start for home myself. I just need a few minutes to get everything together."

"Why don't you stay the night and then leave early in the morning?" Clarice asks, mimicking Jake.

"I… I don't know. I just feel the need to go, to get home."

Ben nods and says, "Yeah, I'd probably feel the same way. What can we do to help?"

On my drive back from the convenience store, I started thinking of my route home. The quickest way would be to catch Highway 30 East, north at Longview, then catch I-5 North to Seattle. Exit 142A is the bypass to I-90. Then it's I-90 for almost eight hundred miles. Getting off I-90, I'm less than two hours from home—easy peasy.

But I'm concerned about being on I-5 for that long. I may be paranoid, but feel the I-5 corridor, and maybe even I-90, could be dangerous. Either as targets for attack or from general bad guys. I fear people may take an opportunity to do whatever they want during a time like this.

"Can you grab the suitcase I left here last year?"

"Sure, it's in the storage section of our game room. Give me a few minutes and I'll bring it to your room."

"Can I help you pack?" Clarice asks.

"I'm not sure how much help I'll need, but I wouldn't mind the company. Unless you're ready to head to bed?"

"No, I don't think I can sleep."

"Yeah, another reason I might as well leave tonight."

In my room, I ask Clarice, "Can you pull up an online map? I'm going to head down the coast and then cut over to Eastern Oregon. Can you find the best route for me and write down the directions?"

"Sure. Or I could pull it up on my computer and then print out the directions. Which do you prefer?"

27

"Hmmm. Just write down the highlights. I have a paper map of Oregon in the suitcase Ben is grabbing. I just want a cheat sheet I can refer to."

"Okay, that makes sense."

Even though the door is open, Ben knocks on the frame before stepping in. He sets my case along the wall and asks, "How are you covered for protection on the way home?"

I don't quite understand his question. My face must have a blank look because he says, "Do you have a gun?"

"Oh... yes. I included a handgun in my checked bag. Of course, my concealed carry permit isn't any good in Oregon. It's not a reciprocal state," I say, shaking my head.

"Yeah, well... I'm sure you know what I think about that. I'm going to send you with a rifle also. I doubt you'll have any trouble getting home, but I'd feel better knowing you're well protected."

Like us, Ben is an avid hunter. While we hunt to fill the freezer, Ben likes to find the biggest bull or buck he can. He not only hunts in Oregon but he also hunts Montana, Idaho, and even Wyoming, whenever he can get the out of state licensing.

He spends a lot of time practicing and has invested in several long-range rifles and specialty scopes. In addition to his love of hunting, he enjoys target practice with a variety of weapons, from rifles to shotguns to handguns. His gun room reminds me of a small gun store. He returns a moment later toting a rifle.

"It's only a .22. I know that's not much, but I don't have anything larger I feel I can spare. We have a few of these, so this one is kind of surplus. Plus, it's a little smaller in stature than some of the other guns, and you can tuck it in the car easier. I know you're used to hunting big game, so I figure you can handle this fine."

I smile, thinking how Ben and I share hunting stories each year. I've only been hunting a few years, but I do enjoy it. I'm not a trophy hunter like he is, but I did enjoy sharing pictures of the nice buck antelope and deer I harvested last year.

"Thank you so much. This is a scary looking black rifle," I say jokingly.

"Yep. Sure is. It's a Mossberg semi-automatic with a 25+1 round magazine. Some people would have a fit just over the way it looks. Doesn't even matter it's only a .22 plinking, or small varmint, rifle. Sorry, I don't have a second magazine for it."

28

I take it from him and am slightly surprised. "It's super light."

"Less than four pounds, if I remember right. I kind of bought it on a whim off a friend who got it for his kid. The kid didn't like it. I gave him fifty bucks for it. Shoots good for what it is. Of course, you want to be fairly close. Fifty yards or less with the open sights, I'd say."

"Nice. Always good to get a deal. I can pay you for this."

"No way, Mollie. You can just give them back when Clarice and I come to visit later in the summer. Of course, I think we both know things will be very different after tonight. For sure in the US and maybe the entire world. And if we find out who's responsible and retaliate... we could be looking at World War III," Ben says with a sigh.

"You're right, Ben. Things may never be the same. Do you think you and Clarice will be safe here?"

"Will we be safe anywhere?" Clarice asks.

Now it's my turn to sigh. "Good point."

"I have to admit, part of me wishes we would've gone through with buying property when we visited you last time. There are a lot fewer people there. That alone makes me think it'd have to be safer than here," Ben says.

"You know, property or no property, you're always welcome to join us."

"Yep. I know. Of course, we're not to that point, and I hope we never will be. I'll let you finish up. You want me to take this down to the car for you?" He motions to the rifle.

"Not yet. I'll get everything situated first."

Ben excuses himself to check on Liam.

"I've found the route and made your notes. What can I help with next?" Clarice says.

"I'm finished with my carry-on. I pulled out a few things I brought last year that I want to put in the backpack, so I'll get started on organizing."

I open up the large suitcase. Bringing this seemed very silly at the time—especially since I packed a handgun in it and went through the rigmarole of flying with it. As I pull things out, I'm kind of surprised at my finds. I did a better job putting things together than I remember.

"Nice backpack," Clarice says.

"Yeah, it's a decent one. I tried it out and it balances well."

29

"So, instead of packing it up, you just put everything in the suitcase and left the backpack empty?"

"Uh-huh. It fit better that way. I tried it with the pack full, but it was too oddly shaped to fit in the suitcase."

"Jeez, it looks like you brought just about everything. Tent, sleeping bag, tennis shoes… what's this?"

"Water filter. The straw kind. There's some iodine capsules too."

"You even have clothes in here. Smart, Mollie."

"I tried to put in everything we'd use on a backpacking trip. Then added a few extras like the maps of Oregon, Idaho, Montana, and Wyoming."

"Ha. I see you even have a coffee maker. That sounds about right."

I laugh. "Yeah, I guess you know me pretty well. The pour-over coffee maker actually makes a decent cup. I'll need to buy a camp stove tomorrow since I didn't pack anything like that, you know, because of the fuel not being allowed on airplanes. I'll get a couple of lighters also. But I was able to pack my multi-flame mini-tool without having a TSA issue."

"Your what?"

"This," I pull out a little black pouch, "I have a friend who makes these. Its main function is a fire piston, giving me an option for starting fires."

"Huh. Looks complicated."

"Not really. It needs a little piece of char cloth—which I keep in this old mint tin—and I put the piston together and get a spark. Easy peasy. The tool can also be used as an auger when adding a bit so I could do some drilling. I don't have any bits, though," I shrug.

Clarice gives her own shrug. "Sunglasses?" she asks, holding up a plastic glasses case.

"Just regular glasses—an old pair. The prescription isn't exact, and they're single-vision only instead of the progressives I'm now wearing, but I figured they're better than nothing. I've worn glasses since first grade and my far away vision is terrible. Up close, it's not as good as it used to be, but I can get by. Forget it if it's more than twenty-five feet away. I have prescription sunglasses in my purse, but you wouldn't know that since the sun hasn't been out since I've been here."

"True," she says, and we both give a small laugh.

I take my handgun out of the TSA-approved locked case. It's a Taurus 9-millimeter Slim. I have two loaded magazines along with a full box of ammo in a second case. Taurus is a brand people either love or hate. It's reported to have more issues than a Glock or Beretta, and I've heard from several people they'd never own one... and they never have.

I also know people who do own a Taurus and have never had a problem. Our neighbors, firearms instructors who I've taken several classes through, including my concealed carry permit, own Taurus firearms. They have never had an issue and look at them as what they are... an affordable option.

I purchased mine from a local gun dealer on clearance for $197, specifically to add to this get-home bag. After purchasing, I practiced with it, sending several hundred rounds through the barrel. I feel confident this will work fine as part of my personal protection to get me home. Of course, I anticipate an easy drive without even having to think of taking out my weapon.

I brought along two holsters. One is a belly band style with a hook and eye closure. It's very comfortable and works well when wearing a dress, skirt, or leggings—my preferred clothing in my everyday work-from-home life. The comfort level of a casual dress or skirt with leggings underneath, can't be beat.

The second is a standard hip, outside the waistband, or OWB, holster. It will work with my quick-dry hiking pants, also included in my get-home bag, or the single pair of jeans I brought along for working in the shop. This is the same type of holster I wear when we're hiking or hunting, so I'm quite comfortable with it.

I have to admit, I have a fondness for holsters. The way some women enjoy jewelry, I enjoy holsters. Don't get me wrong, I like jewelry also and know the perfect pair of earrings can really change an outfit. But the perfect holster can change, or I should say, save a life. If I find myself with discretionary funds, purchasing a new holster is always a fun way to spend the extra money.

There was a time I didn't carry a handgun and thought a friend of mine, who always carried, was a little over the top. One time, she was on her way home from the firing range in Casper and stopped to visit. She gave me a great introductory course on concealed carry that day.

Up till then, I had no idea there were so many options, and no matter how she was clothed, she could always carry—even going to church. She understood my reluctance to carrying a firearm and understood it was my upbringing more than anything. She never tried to convince me or browbeat me to see things her way, just matter-of-factly shared her thoughts.

It was still several years, and not until we moved up to Bakerville, before I had a desire to carry. It started with wanting protection, in addition to bear spray, from the grizzly bear and mountain lion population. It progressed to realizing wildlife wasn't the only danger around.

My handgun collection now consists of a Ruger .357 revolver, .40 Springfield Armory semi-auto, Ruger LCP II .380, almost brand spanking new Glock I bought a week before this trip, and this Taurus I've been storing in my get-home bag.

"Nice, Mollie. Smart to bring that. Are you going to wear it now?"

"No… I don't think so. But I'll keep it in easy reach."

"Yeah, I guess you should," she says, shaking her head.

I continue organizing things while we talk about nothing. We're both avoiding the terrible realities of tonight. Once I have my ducks in a row, I'm ready to go except for my computer. Packing it takes only a minute. I'll put it in my hard-sided carry-on—the usual way I transport it when traveling by plane.

Ben reappears and asks, "How's it going?"

"It's good. I'm about ready. Umm, Ben, I just remembered, the rental car is on the company credit card. The main email address was used for the reservation. Can you email them and let them know I won't be returning the car tomorrow? They have an office in Prospect, and I'll return it there once I'm back."

"Sure, no problem. I'll take care of it for you. Don't worry."

"Okay, thanks. And I'll take care of the extra charges."

"No, you won't. We'll handle it, but seriously, this is talk for another day. Just worry about getting home. Nothing else."

I nod my thanks.

"Ready to load your stuff?" Clarice asks.

"Yeah. I think so. Can I borrow a reusable grocery bag, a hand towel, and a washcloth? I missed packing those things."

"Of course. Be right back."

"You're sure about leaving tonight?" Ben asks.

"I'm sure. I've decided to head down the coast. It's a longer trip, so leaving tonight will give me a jump on it."

"You think that's better than just making a beeline for home? You can be through Portland within a few hours."

32

"I know… I thought about that. I don't know what's better. I just know I'm… scared, maybe. I don't want to go to Portland."

Ben nods as Clarice reappears with my items. I grab my hip holster, now holding my Taurus, along with the extra magazines and my purse. I tuck the washcloth and towel in my overnight bag.

"Okay, that about does it."

"We'll help you carry things down," Ben offers.

"Thanks. Clarice, the big suitcase is empty. Do you mind carrying it down for me? And maybe this little daypack? Ben, could you get my carry-on and the rifle? And I'll take the backpack, overnight bag, grocery bag, and whatever is left."

At my car, the empty oversized suitcase goes in the trunk. The backpack, carry-on, and overnight bag on the backseat. The passenger's seat, filled with food from the mini-mart, is a mess.

I spend a few minutes organizing it and moving things I don't want up front to the back seat. The handgun and magazines I tuck in the center console. I'm almost finished organizing when I turn to Ben and Clarice. "I worry it's not safe here. Maybe it's too close to Portland. Do you think you guys should go with me? We can get your dad, of course."

They share a long look, and Ben says, "We worry it's not safe here either. I think, if things go bad in Portland, people will start heading this way. Some will probably think they can survive in the forest, and when they can't, well, we're the next populated area. But I'd like to think that isn't going to happen. Remember the comradery after 9/11? Most likely, it will be the same now. There's no reason to think otherwise… as long as nothing else happens. If it does, we can combine forces with the neighbors here, then we can increase our chances of safety."

Clarice nods in agreement.

"I think that's a good plan," I say. "I have to admit, I wasn't even thinking long term, but I'm concerned, if there's another attack, Portland could be affected and whatever happens there would directly affect you."

"Also possible. We're going into town first thing in the morning. We'll be there when the store opens and buy a few things. I think getting what we need just in case is a good idea."

"Good plan, Ben. Maybe get your camping gear in order too. You know, just in case you have to leave your place in a hurry. By the way,

I cut the checks yesterday, so they're ready to be handed out on Monday. I think you should have Jill make them available tomorrow. Since the shop crew doesn't work on Friday, she can call them and let them know to come and pick theirs up. I'd like her to drop mine in the bank, and she can put hers in also. The paranoid part of me wants to suggest they all get cash and buy extra food... but I'll leave that up to you."

"Sure, Mollie. Checks tomorrow are no problem. I suspect a few of the guys are already planning their purchases for tomorrow."

I fiddle with my supplies a bit more. I leave a few things I may want to eat soon on the car seat. The rest goes in the reusable bag and in the back seat. My backpack goes on the floor of the passenger's side and the daypack on the seat. I decide to keep the rifle in the trunk for now. I'm ready to go.

I hug Ben goodbye. "Be safe, Ben. I'll check in with you soon."

"Yeah, Mollie. Call tomorrow and tell us where you are. Use your company card for fuel. You're still on the clock until you get home." He gives me a wink.

"Okay, thanks, Ben."

I turn to hug Clarice. "Take care of yourself," she says. "Let us know when you get home."

"In fact, let us know where you are tomorrow," Ben says. "Oh, hey, did you happen to look and see if your rental car includes an emergency kit? Pop the trunk and let me look. I doubt it does."

I open the trunk, and he reports there isn't one and I should hold on a minute. Ben goes in the house and returns with a premade roadside kit.

"I get these things as gifts but never need them. You take this one just in case."

I take a quick look over it and see it includes booster cables, flares, a few basic tools, and other miscellaneous items.

"Thanks, Ben. I appreciate it."

34

Chapter 11

And that's it. I'm pulling out of their drive and heading toward the highway. I plan to stop at the bank in Alto and pull out more cash. I'll also top off the tank there, even though it's only twenty miles. I'd love to have a gas can, but I don't want to haul it in the car—not even the trunk.

All is quiet in Alto.

I'm feeling pretty good about the cash I have with me. With the traveling money plus what I've pulled out of the ATMs tonight, I have over twelve hundred dollars. I also had three hundred in assorted bills, from singles to twenties, stashed in my get-home suitcase.

Jake and I debated the need for packing some sort of precious metals. Many in preparedness circles believe the dollar will eventually crash and only things like gold and silver will have any value.

On the surface, this sounds incredibly reasonable. But deeper down, I have to wonder, if things were really that bad, if we'd even care about precious metals. Even so, we talked about me taking along a small amount of junk silver.

We finally discarded the idea, deciding if I'm gone from home when fiat currency loses value, I'll probably be in such a pickle it won't matter if I have a few old dimes and quarters.

With my cash on hand, and the thought of taking a little more from an ATM, I have enough to get home, especially since I'll use my company credit card for fuel. I take a few minutes to put money in different bags and assorted places in my car so it's not all in one place. While I'm happy to have the money for my trip home, I want to be smart with carrying this much.

It's 11:45 Pacific—12:45 at home. Jake is likely on the road, heading back home from Prospect and his shopping excursion. I text him.

"Babe. I'm starting home. I'll head down 101 to Florence then over to Redmond. From there I'll figure out where to go next, either north and then east or east and then north. I want to see how things are before I decide. I'll drive a few hours then find somewhere to sleep. I just feel the need to get farther from Portland. I know I'm probably

paranoid. I'm okay with that. Kiss Malcolm for me. If you hear from the girls, give them my love. See you soon."

The first part of the drive is easy. I've driven this road many times over the years. As I drive farther south, I know it's narrow and curvy while it runs next to the Pacific. I'd like to make it somewhere near Lincoln City before I stop. Maybe a little farther. I think I remember a SuperMart in Newport. I could sleep there for a few hours. People do that, right?

There are very few others on the road. When I do finally stop at the SuperMart, along with half a dozen RVs, it's shortly after 3:00 am. I've stopped for gas twice. I was surprised to find twenty-four-hour stations in these sleepy little seaside towns. At the last gas stop, I pulled a sweater out of my suitcase and a fleece blanket out of my backpack. Confirming all of the doors are locked and the pistol is within easy reach, I settle in. I don't worry much about oversleeping since I've parked with my windshield facing east. I'm guessing sunrise is around 5:30. That'll do.

Chapter 12

Friday, Day 2

Sun streaming through the windshield, along with the cacophony of an angry seagull, wakes me up. In those first few seconds of waking, I don't remember the destruction from the evening before. As it all comes rushing back, I'm overwhelmed with grief. I cry for several minutes before pulling myself together.

Last night I was so focused on getting as far away from Portland as I could, I didn't take the time to truly grieve. Pulling myself together isn't easy, but my bladder—screaming for relief—makes going into the store necessary.

I glance at my watch and see it's only a few minutes until 6:00. I'm hopeful the place opens at 6:00 so I don't need to find a tree. I gather my toiletries case out of the overnight bag in the backseat and put it and my small purse in the daypack. I contemplate my handgun and, not wanting to leave it in my car, also stash it in the backpack. The rifle will just have to stay in the locked trunk.

Sure enough, there's a line of several people waiting. Most look about the same as me, obviously crying and upset. I share a small side-smile with a lady. She smiles back, shakes her head, and pulls me into a spontaneous hug. I stifle a cry.

We're soon allowed in, and I head straight to the bathroom. Once my first order of business is taken care of, I wash my face, brush my teeth, and do the best I can with my hair. I keep my hair short, which works quite well for me most days since I can just wash and go. Today, I'm wishing it was longer so I could pull it up in a ponytail. I do manage to get a little water on it, but the sink in here isn't the best for this.

As I was drifting off last night, I decided I'd buy a bike and car carrier. This way, if for some reason I can't drive the car, I don't have to walk. I'm concerned the plane crashes and bombs from last night are a precursor to what will come. I pray I'm wrong and my paranoia comes from too many years of reading end-of-the-world books, articles, and prepper sites.

I find a bike and helmet. The bike isn't very good quality but is an entry-level mountain bike and should be fine. I grab a can of fix-a-flat plus a few other accessories. The car carrier is also not very good quality, but I'm not sure I care about this. As long as I can get it attached and it stays attached, it will meet my needs.

I think about the food I purchased at the gas station last night, plus what's in my backpack. If I were to end up getting stuck somewhere, more food would be good to have. On the flipside, if I don't have a car, I can't pack much more food than what I have with me. I think of meals I pack for us on our backpacking adventures and decide to grab items we'd take on a trek. We can always use these foods at home, so I'm out nothing by buying these today and not needing them on this trip home.

Most SuperMart's have a section of freeze-dried foods in #10 cans in addition to individual meals for camping. I'll start with the camping meals but need a cart and don't want to try to manage my bike, carrier, and a cart, so I take them to the customer service area up front. The attendant there assures me they'll be fine while I complete my shopping.

I head back to the camping section to see what food choices they offer. There's a very small selection, including beef stew, biscuits and gravy, lasagna with meat sauce, chili mac with beef, and macaroni and cheese. I grab two of each. I look for a small backpacker's stove and am surprised to find one with an automatic ignition along with small isobutane canisters. I also grab a larger one-burner stove and four bottles of propane. I'll keep the backpacker's stove in case I end up traveling by foot, preferring the ease of the larger one-burner with propane if I'm traveling by bike or car.

Next, I head to the grocery section to look for larger cans of freeze-dried items. I'm happy to find a decent selection of not only individual cans but also seventy-two-hour emergency kits. The kits are convenient. The meals are packed and contained in a three- to five-gallon bucket, depending on the company. This kit is designed to feed four people for three days, giving just over two thousand calories each day. I've tried some of these meals before, and while not the best food around, it will keep you from starving. I add a pail to my cart.

The #10 cans have a few things I'm fond of for our backpacking trips. Black bean burger, freeze-dried beef, rice, and strawberries. I grab one of each.

My next stop is paper goods. A box each of gallon, quart, and sandwich zip top bags and a roll of paper towels go in my cart, along with a four-pack of toilet paper. In the snack aisle, I add a few bags of jerky, a large container of assorted nuts, dry roasted peanuts, and a good-sized bag of trail mix.

I make my way through the aisles, adding any items that make sense.

I stop by the dairy section for hard cheese. Parmesan and cheddar are cheeses we take backpacking and hold up quite well without refrigeration. String cheese and small, round, individually-wrapped soft cheeses in wax also last a long time in a backpack. I don't like the wax but grab a few individual string cheeses along with a small block of Parmesan and an eight-ounce cheddar.

A few yards down the refrigerator case are lunch meats. Dry, aged salami can last for many days. Genoa salami and whole pepperoni are also very shelf-stable when unopened. Once cut into, they need to be used within a day or two. I add a few of each to my cart. There's a display of shelf-stable summer sausage at the end of an open freezer case. I buy two of the smallest rolls.

I evaluate my cart and decide I have enough—more than enough. Again, I think I'm being a little silly and will never need these things since I'll be home by tomorrow. That said, food is something we'll always eat, and since everything is shelf-stable, I'm not wasting money—just buying ahead for when we may need it.

And, then again, if things go wrong and I get stuck somewhere, I'll have supplies. Realistically, I have too much to carry with me. Thinking of this, I decide to go back to sporting goods to see about a basket or something for my bike. On the way, I detour through the women's clothing section for socks and underwear. I spend a few minutes looking for thin wool socks, my preference, but don't find any. Bummer.

I find a soft-sided, waterproof handlebar bag—looks good. It reminds me of a lunch bag and zips closed, plus has a mesh pocket on the outside. There's also a water bottle kit for the bike. Did the bike I chose have a water bottle? I can't remember so I grab this.

Then I find a good-sized basket for the rear of the bike. I add it along with a rear cargo rack, a small tarp, and a container of bungee cords. How about a small cooler? Not a terrible idea. While the cheese and meats can go without it, they'll keep better on ice. I make a mental note to buy a bag of ice when I'm checking out.

Near the coolers are backpacks. I have my nice backpack and a daypack but think a fanny pack might be a good idea too. I find a style on clearance for three dollars and decide to buy two. Yeah, I'm ridiculous.

As I'm tossing the fanny pack in my cart, I spy a bundle of gray socks. Checking the label, they're a wool blend. While not exactly the sock I prefer, the wool blend beats straight cotton. The wicking offered by wool should help with keeping my feet dry if I end up hiking. Of course, these are only a backup; I brought three pairs of wool socks along with me.

Heading toward the pharmacy, I stop at hardware and buy a baggie of zip ties—I might need these to keep the baskets attached. Then I pop into housewares for a box of matches. I'll pick up a lighter or two at the checkout.

I make a quick stop by the pharmacy. Even though my pack contains a small first aid kit, I beef it up, adding more ibuprofen, acetaminophen, a couple Ace bandages, tape, nonstick gauze, an assorted packet of Band-Aids, hand sanitizer, and a packet of wet wipes.

I stop by the women's products for pads and tampons. My cycles have been irregular for the last several months. I never know when "Aunt Flo" is going to visit. At home, I prefer reusable products, but these are convenient for travel. Plus, since they're incredibly absorbent, they can also be used as an emergency bandage, if needed.

I have more than enough stuff for my trip home. My growling stomach demands breakfast. At the deli they have cheese and salami rollups. I buy several. At least one for breakfast and others for later, and since I now have a cooler, they'll keep well.

Produce is right next door. I pick a small bunch of bananas, a few apples for later, a bag of baby carrots, and a couple single-serve salads. I really wish this store had coffee already brewed. I'll for sure be stopping somewhere for coffee but want some food before I tackle putting the bike rack on the rental car.

At the check stand, I add a few sodas and a couple small bags of chips—another treat. I'd better hurry home. The treats I'm buying... I'll be twenty pounds heavier if I'm not careful. Did I mention how hard I have to work to keep my weight in check?

When I check out, I remember to order my ice, then say a prayer of thanksgiving as my transaction completes. I had a momentary worry my credit card wouldn't work. From my end, there's no reason it wouldn't be fine, but I wasn't sure if there could or would be a problem from the financial institution's end.

I have no idea if my company might be located in one of the affected cities or if this would be a problem for my card if they were. I'm both shocked and happy when the cashier offers to call someone to help me to my car. That never happens at my local store, so I expected to make a couple trips in order to get the bike and everything managed.

Chapter 13

Lindsey

Saturday, Day 10
San Jose, California

With the bike attached to the car and things stashed so I'm ready to roll, I take a few minutes to call Jake. I have no doubt he's up and on with his day. My call won't connect. Likely my coverage continues to suffer here in this small coastal town. I send him a text letting him know where I am, about my purchases, and my next major stop of Redmond, Oregon. Then I'll decide which road to take to head home from there.

With my new bike on the back of the car, I drive slowly around the lot to make sure it isn't moving. Then I search out coffee. A gas station nearby is my coffee answer, and the attendant fills my tank while I go in for my cup. One of the best things about Oregon, in my opinion, is the full-service fuel.

I check my phone. Nothing from Jake yet.

After coffee and gas, I'm back on 101 South. The coffee is nothing to write home about but gives me the jolt of caffeine I desperately need. I turn the radio on, deciding I'm finally ready to hear the latest updates. After listening for just a few minutes, I don't hear about any new problems. I'm hopeful that, while last night's events were devastating, this is the end of the attacks.

In just over an hour, I reach Florence, where I get off the 101 and onto 20 East. I decide to go ahead and top off my tank here. I don't need much, but the towns are few and far between from here until Eugene. I check my phone and see a text back from Jake.

"Glad you're on your way home. No new developments overnight. Decided to head to town to pick up materials to build a greenhouse. It won't be exactly what we've been talking about, definitely smaller

and not a dug out. I don't think the building cost will be very high. We can add the one we want later. Better safe than sorry. Malcolm is good, he misses you. Tate and Sarah bought a camp trailer, they're going to park it here for now. I tried to call you, but phone just went to voicemail. Will try later. We love you."

Tate and Sarah buying a camp trailer is interesting! I look forward to hearing more about this.

I'm getting an eighties and nineties radio station. The music is a nice break from the info on the attacks. I'm confident, if there was something new to report, they'd interrupt with the latest updates.

At the top of the hour, they switch to a national news report. I don't hear anything new about last night's plane crashes or explosions but do hear something which really makes my ears perk up.

"In other news, health departments in about a dozen major US cities are reporting an increased number of foodborne illnesses. Most of the cities are seeing both Shiga toxin-producing E. coli and Salmonella Typhi, also known as typhoid fever.

"Limited cases began appearing a few weeks ago. Yesterday, there was an estimated 137 E. coli and 268 typhoid cases. There have been at least six deaths associated with the E. coli outbreak and eight from typhoid.

"While E. coli has made the news many times in recent years, typhoid fever tends to be related to developing countries or people recently visiting these places. It's closely related to salmonella, which typically causes food poisoning as it can only affect the stomach and digestive tract. S. Typhi, on the other hand, causes a body-wide and life-threatening disease because its toxin can enter all of the body's cells and cause infection.

"There have been recent reports of typhoid fever incidences in homeless camps. The incidences from the last several days are believed to be unrelated to those occurrences.

"Please visit our website for information on symptoms for both E. coli and typhoid fever. Early diagnosis can help with a full recovery. We'll update this story as more information becomes available."

Interesting. I know someone who had Shiga toxin-producing E. coli, so I do know a little about this. It's more common than people think and can't always be traced back to the source. In fact, it's more common to not find the source.

Typhoid, I believe, is often referred to as Montezuma's revenge. I went to Mexico many years ago and was cautioned to not drink the water, use the ice, or eat the salads. I don't think typhoid is common in the US at all, other than of late. I remember reading about several LAPD officers coming down with typhoid fever symptoms after patrolling homeless camps.

Chapter 14

My drive to Redmond is completely uneventful. It's about 1:00 pm when I reach the town. I've stopped for gas once along the way and fill up again in Redmond. I'm very conscience about keeping my tank from getting too low. When it's about three-quarters of a tank, I start looking for a gas station.

Ben called earlier. He and his dad did go into town. They took out cash and stocked up on groceries, along with filling up all of their vehicles and our company semi-truck—going to be quite the fuel bill when it comes in. Paychecks were distributed to all and my check was dropped in my bank account.

There's a diner across the street from the gas station in Redmond. A sit-down meal is in order. As I'm pulling in the lot, I remember the news report about the food poisoning cases. Could these be intentional?

My sit-down meal doesn't sound quite as appealing. Instead, I'll find a park and eat some of the packaged food I have in the car. Redmond, like many Oregon towns, has several parks and green spaces, so it's easy to find what I'm looking for. I spy a picnic table and park near it.

While eating, I try Jake and reach him this time. I talk to Malcolm first. It's so good to hear his voice, but it really makes me wish I was there with them. I have a hard time not crying while we're talking.

Jake comes on the phone and shares about his day. He's been to town and back, picking up a few more items he thought we could use plus materials to build a basic greenhouse. He says he even found three greenhouses in boxes, which are small but may be useful.

We don't really need the greenhouse until fall since summer is in full swing and our regular garden is planted, so he'll put off construction for now. The greenhouses in the boxes… I'm not so sure about, but he insists they were too good of a deal to pass up, and if we don't need them, we can gift them to a couple of the girls.

"So, while I was in town, Bubba Larson called," Jake says. "He's repossessing a small prefab cabin and thought we might be interested in it."

"Okay... and?" I ask warily.

"And it was too good of a deal to pass up. He's bringing it over tomorrow."

"So... you agreed to purchase another cabin? Do we need another cabin? And what about our no-new-projects agreement for this year?"

"I'm not sure we need another cabin. But I think the price is amazing, and I could possibly resell it for more than what I paid if we decide we don't need it. Or we could keep it for storage. I filled up the processing shed with the greenhouse materials. I won't take this on as a project right now unless absolutely necessary. It can just sit there and hold our stuff."

Trying to keep my cool, I let a sigh escape. "Hmm. Well, I trust your judgement on this. Do you think we're good now with the purchases you've made and the car full of stuff I have? Should we consider *Plan A* complete?"

"I think *Plan A* is a definite success. Unless something big happens, or should I say, something additional, we should hold off on anything else. You focus on getting home. Keep your gas tank filled and find a place to stop tonight where you can get some good sleep. Leaving so late last night, you must be tired."

"I was doing pretty well, but the longer I sit here, the more I'd welcome closing my eyes. Did you hear about the foodborne illnesses?"

We go on to discuss the food poisoning and how I wanted to stop at a restaurant but didn't out of fear of illness. He had heard about it and found it odd, but hadn't thought much of it.

"Do you really think this is related to the terrorists, Mollie?"

"Maybe? It just seems super suspicious that two different foodborne illnesses are causing widespread outbreaks. Typhoid didn't even used to happen here. It's more of a third world type thing but is cropping up in homeless camps. You remember, we talked about that."

"Vaguely, I remember you mentioning it, but I can't remember the details. Something about unsanitary conditions and people getting sick?"

"Yes, exactly. But the news report said these latest outbreaks aren't related to the homeless camps. It sounds like it's very widespread and feels intentional to me. But you do know, I could be paranoid."

"You could be right. Not about being paranoid... well, that too. But about the illnesses. Something like that would definitely cause more terror."

"Exactly. I was going to go to a restaurant for lunch, thought it'd be a nice break, but the outbreaks made me think twice about it."

"Makes sense. I think that's often terrorists' goal, to stop us from living our life and to make us live in fear."

"Huh. I thought their goal was to kill everyone who didn't believe the same as they do."

"Yeah. Maybe so."

Before we hang up, I tell him I've decided to take 97 to Biggs Junction, cross the Columbia there, and head through Yakima.

"I thought you were going to skip Yakima. Isn't there an Army base or something there?"

"I think there is. I think avoiding big cities is my best bet. Yakima isn't very large. But maybe you're right. I could go to the Tri-Cities instead."

I'm feeling very grateful for the maps and Gazetteers I included in my checked bag so I can see my options for getting home.

"I think it'd be better. From there, it's not too far to I-90. If everything remains quiet, you could hop on there and be home in no time. Tomorrow, even."

"Yes, getting on I-90 would speed it up. It isn't far from Tri-Cities to 90 at all. I think that's what I'll do. Looks like about 250 miles to Tri-Cities. I should be able to make it at least to Spokane tonight and be home tomorrow. I'd better get going. Keep in touch?"

"Of course. Malcolm and I are going to get a load of hay and then a load of wood from the reservoir. Maybe even two loads of wood. I decided against going up in the forest. I don't want to be so far away from home, just in case. Plus, it's already a little late in the day for a trip like that."

"I agree. I'm glad you'll be sticking closer to home. Talk to you soon. I love you."

"Love you too, honey."

I get back in the car and prepare to hit the road. I get a little turned around while trying to find my way from where I am to where I need to be. I'm usually very good at finding my way around, so I didn't take the GPS option on the vehicle. I'm frustrated and wishing I had a GPS.

I'm close to pulling over and asking for directions when I suddenly find my way.

Whew. I hate being lost.

I check the radio to see if there are any new updates or information on last night's attacks or the illnesses. Music is playing at the moment, which I take as a very good thing. It's a country station; not super old country but not new either. Definitely stuff I can sing along with and pass the time during the drive.

Tracy Lawrence is telling me "time marches on," reminding me of the time after 9/11. In the weeks and months following that terrible Tuesday, several country musicians did what they did best. They poured out their emotions, putting to music what so many were feeling but didn't know how to put into words.

"Where Were You (When the World Stopped Turning)" by Alan Jackson really struck many people, including me. I have no doubt we'll be talking about last night's attacks in the same way as time goes on. Asking each other, "Where were you?"

Another song which affected me during that time was Lee Greenwood's "God Bless the U.S.A." The days following the Twin Towers coming down seemed to be filled with people banding together. Uniting in the loss we felt. Of course, in the years following, things have changed. And some of the information which has cropped up since...

My tears start again. I wonder if we'll be banding together after this attack. Our country has felt very much divided for years. Everything seems to be "us" against "them," with divides among many factions— politics, race, Second Amendment, and other ideologies.

Sometimes I wonder if the country is really as divided as it seems, or with the constant news cycle and social media, are we just more engulfed in it? After the last presidential election, there was protesting and rioting. People were sure a dictator had been elected... and on the flip side, others were sure our nation was going to be saved from tyranny.

I read a BBC article a while back which indicated, a few presidents ago, two-thirds of Americans regarded race relations as generally good. Before our most recent president left office, there was a complete reversal. Sixty-nine percent of Americans assessed race relations to be mostly bad. I can't even imagine what those numbers might be now.

My friend Kelley, who's black, once told me nonwhites see racial discrimination more than whites do. She may be right.

All I know is the last several years have felt like we're living in a powder keg. And not just with politics and race relations—the often-violent protests surrounding these issues—but the economy, rumblings of a second civil war, international relations, and increased terrorist activity around the world. Now, with the plane crashes and bombs set off last night, this could be the catalyst that puts us over the edge. And it could be a very long drop.

My country radio station fades out, and I find an oldies station to replace it. Somewhere between the little towns of Shaniko and Grass Valley, the song I'm listening to, "Daydream Believer," is interrupted.

"We're receiving reports of a possible new wave of attacks. There have been explosions on or near several US bridges. Early reports indicate the Brooklyn Bridge, connecting Manhattan and Brooklyn; the Golden Gate Bridge in San Francisco; Mackinac Bridge, which connects the Lower and Upper Peninsulas of Michigan; Seattle's Lacey V. Murrow Memorial Bridge; and Portland's Marquam Bridge.

"We believe these are just a few of the bridges which have been attacked. Even as I speak, I'm being given more information, and additional explosions are being reported throughout the US and even Oregon. We'll return with more information shortly. May God have mercy on us all."

There are a few seconds of silence followed by an instrumental I recognize as "Amazing Grace."

Chapter 15

Sylvia

Saturday, Day 10
Between Shoshoni and
Thermopolis, Wyoming

My vision is immediately blurry. I'm overwhelmed. Pulling off the road is a challenge. The Marquam Bridge in Portland is a bridge I've driven many times. It's a double decker bridge on I-5 going over the Willamette River.

As the busiest bridge in Portland, at a little after 2:00 on a Friday it was likely very busy. Friday rush hour tends to start about 1:00 or 2:00 in the afternoon, or according to some, the morning and afternoon rush hours meld into one with heavy traffic all day. Everyone wants to get an early start on the weekend. Maybe it's quieter today than usual because of last night's attacks.

I've been over San Francisco's Golden Gate before, and the bridge in Seattle is the I-90 Bridge going over Lake Washington. I know both of these are at least as busy as the Marquam. As I'm sitting there absorbing all of this, I realize I have a bridge coming up fairly soon.

Highway 97 crosses over the Columbia at Biggs Junction. I've been over this bridge many, many times through the years. It's not a super busy bridge but it's fairly long and one of the few bridges crossing the Columbia River going from Oregon to Washington.

Nope. No way. I'm going to avoid large bridges. I can't avoid all bridges since there's an untold number of small bridges crossing rivers, creeks, and other items on all roads. But I'm staying away from ones that feel like they could be a target.

The report is over and a song, "America the Beautiful," is now playing. I look at the map and try to find a new route home. I slide my seat back to give me a little more room. My phone rings about the same time, causing me to jump. Jake.

"Hey, babe." I say.

"Honey! Have you heard? They're blowing up bridges now!"

"I've heard. They said the names of a few. The Marquam in Portland was one of them, the Golden Gate, and the one in Seattle I-90 is on."

"Last night, they took out air travel. Today, they're taking out our bridges." Jake lets out a big sigh. "They're also possibly connected to the food poisoning stuff. People are going to be too scared to leave their homes."

"True. I'm not far from Biggs Junction and the bridge over the Columbia. I'm scared to drive over the bridge."

"Oh, jeez! It seems like it may be a good target since they hit the two bridges in Portland going over the Columbia."

"Jake, hold on a second. The radio announcer is back."

"We have confirmed reports, the Sellwood and Fremont Bridges in Portland have been destroyed, along with the double-deck Marquam. The Interstate Bridge and the Glen Jackson Bridge, connecting Portland to Vancouver, Washington, have also both been attacked, but are still standing. These bridges are closed until the extent of the damage can be assessed.

"Across the US there have been over forty-five bridges hit so far. It is believed a truck loaded with explosives drove onto each bridge and then detonated a bomb. This type of attacker is often called a suicide bomber. The results of these attacks vary in degree from minimal damage to total destruction. This attack, on the day after five airplanes were brought down and five of our US cities were affected by weapons of mass destruction, is surely related. We're expecting an address from the president shortly."

"Ah, Mollie. This is bad."

"I know," I whisper through my tears.

"Where are you?"

"I don't know. Somewhere on 97, a ways from Grass Valley, pulled over on the side of the road. I stopped when I first heard the report. I was going to take a look at the map and find a new route home without big bridges. Do you think any of my Portland friends were killed today?"

"I don't know, honey. I can't even imagine the number of people who died today and yesterday. I haven't really heard many numbers yet from yesterday. Nothing firm, anyway."

"It's terrible. No, that's not even the right word for it. It's beyond terrible, but I can't think of a better word to use. I want to get home. Do you think I should just stay on this road and get to I-84, then take it to Pendleton? I can go north there, I think, and hit 90."

"Pendleton is past the Gorge, so you wouldn't have to cross the Columbia that way?"

"Right. Let me pull out the map and take a look. There's still a bridge I'd have to cross. It looks like it goes over the Snake, and it looks like a good-sized one."

"Maybe you should find somewhere to stay tonight? Let the bridge activity calm down and then we can find you a good route tomorr—"

"Jake, I need to be home."

"I know, and we need you here… want you here. But I feel like you should stay off the interstate for now. Maybe take one of those backroads to get to Pendleton and sleep there tonight. Don't want you too tired to drive.

"I'm fine to drive. I'll stop…" I break down in tears. Neither of us says anything for several seconds.

"Mollie, I'm sorr—"

"It's fine. I'm tired and upset and… just… I'm just so overwhelmed and sad—so incredibly sad—about all of this. The planes, the bridges, me not being home with Malcolm. With you. You could be right; I might be more tired than I realize."

"I think you can get from 97 over to the road Condon is on. Can you take a look? Then from there get to 395? I think Pendleton is on 395."

"Jake! *Seriously*? I'm telling you how I'm feeling and you're giving me directions?"

He's quiet for a long beat, then softly says, "Sorry, honey. I was just so focused on helping you get home, I… I wasn't paying attention to how you may be feeling about all of this."

I know he doesn't mean to be such a… jerk. No, that's not the right word, he's just focused. Focused on me getting home.

"Honey?" he asks.

"Yeah, I'm here. I know you're trying to help." I take a deep breath. "Let me see... Condon is on 19. Pendleton is on 395. It looks like it'd be a maze to get there, but I can. From Condon, I can take a road to Hepner and then from Hepner to Pilot Rock, which is on 395, and then up to Pendleton. I could stay in Pendleton tonight."

"I think that would be good."

"I wish I would've just darted through Portland last night instead of going south. I'd be so much closer to home now if I would've just done it."

"I know, but your instinct to stay out of Portland and Seattle was good. Besides, no use wishing now."

"I guess you're right. I have to admit, I'm so tired I don't know if I can make it to Pendleton."

"You can probably find someplace closer. Maybe Condon or Hepner."

"Maybe. They're pretty small but might have a hotel. And I have my gear, so I can camp. A bed sounds wonderful, though, after sleeping only a few hours in the car last night."

"Don't push yourself or drive when it's not safe. You don't want to risk an accident, which would delay you getting home even more."

"No kidding, Jake. You don't need to state the obvious," I snap. He's completely silent. I soften my voice. "Sorry, Jake. I shouldn't have said that. I'll start looking for a place and will let you know. Have you talked with the girls?"

"I've talked to all of them. They each said they tried to reach you, but your phone went to voicemail. They know how sketchy connections can be. Hey, it sounds like the president is coming on. Let's listen."

Jake turns up his radio a bit, which makes an echo for me, so I move the phone away from my ear and listen to my radio.

"My fellow Americans, it is with a heavy heart I report our nation continues to be the target of terrorist activities. As of yet, we have not identified the culprits but believe we're getting closer to knowing who is responsible. Today, many of our nation's bridges have been attacked. Some were devastated by, what we believe to be, suicide bombers driving panel trucks loaded with explosives. In many cases, these trucks caused severe destruction. Other bridges were targeted by handheld surface-to-surface missiles with devastating results. As of now, we have confirmed reports of forty-eight bridges affected, with varying degrees

of damage. We'll provide the list of these bridges after I have finished speaking with you.

"Due to today's attacks, we are closing or limiting access to other bridges across the nation which we've determined to be likely targets. Last night, our nation came under attack with the deliberate crash of five airplanes while attempting to land. This was followed by the detonation of multiple explosives at and very near each airport experiencing a crash.

"Today, we continue to see evil with the destruction of our bridges. The loss of innocent life is staggering. Immediately following last night's attacks, I implemented our emergency response plans. Our emergency teams are working at all five cities which were attacked. These cities are Queens, New York; Miami, Florida; Los Angeles, California; Chicago, Illinois; and DFW Airport in Texas.

"With the bridge disasters, we are distributing teams as we can to all affected areas to assist the local fire and rescue departments. I ask for your cooperation, as citizens, to help where you can and obey all requests from your local government. Let us come together during this time of tragedy and show those who oppose our very way of life we cannot be broken by their cowardly acts. We will find those responsible and bring them to justice. None of us will forget these times, but we will persevere. God bless each of you. God bless America."

"So, they're closing other bridges? That sounds smart but could make it harder for me to get home."

"Yeah," Jake sighs, "I agree on both accounts."

"And it doesn't sound like they know much more about who's responsible."

"Don't think they do. But then again, if they did, they might not say anything if they're planning something."

"I guess that's true." We hear a new voice on the radio.

"Please listen closely while we read the list of bridges targeted today and the towns affected. We ask if you are in these towns to please follow the instructions of your local officials. Staying at your home is safest, but please do heed calls to donate blood and requests for any trained first responders or medical personnel."

As she goes down the list, we hear the places we knew about and many we didn't. We specifically listen for bridges in places we're familiar with. The Lewis and Clark Viaduct—connecting Kansas City,

Kansas, and Kansas City, Missouri—and the Speer Boulevard Bridge in Denver were both hit. It does seem the terrorists are doing their best to halt transportation and scare people into staying home.

"Do you think we should see if Katie wants to come home? It might be a challenging trip for her, like it is for me, if she's avoiding bridges."

"I'll call her. You should get on the road and find someplace to rest up. Hopefully, by tomorrow, the bridge destruction will be done and you can make some good time getting home. Let me know when you find a place to stay. I love you."

"I love you, and… Jake, I'm sorry I was so snappy."

"This is a hard time, Mollie. You'll be home soon, and you can make it up to me in person."

I can't help but laugh. "Sure thing, Mister. Please call all of the girls, just to check in with them. Let me know how they are when we talk again. And hug Malcolm for me."

After disconnecting, I wonder how the conversation with the girls will go. Will Katie think it's time to head to our place, or will she want to stick it out a little bit longer? It's a fifteen-hour drive, if all goes as expected.

I'm pretty sure Sarah, being so nearby, will delay as long as possible. Angela is just under five driving hours so will also likely wait. And, of course, I have no doubt Calley won't head our way unless she and Mike have determined there are no other options.

Please, Lord, be with those who have lost loved ones. Be with us all. Please, Lord, protect us all.

Chapter 16

It's not long until I reach the little town of Grass Valley, Oregon. My turn should be in a few miles. I don't want to miss it, so I start paying attention. Even so, it's hard to keep my mind from wandering to the recent events. *Please, Lord, watch over us. Comfort those who have lost loved ones...*

I find my turn and eventually make my way to Highway 206. I'm only on 206 a few miles when a State Park sign with a camping emblem appears.

I've been down this road years ago and don't remember this park. It's still early, and I was thinking of a hotel room with a bed and shower, but I'm so tired the campground sounds incredibly appealing.

The information kiosk tells me why I don't remember this park. It was only opened in 2013, well after we moved from Oregon and last traveled this road.

This is a first-come, first-served campground with twenty-one sites available and another seven backpackers' sites. I'll be looking for something I can drive my car directly up to. I'd also like to camp near a family, thinking, as a woman alone, this is safer for me.

The FAQs placard indicates there are vault toilets only and community potable water, but no showers and no cell phone coverage within the park. There's an asterisk indicating service may be available at the kiosk.

I test it by trying Jake, and sure enough, I'm unable to connect. I'm able to send a text letting him know where I'm trying to stay tonight and the lack of coverage.

Cottonwood Canyon State Park turns out to be quite a lovely spot along the John Day River. I try for one of the seven riverfront sites but all are occupied. In fact, all of the sites I've driven past are full.

The campground loops away from the river, with additional sites on the other side of the road. The second site on the left, number sixteen, is the first empty one I find. Sweet sixteen looks like a winner, especially when I notice a family at number fourteen next door and also at fifteen across the road.

I take my daypack out, lock my car, and walk to the registration area. There are three additional empty sites along the way, but I'm sticking with sweet sixteen.

Setting up my camp takes only a few minutes, and once I'm done, it's nap time. It's almost 4:00 pm, so I set my phone alarm to go off in forty-five minutes. I lay there for a few minutes, thinking about the events since last night. Not even twenty-four hours ago my world, the world, seemed mostly normal. Today, it is forever changed.

When the alarm goes off, I hit snooze two more times before finally deciding to get up. As I'm waking up, I remember snippets of my dream.

Prospector Peak, the mountain rising up out of the basin near my home in Bakerville, was the focus. In my dream, Jake and I were driving home—likely from Casper or Thermopolis, based on the view of the mountain. My first glimpse of Prospector Peak, after I've been away, is always wonderful. It's like a beacon calling me home.

In my dream, Jake says, "There she is. There's our mountain. It won't be long now."

The dream is a reminder, a harbinger, of my need to get home. To see our mountain again. To hug my son. To kiss my husband.

Chapter 17

I have a snack of macadamia nuts and Gatorade, purchased from the gas station last night. One sip of the Gatorade reminds me why I rarely buy this. Ick. I drink it anyway.

Three young children are playing next door. At first glance, I think they're all girls. But looking again, I decide one is a boy, less than two years old with longish curls. He's been playing hard, and his clothes and face reflect this. He has a dustiness about him, almost looking like he's been playing in flour.

The girls, a few years older, look about the same—covered in the dry, fine dirt. Two adults are sitting at the picnic table. I give them a wave.

When I registered for my site, I'd picked up a hiking brochure, showing two trails in the park. One connects with the road and then loops over to another trail running near the campgrounds. About two miles combined, and a perfect short hike to pass the time and exercise my road-trip-weary muscles.

I start out with the trail along the John Day River, known as Willow Flats Trail. It's a smooth, easy walk and obviously well used. I meet several others on the trail or along the river. One couple stops me and asks, "Have you heard anything new about the terrorist attacks?"

"You know about the bridges?"

"Yes, heard about those from someone else. We had the radio on for a bit to listen for the details and heard the president speak—not that he sounded like he had much of a clue," the woman says.

Oh, goody. One thing I don't want is to get into a conversation about how the president may or may not be handling things. I don't mind a good political discussion, in the right circumstances, but I'm increasingly disillusioned over the insanity of the political propaganda machine. Seems the old adage of "lesser of two evils" applies more and more at every level of government.

"Sorry," I say with a small smile, "I don't know anything more."

The woman gives me a dirty look—why, I'm not sure—while the man says, "Okay, well, thanks for stopping. We'll let you get on with your walk. Have a good one."

"Yes, you also. And God bless you," I say. I'm not really sure why I added that, not a usual thing for me to say.

I get an even dirtier look from the woman, then she opens her mouth to speak as the man touches her arm.

"Uh, yeah. Sure," he says, hustling them away.

I try not to laugh out loud. What just happened there? I'm not usually so surly.

There are several people fishing along the riverbank or fly fishing in the river. A hooked-beak raven startles me with a thick throaty hackle. At home we have an overabundance of ravens. They're beautiful to watch as they soar through the air, and I love the way they fold their wings and seem to just drop, almost dive bombing through the sky.

While beautiful, they're also a bit of a nuisance, bothering our chickens, stealing eggs, and even sometimes young chicks. They do have a purpose, though. Both the ravens and crows do an excellent job of cleanup. They're scavenger birds, important parts of the ecosystem, cleaning up roadkill carcasses before they have a chance to rot.

The trail takes me by the day use area, not in use today, then continues on. I cut through the day use area to connect with the Sage Steppe Trail.

Off the Sage Steppe Trail is the Sage Knob Trail which, according to the brochure, has a nice sitting area and photo spot.

I'm not disappointed in the view from the benches. The view looks back over the day use area and the river. There's a grove of locust trees just below the lookout and some kind of flowering trees.

I'm back on Sage Steppe Trail when a herd of antelope drift over a nearby ridge. For a moment, I feel like I'm home.

Then I'm sad that I'm not and think I should be on the road now instead of wasting time here. I made a mistake not taking the fastest route home last night.

My paranoia about going through Portland and the I-5 corridor, while accurate, was too soon. I would've been well away from today's devastating bridge disasters and much closer to home.

For a few minutes, I ponder taking down camp and hitting the road again. My short nap gave me a second wind, and I'm feeling pretty good right now.

Should I start out? Maybe drive all night and get home sometime tomorrow?

Or, as soon as I get behind the wheel, will I tire out again? I've experienced driving fatigue in the past and know how unsafe it is.

As much as I want to get home, a good night's sleep is the best way to get me there safely. While I'm here, I may as well enjoy this wild, remote, and breathtakingly beautiful place.

I'm soon back to the campground and discover all of the spots previously vacant are now filled. This is a pretty common thing across campgrounds in the US on Friday nights. I'm heartened to see this, thinking people aren't giving up their plans and cowering to the terrorists.

People are beginning their meal preparations. There are several signs around—at the kiosk, registration area, and even in the campground—indicating a campfire ban.

I'm happy I bought the stoves this morning so I can cook a hot meal. I'll use the one-burner and heat up a can of soup. First, I'm going to drive out and try to find some cell service.

I'm rewarded a few minutes later with the notification ping, not just once but several times. I have text messages, one each, from Jake, Sarah, Angela, Calley, Katie, and my neighbor Doris.

I start with the message from Katie.

"Mom, I tried to call you, but my call just goes to voicemail. Jake tells me you're in a bad coverage area. It's so hard to know what the best thing to do is! I've decided to stay in Manhattan for now. It's still safe. There isn't anything happening here. Kansas City and Denver are a little too close for comfort though with the bridges being attacked there.

"My internship closed work today. I logged on to the school chat and many of the professors were encouraging unity and saying this needs to bring us together like 9/11 did. Most of us are too young to really remember 9/11 other than what we know from textbooks. People I know think it may result in riots more like Ferguson than the unity of 9/11. If rioting happened here, I'm not sure what I'd do. I know I wouldn't be involved in any riots or protests and would try to stay in my apartment. Being on the second floor is a good thing, I think. Last night Jake said I should hunker down. I'm going to stay with that for now. Yes, I have plenty of food and water. Enough for several weeks.

"If it seems something more widespread has happened or could happen, I'll get to your place as quick as I can. I hope you get home soon. Jake is doing okay but he really needs you there. I love you. I have a shift at the restaurant. I'm leaving shortly. I should be off by 11. Try to call me if you can."

I finish the text with tears in my eyes. I hope Katie's friends are wrong and the professors are right. I pray for unity and not rioting. There have been so many riots over the past few years.

I decide to read all of the texts before replying to any, that way I have all of the info I may need to formulate my responses.

I read the text from Sarah next.

"Hey, Mom. Tate and I bought a trailer and took it to your house. His folks are here now, and they, like everyone, are worried. His sister came along. She was able to work it out at the last minute and wanted to surprise us. We were going to go up to Bozeman for the weekend but have decided just to stay here. It doesn't sound smart to travel with everything going on. We might go down and visit Jake and Malcolm. Wish you were here. Be safe and get home quickly. It's so scary having you gone with everything going on. Tate is really glad his family is here. It's a relief. I'll feel better when you're home too. And Katie, I hate her being so far away. Talk to you soon."

Calley's text was short and sweet.

"Where are you, Mom? It's not good for you to be away from home with everything going on. Jake said you're in Eastern Oregon somewhere. Stay away from bridges and big towns but try to get home soon. Mike says he thinks you should avoid tourist areas too. I think he's right."

Angela's was even shorter.

"Tried to call you and wouldn't ring. I think you need a new phone. When will you be home?"

My neighbor Doris had only a little more to say.

"Mollie, I know you are doing your best to get home. Jake says you're taking back roads, avoiding bridges and cities. Smart. Let me know if you need me to help you find a route."

Jake's text is the latest to arrive.

"Honey, it's good you stayed off the interstate and stopped before Pendleton. They're showing video of interstates all over the country that are bumper to bumper parking lots. I-84 is one of these. Pendleton is full up with people leaving the Portland area. Gas is even becoming an issue since there are so many people on the roads. You might want to find gas as soon as you can just in case. Call me if you can."

Argh. That adds a new wrinkle in getting home.

I'm fairly confident trucks will be rolling to refill fuel stations, but it could take a couple days for this to happen. I filled up while in Redmond and am now just above a half tank.

I make a quick decision to pack up camp and get on my way. I think briefly of driving to Wasco, which is north on 206, but it's quite a bit closer to I-84 and people could, conceivably, be going there for gas and lodging.

And now I'm wondering if any of the campers are people leaving Portland instead of just weekend vacationers. I'll continue on my planned route, at least to Condon. After filling up my gas tank, I'll look over the map and decide how to proceed. My short nap will carry me through for several hours—at least I hope that's the case.

Back at my camping spot, I start packing up. I decide to have a quick, hot supper before taking off. Chicken and dumpling canned soup, saltines, and an apple goes together quickly.

While I'm eating my supper, I compose return texts to everyone and save them to drafts. I plan to try to call Jake but have the text ready to go in case reception is bad. I'll try to call each of the girls, also knowing text should go through if voice doesn't.

I take advantage of the water in camp to clean up my soup pot—which will also be my coffee pot as needed for this trip—and fill all of my water bottles.

Jake always makes a big deal about us having fresh, clean water, so this is a natural thing for me to do. I use the vault toilet on my way out and wistfully wish this was a full-service campground and I could take a quick shower. Once more, I bring the daypack with the toiletries bag inside it and a water bottle.

I wash my face, then brush my hair and teeth. The silver nonglass mirror helps little. I can see enough to know I look stressed and tired. Good to know I look the same way I feel.

Chapter 18

I stop just down the road from the welcome kiosk, trying to call Jake. The call won't connect, so I decide right then to send all of the texts before getting on the road. The texts are all pretty much the same, letting them know I'm driving again and avoiding the freeways, cities, and bridges. I hope to fill up in Condon and figure out my route.

It's not long until the response texts are going off. I'll wait and check them at the gas station. As tempting as it is to take a look on this quiet road, the risk isn't worth it.

I listen to the news on the radio. Nothing new on the plane crashes or bridge explosions. There's an update on the food poisonings, with reports of several thousand people affected with E. coli and at least fifteen hundred with typhoid.

The source of the illnesses has yet to be traced, but it's expected to be a widespread contamination of some sort, possibly intentional and related to the recent terrorist activities.

Yep. Saw that one coming.

Just over thirty minutes and I'm in Condon, finding a small service station to fill up. After the attendant finishes my fueling, I pull over to check my texts and maps. Jake's text says he'll try to call me, and everyone else asks I keep them posted.

While I was driving, I was thinking about a camping trip we took several years ago when Sarah graduated from college at Western Oregon. After the graduation we spent a few days camping on the coast, then camped our way home.

One of the places we stayed was Lake Owyhee State Park, very near the Oregon/Idaho state lines and very, very remote. The road in was very narrow and windy. We thought we were never going to get there. When we did, it was well worth the effort.

Such a wonderful place to camp. While I don't want to actually go to Lake Owyhee State Park, I do think the small roads we used to get there can help me get home.

I find Lake Owyhee on the map and trace a route from Condon to Vale, a town nearby. I'm happy to see this route takes me through John Day, Oregon. I've been on these roads a few times when I went elk hunting with Jake. I try to call Jake before heading out. I'm ecstatic when my call connects.

"Honey! Are you in Condon?"

"Yes, I just fueled up and am getting ready to be on my way. I'm heading toward Lake Owyhee, you know, where we stayed that one time."

"Uh, yeah. But you don't want to stay there. Remember how far it is off the main road? It took us forever to get to the campground."

"You're right. But it's nice, quiet roads that'll get me closer to home. My goal is Vale, which is near there. I'll go through John Day and Prairie City, so I'll have fueling options."

"I think that's a good plan. Did you look ahead on how to get home from Vale?"

"Not much. I'll be pretty close to Ontario. I think there's a highway running north from there I can take. I think it's the same one we took when we camped near there that time."

"Okay. I'm pretty sure the road goes up to Moscow, Idaho. You can probably find some small roads off it to continue east toward home. It's going to be a long, slow haul for you."

"For sure. I'm pretty happy to be off the interstate, though, if they're still parking lots. Are they? Or are things moving better?"

"Parking lots, last I checked. Many places with gas and hotel room shortages. Some towns are setting up emergency shelters in schools and such."

"What a mess."

"It's for sure a mess. I'm glad you're not caught up in it."

"Me too. The people ending up in those towns could be a lot like refugees. The little towns won't have the resources to sustain the sheer numbers."

"They don't. It's already to that point. You'd better get on the road so you can get somewhere and get some sleep. Do you want to say a quick hello to Malcolm?"

"Yes, I do. Can you put me on speaker phone?"

"Okay, I'm trying to switch to the speaker," Jake says loudly, without the speaker function engaged.

Malcolm's in the background. "Dad, the button is in the middle."

"Yep, there it is. Can you hear us, Mollie?"

"Perfectly," I answer. "Hey, Malcolm. How are you?"

"I'm good, Mom. You driving okay?"

"I am! Everything is good. I took a little nap at a campground. You won't believe this, but there were antelope at the camping spot."

"Antelope in Oregon?" Malcolm asks with disbelief. "I thought all of the antelope lived here."

"Most do," I say, "but there are some in Oregon, California, and remember we saw those ones up in Montana? They live in other places too."

"Neat. Did seeing the antelope make you miss home?"

"I missed home already. I can't wait to get there and hug the stuffing out of you."

"Okay, Mom," he answers with mock indignation. "I'll let you hug me when you get here."

"Well, thank you very much, Mr. Malcolm. I'm going to get going. I'll send you guys a text or call when I stop again. I love you both."

"I love you. Be safe," Jake says, while Malcolm says, "Love you too, Mom."

Chapter 19

In a little over two hours, I'm in John Day with a full gas tank and a cheap motel room. Parking directly in front of my room, I stash the handgun in my suitcase to take into the room but leave the rifle in the trunk. Part of me feels a little weighted down by these two items.

At home we have a funny saying, "Welcome to Wyoming, consider everyone armed." There are even bumper stickers with this on them. Oregon doesn't share this same motto. Keeping the guns out of sight, yet available, is my plan.

I waste little time heading for the shower. Afterward, I take a few minutes to wash the new socks and underwear I purchased on my shopping excursion plus ones I have in my suitcase. I use the free Wi-Fi to check current events, then turn on the TV for the same reason, and, finally, call Jake.

It's late at home. I'll wake Jake up but really want to talk with him. The phone goes to voicemail before he answers. I hang up without leaving a message, thinking I'll try again in a few minutes. Instead, he calls me.

"Hey, Jake. I'm in a motel in John Day."

"Super, honey. How was the road there?"

"It was quiet. John Day seems quiet. I guess people aren't coming here or haven't thought to come here yet, anyway. I'm just logging on to my laptop to see what's up, and I have the news channel on TV."

"I went to bed a while ago but had the phone by the bed so I'd hear when you called. I haven't looked at anything on the computer for an hour or so. Anything new?"

"I'm looking at a Portland news channel. They're reporting a confirmed death toll of 358 but expect the number to rise considerably with so many bridges affected. People are being advised to stay in their homes and to not try to exit the city.

"There are shortages of gas in and around Portland, plus I-84 and I-5 South aren't moving at all. I-30 and I-26 West are also parking lots. All the little towns dotting the coast, including Alto, have been inundated. Alto, Jake. I guess I shouldn't be surprised, but I worry about Ben and Clarice."

"Have you talked to them?"

"Earlier today, to Ben, before the bridges. They're announcing no lodging available in these towns and none anywhere along I-5 or I-84 within the state, plus the gas shortages. Jeez, I suspect John Day will be hit soon by travelers, if that's the case."

"Did you fill your tank when you got to John Day?"

"Yes, I did that before finding a room. I want to be ready to jet out of here in the morning and not worry about fuel. With fuel shortages, people will start getting desperate. Depending on where I end up tomorrow night, I may have to worry about my gas being siphoned—you think?"

"Gosh. I guess so. Remember when gas prices were really high and I had a friend who did have his gas siphoned? Lots of people installed locking gas caps during that time. It makes sense. If stations are out of gas, people could start stealing gas from car tanks."

"I need to get home. This just gets crazier and crazier."

"You need to sleep. Then get back on the road early tomorrow. Did you bring your map in?"

"I did but I'm going to look on MapQuest and see where to go from Vale. I'll spend a few minutes before bed figuring it out, then trace it on the paper map."

"Sounds like a good plan. Call me tomorrow once you're on the road?"

"I will. Sleep well, my love."

"You too, Mollie. Goodnight."

I spend a few minutes looking at the online map and matching it up to my paper map. Jake was correct about a road going north to Moscow, Idaho, from the Vale area. I'd have to cross over Interstate 84 around Ontario, Oregon, on her path north.

The news had said I-84 was clogged through to Pendleton. I wonder if it will reach as far as Ontario by tomorrow? I'm hopeful, with Ontario being on the very far-east side of the state, only a few miles from the Idaho state line, it will be less congested than places farther west.

I start to shut down the computer and stop while I think about the attacks. With the plane crashes and airport explosions yesterday, then the bridge explosions today, which have caused so many people to flee the affected cities, and the foodborne illnesses being reported, I have to wonder what may be next. Hopefully nothing. But something more wouldn't surprise me.

I take a few minutes and look for new books for my eReader. While I haven't spent much time reading in the past thirty-six hours, it's something I very much enjoy: spending time each day reading. I want to order a few books I've been thinking about.

I have over three hundred books on my device, which are accessible to me now, plus about three times the amount in the cloud. I'll order a few books I've had my eye on and also scroll through the cloud to see if any books in there should be on my device.

Jake and Malcolm also have tablets for reading, plus we keep a backup eReader—a very basic one for books only, not surfing the internet—in the basement within a garbage-can-turned-Faraday cage. We hope this made-from-internet-instructions Faraday cage will work if there's ever an electromagnetic pulse or coronal mass ejection.

My hope is we'd still have access to the mass amount of books we've collected, books which cover just about every genre in both fiction and nonfiction, both for entertainment and education. We also have lots of paper books, but these electronic books are terribly convenient. I designate my new orders to go to this eReader also. As I finish ordering, I find a few books for Jake and send them to his tablet, as well as several for Malcolm, which I send to his tablet. Tomorrow I'll have Jake turn on the wireless connection on each of the devices at home, including the backup in the Faraday, and they'll load up.

I finally shut down the computer and turn off the lights, but leave the TV on, finding a home remodeling show for background noise.

Chapter 20

Saturday, Day 3

My eyes pop open. The room is still dark. This room, like so many these days, doesn't have an alarm clock, so I reach for my phone. 3:03. Yeah, it's early all right.

Might as well get on the road. I can drive in the dark as well as the light, as long as I'm careful of wildlife. This area is rather sparsely populated with humans but has plenty of deer and elk.

Before leaving town, I stop at an all-night gas station with a mini-mart to get a little caffeine in my system. I'm on the road and the coffee has barely cooled enough for me to drink. The first sip hits my taste buds and the experience is less than pleasant. I know by the third or fourth sip my tongue will be numb, and I'll have no trouble gulping down the rest.

The road from John Day to Vale is quiet. Even though my tank is still at about three-fourths, I fuel up. I'm not sure what I'll encounter as I near I-84, so I figure better safe than sorry. I find a second cup of gas station coffee, so I'm also well fueled up for the day.

I reach Vale around 6:00. This small town's claim to fame is as the first stop in Oregon along the Oregon Trail, with many murals depicting the town's history on the Oregon Trail. I decide to find a nice place to park and have some breakfast and then pull out my maps to plan the next section of my journey.

I refilled the ice in my cooler before leaving the motel, so my breakfast consists of a chilled cheese and meat roll along with a granola bar and half a Gatorade. Once I've eaten, I give Jake a call.

"Hey, honey!"

"Hi, Jake! Guess what?"

"What's that?"

"I've crossed over to mountain time."

"Wow, you must have got an early start."

"I did. I think I left the hotel just after 3:30. I'm in Vale now and stopped to look over the map. My plan is to go from here up to Ontario and then head up Highway 95. Can you look on the computer and see if there's any reason not to do this? I could pull mine out and use my hotspot, but if you already have yours handy…"

"Yeah. Give me just a few minutes. We just came in from doing the chores."

"Thank you, Jake. What are your plans for today?"

"I have to dig some holes. I bought a few clearance vines the other night. Malcolm and I started digging the holes to plant them, but I'd forgotten just how rocky it is there, you know, along the front line? I'm going to see if Noah can come over and help dig."

"I suspect he will. He's often looking for ways to make a few bucks. You putting them in the sections that are a little bare? What are they?"

"Yeah, I'll fill them in where needed. That one spot where we lost the raspberries is where I started digging last night. I bought an assortment—ten total. Found a few gooseberries. I was surprised about that."

"That's great. I'm glad you found more gooseberries. The two we planted are doing well, and with their sharp spines, they really serve well as a deterrent."

"You want to talk with Malcolm for a minute while I finish getting the computer going?"

"Yes, I definitely do."

"Hey, Mom," Malcolm says, sounding tired.

"Hey, Malcolm, sounds like you two have a busy day planned."

"Yeah, Dad says we have to go to a wedding today. Annie is getting married. At least I can play with her brother… what's his name? Tommy?"

"Tommy is her youngest brother. He's eight, I think. The one just older than you is Josiah."

"Oh, yeah. I always forget their names."

I laugh a little at this. Malcolm loves people, and he loves doing things with his friends, but he rarely remembers the friend's actual name. He'll say something like, "You know, the one with the yellow hair," or, "The one that likes Minecraft," or something similar.

"Think you'll be home today?" Malcolm almost whispers the question.

"I don't think so, sweetie. It's still a long drive, but I'm going to get closer, and I should be home tomorrow. How does that sound?"

"That sounds good, Mom. Today would be better, but tomorrow will be okay. I think Dad is ready to talk to you again."

I swallow the lump in my throat. It's so hard not being home with Malcolm with everything going on. I know he's fine, but I still hate it.

"Okay, honey," Jake says. "I'm checking I-84. It's still terrible to Pendleton, and even a little beyond, but clears up around La Grande. I think you'll be fine crossing I-84 at Ontario."

"All right. That's good. I'm going to go ahead and get on the road, then. I just had a yummy breakfast of a cheese and meat roll plus a granola bar."

"No coffee?"

"Two cups of gas station brew along the way."

"Ah... I know how you love gas station coffee."

"I was thinking it was better than nothing this morning."

"Stay in touch. I'm thinking these nuts aren't finished yet. I disconnected the solar system yesterday, just in case."

"Just in case? Oh... you mean in case of an EMP?"

"Right."

"Does that seem like something terrorists would do? It seems to me they'd want to continue to cause terror. Not do something so final. What could they hope to gain by an EMP? And where would they get a nuclear weapon?"

"I suspect they have connections. And we're assuming these are regular terrorists, like Al-Qaeda or ISIS. What if this is North Korea doing these things?"

"North Korea? Wouldn't a country acting like terrorists be a little odd?"

"Yes, it would. But the end result would weaken us so they could come in and take over," Jake states firmly.

"They don't have near the people needed to come in and take over," I counter.

"Not on their own. But what if they aren't acting on their own?"

I have to admit, I'm a little irritated with Jake. He's sounding like he needs to tighten his tinfoil cap—even more than I do. "Jake, you're sounding like you've been spending too much time on the internet."

"I haven't. I've been thinking of these things on my own. I might do an internet search, though. Just to see if other people are thinking the same thing."

"I have no doubt you'll be able to find others thinking as you are. You can corroborate anything you want with the right searches. That doesn't make it true," I snap.

"Honey," he says with the patience of Job, "all I'm saying is it seems a little too organized. Too well planned. Could a terrorist cell plan and institute these things that have happened?"

"Why not? They've done things on a smaller scale. What if those were all practices leading up to this?"

"Hmmm. Maybe. Whether it's terrorists or some country attacking us in a nonnormal way, I think we should be ready. We've been storing food and materials and building our place just in case something like this happens. It'd be silly to stop thinking through the possibilities now. Speaking of, I thought I'd contact Dwayne and see if he has a used inverter and controller for sale that I could hook into our system."

What? He wants to buy another solar system. No. No way. With as much patience as I can muster, I say, "Jake, we've spent so much money the last few days. And you know how much those are. We decided not to buy a backup for the house because of the cost and Operational Security. The small system backups were expensive enough."

"They were. And it seems that you talked me into those. I trusted you knew best when we decided to buy them. And it's not just their cost, but the cost to put together the Faraday cages, while not super high, does add up. This is something I think is a good idea. You should trust me on this."

Jake's right. I should trust him. Most of the prepping we've done has been at my urging. I doubt we'd have near what we do have if I wouldn't have pushed Jake into some of the purchases. Many of the items, like the food and toiletries, simply make sense, as we can always use them. But the backups of the small solar systems and other things are a little more controversial. Sure, if the cistern pump system goes out, we can simply go down to the basement and get a replacement. Seems a backup to the main solar system would also make sense.

I let out a small sigh while I compose myself. "You're right. I do trust you. It's smart to disconnect it. Go ahead and check with Dwayne. If he has something he's looking to move from his inventory, he may give us a good deal on it. Speaking of, you're still expecting Bubba today with the new cabin?"

"Far as I know, Bubba should be here around noon. He said he'd call me from the pickup place if it wasn't what he expects. I'm kind of wishing I would've passed on it. Then the idea of a second solar system wouldn't be so bad."

"The second system is going to be more than the cabin by a long shot."

"Yes, it will. And I hope Bubba is on time. I completely forgot about Annie's wedding today."

"Me too, until Malcolm mentioned it. I'm glad you two are still going. Be sure to pass along my congratulations and regrets for not being there."

"Alex already knows. I saw him yesterday evening. He stopped by for a minute while Malcolm and I were trying to dig those holes. I let them know you aren't going to make it. Quite a few others aren't making it, either, with the flight cancellations."

"The gift I bought for Annie and Kaleb is in the gift closet. I wrapped it before I left. There's a card on it. You can't miss it."

"Great. I'll make sure I get it. You think Malcolm can just wear his black Wranglers and a button-up shirt? Me too?"

"Yes, that should be fine. It's an outdoor wedding and during the afternoon. I think there will be cake and punch afterward. No dinner."

"Right. Maybe, when Katie gets married, we can do a nice afternoon one. Speaking of, she told me last night she loves Leo. I got the impression once she finishes school, we'll be planning a wedding again."

"I've wondered. More because of what she doesn't say than what she does. I feel a little bad I made such a big deal about needing a break from weddings. That probably wasn't fair to her."

"We did need a break from weddings. Even though they were all wonderful and we're happy about them, three weddings in three years was a lot. But if Katie does want to get married, we'll help her with the wedding just like the others."

"Of course. I hope we can meet him before wedding plans are started."

"Yeah, me too. I'm going to take care of paying all of the bills. I only left a hundred in savings yesterday. I know you said you'd take more cash out of checking today, but how about I move additional to savings so you can withdraw from there also—you know, to beat the daily limits, just in case?"

"I think it's a good idea, but I'm not sure when I can get that out. There may be a rule I have to wait twenty-four hours from the last transaction. I'll keep an eye out for an ATM and try it. I didn't even think about it, but I suspect ATMs are out of money in the areas where the crowds are. Cash on hand is probably a good idea. And we can always put it back in the bank when I get home and this whole ordeal is over.

"Oh, Jake," I say all excited. "I just remembered, I sent a bunch of books to yours and Malcolm's tablets and the spare eReader. Turn all three on and connect to the Wi-Fi so the books can download, okay?"

"Yes, sure. Good idea. I'd better let you get on the road. Call me later?"

"I will. I love you. Remind Malcolm I love him."

"Ah, honey, he knows. But I'll tell him anyway."

As Jake and I disconnect our call, I think about what he said. Is there a chance this isn't terrorists?

Chapter 21

I've always assumed this was terrorists. I thought they might not be done after the first night but wouldn't expect them to do something like an EMP. Why would they? I've always thought terrorists wish to cause terror and watch the reactions.

If there was an EMP, how would they witness the terror? There would be no twenty-four-hour news stations broadcasting the carnage.

But if, like Jake said, a country was behind these events, things could be very different. An EMP, or even ground detonation nuclear weapons, could be planned.

If they did that, we'd do the same right back, so it wouldn't make any sense. Of course, things sometimes don't make sense. And the president did sign the Executive Order recently for the government to harden against an EMP... I wonder how they're moving on this process?

I need to drive and stop thinking about this. My main goal right now is home. I should be to Ontario within a half hour. And out of Oregon shortly after.

If all goes well, I'll make it into Montana today. If I can push for a really long day, I could even make it home.

Home. My foot becomes heavy on the accelerator. Home. The temptation to rush, to speed, to fly down the road is strong. Home. I set the cruise control. A ticket would be bad. Ontario soon appears.

The town looks quiet. Should I get fuel? My needle hasn't moved off the full mark. I'll wait. I find a bank and pull the maximum cash out of both savings and checking. If nothing else, I should be set on money. I'm soon on US-95 North and in Idaho. As much as I love it, I have to say, it's good to be out of Oregon.

My windshield time allows my mind to wander.

I'm disappointed I'm missing Annie's wedding. Alex and Natalie MacIntyre have a homesteading and permaculture school, which is how we first met them—by taking a Saturday workshop.

Besides for the Saturday workshops, they do immersion programs. People from all over the country visit for a week or longer to learn the basics of running a sustainable farm. It's a great way for people to see if the farm life is really for them, or if the novelty is a whole lot better than the actual process. Something like this wouldn't have helped in our case since we loved our little homestead until recently. And there are still many parts of it I continue to love.

I have no doubt Natalie will be well prepared for the wedding guests delayed in leaving. She's not only a great teacher but an amazing hostess. I want to be sure to ask Jake about the wedding and Annie's dress.

It's a casual, outdoor wedding. My daughter Calley's outdoor wedding last summer was a much more elaborate affair than Annie's is supposed to be. Where Annie is having an afternoon wedding, Calley's was shortly before sunset followed by a full dinner. Calley wore a long dress with a train, which could be bustled at the reception, and a veil. She was lovely. The ceremony was short but very sweet and the reception went well into the night, with the DJ playing until almost eleven o'clock.

Two summers before, Angela and Tim were married. Their wedding was also an outdoor event held at a lake. It was casual and lovely, fitting the bride and groom.

Angela wore a long, pale-green dress with a white lace overlay and veil. When we went dress shopping, she said "Mom, I want a white dress, no lace and no veil." We both laugh now about how her perfect dress wasn't at all what she thought she wanted. Tim wore shorts and a casual button shirt. Both wore flip-flops. It was perfect.

A few months prior, over Thanksgiving weekend, Sarah and Tate were married. Their original wedding plans were for June of the following summer, allowing almost fifteen months to plan the perfect wedding.

While Jake and I were contributing a small amount to the wedding budget, they were footing the rest of the rather large bill. One day in mid-September, Sarah, living in Oregon at the time, called and asked if I thought we could put a wedding together within a couple of months.

She assured me she wasn't pregnant but just couldn't see planning, and paying for, a big wedding. They really wanted to buy a house and start a family as soon as they could and thought their money should go to housing. She'd already purchased her wedding dress and had some ideas.

Sarah made some calls and settled on Thanksgiving weekend because no one else was getting married then. She was able to get an extremely discounted venue at the historic Benson Hotel in downtown Portland.

The guest list was kept to thirty-five, which was a perfect fit for the venue. The meal was fully catered by the hotel, and they even included a honeymoon suite for the bride and groom. Jake and I were surprised to discover our limited contribution to the wedding covered almost everything. Sarah said it was exactly what she dreamed of but never thought she could afford. I often tell people when planning weddings to look at holiday weekends. You never know the kind of venue deal you can make.

Katie hasn't mentioned marriage. I do know she's very fond of Leo, her boyfriend, and suspect they're likely living together, though she's not admitted to it. Of course, I haven't really asked.

Until recently, she talked about going on a mission with her Kansas church after graduation. Now, she doesn't mention it, and the last time I asked, she changed the subject. While I want to be involved in my children's lives, there comes a point when they're adults and should be allowed to have some privacy.

I try not to be hurt when Katie, or any of my adult daughters, don't fully share their lives with me. Part of me wants to be their "girlfriend" who they tell their secrets to, but most of me knows I'm the mom and I react as the mom. They often play things close to the vest because of this.

Katie will tell me when she's ready. For now, I listen to the hints she drops and the things she doesn't say. And I pray. I pray for each of them.

A few months ago, after we gave each of the girls and their spouses bug-out bags, Katie started sending food storage items to us. She had dehydrated and bulk orders shipped directly to us from the companies. She said she wanted to contribute to our food stores in case she did ever have a need to live here. One of the orders had the name Leo Burnett on it... Katie's boyfriend. This was a pretty good clue as to how serious they are.

Sarah and Tate, along with Angela and Tim, have also been adding to our food stores, either with food itself or cash earmarked for us to buy extra. As a result of these contributions, we've had a great increase in our stored items lately.

We already had a one-year supply of food for fifteen adults. With the additional items, we estimate we're pretty close to having enough for eighteen adults. Their contributions also came at a good time for us.

In addition to wondering if we wanted to continue with the farm, we've also been wondering if we're plumb nuts for prepping. It's not the first time we've had the conversation, but it had been coming up more and more often over our "winter of discontent" with farming.

In the past, we'd get to a point we felt we were pretty well stocked with food and other supplies. We had a decent amount of knowledge and a plan for dozens of different scenarios. We'd start to relax a little and decide to move into a maintenance mode.

Then, something would happen—stocks would plummet, rioting, strike threats, etc.—and we'd rethink things, discovering we could really use more of X, Y, or Z or another thingamajig or widget.

This past winter was different. While I felt a burning need to provide the bug-out bags for the children, I had a hard time wanting to add anything additional to our place.

The past couple years left us in a mess, and we were just digging our way out. After a considerable amount of work, our marriage was improving, but we were both questioning our little farm and our prepping ways.

A few weeks ago, I restocked some of the things we were low on… more out of habit and a sense of obligation than desire. But for the most part, we're in a holding position, similar to the philosophy of our farm. Just keep it going but don't exert much effort.

Chapter 22

My daydreaming makes the trip go rather fast. In three short hours, I'm in the town of Grangeville, Idaho. This is one of the towns I've dubbed a "deciding town." Here, I can continue north on US-95 or I can take a smaller road heading east.

Staying on 95 would eventually put me on I-90 and likely end up putting me home quicker. The smaller road will keep me off the interstate for now and take longer but may be a better choice depending on what's happening.

I've been listening to the radio off and on all morning and have heard plenty of updates about yesterday's bridge attacks and the airplane and airport attacks from Thursday night, but I've heard nothing new making me think anything additional has developed.

Of course, that may not be entirely true. There are now many thousands of cases of E. coli and typhoid throughout the US and even in Canada. The list of affected cities is in the high hundreds.

It is now being called bioterrorism since the only explanation can be a deliberate outbreak. The cases are too widespread to be anything else. How these are being spread is still unclear, but people are being cautioned to wash fresh produce, fully cook their meats, and drink only bottled water or water which has been filtered or boiled to remove pathogens.

Argh. I'd better fuel up and buy more water in Grangeville. My early morning seems to be catching up with me, so a cup of coffee or stopping for a short nap might be warranted. Maybe both. I'm thinking fuel up, buy water, find a spot to nap, and then grab a coffee.

That is sounding very much like the winning combination.

After filling up, I move my car out of the gas lane to the convenience store spot. Like many convenience stores, they have cases of bottled water sitting on the front walk. The stack, which I assume is usually quite large, has a dozen cases left. I grab two of them, which isn't an easy feat. I set them on the counter and ask the clerk if he minds if I grab a drink out of the cold case before I pay.

"Don't mind at all. But I can't guarantee these waters."

"I'm sorry?"

"They're going like hotcakes since the alert came out. Someone else wants to buy them, well, I'll let them."

Interesting. I'm kind of surprised the guy is being such a dolt. "Okay. No problem. I'll pay for these and be on my way."

"That's fine. It's twenty-two dollars. Cash only."

Whoa. He's more than a dolt. My first thought is he's running a little side biz today, taking advantage of the situation. "What's that? The sign outside says $3.99 a case."

"It was, but now it's not. Twenty-two bucks. Cash."

"Ah, I see. Can I ask, is this your store or are you an employee?"

"I work here."

I smile, what I hope is a sweet smile, but suspect it may be more of a grimace. When coming in the store, I noticed the phone number for the franchise owner on the door. I love it when they do that.

I've never needed the number of a franchise owner before but consider using it now. I'm toying with finding out if the franchise owner is behind the price hike or if this is an enterprising clerk.

I'm totally in favor of capitalism, and if it's the owners, that's one thing. If it's a guy trying to line his pockets… I'm not sure I'm okay with that. Then again, what do I really care? I make a snap decision and decide I do care.

"Sure. Just give me a second. Looks like this store is part of a franchise owned by GI Enterprises. I'm sure you won't mind if I give them a call and find out when the price increase went into effect and when the water sales became cash only," I bluff.

I have my phone out to make the call. I can almost make out the numbers on the door from here.

"Listen, lady. If you don't want the water, fine. There are plenty of *local* people here who'll appreciate these two cases you want to hoard."

Hoard? Is that what I'm doing? I look at it as giving myself the best shot possible to get home. I take a second to look the clerk over. He could be anyone. He's average height with a medium build. His brown hair is cut in a typical no-style style. His polyester shirt, supplied by the mini-mart with their logo, is one size too large.

"I didn't say I don't want the water. I said I'm following up with your employer on the cost of the water and their business practices. I'll be purchasing the water once I get a straight answer," I peer at his name tag and add, "John P. This will only take a minute."

"Get out."

"I'm sorry?"

"Get out of here. Now. I will not tolerate your threats, and we have the right to refuse service."

"No problem, John P. But I'm still calling your boss and making sure they know you're gouging people and pocketing the difference. You have a nice day."

I'm backing toward the door, thinking I'm an idiot for causing trouble. I should've gone with my first instinct of not caring. The guy looks like he's going to wallop me. Not to mention, I'm missing out on the water.

"$7.98 plus tax, and your card is fine," he hisses.

"No, thank you."

I'm out the door and in my car with the doors locked faster than I thought possible. John P. is coming through the door as I tear out of the parking lot.

What were you thinking, Mollie? You should've just paid and kept your mouth shut. Now you have no additional water and a guy that wants to knock you from here to Tuesday.

My flip phone is still open and in my hand. Several blocks away and heart pounding, I pull over. The number to the store owner is punched in. I deliberate for a moment but choose not to call the franchise owner's number.

I had my answer when he gave me the actual price and told me I could use my card. Of course, maybe my calling him on it will deter him from trying it again on the next stranger visiting the mini-mart.

It's easy to cross a line, especially if it's with a stranger. I suspect he'd never think of doing what he just did to one of his regulars—his neighbors. I'm sure glad I fueled up using the credit card machine. He may have tried something there also. I decide to let it go. Not easy for me since I tend to overreact to things and really like to make a point. One of my many character weaknesses.

I'm still conversing with myself about what I wish I would've said to John P. when I see a warehouse-type store, one which advertises "pay cash and carry it out." I'm not really sure what that means but give it a try.

They do have water. Not the individual bottles like at the convenience store but gallon jugs. I buy four, even if it does make me a hoarder. I'm not the only one buying water. I momentarily ponder buying more food. They have large cases of things like granola bars and breakfast bars. I decide on a twelve-pack of breakfast bars and a twelve-pack of packaged muffins. The whole John P. thing has me looking for comfort, and food seems a good solution. I'll definitely need to go on a diet when I get home.

At the check stand, I find out they take only cash or checks every day, and they don't have any one to help you out—hence the cash and carry motto. I'm good with both.

After so much excitement, I'm not tired and decide to forgo the nap. There's a coffee hut across the street. Yay! Coffee.

First, I try Jake—no answer. I pull out my computer and hot spot to go on the internet. My girls make fun of me for having a hot spot device instead of just switching over to a smartphone. I just can't bring myself to change from my trusty flip phone and be "connected" all the time. The hot spot does exactly what I need it to do: get on the internet so I can see what I-90 looks like. And what I see it not good.

Not good at all.

Chapter 23

Washington State has a great website for traffic conditions, which shows I-90 is a mess. All of I-90, plus many other roads, are showing "highest impact" with multiple warnings. Once in Montana, the interstate is still bad with several "road incidents" in the Missoula area. The information indicates slow or stopped traffic. The interesting thing is the interstate looks terrible in both directions. I briefly wonder how people got so far from Seattle. Especially since the I-90 bridge was one of the bridges taken out.

The people of Seattle have few choices but to head east. South on I-5 takes them to Portland, which was hit harder than they were. North gives few options other than Canada. West is small towns and then the Pacific. Yeah, east is likely the best choice with the most opportunities.

I'll stay off I-90 and continue to use the state and county highways to make my way home. Prospector Peak pops into my head. My beacon of home, and my signal I'm near my family.

One of the things I love about the mountain is the way the views change depending on the perspective. When we're heading home from the south, it looks like a normal mountain. Beautiful, but nothing terribly special.

From the east, it shows more of its jagged side—a bit of personality. My view from Bakerville is the most amazing. From our angle we see the surrounding area, what some people refer to as the "wasteland." It's a rather barren-looking area of public land owned by the Bureau of Land Management, the BLM. The BLM owns something like 50 percent of the land in Wyoming, and a good portion of it looks like wasteland.

When the sun hits Prospector Peak and the surrounding area just right, it all lights up and glitters like gold. While most people look to the west to enjoy a sunset, I always check the east, in the direction of our mountain, and enjoy the light show the mountain and the wasteland provide. Some evenings, it will look almost like fire sparkling and dancing across the land.

Oh, and that wasteland? It may look like nothing from afar, but going into it, the land is amazing. While most of what grows is sagebrush and cactus, it's teeming with large and small wildlife. From a distance it looks flat as a pancake, but up close, there are amazing rock formations, hills, gullies, and more. We hunt and hike in the area, always amazed at the beauty.

The beauty is a big draw to home. The biggest draw—my family.

I let out a big sigh and shut down the computer. As I'm putting everything away, my phone rings.

"Hey, Ben. How are you?"

"Hi, Mollie. Things are a mess here. The highway is full up. Some idiot tried to get around it by driving on the shoulder. A few others followed him. When he crashed, it caused a small pileup from the followers and even pushed them into the regular lane. Emergency vehicles had a tough time reaching them because of the traffic. I think there were several fatalities. That happened just down the road from here, which made the back up even worse."

"Oh no."

"Yeah. The county folks are talking about closing the east bound lane in Alto so west bounders can drive on both sides. But when they get to Alto, they have to just keep going. There's no services available now.

"The station near my house, the one you used before leaving here, closed about an hour ago. The owner was smart and shut off the self-serve option when he closed last night. He opened up at 6:00 and was immediately hit. Food and water in the convenience store too. Adam, the owner, locked the doors and even hired a guard. There may be a little fuel at Stumpy's place in Alto since he closes overnight and doesn't offer self-serve, but the all-night places are dry. I suspect Stumpy won't be far behind."

"What a mess. How are you and Clarice? And your dad?"

"We're waiting it out. Glad we filled up the vehicles yesterday before the bridges were hit. Hey, even the cardlock by us is dry. The rumor I'm hearing is, someone decided to become an entrepreneur. He used his card to give people gas and took cash in payment. Ten dollars a gallon. It's Burdock, you know, the log truck driver who was arrested for poaching a few years ago? Him. And apparently, when his fuel-lock card stopped working with the built-in limit feature, he called his buddy Hank and they continued the deal. At that point, they increased the cost per gallon to fifteen so they could both pocket some. I'm sure people were happy to pay it."

"Wow. People are already taking advantage of this. I had a guy try to charge me eleven dollars for a case of water."

"Where are you? About home?"

"I'm in Grangeville, Idaho. I've been taking back roads the whole way. I didn't get very far yesterday. I had to keep changing my path and stopped for a nap. I stayed in John Day last night. Left a few minutes after 3:00 this morning. I was thinking I needed a nap, but the water guy got my adrenaline up enough so I'll be okay for a while. I was just checking my maps and the roads to see which way to go. I planned to hit I-90, but it's terrible."

"Most freeways are terrible, all across the US," Ben says. "People are fleeing the towns where the bridges were hit. Even though officials are telling people to shelter in place, it's not happening. With so many people on the road, there's a fuel shortage just about everywhere.

"People are trying to fill up when they leave the city, but those stations were hit hard yesterday, and suburbs and little towns along the edges too. Some people are turning around and going home. Since so many people run their cars on empty, they have no way to leave town to begin with. Probably best. With the number of people on the roads now, they can't get anywhere. Hopefully it will start to calm down. Oh, and wrecks like we saw are everywhere. You can't have that many people on the road without troubles. I've even heard of shootings in some places. You definitely want to stay away from the hordes if you can. You having any trouble getting fuel?"

"No, I've been in small places that haven't been affected yet. I thought I might have some trouble when I crossed over 84 at Ontario, but it was quiet. Far enough away from Portland, I guess."

"Think you can make it home today?"

"I don't think so. I mapped out a route, and it looks like sixteen hours or so with staying off the freeway. I'll have to stay somewhere tonight, or at least get in a few naps."

"I hope the terrorists are done."

"Me too," I agree with a nod, even though he can't see this action. "Any news on them?"

"Yeah. Some. Still no one claiming responsibility. But you know how they originally thought suicide bombers detonated the bombs while they were still in the vehicles?"

"Yes?"

"They aren't so sure anymore. They believe all of the bombs were detonated remotely, even the ambulances filled with explosives at the airports. They found evidence of detonators. It's not as easy on the bridges, but there are a few reports indicating bombs may have been left. And several 911 calls about stalled vehicles. In fact, about a quarter of the bridges hit had these calls. There's even some suggestion missiles were used, like the kind used to bring the planes down, especially in the cases where the bridges were fully destroyed."

I'm having a little bit of déjà vu after the conversation with Jake earlier this morning. "Huh. I thought terrorists were all about suicide bombing."

"I guess that's assuming these are the usual terrorists. Maybe they aren't?"

"Maybe not. But if not, then who?"

"That's the million-dollar question."

"For sure. Hey, Ben, I'd better get on the road."

"Sure, Mollie. Take it easy and stay safe. Oh, and... I think some of your paranoia may have rubbed off on me."

"Oh?"

"Yeah. Dad and I came up with a plan in case we have to get out. As soon as we heard about the bridges yesterday, we got more fuel. We'd already filled up our vehicles and the semi-truck, but we bought an auxiliary tank and secured it to the small flatbed trailer—not the semi one but the one we use with the red pickup truck—then we made a few adjustments so the semi could tow it."

"Okay? So... what? You're thinking you'll use the semi as your bug-out vehicle? The truck gets, what? Five miles per gallon?"

"About that, little less probably. The tanks hold three hundred gallons, which should be enough to get to your place, especially with the auxiliary tank. Provided, of course, the offer is still open."

"The offer is always open. But why the semi? Just for the fuel distance and not needing to fill up?"

"That... and the modifications we made. Owning a machine shop does have its perks, you know."

"What modifications?"

"We Mad Maxed it."

"You Mad Maxed it? I have no idea what that means."

"We dressed the front up a bit. Added a... well, something resembling a brush guard. With it, we can push stalled cars out of the way. You know, gently nudge them aside so we can get through. Kind of like one of the trucks from the Mad Max movies."

"Ohhh. I see. Was that your dad's idea?"

"How'd you know?" Ben asks with a small laugh.

I can't help but laugh in response. "Sounds just like him."

"Yeah, well, my idea was to also bring our ATVs. Both of my side-by-sides and four dirt bikes."

"How'd you fit those? On the trailer?"

"Yes, the ATVs fit fine. Two of the dirt bikes also fit on the trailer. The other two we were a little more creative with. I have a couple of hitch-mounted carriers. One we attached at the end of the trailer, no problem. The other is welded to the front of the trailer."

"Why both ATVs and dirt bikes?"

"Figured we didn't know exactly what we'd encounter. We'd like to be able to just take the truck, and the second choice is the ATVs. But if we end up needing to be fully off-road, the bikes make the most sense."

"And fuel?"

"Yep. Several cans of gas."

I don't say anything, weighing my words in my head before I speak. Finally, he says, "You think we're being a little nuts?"

"You're asking me? Did I tell you about all of the stuff I bought this morning? I'd win the award for being most paranoid. Though, I have to say, you might be giving me a run for my money."

We both laugh. Then Ben says, "Yeah, well, I think Dad just really enjoyed the project. We talked about it last night and he had it almost finished by the time I got to the shop at 7:00 this morning."

"I'd better get going. Ben, seriously, if you decide you need to go, you should go. Your Mad Max truck sounds like it's up for the task."

"Yeah. No doubt about that. Hopefully the terrorists, or whoever they may be, have nothing else planned for us and we'll be just fine in a few days. Then we can laugh about our silly truck."

Chapter 24

As we disconnect, I think about how much I hope he's right. Things are such a mess now, but could certainly become worse if the terrorists have additional attacks planned. I think about how these are not suicide bombers, or possibly not, and wonder if we're way off the mark on what's happening.

With the firsthand account Ben gave me of what's happening where he is, I think about my fuel. I just filled up before my run-in with John P., but now think maybe I need an alternate plan for fuel.

As part of the bug-out bag we sent to Katie, we suggested she buy a couple fuel cans and figure out a way to tie them on her bike rack. I decide to take this advice and stop at an auto parts store before leaving Grangeville.

I find two flat five-gallon gas cans; another container of zip ties, which are larger than the ones I bought at SuperMart; and another assortment of bungee cords. Not liking the red color, which screams "gas can," I also buy a couple rolls of duct tape in a color somewhat like my gray rental car. I love how duct tape now comes in colors instead of just silver.

Back at my car, I cover the cans in tape and secure them to the bike rack using the zip ties and bungee cords. While it's definitely a rigged job, it seems fastened tight. I find a different gas station than the one John P. was working and fill both cans. In this economy rental car, I should be able to get an extra two hundred miles, give or take, with two cans. And if I don't need them, the gas can always be used at home and the cans added to our stash.

This town stop has taken me much longer than I would've liked. It's almost 11:30 before I'm finally on the road again, taking Idaho 13 to US-12 East. I decide to see if I can find any new information on the radio.

Scanning the channels, I finally find a station with the news. I listen for many minutes and learn nothing new from what Ben told me. There's more info on the food poisonings—they've spread even more. There are many deaths now, mostly from E. coli but some from typhoid where people were too sick for the treatment to work by the time they got to the hospital.

I listen for another hour or so as a talk radio host does his show, then the station starts getting static. I'm still catching most of what's happening when the radio host mentions the shooting in Wyoming last month.

"Here's some new information on last month's shooting at Grover Elementary in Grover, Wyoming. After killing several at the school, the shooters were stopped by a husband and wife, the Mitchells, visiting their child's class. In violation of the posted Gun-Free Zone, the parents were carrying weapons.

"Wyoming enacted the School Safety and Security Act in 2017, which allows local school boards to decide if district employees may be armed in school buildings, but this district said they didn't want the new act and would remain gun-free, feeling confident local police could respond quickly as needed. The police weren't even called before the Mitchells ended the situation. They were able to kill two of the shooters. Sam Mitchell killed one of the shooters using only a small pocketknife. A third suspected shooter was found dead near the office.

"Interestingly, the third shooter, who the Mitchells say was dead when they found him, was the only one with ID. He was a young kid from the area, known to be a bit of a troublemaker, whose mother was found dead at their home nearby. We're now hearing rumors that, while the other two shooters' IDs have not been definitely established, they're believed to be European residents."

I decide I need to pull over so I don't lose the station. I know this talk radio host has a tendency toward theatrics and is considered a bit of a conspiracy nut, but I hope there may be some good information. Besides, Jake and I already have our own conspiracy theories on this shooting. Everything is a little too disconnected.

"Now, it's all a little strange," continues the talk show host. *"After the shooting, one of the teachers from the school, who corroborated the Mitchells report of finding the kid dead in the hall, died in a car accident. Then the school secretary, who had backed up the Mitchells using the gun she knew the principal had hidden in his office, committed suicide. The Mitchells have disappeared.*

"Dr. Mitchell walked away from his successful medical practice without telling his office partner, staff, or any of his patients. Everyone

who knows Dr. Sam Mitchell says leaving without warning is not in his nature. A retired Lieutenant Commander in the Navy, he was known as being a man of his word.

"Mrs. Mitchell, who studied medicine and went on to become a Doctor of Chiropractic—yes, a chiropractor who I should also refer to as Dr. but have avoided doing so to help cut down on confusion—worked in conjunction with her husband's practice and also left without giving notice to anyone. Their children were whisked away and none of their friends, teachers, other family members—no one—knows where they may be.

"Earlier this week a deputy sheriff was killed in the line of duty. I have to wonder if this is all connected. Is someone trying to silence those at the school for a shooting that was supposed to look like a 'Lone Wolf' killing by an unstable young guy? And if so, who?

"Then you add in the attacks we've had the past couple of days. These attacks originally looked like terrorist attacks. We were told they were suicide car bombers. Now it seems the car bombs had detonators. The backpacks and other items with bombs at the airports on Thursday night were also detonated from afar. Same thing on the bridges. Cars were abandoned and exploded, or the bridge was hit by a surface-to-surface missile. This is not the behavior we usually see from known terrorist groups.

"And I have to wonder, are these events related? Of course the events of Thursday and Friday are related, but what about last month's shooting? Could it play into this? Is it possible these other 'Lone Wolf' events we've seen over the last several years are also related? What if a, possibly, foreign government is behind these? Our government tends to respond to these shooting massacres with a knee-jerk reaction of increasing gun control. Seems to me that would play right into our enemy's hands. An invading force wouldn't want an armed populace. The fewer guns in citizens' hands, the better a target we look. I'll be back after this short break to take your calls on this subject."

Holy buckets. Maybe Jake was right. As much as I'd like to sit here and listen to the call-in portion, I need to get back on the road. Before I start up again, I check my phone for text messages and missed calls. With the radio on, it's likely I didn't hear the indicator go off.

I have a missed call from Jake and a text from Katie.

"Mom, hope your trip is going okay. Jake told me you're in Idaho. Yay! That's so much closer. Things got kind of bad in Manhattan. Not

90

super bad but a lot of people came in from KC. People are camping in the city parks and they opened up the college to house them. I decided to head to your place. Leo is with me. I talked to Jake and he knows we're coming. Hopefully it will just be a few days' vacation at your home and we'll be able to go back. My restaurant is likely going to have to close until more food gets shipped in, which doesn't seem possible right now with the freeway clogged up. We're on a highway now, it's moving but not very quickly. Leo says maybe when we get farther from I-70 it will thin out. We hope to be to your place by tomorrow. Maybe you will be too. See you soon!"

I can't believe I didn't even think about Katie being affected by this. I should've checked to see what I-70 looked like. I'm so glad she was keeping abreast of the situation and knew when to leave. Or maybe Leo knew when to leave. Either way, I'll feel so much better when I know she's at our place.

I try to call Jake and his phone goes straight to voicemail. I send him a quick text, letting him know where I am and that I hope to drive straight through with only quick stops to nap. I'll be home soon.

Chapter 25

I've been on US-12 East trying to find a road to take me through a stretch of national forest and put me on US-93. So far, I've not found a road I can be sure of. If I stay on this, I'll end up in a little town about ten miles south of Missoula. Ten miles—is this far enough from the interstate not to be affected by traffic? My gut tells me no.

Several miles outside the town, traffic increases. I'm soon stopped by a police officer a few miles before US-12 intersects US-93.

"Hello, ma'am. Can I ask where you're headed?"

"Bakerville, Wyoming, I'm trying to get home. I'd like to get on 93 and head south, then make my way east a little farther down. Can I get through here okay?"

"Well, you can. But you won't be able to stay here. We don't have any services available. You'll be able to go south on 93. We're trying to keep the roads cleared to through traffic only, so you'll see several officers directing you along the way. You'll have a slow drive through town and then another forty miles south. The county sheriffs are helping with the traffic control."

"Okay. And I'm guessing I-90 is a mess, so 93 is my best option?"

"Yeah. You don't want to go on 90. It's okay closer to Bozeman but between here and there," he shakes his head, "you won't even be able to get on."

"Thank you. I'll stick with 93, then."

"Yep. Just keep going and follow the instructions from the officers. And remember, you won't be able to stop in town. They'll direct you through town."

"Sure. Thank you. Can I ask, where are all of these people from? This seems quite a ways from Seattle to have so many people here."

"Seems not just Seattle people fled their homes. We can't really understand why, but there are people from all over here. Instead of staying put, they thought it'd be better to look for greener pasture, I guess. Doesn't make much sense," he says with another head shake.

I nod in agreement and make my way through town. He's right. The police presence is heavy. So is the civilian population. The town is full. Tents are even on several expanses of green lawn.

The drive through town is slow. As I continue on, stopping periodically to be given instructions by city police or sheriff personnel, I consider this route may not have been the best way to go. I should've gone east somewhere farther south. Maybe even gone through Yellowstone.

An hour later, I'm still driving at a snail's pace and being ushered along by the occasional police officer, with the radio on low. Things may get even worse.

"We're receiving reports of computer networks running dozens of financial intuitions offline by what is believed to be the result of a malware cyberattack. The affected banks are unable to offer any online services, which has shut down credit and debit cards, online banking, and ATM machines. While it is a Saturday and most bank branches are closed, people are prevented from withdrawing money directly from branches since the computers cannot be accessed for these records. We're assured these attacks are being addressed and services should soon return to normal.

"In addition to financial institutions going down, social media giants Facebook and Twitter, along with YouTube, Google, and Yahoo, are unavailable due to what is believed to be a distributed denial-of-service taking these out. With so many people turning to social media and online searches to stay up to date on the latest news, this is causing extra panic.

"The affected sites hope to resolve these outages as soon as possible. 911 operators are being inundated with calls reporting downed status of websites. Please do not call 911 to report any websites being down. Please reserve 911 for true emergencies only. We'll have more on this developing story as information becomes available."

Huh. Credit and debit cards not working, along with ATMs going down, is a huge deal. The report didn't say which financial institutions are affected, only "dozens."

This certainly complicates things even more for the people fleeing the bridge collapse towns. Even if wherever they stopped still managed to have resources, can they buy these resources?

What a mess. And surely it must be related to the terrorists... or whatever they might be.

A little over an hour later and I'm out of the worst of the traffic. It's taken me about two and half hours to go less than sixty miles. I sure hope Katie's trip is going quicker than mine.

93

I'm pretty sure I'm a good ten hours from home here, if I don't run into any more stuff like I just got through. I've decided I'm going to keep going as best I can and only stop for short naps. No more hotels or campgrounds—simply rest breaks.

Of course, since I've been up and driving since 3:00 am and it's almost 5:00 pm, I could use a break right about now.

And my fuel is getting low. None of the small towns I've gone through during the previous couple of hours had fuel. I'm hopeful the next town up the road will have gas stations open. I do still have my filled gas cans but would rather not dip into them unless absolutely necessary.

I soon reach the little town of Sula, Montana. Yay! An open gas station.

I'm the third car in line. While everything looks fine here, I make sure my pistol is within easy reach. I also leave enough space between my car and the car in front of me so I can bolt if necessary. I have about a ten-minute wait before it's my turn.

"Afternoon, ma'am. Need some fuel?"

"Yes, I'd like to fill up."

"Can't fill you up. We've got a ten-gallon limit. The price is five dollars a gallon. Can't take cards since the machine's not working, so it'll have to be cash."

"Okay. I think I have that much, if you don't mind small bills and change?" I still have quite a considerable amount of cash on me, stashed in various places, but don't want him to know this, for my own security.

"I'll need the cash, then I'll take care of handling the pump for you."

I get him the money from my wallet in small bills and change. I make a point of him seeing that he's just about cleaned me out and even take the last few wrinkled bills out of a pocket in the purse along with three quarters, a dime, and three nickels.

"Thanks, ma'am. Let's get you fueled and on your way."

A few minutes later, I'm all set and ready to go.

"Be careful, ma'am. Since you came down 93, I'm sure you know what all is going on. If you're heading toward Dillon, it's okay until just this side of Dillon. Then you'll be in it again. They've got people directing traffic to get through. You'll want to stay off I-15 if you can. It's a mess."

"Thank you, I appreciate the information."

I have to admit, while I really do appreciate his information, I'm a little paranoid it's completely obvious where I'm headed. This can't be avoided with limited roads and options through this rural area. Again, I'm thinking I made a mistake picking my route. Could've, should've, would've. No sense lamenting on what can't be changed.

Chapter 26

As soon as I find a spot, I pull over to take another look at my map. Seems this road I'm on, 93, continues south. I could possibly stay on this instead of getting on 43 and heading toward Dillon. Maybe this would help me avoid the issues around I-15.

I spend way too much time looking over the map and determine there's really no good way to get home from where I am. Home. The need to be there is sitting like a pit in my stomach. It feels of desperation.

Beam me up, Scotty. The fictitious transporter could take me from this road in Idaho to my home in Wyoming in seconds. By car, I'm still hours and hours away. So close, yet so far.

My best bet is to go through Yellowstone Park. It's not a transporter, but it's the most direct route from here.

I really don't like the idea of this, knowing the park is likely well populated with the summer tourists. And I suspect many of them are ready to get out of there but don't want to risk leaving until things calm down. I worry people will be short on food and patience.

We tend to avoid Yellowstone during the rush. Ben and his family visited Yellowstone during peak season a few years ago. He told me about waking up early and driving the park right around daybreak. He said he was the only one on the road. During daytime, travel was terrible, but the early morning trip was perfect.

I decide I'll do the same thing. Stay outside the park and plan to get to the entrance right at daybreak.

My ten gallons of fuel gives me just over half a tank. I'm going to need to find more fuel in order to make it through the park and home.

Hopefully the next town down the road will have a station. Just in case, I put more cash in my purse from one of my stashes.

Before I take off, I try to call Jake. The phone doesn't even ring, just disconnects. I try again with no change. I try to text but get a message failed notice. Maybe too many people are using the circuits or towers or whatever.

Then I wonder if the attacks have affected cell phone service. Either is possible, I decide.

Back on the road, I'm not the only one traveling this route, but at least it's not super busy.

Less than an hour later, I'm in a little town with an RV park, hotel, convenience store, and gas station, all in one.

Again, there's a person out at the pump helping another person. Again, I take precautions, making sure my pistol is hidden yet available in case I need it. There are a fair number of people milling around, so I want to try to pay attention to everything going on.

Once the guy finishes talking with the other car, it's my turn.

"Hey there. We have fuel. Fifty dollars for five gallons, cash only since our card reader isn't working. You want some?" asks the man, who isn't much out of boyhood.

Half as much fuel for the same amount of money as my last stop. I guess that's how it's going to be.

"Yes, please. Can you fill me up?"

"Nope. I can give you five gallons. That's it. You got the cash?"

"I can pay, if you don't mind small bills and possibly change."

"Don't matter to me. I just work here and take the money into the boss," he gestures at the store.

I get the money for him.

As he starts to walk inside, he says to me and the person at the next pump over, "I'll holler out when the pump is on. It will stop automatically at five gallons."

I let him walk away, then remove the pistol from the holster and consider tucking it into my leggings. I'm wearing a dress, which will cover the pistol, but it's also going to be a pain if I need to get it out in a hurry, and I really wonder if it's going to stay put with leggings. Why, oh why, didn't I put my leggings-approved holster on? With a sigh, I leave the gun in the car. I try to move it so I can get to it in a hurry but have my doubts.

My worry is unnecessary, and I'm soon fueled up and on my way. Before leaving, I briefly contemplate going in the mini-mart but decide against it.

I'm not comfortable leaving my car with the number of people around and the feel of things. There's a vibe in the air. I'm not the only one on edge.

Outside of town, I pull over and put my belly band holster on. I don't put the Taurus in the holster, instead leaving it in the other holster it's been in while it rides in the car, but at least I'm now "dressed" for the occasion of carrying my weapon.

Another hour and I'm nearing another small town. The closer I get, the heavier the traffic heading west is.

There's a gas station, only this one has a big sign out front: NO GAS. Farther down the road is a second station. This one also has a sign: GAS 2 GALLON LIMIT $30 CASH ONLY.

Cash only is underlined two times. There's also a sign indicating the entrance is farther down and the outlet next to me is the exit. I pull out a ten and a twenty and pull up.

There are half a dozen cars in front of me. Could these be people who've made their way from I-15? I think it's only a little over an hour to 15 from here, under normal conditions.

Today… who knows? I'm hopeful, since I'm heading toward 15 and not away, the traffic won't be terrible for me.

When I reach the front, the attendant declares, "Thirty cash." I hand it over and he handles the pump. There's a second person on the other side of the pumps telling a person in a pickup truck, which just pulled to the front of the line, the same thing.

"Just how do you think two gallons is going to help me?" Mr. Pickup Truck yells loudly.

"Hey, friend, I just work here. We're doing what we can to help everyone get where they need to go. The other station in town is already out of fuel since they didn't put limits in place."

"So what? What makes you think I care about you helping everyone else? What are you, a socialist?"

"I just work here. Do you want your fuel or not?"

"I want you to fill up my tank. Do it now. And you will take my credit card," Mr. Pickup Truck says, while punctuating each word with a jab of his right index finger.

"Can't do it. The card reader isn't working. Either two gallons for thirty cash or nothing."

At this point, all I want is my gas finished so I can leave. I look in my side mirror and see my gas guy isn't even there. Glancing at the pump, it's turned off.

Mr. Pickup Truck is still yelling. I slide my seat back and slip the pistol in my belly band holster, then carefully get out of the car to detach the hose from my vehicle.

I have the hose hung up and am putting the gas cap back on when there's the unmistakable pump of a shotgun. I immediately crouch down and move quickly toward my car door.

"Mister, get back in your truck and hit the road. We don't have any fuel for you. MOVE," a new voice yells.

"You go to—"

I start my car and take off as the shotgun goes off and, almost simultaneously, what sounds like two shots from a semi-auto handgun.

I scrunch down, straining to reach the pedals after moving the seat back, with my eyes peering through the steering wheel, as I screech out the exit.

Chapter 27

Holy cow. That was close. Holy cow. I suddenly have to go to the bathroom super bad. I guess getting the pee scared out of a person is a real thing. No way am I stopping.

About five miles down the road, I find a place to pull off. Traffic heading into the little town is quite heavy, so I do my best to park so I'm off the road and not super noticeable.

I briefly consider finding a road leading me away from this little highway, but my need is much too urgent. I open both car doors to provide a privacy screen of sorts and complete my business.

After I'm done, I check the car to make sure a stray bullet hadn't hit it while I was making my getaway. Everything looks fine with the car, the gas cans, and the bike. My nerves, however, are still shot.

I take a couple of snacks and a soda out of the cooler. I still have a decent amount of food in the car and a considerable amount in the trunk. I'm glad I got the two gallons of gas before things went to pot. I'm hovering just over half a tank. Hopefully the next place won't have a limit and I'll be able to fill up.

I need to just get through it and up near the Yellowstone entrance. Then I'll sleep and start early tomorrow. *Please, Lord, let me find more fuel.*

Within an hour, traffic is congested going my way also, but we're still moving along between thirty and forty miles per hour.

A good hour later, I finally see a sign letting me know I-15 is twenty miles ahead. Traffic is now stop and go, crawling occasionally at ten miles per hour. Will this road ever end?

I've had the radio off since the shooting incident. I decide to check in and see if there's anything new. There is.

The cyberattacks have increased to the point the entire internet has been taken down by the US government to prevent any further breaches.

Apparently, traffic lights, which are computer controlled, had been hacked and many accidents were caused in cities and towns across the US. Power plants have also been affected.

Elements of power grids have been taken down en masse, which has caused what's described as a "cascading" outage, in which a power overload spills over from one region to another to another.

Blackouts and brownouts are being reported throughout the US. And not just power outages are reported; several power plants had what's being described as a type of malware attack their digital relay and backup generators.

The code opened a circuit breaker in the generator's protection system, then closed it just before the system responded, throwing its operations out of sync and destroying the generator.

There are even reports of similar events happening to transformers across the US where the malware code caused a power surge and blew the transformer.

And they do mention cell service is spotty, with many carriers and some of the smaller carriers down completely. Yep. Thought so.

In addition to the new cyberattack, there's more info on the original plane crashes and explosions from Thursday night, as well as the bridge explosions yesterday—nothing new, really, just updated estimates and more pondering on who and why.

It's hard to believe this all started only forty-eight hours ago.

10:15 and full-on dark.

I've been on the road almost nineteen hours. I could really use a break but don't want to pull over in this traffic. I should reach I-15 within the hour at the speed we're moving.

I suspect it's going to be even worse trying to get past 15. I remember I've yet to drink the soda I pulled out of the cooler. It's a cola, maybe the caffeine will help keep me going.

At 1:00 am I reach a small town. Every gas station I've seen has a big NO GAS sign.

From here, it's just over eighty miles to Yellowstone. I'm so tired I can barely stand it. I get out of town, then find a road to pull off on and walk around a bit.

This road doesn't have the traffic I've been in the last few hours. Maybe I can make good time. I need to sleep at least a couple of hours before going through Yellowstone.

I also need fuel.

I'm down to under a quarter tank and the info button indicates I can go sixty-two miles on what I have left. I add one of the five-gallon

101

cans to the tank. Once it's in, I rehook the can using a fresh zip tie along with the bungees.

I have one soda left in the cooler along with one meat and cheese roll. Good thing since the ice is mostly melted. A couple of hard cheeses are still in the cooler, but they'll be fine without ice.

I dump the ice out and put the cooler away, then cut the roll into pieces and pop open the soda. I'm on the road again, enjoying my snack. My fuel info button now shows 165 miles.

I check for gas stations in every small town I come to. At each I find out of order or NO GAS signs. Looks like these towns have been affected by the cyberattack blackouts, since they're completely dark.

I reach West Yellowstone at 2:45. This town is also dark and all gas stations I've driven by are closed.

The road takes me through what seems to be the edge of the downtown area, where I find a gas station and travel mart combination. This is as good a place as any to take a nap.

Maybe they'll open up before I leave and I can get some fuel. I pull up and look for the hours on the door. They open at 5:00. Perfect.

My fuel info button is down to eighty-three miles plus I still have a five-gallon can left. Hopefully they'll have the fuel pumps working in the morning.

As it is, with the gas can, I should have enough to make it home.

I move to the edge of the parking lot, lock the car up tight, and set the alarm on my phone. I'm thankful that, even if calls can't be made or received, the time and alarm are still working.

I pull my blanket out, spend a few minutes adjusting, and settle in. This sleeping in cars business is getting to be a habit. A habit I'm not fond of at all...

I try to text Jake before I go to sleep. I'm pleasantly surprised the text appears to have been successful. Hopefully he'll receive it and know where I am, and know I'm okay.

Chapter 28

Sunday, Day 4

When my alarm goes off, I feel like I've not slept at all. It's still fairly dark, but I can see the sun trying to peek over the mountain range. Today is the day. The day I make it home. Jake, Malcolm—I can't wait to see them. Katie should also be home today. I wonder about my other girls. Is Sarah okay in Billings? Are Calley and Angela fine in Casper?

Casper isn't very far from Denver, which had a bridge attacked. Are they seeing people fleeing from Denver for someplace perceived safe? Hopefully Casper isn't being affected as severely as some of the towns I've driven through.

I dig around in my large backpack and pull out a ball cap, which I'm happy to have in my get-home bag, then grab the other items I'll need—including a flashlight—and tuck the handgun snug in the belly band holster. I pull my car over to a spot in front of the door to the mini-mart.

There's a guy inside. I try the door: locked. I give it a rattle. He sees me, walks over—taking his time—adjusts the lock, and pokes his head out.

"No power. Can't help you with gas and I can only take cash for anything you want to purchase."

"Okay. Can I use the bathroom?"

"Yeah. I think you can still flush even. The sinks have water. It's a little slower than it should be but still running. But, hey, how about only flush if it's absolutely necessary, to help conserve."

"Sure. That's fine."

"Well, come on in, then."

I freak out a little when he locks the door behind me.

He notices my reaction and says, "Oh, hey, I just thought it'd be safe to not have an open door today. I'll leave it unlocked for now."

He unlocks it as I hurry back to the bathroom. I decide I'll do what I need to do as fast as possible.

Less than five minutes later, I'm in fresh clothes. I buy a cold coffee from the fridge case—at least it's supposed to be cold. Without power, it's cool, but that is all. I also buy a few cheese sticks and a packet of jerky. I'm way okay on food but am taking the easy way out and not digging in my supplies.

"Do you know how far it is from the west entrance of the park to the northeast entrance at Cooke City?"

"Hmmm. Let me think. Around ninety miles, I guess."

"How about to the east entrance?"

"Less. Maybe sixty-five."

"Super. Thank you."

"You trying to get home?"

"Yeah, I am. You hear anything about how things are in the park?"

"Not much. There were quite a few people who came out Friday morning after the first attacks. We quieted down by afternoon. Didn't notice much after the bridges were taken out on Friday afternoon. Sold out of fuel that day. Thought we'd have a truck late Friday night or early Saturday, our usual schedule. Nope. Guess it doesn't matter now with the power out. Haven't heard anything after the phones and power went out last night."

"You know if any of the gas stations in town are working? I really need more fuel to make it home."

"I don't think so. I went over to the Exxon last night. His truck did arrive on Friday, before the bridges were hit, so he didn't sell out. He said he was going to try to find a generator to get the pumps working. Last I heard, he hadn't found one that could do the job. He suggested I contact the owner here about doing the same thing, but with the phones not working right, I couldn't connect." He glances at his watch. "He should be there now getting ready to open up. Doubt the phones are working this morning, but let's try."

He picks up the store landline and dials from memory. Shaking his head, he says, "Nope. Let's try my cell." He can't connect via cell either. "Why don't you drive on over there? Knock on the door, tell him Bernie sent you."

He gives me directions to find my way.

"Thank you."

"Sure, hope you make it home okay. If he can't help you at Exxon, maybe you can find fuel at one of the park stations. 'Course, I suspect they were slammed with people filling up on their way out. Probably affected by the blackout too," he says, walking me to the door and locking it behind me.

I check my phone to see if there's anything from Jake or the girls. No texts, no messages. I try to call Jake but can't connect. I try to text but get a failed signal.

Maybe last night's went through and he'll at least know things are okay on my end. I can only assume everything is fine on his end also.

I find the Exxon. It's still closed but someone's inside using a flashlight to get around. I knock tentatively on the door.

The man walks over, and reading his lips, I can see he's saying, "We're closed. No power, so can't help you."

I motion to the gas pumps. He shakes his head and yells so I can somewhat hear him, "Sorry. Can't get the pumps working."

I nod and make my way back to my car. There are now a few people around, so I decide to put the remaining five gallons in my car farther up the road where it's a little more private.

I check my maps before starting out. A quick look confirms my best choice is to take the Northeast Exit out of the park near Cooke City, Montana. This is the least mileage to home.

I make my way through phone calls, trying Jake and each of the girls. No success. I repeat with trying to text, only to encounter "message failed" with each attempt. At this point, exasperated and fighting tears, I stop trying.

I listen to the radio on my short drive to the park entrance. The cyberattacks continue. Power is out across the US, with the number of places unaffected being a very small portion. Cell phone service is still spotty, with some carriers completely down. All banks are completely offline, along with the entire US internet.

Commercial transportation is even at a standstill. With trucking companies and rail cars running on computers, deliveries are a mess. Of course, the trucks are sidelined anyway with the power outages affecting the fuel stations. Seems I'm not the only one running on empty. People are stranded throughout the US. The radio station is on backup power and will begin to limit its broadcasts to the top and bottom of the hour with news only.

The entrance to Yellowstone is unmanned, with a sign saying to pay upon exiting. There's a stack of Yellowstone newspapers, but I don't see any of the nice maps they usually hand out. I've been to Yellowstone several times, but a detailed map would still be helpful. The newspaper has a general map. I'll use that. Grand Loop Road is quiet; so quiet I'm the only one on it.

Shortly after Madison, as I'm admiring the beauty of Yellowstone—the lush forest along the Gibbon River and the wonderful smell on this crisp morning—my rental car beeps at me. *Low fuel.*

I ignore it for now and keep going.

With the reduced speeds through the park, it takes some time to reach Norris Canyon Road. A mile or so farther, just past Virginia Cascade, is a picnic area. This looks like a good spot to put in my last five-gallon can of fuel.

As soon as I get to the gas can, I can see I have a problem. A big problem.

Chapter 29

One of the zip ties is undone. I wiggle the can and know it's way too light. Did someone undo my can and steal my gas? Even though one zip tie is missing, the other three are in place.

Tears immediately well up in my eyes while I try to figure out what has happened. It takes me only another few seconds to realize someone punched a hole in the bottom of the can and drained it out.

Anger, frustration, and desperation. My tears are now full force. When could this have happened? While I was sleeping? My sleep last night was terrible. I should've heard something like this happening.

Could it have happened when I was in using the restroom at the gas station? I moved my car up front. They would've had to be very sneaky for Bernie, the clerk inside, not to have seen them.

Either that or he was involved. He was very nice and tried to be helpful; I don't want to think he's involved.

Beam me up, Scotty. I really need that transporter now.

I could dematerialize here and rematerialize in my kitchen. Oh, I guess Scotty would need to take me to the ship first. I don't remember Captain Kirk ever beaming anyplace other than to or from the ship. No matter, I can allow a few extra seconds to stop by the ship before they send me home.

I stifle a giggle. It doesn't work. Another giggle escapes. I cover my mouth to hold any future snickers in. Why am I laughing? As quickly as the stress laughter started, it stops. The tears return.

I allow myself a few more minutes of sniveling, then start to pull myself together.

Do I have enough gas to make it back to West Yellowstone? I'd probably come up a little short and have to finish on the bike. Not terrible. Though, who knows how long it will be before the gas stations are working again. I'd need to find a place to stay and wait it out.

I definitely don't have enough fuel to make it home. I check the makeshift park map. It lists distances between major points. While not exact, it's helpful. Looks like about forty miles to the Northeast Gate.

I dropped below the fifty-mile indicator just past the Madison Junction. I'm kicking myself for not stopping then, when it was an easy trip back to West Yellowstone.

Maybe it's better this way. This far inside the park, I can't bring myself to turn around and go the opposite direction from my home. I'm going home, even if it means biking farther than I thought I'd need to.

According to the map, Madison Junction was about sixteen miles ago. I should still be able to travel around thirty-four miles. Where does that put me?

On the other side of Tower–Roosevelt.

Can I make it to Slough Creek Campground? Probably not the campground itself; I think it sits well off the main road. But I remember a pullout near there. We've stopped for a picnic lunch overlooking a stream and meadow on the road to Slough Creek. That might be a good spot to leave my car.

If I can make it that far, it's another twenty miles to the Northeast Exit. Cooke City, and a gas station, is a few more miles down the road.

Gas stations… where are the ones in Yellowstone? I looked at the Madison and Norris junctions and didn't see one. What's next? Canyon. The map doesn't show anything about a station. It does show road construction in the area. Great.

I flip through the newspaper and find the Canyon village information. Yes! A twenty-four-hour station… using a credit card. Argh. Maybe it's open with someone taking cash like some of the other towns. And farther up the road, at Tower–Roosevelt, I know there's a station. I pointed it out to Jake last time we were in here. *Please, Lord, let one of them have fuel.*

At the moment, I'm in desperate need of the toilet and a cup of coffee. After using the bathroom, I fire up my little propane stove. Pour-over coffee is pretty trendy right now. With fancy coffee shops grinding just enough beans for a single cup, then using a cone-shaped dripper—usually made out of glass or ceramic—and a special slow-pouring kettle.

That's not what I have.

I have a cheap plastic thing, with a cheap coffee filter, and a small pan for boiling water. Instead of grinding just the right amount of coffee, I open up a pod.

Immediately after I pour the water over the grounds, the aroma hits me. Yum. As soon as it drips through, I take my first swallow. And scald my tongue.

I heat up a can of soup while the coffee cools enough for me to drink. It's slightly bitter, but not in a bad way.

After coffee and breakfast, I make my preparations.

Hopefully, I'll find gas in the park. Otherwise, I'll continue to the Northeast Exit, taking the car as far as I can. I'll try to find someplace I can pull it off the road so Jake can bring me back to get it and I can return it to the rental company. Ugh. That invoice is going to be crazy high if things don't straighten out soon.

It's been a long time since I've run a car out of gas. In fact, the last time was when I was a new driver.

I had a Ford, which was several years old. I can't even remember what model it was, but remember it had a three on the tree shift pattern and was a two-door. It got terrible gas mileage, but I'd bought it for three hundred bucks, and it served my needs of getting me to school and my afterschool job.

I'd yet to realize the gas gauge wasn't completely accurate.

On my way home one Saturday, it coughed, sputtered, and died. I coasted to a stop shortly thereafter. I hope I have a little more warning with this car so I can find a good place to leave it.

I need to get things as organized as possible while I'm here, in a comfortable location. The bulk of my supplies are in the trunk, which means I'll need to take the bike off the rack and remove the setup in order to access my supplies.

As I'm contemplating this, I remember Sarah's car has access to the trunk via the backseat. Malcolm discovered this while riding back there one day and thought it was pretty neat. Sarah, of course, knew about it and told him how handy it is.

Yes! This rear seat folds down to access the trunk. Pretty neat and a helpful feature. At home, I drive what people refer to as a crossover, which has a hatchback. I never even think about a backseat with trunk access.

I'm able to move the trunk cargo out of the car and have everything set out on the picnic table.

I packed up my backpack at Ben's house, so I'll only need to make a few adjustments, then figure out how to pack everything onto the bike. First, I take care of my clothes. I'm going to change clothes, putting on my quick-dry pants. They're the kind with zippers on the legs so they turn into shorts. I'll leave them as regular pants. I pull out a T-shirt and the athletic shoes, which were in my carry-on. I have a second pair of athletic shoes from my get-home bag, which tie on my backpack.

My backpack still has a decent amount of room and is still on the light side. I start adding food. During my drive, I ate most of the snack foods I'd purchased, so I pack the individual dehydrated meals. When I reach a point where it's getting close to as full as I want it, I start working on the other bags.

I can pack up the back basket here and then attach it to the rear rack on the bike easily, even when it's loaded. At sixteen-inches long, twelve-inches wide, and twelve-inches deep, I can get quite a bit of stuff in it.

I wish Katie was here. She'd know how best to load the bike. As an avid cyclist, she's taken a few overnight trips on her bike. Biking isn't my forte. Figuring out how to pack the bike is a bit taxing.

I load up the basket with a couple water bottles, two Gatorades, fix-a-flat, and continue with food items as space allows. I have cans of tuna, salmon, and sardines I picked up at the convenience store Thursday night, along with the small bottle of malt vinegar. I briefly wonder why I bought malt vinegar; it must have seemed like a good idea at the time.

I remove the freeze-dried items from #10 cans and transfer these to zip top bags. While they aren't at all heavy in the bags, they are space hogs.

I put a generous serving of the beans along with the dehydrated rice in an empty peanut butter jar, brought along in my get-home bag specifically for this purpose, with water to rehydrate for a snack or lunch later.

Strawberries without water are put in a second bag and a serving of meat, also without water, goes in a third to be for a meal later today.

The three baggies will go in my daypack for easy access, while the bulk supply of the freeze-dried items stays in the back basket. The family-size dehydrated meals go in here also.

Once I have this rear basket attached to the bike, my pack will attach to the basket. I'm hopeful my center of balance will be better without the large pack on my back. I plan on wearing the smaller daypack and possibly one of the fanny packs. I'm sure I'll be a sight.

In the front basket, I add the first aid supplies along with two more water bottles, the pour-through coffee filter, plus several coffee pods. Easy access to my coffee sounds like a good idea.

I put the ammo Ben gave me for the rifle in one of the fanny packs along with the second magazine for my handgun—I'll be wearing this fanny pack. I add my multi-tool and take some of the items out of the roadside kit Ben gave me.

I load the second fanny pack, which I'll attach somewhere to the bike, with more food. The daypack gets the food I plan to eat today. When I'm done, there are still several things loose and unpacked I'd like to take along.

I'll spend a few more minutes attaching things using bungee cords and zip ties before I take off. Again, I wish Katie was here so she could give me pointers on balancing my load. I do still hold a small hope one of the Yellowstone stations will be open for business.

The activity in the park, while not super busy, has picked up slightly since I first arrived at this picnic table.

There's been a couple of cars that drove by. One even slowed down quite a bit and seemed to be checking out what I was doing. I check the time on my phone. It's a few minutes after 8:00 am.

I guess Bernie from West Yellowstone was right—people did leave the park. Last time we were here in summer, even at 8:00 am, there was a decent amount of traffic.

I move the car as close as I can to the bathroom. I'm going to change my clothes so I'm ready to ride. I lock the car and leave the bathroom door slightly ajar while I get ready to go. I can't afford to lose my bike and plan to keep an eye on it. Thinking about losing the fuel in my gas can has me angry all over again.

111

Chapter 30

I'm dressed and ready to go in just a few minutes, including wearing my belt, holster, and sidearm. I'm carrying protection from here on out. I've been thinking about how to transport the rifle and have decided to bungee it to the pack on the back of the bike. I'm very thankful I bought several bungees and had a few more in the roadside kit. They'll come in very handy.

I find a radio station to catch up on the latest events. Nothing new, just more of the same.

The internet is still out nationwide, and even several other countries were peripherally affected. The stock market will be closed for the week, as will all banks. More people have died from E. coli. There are many, many thousands of cases of typhoid also, but most people are going in for treatment early.

Of course, the hospitals are operating at reduced levels with the cyberattacks and power outages. They're relying on backup generators. Many are calling for fuel help. There's a belief the illnesses were acquired at salad bars and buffets. And these were also deliberate attacks. Big surprise.

Nothing new on the plane crashes and explosions from Thursday night, other than an updated number of confirmed dead. Same with Friday's bridge explosions. There's still considerable speculation on who's behind these attacks.

I'd love to be able to get on the internet and look at a variety of sources to see what people are thinking about who's doing this. Not that it really matters. I'm pretty much wrapped up in my own issues and wondering about my family and friends.

Sunday morning… I'd like to think Katie is only a few hours away by now. I wish I could call and ask.

And Sarah, how's she faring in Billings? With a population of over 100,000, could they be having trouble? Even though there aren't any affected bridges nearby, I still wonder. Like the officer I talked with yesterday said, I wonder how many people left perfectly safe locations "just because."

Casper, where Angela and Calley live, is close enough to Denver—which did have a bridge destroyed—to see fleeing people. I say a quick prayer for all of my children, their spouses, and my little grandson, Gavin.

Jake and Malcolm. My men waiting for me at home. Did Jake get the most recent text I sent? Does he know how close I am? How hard I'm trying to get to them?

I see two oncoming cars before I reach Canyon Junction, and none behind me.

Usually bustling with activity, it's a ghost town. There's a sign on the road indicating all services are closed. There are also several people standing around holding their own signs. Jumping up and down to attract my attention.

"Employee, anywhere you're going."

"Employee, heading east."

"Employee, want to go home. East."

Sorry, friends. Can't do it. Besides, I'll soon be walking also.

Driving toward Tower–Roosevelt is a steep incline. I'm nervous, thinking how much extra fuel I'm burning while going up, up, up. I breathe a sigh of relief when I reach the top and begin the descent. Maybe I can keep my foot off the gas and coast down. Will that help with fuel conservation? I doubt it.

There are several people walking and hitchhiking along the way but, again, very few cars.

The sign for Tower Falls suddenly appears—a place I've yet to visit because the parking lot to view the falls is always so busy. Today, the lot is completely empty. Not even a hitchhiker.

I'm almost holding my breath as I continue to the junction. The gas station is just beyond the turn to head to the Northeast Exit.

While this area isn't usually as bustling as others, it's completely dead today. My heart falls when I see the large SERVICES CLOSED sign.

I turn around in the parking lot, making my way to the junction toward the exit. I've only gone about a hundred yards when the car starts making a beeping notice and gives me a gas alert. I guess this beats a cough and a sputter.

I start looking for a place to leave the car. Maybe a mile farther is a picnic area. I didn't make it to Slough Creek and the road I was hoping to leave the car on, off the main road. But the picnic area is better than parking on the shoulder.

How long will it take me to get home? When Katie did a bike camping tour with a few friends, she rode around seventy miles each day. It's very unlikely I can do any more than forty miles per day, and that's probably pushing it.

I'm pretty sure I'm around a hundred miles from home. Today is Sunday. I can maybe be home Tuesday. We could come back up Wednesday to get the car. Three nights in this picnic area, that should be fine. Especially considering no one is around.

I get the bike off the back, stow the bike carrier in the trunk along with the already packed large suitcase, and begin the loading process.

Everything goes pretty much as I hoped. I have the basket on the back with my backpack attached to it. It's a little awkward, but I discover putting the straps up helps stabilize the load.

I'm able to attach the second fanny pack with the food in it here also. I find spots on the pack to attach a few more things. The pack has built-in bungee cords I can manipulate, and I attach packs of crackers using the extra small bungees I'd purchased.

I attach the rifle to the top. Once it's on, I cover everything with a small, folded tarp. I test to see if I can still get the rifle off in a hurry if I need to. I'm not pleased with the time it takes, so I make a few adjustments.

Even though the bike did include a water bottle, I purchased a second one. I fill both from a gallon jug I bought at the warehouse store back in Idaho. I have enough water, plus I know there are streams and lakes aplenty on my route I can use with my filtering system. There are a dozen individual bottles and one-gallon jug leftover, which I leave on a picnic table for someone else to use.

I have all of my food packed or hanging off me or the bike somewhere. I contemplate a snack but decide against it for now. I've no doubt I'll need a break before long and can snack then.

I take a quick look at the newspaper map. Twenty-nine miles between Tower Junction and the exit. Another five, or so, from there to Cooke City. I can do that today and stay tonight in Cooke City.

I'm ready to go. I've organized the car trunk as best I can. The suitcase I'm leaving is packed with my laptop and other work items. I pack my eReader in the daypack and slide it inside my purse, already in the daypack. I switch out my regular progressive lens glasses for the single-vision sunglasses in my purse. I can't imagine riding the bike with the progressives. I usually swap them for single-vision lenses any time I'm doing things like hiking, skiing, or martial arts. The multiple lenses just make things too wonky for sports.

There are several empty boxes from when I consolidated items to fit in my packs, plus the three #10 cans. I've packed one roll of toilet paper and tore off many sheets of paper towel. The remaining roll of paper towel and three rolls of toilet paper I put in the suitcase.

I've used most of the zipper bags I bought and have put in an empty gallon, two quarts, and half a dozen sandwich size in one of my packs. The rest are left in the trunk. I want the main part of the car to look like there's nothing interesting, and decide it's okay.

After locking the car, I walk the bike to the restroom. I take my bike into the bathroom with me. I'm not even going to risk losing it.

The road out is pretty rough, so I decide to walk my bike. While I'm doing this, I suddenly remember I'm in bear country.

Grizzly bear country.

I live in bear country and am quite aware of them, but with the fuel situation and wanting to get home, I've forgotten.

To make things even more fun, I'll be in bear country the entire way home, I don't have any bear spray, and my only weapons are small—way too small for encountering a five- to six-hundred-pound bear. A 9-millimeter or .22 would be little more than a bee sting, unless I managed a pretty amazing shot while being charged.

Suddenly, all the food I was so pleased with myself for finding space to carry feels like a bear magnet.

Will the sound of my bike be like ringing a dinner bell?

I suddenly wish I would've returned to East Yellowstone and kept trying to reach Jake. Then he could've made his way to me and picked me up. I could've easily holed up in a hotel for the duration of the cyberattacks and things going on now.

My tears are threatening to fall again. I take several deep breaths. I'm committed. At the very least, I need to get to cell service and try to call Jake, assuming the phones will be working once I get out of the wilderness.

On the bike, I'm a little wobbly at first. It's been a while since I've rode, and the balance is a little off since I'm so heavily laden.

115

After a few miles, I begin to get my sea legs and start feeling pretty good. I'm pretty nervous when I hear a car behind me, praying he pulls over and gives me plenty of room. He does.

Cooke City. At least it's not too far. Maybe I can call Jake from there. It's an easy drive for him to come and retrieve me. While we have rules about getting home in case of an emergency, we made those rules on the assumption there would be no contact.

But if I can reach him and tell him where I am, things change. I know he has plenty of fuel stored at home for the truck, and he can bring fuel for the rental car. And I won't have to think about meeting up with a bear on my trek home. This idea is definitely a winner.

I'm several hours into my ride. Things are going well, and I'm pretty sure I'm nearing the exit of the park, maybe only another hour or so. I've passed the road to Slough Creek Campground, then saw Pebble Creek Campground. Shortly after passing Pebble Creek, I had a slight scare.

A bear was in the field across the road. It was a young-looking black bear, very cute, but I still panicked. He didn't notice me at all.

A mile later, I start up a steep incline. This hill is a killer. I'm not even halfway before I need to get off and walk. I'm fully winded when it finally starts to even out. Once I'm back to breathing normal, I hop on the bike. I think to myself how nicely everything is going. In an instant, things change.

Chapter 31

A rabbit darts out in front of me. I swerve just enough to lose control. Stupidly, I yank the handlebars to try and correct. The next thing I know, I'm a heap in the ditch.

I stay on the ground for a minute doing a mental check. I can move all of my limbs, so assume nothing is outright broken. I'm definitely banged up. My sunglasses were knocked off in the fall, snapping one of the bows and popping out the right lens. I touch a sore spot above my eyebrow. My finger returns bloody.

My right side has taken the brunt of it. My knee is scraped up and my pants are ripped. Glad I learned in my martial arts training not to stick out my hand to break my fall, I'm pretty sure I'd have a busted wrist if I'd done that. Instead, I have a decent road rash the full length of my forearm.

My nose is running. I wipe my good arm across it and come back with a bloody streak. Ugh.

I carefully get to my feet, then pick up my bike. Other than crushing one of the packets of crackers hanging off the pack, everything with the bike seems okay.

Now that I'm upright, I discover a bit of a headache. Good thing I was wearing a helmet.

I find my backup pair of glasses, then spend a few minutes cleaning up using the wet wipes, taking care to pick the small pieces of gravel out of my forearm, elbow, and knee. One of the first aid kits has individual packs of antibiotic cream, which I apply liberally, then dot my elbow and arm with Band-Aids. I don't have a Band-Aid large enough to cover the knee scrape so make one out of a nonstick pad and some tape.

I'm hurting and hungry. Pushing my bike, I hobble to a better place—than the ditch—for lunch. From my daypack, I pull out the bag of tortillas and now-rehydrated bean and rice combination, plus the saltshaker. My bandana becomes a tablecloth to assemble my lunch. I spread the bean mixture on a tortilla, break up the string cheese and put it on top, sprinkle with salt, drizzle a smidge of olive oil over it all, then roll it up.

This is one of my favorite hiking meals, and it never disappoints. It even provides a serious measure of comfort after my crash. I try to eat an apple and discover a slight pain in my jaw. I toss it aside for a chipmunk treat. I try a few of the freeze-dried strawberries—no problem with them. At the end of my meal, I choke down a Gatorade.

When I'm done eating, I look over the bike again. It seems fine. *Thank you, Jesus.* Back on the bike, I'm stiff, and getting going again isn't easy. The combination of stiffness, crashing, and not being used to bike riding—I'm starting to think I might need to stop and rest, when I see the exit out of Yellowstone.

Yay! I suddenly have a second wind. I can make it a few more miles. Then I'll start looking for a place to stay. Maybe Cooke City even has power and I can get a hot bath. That'd be amazing.

At the edge of Cooke City is an open gas station. I pull my bike up to the front and poke my head in the door.

"Hello?"

"Hello," a lady around my age answers, while giving me a strange look.

"Do you have gas?"

"Nope. We're out. Should've got our truck in on Friday—didn't show. We were hit hard yesterday by people leaving Yellowstone. Then, when the power went off last night, the owner hooked up a generator. That lasted about an hour before he shut it down. He's trying to get our genny working at the other station down the road. Not sure how that's coming along. But they're probably short on fuel also, since their truck didn't get here either."

"I was just wondering. My car ran out of gas in Yellowstone."

"Good thing you had your bike with you."

"Yes. For sure."

No way was I telling her about my planning to have this bike with me. "You think I'd be able to find a hotel?"

"Maybe. Heard the Cloud View is open. At least, they were still renting rooms last night after the power went out. Cash only, I suspect, since the machines are down. Just keep riding. It's not far down the road, on the left. You can't miss it. And I think the Grizzly Paw restaurant might be open. They have a gas grill and teamed up with a couple other restaurants in town to use up their fresh food instead of letting it spoil."

"Good thinking on their part. Thank you."

"You betcha. Have a good afternoon."

My body protests when I attempt to mount my bike. I decide I'll simply walk it. She's right—I can't miss it. I stick my head in the door and ask if they're renting rooms. The man inside answers with a hearty, "You better believe it."

"Super! You mind if I roll my bike in?"

"Nah. C'mon in. Room's $140 for one person. We're only renting out a few on account of the power being out. I can take your card if you have ID with your current address, and I need a phone number. Machine's out but we're recording the numbers manually. No power in the rooms but I'll give you a flashlight, and it doesn't get dark until late. You want just one night?"

Ouch... $140 a night. I think about this for a minute. The little time I've spent on the bike since the wreck has me thinking I might need two nights' rest. Or maybe I can reach Jake for a ride home. But I can't commit.

"I for sure want to stay tonight. I took a tumble a while back and may wish to stay a second night."

"Yeah. Thought you might have. You have a bit of blood on your forehead and your nose. Well, your shirt too."

I look down at my shirt, which is well-dotted in blood. I also catch a glimpse of the holster on my right side. Oops. I didn't even think of it when I rode into town. I'm in Montana. Open carry is fine here, last I checked, plus I have my CCP. I choose to assume it's okay to open carry and not say anything to the gentleman, who I'm sure has also noticed my weapon.

"I'm a bit of a mess. Are the showers working in the rooms?"

"Nope. Sorry. Water's shut off. The town shut it down. They're on generator also. They'll be turning on the water at 5:00 and 7:00 this evening for thirty minutes each time. It'll be cold water only, on account of the hot water heater being electric. So you still won't be able to shower. Sorry. But collect as much as you need to hold you over. You have something to store water?"

"I have water bottles."

"Get what you need for the night. They'll turn it on again in the morning, 6:00 and 9:00, if the power is still out. I've got a camp stove out back you can use to heat up water. Just let me know and I'll help you out. You can use the microwave too, if I start the generator for you. We put a couple buckets in the room for the toilet. Please refill

119

these when the water comes on if you empty them before then. Hold your flushes unless absolutely necessary. You need a sewing kit to fix your pants?"

"Oh, yes. If you have one, that'd be great. Do you have something I can use to heat water in the microwave? I'm not sure a water bottle will work."

"Yep. I can get you something. You get your stuff settled in your room and come back. I'll have it ready for you. I have a little water stored from earlier, so you can get cleaned up now instead of waiting. It's still a while until 5:00."

"Thank you. I appreciate it. I'm impressed with how well-organized everything is, with the water and you even being open. Let me get registered. Oh, I'll be wanting to take my bike in the room, is that okay? I'll make sure the tires aren't a mess before I roll in."

"Of course. Good idea. Weird things are happening."

I decide not to lament on my punctured gas can and simply nod. The registration takes only a minute. Instead of using my card, I pay with cash. Who knows when they'd be able to collect on the card. He gives me a battery-powered lantern and a regular, old-fashioned hotel room key.

As I'm leaving, he says, "If you're hungry, the restaurant across the street is serving. Don't know what exactly. Couple of places got together and are cooking up whatever they can. You'll need cash there."

"Thanks. I might give it a try."

The room is fine. While rather rustic and outdated, it's quite clean and spacious. The bathroom has a window, for which I'm thankful, until I look in the mirror.

Holy buckets, I *am* a mess. The startled look the woman from the gas station gave me makes sense now. I knew I'd hit my nose and had a cut above my eyebrow. I didn't know I had a cut across the bridge and between my eyebrows. Each cut is well-crusted in old blood.

The two five-gallon buckets, both full, are sitting in the bathtub. The room still includes the little soaps and shampoos on the counter, plus towels and washcloths. Back in the main room, I try to call Jake but get a no service note on my phone when I open it up.

I'm grabbing the room key to head back to the office and heat up some water, maybe I can make myself look a little less scary. As I reach for the door, I'm startled by a knock.

"Miss? I brought warm water over to you. I'll just leave it right outside the door. Thought you might feel a little poorly and wouldn't want to carry it back here."

I look out the peephole and see the gentleman who checked me in. I don't open the door but do speak loudly through it. "Thank you so much. I really appreciate you bringing it over. I'll return the container shortly."

"No hurry, Miss." As he walks away, I notice his limp. I figure he's in his mid to late sixties. His very short hair makes me wonder if he's former military.

I keep watching the peephole until I can no longer see him. I don't see the water, but it may be out of range. I cautiously open the door. Sitting in front of the door is a five-gallon bucket about three-quarters full of water. I quickly and carefully move it inside and relock the door. I test the water, and it's on the hot side. I'm almost elated at the thought of something resembling a bath. Less than five gallons isn't much, but I can make it work and have no doubt it will be glorious.

Using one of my empty water bottles, I add a little water from one of the buckets left in the tub to bring the temp down a bit. I remove the buckets from the tub, undress, and climb into the tub, setting the plug. I take an almost luxurious sponge bath. When I determine most of the dirt and gravel I picked up in Yellowstone is gone, I drain the water and reset the plug. Then finish my bath by pouring some of the remaining water over me using the water bottle. Amazing.

I dress in jeans, a top, and athletic shoes, then wash out the clothes I was wearing, plus a few other things, with the saved tub water and a final rinse in the remaining water from the bucket.

Without air conditioning, the room is warm. This should help everything dry quickly. Once the pants are at least to the point of not dripping, I'll stitch up the tear with the sewing kit the gentleman gave me.

I consider if I want to go to the restaurant. With the foodborne illness transmission now suspected as intentional through salad bars and buffets, I feel somewhat safe with the idea of eating out. Somewhat. Not entirely. I'm not very hungry right now so decide to put off deciding. I'll take the bucket back and then maybe take a nap. I slip on my holster and sidearm.

After thanking the man profusely and offering a tip, which he waved off, I'm back in my room and snuggled in the bed, my holster and handgun now resting within easy reach on the nightstand.

I take out my eReader and go back to reading the book I last looked at Wednesday night when going to bed. It almost seems like a lifetime ago. With the internet now out, I'm very glad I decided to load some extra books on to my reader when I was in John Day. And I have a decent-sized library of "real" books at home.

I don't make it through the chapter before I'm asleep.

I wake up with a jerk.

Chapter 32

I think I was dreaming of my bike crash. I find my phone and check the time. 4:18.

What are Jake and Malcolm doing? Katie should be home, or getting close, about now. I haven't heard from Angela or Sarah to know what they're doing. And Calley... I hope she's being safe and smart.

Calley was so adamant about not leaving Casper to head to our place if something happened, so sure things could never get that bad. I think back to the shots fired at the gas station and know they can get that bad—and worse. They live several miles out of town and will hopefully be fine.

Plus, our friends Sue and Adam next door will keep an eye out, along with Mike's parents on the other side of them. I take my phone out to call Calley, just to check in, but have a *no service* notice.

I move to my knees and begin to pray for my children. For their safety, for Jake and Malcolm, and for my own safety to reach home. After several minutes, I'm back on my feet. I feel surprisingly rejuvenated.

I check my wet clothes and am surprised how dry things are already. While not yet suitable for wearing, the pants can now be stitched. While I'm doing that, I think about preparing a group text to Jake, Sarah, Angela, Calley, their spouses, and Katie. Maybe one of the messages will go through and that person can then reach Jake. It's unlikely but maybe.

I formulate my text in my head. They need to know where I am and my route home. I want them to come looking for me—to find me. As I tie off the thread with a knot, my stomach growls. I'll check out the restaurant and work on my text from there.

I get myself together, holster my sidearm, and grab my daypack. The restaurant is easy to walk to: across the street and down two buildings.

I pull open the door and step inside, waiting a moment for my eyes to adjust. It's lit by a variety of lanterns, both battery-operated and oil, but is still somewhat dark, even with the large windows. The place is full up, so I'm offered a seat at the bar.

The friendly bartender is noticeably tired. She's a few years older than me with a gravelly smoker's voice. "Whatcha drinking? Nothing's really cold, but it's not hot either."

While I'd love a beer, warm beer isn't my thing. I'm not much of a drinker to start with, but a nice cold beer would sure hit the spot right now. Instead, I ask, "You have bottled soda?"

"Sure do. What kind?"

"Root beer?"

She doesn't answer but comes back shortly with a can of root beer. Close enough to bottled, I decide.

"We don't have our regular menu today. We're grilling burgers, making tacos, and can even do gyros. Tell me what sounds good, and we'll see what we can do."

"Uh, sure. How about a gyro?"

"Yep. Lamb?"

I nod.

"You want a side salad?" she asks.

I think for a minute and decide not to risk lettuce or uncooked veggies with the food poisoning outbreaks. "No, thank you. No salad and no raw veggies with the gyro. Can you do grilled onions and peppers?"

"Onions for sure. Not sure how we are on peppers, but I'll check. Be a few minutes."

As she walks away, I survey the place. While there's quite a few people, it's not very loud. Definitely not a typical busy bar and grill feel, more like a coffee shop on a Tuesday afternoon.

The guys next to me are talking about the president speaking later tonight. Both have a carefree look I'm familiar with—several days' growth on their face, dressed in cargo shorts and T-shirts.

What's that smell? Fish? It's faint, but I pick it up. The one nearest me is a redhead, and the other one's more gray than brown. Both are rather ratty and disheveled. I try to eavesdrop on what they're saying. I finally decide to ask if they know of any updates.

"Excuse me. I overheard you say the president is speaking later. Does he have new information on the cyberattacks?"

The redhead closest to me turns and seems to evaluate me. I suddenly remember how I looked when I peered in the mirror earlier.

He gives me a nod and answers, "Not sure. I think he's going to talk about the explosions."

"The bridge explosions? Did they figure out who did it?" I ask.

"Not those. Today's explosions. The refineries?"

"What?" I ask. "I'm sorry, I was on a bike. I haven't kept up on what's been happening. Can you tell me?"

The other guy jumps in. "Sure can. Those terrorists wiped out the gulf. All of our refineries down there are gone... blown to smithereens. They got some of the others too. Ones in California and a few of the other big ones. Probably going to be a long time before our gas stations get a shipment."

"Oh no." I can't think of anything else to say. I weakly add, "Thanks for telling me."

"Sure thing. Probably good you're on a bike. But it does look like you took a tumble. Notice you're walking with a bit of a limp too. You have far to go?"

"Not too far," I say. "When is the president speaking?"

"7:00. Pretty sure Thelma will have the radio on so we can listen." He motions toward the bartender who took my order.

It's not yet 5:00, so still a while until the president comes on. With this newest attack, I wonder if it'd be best for me to simply bike home and not try to reach Jake for a ride, but conserve our fuel. But the guy here is right. I'm walking with a limp. And I do hurt quite a bit.

While I really want to get home, I don't think I'm going to be able to ride tomorrow. I know riding injured could be a recipe for disaster. Staying here a second night is the smartest thing to do. I look at my meal and rapidly blink my eyes, trying to keep the tears away. I want to be home so badly. Smart or not, I'm leaving tomorrow.

Maybe I can reach Jake and he can come and get me. By car, I'm only about two or so hours from home. On the bike it'll take me two, probably three, days. I decide to write out my text to send to the family. With paper and pen from the hotel room, it takes me a few drafts to put together what I want it to say.

It's Sunday evening and I'm in Cooke City. I'm on my bike. Took a tumble on the way. I'm okay but sore. I have a motel room and will stay here tonight. I'll start home Monday morning no later than 7 am. I'll take the pass home by where we cut wood. I should be home Tuesday or Wednesday. Jake, if you get this, feel free to come and get

125

me. I'll be ready for a ride. Girls, if one of you gets this, please try to reach Jake to let him know where I am. I love you all. See you soon.

Before I can put the text together on my phone, my food arrives. The gyro, which does include both cooked onion and pepper, is very good. I have to wonder how long it will be until I have another meal in a restaurant.

Are restaurants now a thing of the past?

My next few days will be cold foods only—with the bear habitat, I'm not sure I want to risk cooking and introducing food smells. I know most bears avoid people and the chances of an encounter are slim, but it's something I prefer to limit even further, if possible.

We've had a few bears near where we live. Each spring to fall, several bears live on the river near our house. We know of people who've had encounters. I have a healthy respect for bears and will be sure to practice smart camping.

Thelma comes back around to see how my food is. A guy nearby asks her if she'll have the radio on for the speech.

"Sure, enough. Hank even found some speakers he can hook into it. Everyone will have to be quiet, but all should be able to hear. 'Course, it's pretty quiet in here anyway. You staying in town, honey?" She directs her question to me.

"Yes. I'm in the hotel across the street."

"Thought so. Ol' Harry told me he had a girl come in who'd wrecked her bike. I suppose that's you, but I have to say, you're a little older than I expected from Harry's description."

I laugh. "I suppose I don't really qualify as a girl, but I did wreck my bike. I know I look a little banged up."

"You look like you could use a good, long rest. 'Course, with everything going on the last few days, I suppose we all look like we need a long rest. Now, with the refinery explosions… things could get interesting. You want anything else?"

"No. I'm fine. I think I'd like to walk around a bit, see if I can get some of the stiffness from the accident out of my knees. Okay if I come back to listen to the radio?"

"Of course. Not sure there'll be many seats available, but there'll be standing room."

"Do you know if anyone is getting cell service?"

"Honey," she says patiently, "we don't have cell service on a normal day. The town just doesn't have it. There's still payphones

126

around, but I don't think they're working. You might be able to send a text, sometimes text works, but usually not."

"Oh." I don't know what else to say. Now that she mentions it, I do remember from previous stops in Cooke City about the cell service problem. I'll go ahead and put my text together and try to send it. At least my phone will save it if it doesn't go out and I can try again later. I also decide to try the payphone.

Instead of walking the stiffness out of my knee, my walkabout leaves me achy. I try four different payphones—none have a dial tone. My text failed but is now held in the phone's outbox to try to send later.

Walking back toward my motel room, I see Ol' Harry, as Thelma called him, standing in front of the office.

He flags me over and says, "I was thinking, I'm not sure how you're set for food, but you might want to see if you can pick up a few things for while you're here and your trip home. The restaurant's not likely to have much left after today, especially with the power out and all the fresh stuff needing to be cooked right away. They might have a few things tomorrow, but your choices will be limited."

"What do you suggest?" I ask.

"We have a small grocery store but they've already been hit pretty hard. Might take a look anyway and try the gas station up the block. They'll have soups and things. You can heat the soup up in my microwave while you're here. With the refinery problem, I'll limit how much I run my generator, but we'll work it out. Maybe you'll find some jerky or something for when you're on the road. It might be a good idea to get what you need before the president's address. Who knows what he'll share and how people will react."

"Thank you. Good idea."

I don't want to mention I have, what is likely, plenty of food to get home, provided all goes well. I do have one can of soup left. Maybe it'd be a good idea to get another couple for tomorrow.

Chapter 33

I limp down to the gas station. While they do have food available, it's obvious they've sold quite a bit and there are many empty spaces. I buy three cans of soup, a package of jerky, several cans of fruit, a few cans of vegetables, a package of Fig Newtons, and assorted individually-packaged pastries. It's getting close to time for the president's address, so I decide to forgo the grocery store. I hustle as best I can back to my room to stash my food.

Thelma is right—the place is full up. I'm able to find a chair against the wall near the bathroom; likely put there when it wasn't needed at a table or to pull over when needed. We're not exactly crammed in like sardines, but it's close.

The noise level in here has drastically increased from earlier. It reminds me of a rowdy restaurant instead of the more coffee-shop-like feel of two hours ago. I look around. There aren't any children. Are they somewhere else? Did the parents send all the children someplace where they can have fun and be sheltered from hearing about the latest disasters?

As the seven o'clock hour approaches, the room becomes uncomfortably full. The power has only been out for a day, but there's a distinctive body odor in the room. I can only imagine the aroma which would accompany a meeting like this next week. The heat of the room isn't helping anything.

A minute or so before 7:00, Thelma begins to shush the crowd.

"All right, all right. We have the radio on and think we're getting a signal, but you all need to hush up so everyone can hear."

The entire room is instantly quiet. Thelma's pretty good at this.

We listen as the president recaps the destruction of the bridges, which resulted in the mass exodus from the affected towns. He then talks about the cyberattacks, which started yesterday, and today's refinery attacks.

The refinery attacks are worse than I feared. More than half our US refineries were destroyed, and refineries in other countries were also hit. The gathered group lets out cries and gasps. Apparently, the severity of today's attacks was news to most everyone in the room.

Oh, sure. He promises we'll rebuild and be as good as new… but I guess we all know that won't be any time soon. He reminds us about the banks and stock exchange being closed, power being out, and to wet a T-shirt to help stay cool. Mm-hmmm. Sounds like some interesting advice, Mr. President.

He finishes by promising to bring those responsible to justice and reminding us not to kill each other during this time. Yeah, he says it a little different, but that's the gist of it. He signs off with, "*We will never forget. We will move forward and come together as one nation, indivisible. Thank you. Good night. God bless the United States of America.*"

The crowd is in immediate disarray. The tears, which were likely silent during the speech, become wails. Thelma is yelling for quiet, and as the crowd lulls slightly, the radio continues, "*…we are operating on backup power. In order to conserve our power as long as possible, we'll be broadcasting at noon and 7:00 pm to bring you brief updates. We'll also broadcast any additional addresses from the president. Thank you. God bless Montana.*"

The wails are now sniffles. A new person steps up near Thelma. At first glance, he doesn't look familiar, but when he speaks, I realize he's the redhead who was sitting next to me when I had my gyro. He's shaved and put on fresh clothes, replacing his disheveled look with a look of rugged authority.

"Okay, friends. I know this isn't the news we were hoping for. We all hoped that when the president spoke, he'd tell us things are on the mend, they had a backup plan for the refineries, the cyberattack had been stopped, and things would soon be back to normal. Even though he didn't tell us these things, he didn't say all hope was lost either.

"Our community is really in pretty good shape. We weren't affected by the bridges collapsing. We saw a lot of traffic on Friday and Saturday morning with people leaving Yellowstone, but it's now a trickle. We have a few guests in town right now who have been affected by the difficulties, but for the most part, it's just us.

"Several of us in the community have discussed the possibly of something like this happening. Many of you are aware of some plans we've put in place and provisions to carry us through for a while. Tonight, we need to make some decisions. The first thing I'd like to discuss is closing down our town."

Everyone starts talking at once. For the most part, it sounds like people agree. I know now why Ol' Harry suggested I buy some food. He must have had an inside track on the plans in progress. In fact, it sounds like they may have had a town meeting, sometime in the past, to plan for an event like this.

A town full of preppers? Interesting.

I look around the room to see if Harry's here. I spy him almost directly across the room from me, holding up the wall on the other side of the building. He catches my eye and nods, giving me a small smile and what may have been a wink. The lighting isn't great, so I'm not sure.

"People, people," Red tries to quiet the crowd. "C'mon. Let's quiet down so we can discuss this."

An ear-piercing whistle carries through the building and does what Red couldn't do. He looks at Thelma, while rubbing his ear. "Thank you, Thelma."

She gives a smile and a slight curtsey in response.

"You all know, with our summer people here, our community is about three hundred strong. Harry Richardson put a group together today who went out and checked on some of the summer folk we weren't sure about. Our best guess is, with us, Silver Gate, and Colter Pass, we're actually more like 250 for residents.

"And we have…" he pauses to look at a piece of paper he's pulled out of his pocket, "twenty-eight people who were passing through and are currently with us. A few of those are hikers or bikers who are able to continue on in a few days. The rest are essentially stranded. We don't have fuel to offer them to help them get home. We're counting them in our community numbers at this time."

More murmurs and more than one person look my way. I consider slinking out, getting my bike, and hitting the road while everyone's in the meeting. I decide my earlier determination of not being physically ready to ride is still accurate. Besides, so far, it's not sounding too bad.

I notice there are several hands raised. Red calls on a man near the front.

"Peter, I'm not sure I follow. How are you planning to shut down the town? And is it even legal? Isn't this a state highway going down the middle of our town?"

"Yep. It is. We're not talking about keeping people from using the road. What we were thinking of doing is escorting folks through town.

130

We figure we can give people water and, if it's appropriate, provide them a place to sleep overnight, but we'd like to keep the rest of our resources for our community."

"No way," someone yells out. "We'd have to monitor the road twenty-four hours a day. Besides, what would people think of us?"

Red/Peter says, "You're right, Bob. We'd have to have people monitoring the roads twenty-four hours a day. We'd need to set up a schedule. And I'm not sure what people would think of us. Not sure I really care. What I care about is my wife and my children, Bob, and your wife and your children."

I raise my hand without thinking. I'm mildly surprised when Peter calls on me.

"Yes. I didn't ask your name earlier. Bike Wreck Girl?"

Bike Wreck Girl. I guess that's better than Bike Wreck Old Lady, but still... I'll remember to introduce myself properly next time I'm sitting next to someone on a barstool.

I stand up and raise my voice. "Uh, yes, Mollie Caldwell. I'm one of the extra people here now. I'm a temporary. I crashed my bike earlier today and just need a day to rest up.

"Before I was on my bike, I was in my car. I went through several towns affected by the multitudes of people leaving Seattle... or somewhere. A few of the towns had police guards at the beginning and at all the major intersections. I was told by the first officer, and about every third thereafter, I could drive through but couldn't stop. They had no facilities available. Personally, I thought they were smart to do this.

"They were also too late. Their towns had already been hit hard. The... I don't know what to say—refugees? That's what it seemed like. I drove by a few green spaces covered with tents. There were so many people, and I'm sure those who didn't have tents were staying in cars. They were out of fuel, and this was before the power went out. I can't even imagine what it might be like in those places now."

I sit back down.

"Thank you, Mollie. It's good to hear what other towns are doing," Peter says.

"But she said it was the police doing it. We don't have a police department. Is the sheriff going to help us?" This is from a lady in the middle of the room.

Harry speaks up from across the room, "They've got their own troubles. All of their patrols were called to help with the horde affecting them from Seattle and who knows where else. I don't think it's as bad in Livingston as where the little lady over there went through, but they were seeing their fair share of people yesterday before we lost the phones.

"I was able to get Bud Hansen on the radio earlier today. I told him what we're thinking. He said lots of towns are doing something similar. I set up a time to talk with him tomorrow, and we can share our plan with him."

Peter starts talking immediately, most likely to keep from losing control of the crowd. "Okay, Harry. Good. So we have two sources, one law enforcement and one with firsthand experience, telling us people are, essentially, shutting down access to their towns. Because we're pretty isolated and have only the one road to deal with, it shouldn't be difficult. Putting people on each end should do it.

"We already mentioned giving out water, and we could put a porta-potty at each end. If it's getting close to nighttime, we can put them up for the night. We'll need to make it clear it's only for the night. We simply don't have the resources to add to the community on a permanent basis.

"The trouble I see is, since our only road goes smack through the middle of our towns, we need to monitor the people going through. It's over five miles from Silver Gate to Colter Pass. That's a lot of distance where people could get lost. Mollie said they had people set up every few blocks. I'm not sure it'd work for us. I still think we'd need to escort people through."

"Yoo-hoo, Petey," a dainty, yet surprisingly loud, female voice calls out. "Oh, Petey!"

A groan from the guy next to me, as Peter says, "Yes? Stella Jean?"

"Petey, dear, is this like that book you gave Sandy and me to read?" Her dainty voice has a smooth southern drawl, reminding me of my friend Sue who's originally from Tennessee. "The book where the lights go out and they don't let people go in their town?"

I strain to see the speaker, but she's blocked by a huge guy. Not just huge. Colossal. Ginormous. Another groan, and a murmured, "*that woman,*" from the guy to my right.

"Pretty much. Same general idea," Peter says with a nod.

132

"Will you have them in the same white suits? Like the kinds the scientists wear? I think that would be a very good idea, look right smart and a little menacing."

The guy next to me leans in, fully assaulting me with his rank body odor and even ranker breath, as he whispers, "I doubt that ditzy woman even knows what menacing means."

"Not sure we have anything like that, Stella Jean," Peter says. "But maybe some kind of uniform would be a good idea. We'll see what we can come up with."

The gruff guy next to me yells out, "Can't believe you of all people would be in favor of this, Stella Jean. Doesn't it go against your *Christian* values?" He spats out Christian like it's a dirty word. "Aren't you one who's always wanting to help the poor and less fortunate?"

The big guy blocking my view of Stella Jean gives the gruff guy a stare, the shooting daggers type of stare.

"When you thinking we should start this?" Bob, from earlier, gruffly asks.

"Tonight," Peter says immediately.

This causes complete pandemonium. Too soon seems to be what I'm hearing. I'm not really sure why they think it's too soon. They already said there are twenty-eight of us here who aren't residents. More than 10 percent of their total summer population at home—a pretty large number in my opinion.

Peter and Thelma are quietly talking up at the front while the crowd has its own multitude of conversations. Harry walks up to the front along with several other people. Harry soon begins to make a motion requesting quiet by putting both hands out in front of him and motioning them downward. It takes a few moments but is effective.

"All right, folks. There seems to be some questions floating around. One I heard was, 'What about the people who own homes here and aren't here right now?' This is easy. When they get here, they can go to their home.

"I also heard a few of you are hoping your family or close friends will come here if things get bad where they are. We hope they will too. This is probably one of the safer places to be in a situation like this. I, for one, can't imagine what it's like in the cities tonight. Even though many of the cities saw people leave when the bridges went down, I'm sure it's still a mess. You heard the president about the

133

looting. Your families are welcome here. We'll verify who they are before we let them in. You'll have to vouch for them.

"Chances are good, if this goes on too long, we're going to be thankful for a few more people. We're all going to be busy cutting firewood and finding food. Even day-to-day things we take for granted now, like doing the dishes or laundry, will take extra time. I know we've all heard the phrase 'many hands make light work' and it will be true."

"So, wait a minute," this is from Bob. "Now you're saying you want more people? I thought Peter just finished telling us he wants to close the town down and not let people in."

"Right, Bob. We're specifically saying anyone who doesn't own a place here, doesn't have family here, or isn't already here today. While a few more people would be fine, we need to know our limitations. Defining who we'll allow to stay is part of tonight's conversation."

"So, you've already decided you're shutting the town down?"

"Not decided, Bob. That's the first thing we're discussing. We could take a vote on it. But first, does anyone *else* have any questions? We're specifically talking about setting up a gatekeeper on either end plus having an escort to accompany anyone going through our communities. Any questions on this?"

"Okay, then," Harry says, glancing around. "Should we vote on it?"

Chapter 34

There's a general agreement to vote. Someone suggests the vote should be private, but she's overruled by people saying a voice vote is fine. When the vote is taken, there are only Ayes. Probably some Nays who chose not to speak up after the overwhelming majority.

I'm not at all surprised when Bob speaks up again, "Okay. You closed down our town. Now what?"

Peter takes over, "Now we'll put together a schedule to have sentries posted at each end. After we're done here, Thelma will set up at the cash register and you can sign up with her. Men and women are both welcome.

"For tonight, we have a few volunteers but could use a few more, especially for shifts starting now and early morning. If you can help with one of these shifts, see me directly after we're done."

"Who's making up the schedule?" Bob asks.

"I'll do it for the first few days," Peter says. "And, hopefully, we'll only need a few days. If they can get the power back on, I suspect we won't see much trouble up here. If the power stays out... well, that could change things."

"You know, Peter, before I moved up here, I was the logistics and supply chain manager for Tyson. I kept everything running like clockwork there. It'd be in everyone's best interest to put me in charge of schedules. Not just for our security force but for any other jobs needing to be done," Bob announces with sonorous pomposity.

From the quiet groans, head shakes, and eye rolls I catch, I think Bob is the only one who thinks it'd be in everyone's best interest to put him in charge.

I take a good look at Bob. His hair, which was likely a short buzz cut at one time, has grown out to an unkempt, stringy helmet. His belly hangs over his too small denim jeans, with his too small T-shirt providing more than a glimpse of a white band of belly. I suspect the person behind him is getting a partial moon every time he sits and stands.

135

"Thanks for the offer, Bob," Peter graciously responds. "We'll definitely be looking for people's strengths and things moving forward. For now, we'll do our best to muddle through."

This results in a few chuckles, which seems to lighten the mood a bit.

Harry takes over again, "As we mentioned earlier, those who own homes here and aren't home right now will be welcomed back. As will any family or friends. We'll verify who people are and do our best to help them get set up, if needed. Today, we have a few extra people here. Some are only resting up before making their way home, but five families don't have the ability to get home until things change."

"Can't those families travel by shank's mare? Seems it'd be better for them to head on down the road instead of relying on us and our limited resources," Bob arrogantly announces.

I have to wonder if Bob is always like this or if he is on a roll tonight. Considering the number of other people here and how little they've said in comparison, I find it interesting. I do, however, see more than one head nod and a few vocal agreements after his latest proclamation.

This time, Thelma speaks up, "These are families, Bob. They were either here or in Yellowstone vacationing when everything started. I've spoken with all of them. They'd love to go home but all are from several states away. Until they know they'll find fuel along the way, it's safer for them to stay here than try to make it home. Walking a thousand or more miles isn't realistic when young children are involved. I'm sure you wouldn't want RJ and Ava trying a hike like that."

Bob, looking less than pleased, says nothing. The woman sitting next to him, his wife I'd guess, pats him on the arm and whispers in his ear. He nods woodenly.

"Each of the families has suitable lodging right now," Thelma says. "Over the next few days, unless things change suddenly, we're going to figure out something more permanent. There are a few other individuals and couples who, at this moment, do plan to move on when they're able to. However, if any of you decide you can't or shouldn't attempt your trip home please come see me tonight or tomorrow. We'll figure something out for you."

I glance at Bob to gauge his reaction on this. He doesn't look happy but doesn't say anything. There are a few other murmurs, sounding less than positive about people like me staying past our welcome.

Someone other than Bob speaks up, "Thelma, you sound like you have this all planned out. Did you, Peter, Harry, and the rest of your crew spend your day planning everything for *our* community?"

Now there are several people visibly and vocally agreeing. None of which seem very happy.

Peter takes the floor. "Not at all. We put some plans in place in hopes of making things easier for all of us. It's true—several of us discussed this earlier, and a few of us were in favor of encouraging everyone who isn't a resident to move on. But we tried to put ourselves in their shoes. How would you feel if you went on vacation and the world suddenly changed? You're a thousand miles from home and everyone you know. The prospects of getting home right now are slim. It doesn't sound very good.

"We also know some of the area residents were gone from here on vacation. The Lewis family went to Maine, I believe. I hope, wherever they find themselves right now, people are offering help and kindness to them. I think the least we can do is show the same kindness to the people stranded here."

The same guy gives a huge sigh and says, "Okay. You have a point. And I also hope Frank, Sally, and their children are in a safe place. But what's the difference between allowing these people to stay and not letting more people in? Isn't that a bit of a double standard?"

"Yes, I suppose it is," Peter says with a nod. "But the truth is, we have to draw the line somewhere. And maybe we should allow more people to stay. That's one thing we discussed today and wanted to have more input on. We could let more families stay or even couples or individuals, if we think they'd be a good fit. I suspect there will be others making their way out of Yellowstone and not able to continue to their homes.

"How do we decide who we let stay? Should we determine how many people we can accommodate and the first X number asking to stay we say yes? Or should we look for certain skill sets to try to fill our needs? And if so, what are those needs? Truthfully, I'm not sure tonight is the time to have this conversation. And maybe, tonight, if we have people coming through, we find a place to put them up and deal with it tomorrow. We still put guards out so we can monitor the situation, then we escort them to a motel room for the night at the regular nightly rate. We can make it seem something like business as usual while we come up with a plan."

There's lots of commotion now with Peter's newest suggestion. Personally, I think they're on the right track with keeping people out. But at the same time, I'm very glad to have a bed to sleep in tonight, and I can imagine the twenty-seven others are also. All of this makes me wonder what's going on at home.

While our community isn't on a main highway bordering a national attraction like this, we do have a state highway running nearby. I wonder if there have been many people like me, who simply ran out of gas and couldn't go any farther. It's likely that if people ran out on the highway, they'd stop at the small restaurant there, owned by our friend Ian, and he'd suggest continuing on to the nearest real town.

Other than Ian's restaurant on the highway—which also houses a basic convenience store and a full bar—and a small winter ski area and summer zip line tour with a tiny restaurant in the wilderness area, we don't really have amenities. No gas station, motel, supermarket, or any of the things found in towns. We don't even have a post office.

I suspect there are several people who don't live in Bakerville currently stuck there. While we don't have hotels and motels, we do have several vacation cabins that rent by the day or week. My husband is even a caretaker for a vacation cabin. There's also a couple of bed-and-breakfast places and a small hostel, part of the ski area open year round for skiers or hikers. Being on the edge of the wilderness, it's likely there are a few campers this time of year.

Our friends Alex and Natalie MacIntyre host their homesteading immersion classes. And while they have fewer students than usual, due to their daughter Annie's wedding yesterday, they did still have people scheduled. With the trouble, I suspect many wedding guests are now unable to get home.

I wonder if my community is having a meeting like this. If they are, we have our own guy like Bob—more than one, in fact—likely causing plenty of trouble.

I realize my mind has wandered and I'm not really paying attention to what's going on in this meeting. I'm brought back to reality by angry, raised voices.

Bob seems to be arguing with the group at the front again, and a gentleman near me tells him to shut his trap—his opinion is well known and no longer needed. This causes many more voices of support in Bob shutting his trap and a few defenders saying to let him talk.

Then the guy that was whispering to me before about what a ditz Stella Jean is starts yelling. Not at Bob, but at someone else.

Thelma, Peter, and crew are doing their best to regain order when things suddenly come to blows. I'm not really sure who started what, but suddenly, there's pushing, shoving, and fists flying all around.

I know it's time to get out of the room, but before I can, I'm on the ground with my chair on top of me. I attempt to untangle myself and get away when a body is shoved into me.

I'm flung into the wall and then the floor, knocking my head. I try to shake it off but feel myself fading fast. My last thought is, I should've left when they started talking about the extra people in town.

Chapter 35

The first thing I see is a crown of frizzy red hair. I close my eyes again. A few moments later, I open them up and notice a nice smile below the exuberant hair. Big blue eyes and a smattering of freckles round out her expressive face. She says, with way too much cheer in her voice, "Hey there. You're awake."

I don't say anything at first, then make a murmuring noise. My throat is very dry, and my lips feel chapped, but these are nothing compared to the pounding in my head. Suddenly, my stomach goes sour. She must have recognized what was happening as she thrusts a basin near my face.

After I finish heaving my guts up, she says, "To be expected. You got a conk on the head. Knocked you out for a minute."

Without moving my head, I let me eyes travel the room. I'm still in the bar, and it looks like most of the rest of the town is too. Lovely.

"You hurt anywhere... except your head? I bet it hurts plenty."

"Not sure." I start to get up.

"Hold up. We're getting the ambulance, and we'll bring a stretcher to move you. Doubtful you have much more than a bit of a concussion, but we'd like to make sure."

"You have an ambulance?"

"Sure. Volunteer fire and EMS. I'm Penny, part of the EMS team."

There's noise and activity, but I choose not to try to look around at what may be going on. My head... so much pain. The next thing I know, a neck brace is being put on me and a group is moving me to a stretcher or backboard of some sort.

"We're going to take you across the street to the hotel, then we'll see how you are," Penny says.

"My room key is in my bag," I say lamely.

"No need. Harry is opening up another room for us. He didn't want a bunch of people in and out of your private space. Just relax a minute and we'll get you all settled."

I'm soon in the room and moving to the bed. They tell me not to help, just relax. A blond in her midthirties says, "Mollie, is it?"

"Yes," I croak.

"I'm Donna. This guy here is James. We're going to do a quick exam. I'd like to remove your sidearm and holster. Okay?"

"Yes…" What else can I say? I'm currently at their mercy.

"Okay. I'll put it in the drawer of the nightstand."

From there, I zone out a bit while they check me out and talk to me and each other. After a few minutes, Donna declares I'm a little banged up, likely from my bike wreck earlier in the day, and have a slight concussion.

Under normal circumstances, she'd take me to the hospital since I did lose consciousness for a good minute. But, with the way things are, she thinks it'd be best to let me rest and see how I recover. I agree it sounds like a good plan, knowing they don't have the fuel to waste on me when I don't have a life-threatening injury.

"Penny is going to stay with you for now," Donna says. "She'll monitor you, and we'll revaluate as needed."

And with that, Donna and James are gone. I close my eyes to rest for only a minute.

Chapter 36

"I bet you're thirsty," the frizzy redhead from earlier says with a smile, then offers me a glass of water via a straw.

I sip greedily, then attempt to talk. "Thank you. My head sure hurts."

"I suspect it does. You have quite a goose egg on it. Now that you're awake, we'll get something in you to help."

I don't say anything since the little bit of talking I've done reverberated in my head, making the pain almost unbearable. I try to glance around using my eyes only. At first, I have no recollection of why I'm here and why I'm so miserable. I feel like I've been hit by a Mack truck. One thing I do know, I'm going to need to get up fairly quickly and go to the bathroom—my bladder is screaming.

The girl is talking again, "I'm not sure if you remember, but I'm Penny. You met my brother, Peter, earlier today. We all feel real bad about what happened at the meeting. Nobody expected it to escalate the way it did."

Oh, yeah. The meeting. The town was talking about sealing themselves off. I'm here for the night after crashing my bike in Yellowstone Park. I really need to get this headache under control so I can leave. I try to sit up and quickly collapse back onto the bed. The pain is excruciating and the nausea almost immediate. I'm surprised I don't throw up. Then I remember, I did throw up earlier. In front of the entire town. *Ugh.* I'm sure that made an impression.

"Take it easy, Mollie. Let me help you sit, and we'll get some meds in you. Should help alleviate the headache. Harry left a couple of his oxycodone he uses when his back is really acting up. We can give you one of those, if you'd like?"

I think hard about what I know about oxycodone. It's a narcotic, for sure. I don't really do well with things like this. They tend to affect me rather strongly and sometimes upset my stomach. I don't want a repeat of earlier.

"Can I just have Tylenol?" I croak out.

"Sure. Of course. You think that'll take care of the pain?"

"Let's try." I have some in my bag but am in no shape to find it and really prefer Penny not be digging through my things. I hope she has her own supply to offer me. She walks over to the table near the window. I notice the few things I had on the table are no longer there.

"Did some of my things get rearranged?" I ask.

"Your things?" she asks, sounding confused. "Oh! No, not that I know of. We're not in your room, remember? Harry opened up another room for you. He wanted to make sure your stuff stayed private. We brought you in earlier—Donna, James, and me. I've been sitting with you while you napped."

"How long?" I ask, perplexed.

"Oh... not too long," she looks at her watch, "an hour or so. It's normal to be a little confused with a bump like you sustained. It will get better."

She's right. I've had head injuries before. Once, when I was very young, my family went on a bike ride. I was in the seat behind my dad when he crashed. I woke up on the couch at home with no recollection of the bike ride. To this day, I still don't remember the ride, the crash—nothing except waking up and hurting terribly bad. That's one of the last memories I have of my family life before everything fell apart.

A few months after the bicycle accident, my younger sister was killed. It tore my family apart. My parents no longer had anything resembling a marriage and barely acknowledged me. The day after I graduated from high school, my mom woke me just as the sun was rising.

"Mom? What's going on?"

She said nothing at first, just looked at me.

"Mom?"

"I'm sorry, Mollie. I tried. I really did. But after Maggie... left us... I just couldn't be a mom any longer. There were so many times I wanted to just pack up and leave, but I couldn't do it. I had to stay until I knew you'd be okay. Now you're done with high school... and I was so proud of you yesterday. To see you walking across in your cap and gown to get your diploma, it was amazing. You know, I never graduated from high school; it just didn't seem important. But watching you do it makes me wish I would have. But I guess it's too late."

143

I didn't know what to say. I just watched her as she sat there with a sad, wistful look on her face.

"Your dad and I, we aren't really a couple any longer. I guess you probably know that."

I nodded, yeah, it was pretty obvious.

"So, now you're all grown up. I've decided it's time for me to start fresh. Your dad and I have made our arrangements, and I've filed for divorce. Everything will be final in just a few days. We wanted to wait and tell you after school was finished so you wouldn't have any troubles. You're such a good student, and I'm sure it wouldn't have been an issue, but just in case…"

It's not like I was surprised. A long time ago, I figured my parents stayed together only for me or because it was easier. I couldn't remember the last time they'd acted like husband and wife.

"Well, I don't know what else to say, Mollie. I'm leaving. I'm going to travel for a bit and find someplace to settle down. I'll let you know where I end up so you can come for a visit. I've always wanted to see the world, so now is my chance. I love you."

She kissed me on the forehead and gave a quick wave, then left the bedroom, gently shutting the door behind her.

I rolled over and went back to sleep. When I got up a few hours later, my dad was in the kitchen nursing a cup of coffee.

"Morning, Mollie," *he said.*

"Morning, Dad."

"So, your mom is gone. I guess it's no surprise. You've probably seen it coming for some time. We would've told you sooner, but…"

"Yeah. She told me."

And that was that. We didn't mention my mom again, at least not until my dad was on his deathbed. I moved out about a month later, into a downtown Portland apartment with three other gals.

My good friend Sharri, who years later introduced me to Jake, was one of my roomies. My dad stayed at the house in Gresham, and we rarely saw each other. When I married Jamie, my first husband, he didn't even attend the wedding.

When Jamie died, he came around a few times. We were cordial but not much more. A few years later, I married Jake. My dad, Sam, did attend our wedding.

After we moved to Wyoming and Malcolm was born, my dad came for a visit. It was then he announced he had cancer. He ended up

144

staying in Wyoming. Before he died, we made up… not because of anything I did but because of God taking hold of Sam and changing him from the inside out. Those last months with my dad were wonderful.

As hard as my childhood was, Jake's was just the opposite. He has so many fond memories of his parents, younger brother, and the things they all did together: hunting, fishing, camping, even great memories of watching TV. He often says he "had the perfect childhood."

Sometimes I think his perfect childhood, compared with my less than perfect one, is part of our communication issue. Communicating is something we've been working on, realizing silence in our marriage was our biggest problem.

My bladder brings me back to the present.

"I really need to go to the bathroom. Do you think you could help me?" I ask.

"Yes. But if you can hold on a minute, I'd like to get some help. My mom should be nearby."

Penny steps out and returns a few moments later. A slightly heavier, older version of Penny, with the same crazy hair, spattering of freckles, and blue eyes, is by her side. She's dressed very comfortably in a flowy pink shirt, black loose trousers, and flip-flops. When she speaks, it's with a lilt which portrays her Irish homeland.

"Well there, it's good to see you awake. Penny says you have a powerful headache and a full bladder. Let's see if we can help out with both."

"Mom, you think we should go see if Harry has a rolling office chair? Seems he does, and it might make things easier on Mollie to get her to the bathroom."

"Please, if you can just help me. I'm nearing an emergency situation here and would hate to wet this bed."

"Well, then, Mollie, let's just get you up." The nausea is instant, and I swallow hard to keep from throwing up. Penny swings my feet off the edge, and before I know it, I'm up and they're dragging me to the bathroom.

I take care of business. As soon as I'm done, I realize the vomit isn't holding back any longer. I manage to make a sound, which must indicate I'm about to let loose, because a basin appears in front of me.

145

Peeing and puking have left me spent as they help me back to the bed. Penny's mom is cleaning my face with a wet cloth while Penny disappears into the bathroom with the basin.

"What's your name?" I ask.

"I'm Aideen, Penny and Peter's mom. How about we let your stomach settle a little, then try to get some medicine in you? I think I'll crush it up with some applesauce. That might help it work faster and help you keep it in. I'm sorry we don't have better options. Sandy Carmichael sure feels bad about slamming into you. Randy feels terrible for hitting Sandy and causing him to slam into you. Sandy's a big guy. It's a miracle you weren't hurt worse."

I have no idea who these people are she's talking about but assume Sandy Carmichael is the flying body I remember colliding with.

Settled in my bed, my eyes drift closed.

Chapter 37

Monday, Day 5

The next time my eyes open, the room is darker. Not dark like night but dark like dusk. Aideen is sitting next to my bed reading.

"Well, hello again. You had yourself quite the nap. How about a drink of water?" She lifts the glass with the straw to my lips. After a few long sips, she takes it away. "Your head feel any better?" she asks.

"Mmm. I'm not sure. Still hurts a lot. Hard to tell if it's better. What time is it?"

"About 6:00 in the morning. You fell back to sleep so fast and soundly, we never got the medicine in you earlier. Want to try now and see if it helps some?"

"Yes. 6:00 on what day?" I ask.

"Monday."

"Monday," I repeat. I was in the bar on Sunday evening, so I just slept overnight. Nothing wrong with that.

"Yes, you've been plumb out of it and slept quite well. Donna was in to check on you shortly after you fell back to sleep. She said just let you sleep as long as you seemed to be breathing okay and all."

I feel the tears welling up in my eyes as I think about my family and where they all are. I can only pray all of the girls have made their way to our place. I'm sure Jake's a wreck worrying about me, and he doesn't need to be worrying about the children also.

"Here you go, Mollie." Aideen hands me a tissue. "You go ahead and cry. I bet you wish nothing more than to be home. It's doubly hard to be feeling unwell and not be with those who love you. We'll do our best to take care of you so you can get home quickly. Now, how about some applesauce with a little Tylenol in it?"

"Yes. I need to go to the bathroom. Can you help me? I think it'll be a little easier this time. I feel a little stronger."

"Of course. Penny is sleeping in the room next door. You want me to go get her, or you think you and I can handle it?"

"Can we try?"

It takes some effort, and I have to stop several times on the short trip to and from the bathroom, but we finally make it. I'm slightly dizzy still and my entire body hurts.

Once I'm back in bed, she says, "Now, then, applesauce time."

The applesauce is amazingly good. I finish all she offers me, then settle back in the bed. It's not long until I'm asleep.

When I wake up, the sun is fully shining. Penny is reading in the chair near the window. I softly say her name, and she turns toward me. Her previously unruly red mane is now somewhat contained on the top of her head in a messy bun.

I'm much better this time, and the trip to and from the bathroom isn't nearly the event it was earlier. I'm still off balance and not well, with an amazingly bad headache, but am pretty sure I'll be fine in a day or two. Maybe three. This time I notice my body aches something fierce. Likely a combination of my bike accident before arriving here and being bashed into by Sandy Carmichael.

Penny gives me water and I take more acetaminophen, the normal way this time. She also has me drink a little Gatorade and eat a few crackers before I go back to sleep.

Penny is still there when I wake up next. This time I'm starving.

"Hello there," she says with a smile. "We thought you might be waking up soon. My mom is working on some food for you."

"I have a few things in my room," I offer.

"S'okay. We might have Harry grab that later. Mom's making some broth for you this morning. It will be good on your stomach and help get your strength back. She's big on broth."

"Okay. Great," I say.

Penny helps me to the restroom and offers me a damp cloth to clean up. I need a shower, or at least a sponge bath like I had the first night I arrived in this town... when was that? Only yesterday? I know I'm not up for it yet. Back in bed, she gives me water and Tylenol. A minute or two later, there's a knock on the door. Penny lets Aideen in. She's caring a thermos in one hand and a chunky blue mug in the other. Aideen's tresses are partially contained, with a purple and black bandana serving as a headband. She's clad in a black flowy shirt with equally flowy purple pants and the same flip-flops as before.

"Good morning, Mollie. You're looking right chipper."

I'm sure she's lying to me but attempt what I hope is a polite smile.

148

"I brought you some well-salted chicken broth. A good cup of broth is sure to cure what ails you."

I laugh a little since I happen to agree with her. I'm a big fan of broth and its healing properties.

"Is it still Monday?" I ask.

"Yes, it is. Around 5:30 in the evening. You've rested well today. After you have a cup of broth, we can get you something a little more solid if you're still hungry."

The broth was enough, and after finishing the mug and having another dose of Tylenol, I consider sleeping again. I'm feeling pretty good at the moment and am able to visit with Penny and Aideen for a bit. Aideen suggests, next time I wake up, I might like a shower. I wholeheartedly agreed, shortly before slipping back into my slumber.

The next time I wake up, I feel almost normal. At least to the point my head doesn't feel like it's going to explode with movement. It's now more of a dull roar. I move around a bit and determine my entire body has a dull ache to it. Maybe from lying in bed for so long as much as crashing my bike and becoming Sandy Carmichael's blocking pad.

"Hi, Mollie. We thought you might be waking up. Mom went to heat up some water so you can get a shower. She figured it might really help you feel better. We've got everything set up for you as soon as she returns," Penny says. She sounds excited for me to get a shower. I wonder if it's because I'm starting to get a little ripe.

Penny continues, "The president spoke again tonight, but Thelma set everyone up outside where there's a little more room and a slight breeze, hoping to help keep tempers from fraying again. He just finished up, and now the town's continuing the discussion started last night."

"Why'd the president speak? Was there another attack?"

"There was. They hit the railroads today. Took out the tracks in many places, blew up railway bridges, and collapsed tunnels. Looks like they're determined to stop supplies from getting to places. But that's not the worst of it. They started targeting individuals. Many senators and congressmen were killed. It's beyond terrible."

"Oh no." I can't think of anything else to say—she summed it up well. These attacks are leaving us all stuck where we are with what we have. And for them to target our congress, it's hard to even comprehend this evil. "Who?"

"Don't know. The president didn't name any names. There were many assassinated—both in the House and the Senate."

"How?" I can't believe something like this could happen.

"He just said they were targeted. They're trying to find the rest of the legislators and putting them in protective custody." Her voice cracks a little.

I give a slight nod—which reminds me, nodding my head hurts.

"I can't even imagine what it's like in the cities and larger towns," Penny says. "When the television was still on, they showed some rioting the night after the bridges were taken out. That's when the power was still on. I suspect it became much worse after the lights went out. I've gone to a few EMT trainings in other places. Riot response was one of the things we learned about. I'm just thankful we're here."

I'm thankful I'm here, too, even if I was collateral damage at their own little meeting.

A knock and then the door opens a few inches.

"You decent? I have Harry helping me bring in some water for your shower."

"She's fine, Mom," Penny says, giving me a wink.

"How are you doing, Miss Mollie?" Harry asks.

"Better. I feel much better. Just a little headache, and… well, I ache pretty much everywhere."

"I understand," he says. "Sandy Carmichael is a big guy, and he plowed into you pretty good. He feels terrible about it."

I say nothing as Harry takes the water into the bathroom, then says his goodbyes.

While the shower is wonderful, it's also exhausting. Aideen brings me fresh clothes to put on: sweatpants and a T-shirt. They're not mine but fit fairly well, being on the slightly loose side and a little too long.

I have more broth and half a roast beef sandwich. The sandwich is amazing. After a few minutes of talking with Penny and Aideen, I tell them I need to take a small nap. I'm not even sure if they answer before I go to sleep.

Chapter 38

Tuesday, Day 6

I open my eyes to the sound of humming. I look over, expecting to see Aideen or Penny, but find a new lady sitting near me.

She looks similar to Dolly Parton circa 1985—very blond, very big hair, perfectly styled, and a full face of makeup. She notices I'm awake, and when she stands up, I can see her figure is also very Dolly—rather well-endowed with a tiny waist. She's wearing tight jeans, a white off-the-shoulder blouse with lace around the neckline and puffy pirate sleeves, large earrings, and several bracelets. On her feet are sky-high sequined sandals.

When she talks, her voice has a decidedly Dolly twang to it. Very soft with a slight accent.

"Well, hello, sugar. You're starting to look much better. Every time I've been here before, you've been sound asleep. I supposed your body has been healing while you're sleeping, so it's all good."

I give a slight nod and am pleased when my head doesn't feel like it's going to split open from the movement. Even the dull roar has decreased to an ache.

"Have you been here long?" I ask.

"Oh, not long, sugar. An hour or so, I reckon. I try to help Aideen and Penny out by sitting with you so they can get some rest or do other things. After all, my Sandy is the reason you're laid up in this bed and not on your way home to your family. By the way, I'm Stella Jean Carmichael. I'm so sorry Sandy ran over you. Sometimes he lets his emotions get the better of him and he doesn't think before he acts. He feels plumb rotten over it too. Well, now, can I help you to the restroom?"

Stella Jean... the woman who asked about people manning the roadblock wearing uniforms.

After my bathroom trip, Stella Jean gives me more broth from the thermos and the other half of my sandwich from earlier.

"What time is it?"

"Oh… about 1:00 in the morning, I reckon. You slept a good spell."

"Mm-hmm," I answer, as I settle back in for more sleep.

Stella Jean is still with me when I wake up the next time. I only slept for a little over two hours. Even so, I'm starving.

"Now, then, Aideen has put a few tasty things in the cooler. She seemed to know, when you woke up, you'd be dog hungry. Let's see what we have… looks like some kind of muffin, custard, a couple hard-boiled eggs, and canned peaches. What would you like to start with?"

"Oh… sounds wonderful. How about the muffin?"

"Yah, sure. Hmmm. Kind of a strange looking muffin. I think it has sausage in it."

She hands me the muffin, which is really more of an egg and sausage quiche in the shape of a muffin tin.

"That's fine. It looks good."

And it is. I quickly polish it off and move to the rest of the food.

After sleeping so much since Stella Jean's husband ran me over, I'm starting to feel a little restless. My headache, while still there, is more of a nuisance than anything, as long as I don't move too quickly.

Stella Jean helps me to the table so we can play a game of cribbage, even though I'm pretty good to make it on my own. While I've played before, it's been a while and I can't remember the game. I don't think it's because of my head injury—I think it's just been way too long.

While we're playing, she says, "Tell me about your family."

Hmm. Where to start. "My husband is Jake. I have four adult daughters—Sarah, Angela, Calley, and Katie. Sarah is married to Tate. They live in Billings about two hours from us. Calley is married to Mike. Angela is married to Tim, and they have a little boy, my grandson, Gavin. All of them live in Casper. Katie is my youngest. She's not married but has a boyfriend. They live in Manhattan, Kansas."

Stella Jean looks thoughtful for a moment, then says, "Manhattan, Kansas… is that where the college is? The one that burned down?"

My mouth suddenly goes dry. I don't know what she's talking about, but my Katie doesn't live far from K-State, the college she attends. "I… I don't know…" I stammer.

She can see she's said the wrong thing and begins to backtrack. "Oh, honey… I just heard there was a college in Kansas where several refuges were and a fire started. It happened right around the time the cyberattacks began, and they were having trouble getting it out. I'm sure it isn't as bad as I made it sound."

I carefully nod so as not to start my head raging. "Last time I talked to Katie, she was heading home. She didn't mention a fire. That was on…" I stop to think. What day? Saturday? "Saturday, I think. Is that the day the cyberattacks started? It's all blending together."

"That's not just from your bang on the head. We all feel the same way. How could things have gone so wrong so quickly? All of this… mess… only started on Thursday. It hasn't even been a week and the world we used to know doesn't even seem to exist. So many deaths…" Stella Jean says with a small sad smile and a shake of her head.

I say nothing as we continue to play our game. I soon realize this is a little much for me, and I tell Stella Jean I should probably go back to bed.

"Oh, honey, you're probably right. I didn't think much about it. How about I read to you? I have my Bible in my bag."

"Yes, sure. I'd like that."

She starts with John 17. I fall asleep sometime during John 19.

Chapter 39

Daylight. Donna, the EMT, is sitting at the table with her head in her arms, softly snoring. I quietly get up and go into the bathroom. I evaluate how I feel, and while not great, I'm not terrible either. I start thinking, maybe, I can leave today. I only paid for one night here, for a room I never slept in but still houses my stuff while I sleep in a different room. Oops. I wonder how large my bill will end up being.

As I walk back to the bed, I'm suddenly dizzy. Grabbing on to the wall, I carefully steady myself. In the process, I loudly thump the wall. A flutter in my stomach feels like the bottom has fallen out of it, and I do my best not to be sick. Donna awakens with a start and is immediately by my side.

"You should've asked me for help," she chastises.

"Yes... I know. I was fine going in, just got a little woozy on the way back."

"To be expected," Donna says, as she helps me back to my bed. "You'll likely have some lingering headaches, dizziness... things like that for a few days. Like I said, losing consciousness normally would've earned you an ambulance ride to the hospital. Now... I hope you understand we need to conserve fuel in case there's a life-threatening injury. It wasn't personal. Sandy Carmichael offered to drive you in his truck if you didn't start coming around as well as you did."

"I completely understand. To be honest, even in normal times, I wouldn't have wanted the ride to the hospital. I'm sure I'll be fine."

"You will be, but you need to take it easy today. I think we can get you up a little more, but you're not going to be running any races any time soon. I know you're probably thinking about heading for home, but you're not ready."

I know she's right. I don't like it but don't see as I have a choice.

"I see Stella Jean left her Bible in here. I'd be happy to have her come and get it."

"Oh, she was reading from it. I fell asleep."

"Uh-huh. She's pretty... enthusiastic about... what does she say? Sharing the Good Book, I think. Personally, I don't pay her much never mind. She never seems to take offense, but she doesn't exactly leave me alone about it either."

"I'm glad she offered to read to me. I have a Bible on my eReader but, taking your advice, I haven't been reading right now."

Donna gives me a long look, then lets out a small sigh. "Oh, are you one of those Bible thumpers too?"

I can't help but laugh. With my history as a lackluster Christian and having turned my back on God more than once, I'm the last person who should be called a Bible thumper.

"I've never thought of myself as a Bible thumper," I answer. "I'm just an old sinner saved by grace. Now I grow and breathe in freedom."

Donna gives me a funny look and then says, "What?"

"It's a couple of lines from a song, but it's true. My walk with God, with Jesus, hasn't always been pretty, and oftentimes I stumble. But he's never let me fully fall. He's there to pick me back up."

Donna rolls her eyes and quietly says, "Yeah, you're another Bible thumper."

I just give a slight shrug and say, "I know God loves me. I know Jesus died for my sins. If that makes me a Bible thumper then…" I give a bigger shrug and kind of toss my arms out to say, "oh well."

"Yeah, well, okay. Let's just check you out and see how you're doing. We'll talk about this another time… or not."

After a short exam, Donna declares me "much better," and since I'm doing so much better, she lets me move to my original room where all my stuff is. I no longer need a monitor when I'm in the room, but she suggests if I want to go walking, have someone with me.

I'm also supposed to not do things which may strain my brain. Specifically, no reading and nothing more than slow walking.

Harry left a walkie-talkie for me to call him if I need anything at all, and this includes a walking mate. Harry also said he's not charging me for staying any additional days or the second room.

I'm to spend my day resting and taking short walks. I almost make the mistake of trying a simple stretch, but my body immediately rebels. My head is suddenly swimming, and I have cramps in a variety of places. While I'm resting, I think about Jake and Malcolm and what they're doing.

Part of me wishes Jake would come looking for me. I imagine how he drives into town and tells the first person he sees, "I'm looking for my wife. Her name is Mollie. She's almost a foot shorter than me with short brown hair and glasses. Have you seen her?"

Of course, the person just happens to be Sandy Carmichael, who very sheepishly says, "Uh… yeah. I've seen her. Let me take you to her."

When Jake knocks on the door to my room, he says, "Mollie, honey? It's me. I'm here."

I jump out of bed, throw the door open, and melt into his arms.

Of course, it's all fantasy. Jake can't come looking for me because he has no idea where I am. The last communication I know he received was on Saturday and I was in Idaho, nowhere near this hotel room. As much as I'd like to think he could magically appear, we have a deal. He won't come looking for me.

But with the new reality of me being stuck away from home in the middle of a national disaster, I'm hating our deal.

If Jake knew where I was, everything would change. Provided he had the ability to come straight to me—and not spend time looking for me like a needle in a haystack—he'd be here quickly. I still hold a little hope, somehow, I'll be able to get a cell signal and notify him just how close I am. Two hours by car is nothing.

Thinking about how much I wish he'd magically appear reminds me of where we are in our marriage right now. I remember watching a popular movie where one of the main characters was talking about losing his wife. He said, "Every marriage has its good years and bad years. We ended on a great year."

We've had great years, good years, and bad years. We came close to ending it during those bad times.

When our friends Sharri and Kenny, along with their children, were killed in a car wreck, it almost ended us. Working our way through the grief and learning to communicate with each other again was vital.

Learning to lean on and trust in God was what made this possible. If this trust is what earned me the title of Bible thumper from Donna, so be it.

Now, by the grace of God, Jake and I are in a good year… not great, but very good. We still have our little tiffs, but they're fairly infrequent.

There was a time when I dreaded him returning home from work. These days, when I hear his truck pulling up the hill, I get a butterfly feeling in the pit of my stomach very similar to when we first started dating.

While I know a marriage can't be all sunshine and roses, it's been great to rekindle the companionship and romance in our marriage.

I know Malcolm also notices, and he especially likes the time we all spend together. Even though we do try to make a point of doing family activities, Jake and I also prioritize couple time.

I think we're finding a nice balance. Maybe where we are right now is about right; we don't need to get rid of the farm or relocate, just keep on keeping on.

Of course, with the way our world has changed these past few days, keeping the farm is a no-brainer. We'll need the farm—the livestock, the gardens, the trees, and the vines. We'll need it all just to survive.

Chapter 40

In the late afternoon, there's a knock at my hotel room door along with, "Yoo–hoo. Mollie, dear, are you decent?"

Stella Jean. I gladly open the door. She's joined by a bear of a man, who looks very similar to Grizzly Adams from the old television show, only his hair is longer and he's bigger—much bigger—than Grizzly Adams appeared on my 1970s nineteen-inch TV set.

I can only assume he's Sandy Carmichael, Stella Jean's husband and the one who plowed into my chair at the meeting the other night.

The saying opposites attract is very true in the case of Sandy and Stella Jean. Her diminutive stature is magnified next to his largeness. I can see why she feels the need to wear the super high-heeled footwear. Even with the extra four or so inches, he's more than a foot taller.

"Oh! You look great," Stella Jean gushes. "Donna said you're doing really well and should be good as new in a few more days. I'm just so glad. I told Sandy you'd be fine, but we both thought we should come and pay a visit so he can give you his apologies in person. You know, he feels plumb terrible about knocking you out and all. Don't you Sandy?"

"Yes… yes, I definitely do," he stammers.

"Of course you do, Sandy," Stella Jean raves. "I'm sure Mollie knows you didn't do it on purpose… but I do wish you'd learn to control your urges a little bit. You not only toppled poor Mollie but also Ted Dobson. 'Course, he probably had it coming with the way he is."

Sandy shrugs, then says to me, "I'm very sorry you were injured. I hope you can find it in your heart to forgive me."

I have to admit, I'm pretty impressed with his sincerity, as I stutter, "Yes… of course."

"Thank you, ma'am," he says, as he lowers his eyes.

"There you go, Sandy. I told you she's a right nice lady and wouldn't hold a grudge. Mollie, you are just the sweetest thing forgiving my Sandy. He'd never purposely hurt a lady. And to help with saying he's sorry, when you're well enough to travel, Sandy is going to give you a ride down the road a bit. As much as we'd like to take you all the way home, we can't spare the fuel, but we'll get you a little closer. Should cut some time off your trip. Donna says you should be ready to travel in a few days."

Impulsively, I say, "I'm planning to leave tomorrow."

"Tomorrow?" Stella Jean blurts. "Oh no, I'm sure Donna won't want you to leave tomorrow. You need to rest up a few more days."

I know she's probably right, but now that I've spoken it out loud, I really do think I'll be ready to leave tomorrow. Instead of two hard bicycling days, I'll take three easier days, and if I can get a ride part of the way, it will really help.

"Tomorrow. With everyone's excellent care, I feel so much better already. And I really need to get home. I'm sure my family is beyond worried about me."

"Ma'am, I truly am sorry to have delayed your departure. I can give you a ride to the turnoff road… should save half a day or so. We can leave in the morning at first light, if you'd like."

"Oh, Sandy… she can't leave tomorrow. She's in no shape to travel. What if she gets dizzy or sick again? Mollie, really. Stay a few more days."

"I'll take it easy, and if I start to feel ill, I'll rest. It will be fine," I tell Stella Jean with a smile and a nod. The nod immediately causes me a slight dizziness and makes me think she's right and I should rest another day or two.

No. I'm going.

Stella Jean shakes her head and says, "Well, whatever you think is best."

We say our goodbyes, with Sandy telling me he'll knock on my door at 5:30 in the morning. If I'm ready, we'll go. If I need another day, it will be no problem at all.

About twenty minutes later, Donna comes knocking on my door. I can't say I'm surprised to see her.

"Stella Jean tells me you're thinking of heading home tomorrow."

"Yes. I feel so much better, and I really need to get home."

"Well… I think it's too soon but won't try and stop you. How about I give you another quick look over just to make sure things are still heading in the right direction?"

Donna gives me another exam and agrees with her earlier assessment. I'm healing as to be expected. She does say, again, rest is my friend now, and if I insist on leaving, I should take it easy and stop when my body tells me to stop. And since I insist on leaving tomorrow, I might as well feel free to walk around on my own for the rest of the day.

With my somewhat clean bill of health, I start packing up. There's not much to do since I've spent very little time in this room. After determining I'm ready, I decide to look for Aideen so I can return the sweats and T-shirt she loaned me. As I open the door to exit, I'm given quite a fright from Aideen standing on the other side, arm raised to knock.

"Oh my!" she exclaims. "You scared me."

"Same here! I was just going to look for you. Thank you so much for loaning me the clothes."

"I heard a rumor you're thinking of leaving tomorrow," Aideen says.

"Not a rumor. Truth."

"Ah… well, I know you're anxious to get home. Just be sure to take it easy," Aideen says, while embracing me in a hug. "Would you like to join us for supper?"

"Oh… yes. I would. I have a little food. Can I bring something?"

"Nah. You keep what you have for your trip home. It may take longer than you plan, and you could be thankful for every morsel you've packed."

I know she's right, but I've already been fed by Aideen during my recovery time, and with the way things are, she could regret my eating their food at a point in the future. I ask her if I can take a minute to get ready, and she agrees. Five minutes later, we're out the door and on our way.

We take advantage of the short walk to Aideen's home to chitchat. I find out Penny and Peter both moved away to attend school, then moved back. The family owns several different businesses in the area, including construction, snow removal, tourist and hunting guide services, along with a few other things. That tends to be the way in small towns without much industry.

Aideen surprises me when she says, "Penny tells me you're pretty athletic."

"Ha. Well… I don't know about that. I try to exercise, but I'm not a natural athlete by any means."

She nods and says, "Yeah, I understand. But you do martial arts and stuff, right?"

"I'm learning a Korean martial art known as Yongmudo. It's more of a self-defense thing. My husband, son, and I started last fall, so I'm not very good yet. Sometimes I look back on the first class and am amazed I stuck with it. I was definitely a fish out of water. One of the first things they taught us was front rolls, kind of like a somersault. I hadn't done a somersault for over thirty years!"

Aideen laughs and says, "Oh my! I can't even imagine doing one."

"It wasn't easy. Jake had a hard time with it also, getting very dizzy and turning a shade of green. But we stuck with it and were soon doing not only front but also back rolls. It's fun and definitely a workout."

"How'd you become interested in it?"

"Definitely in a roundabout way. Years ago, after my first husband died and before I married Jake, my four girls and I took a weekend self-defense course. It was marketed as a mom and daughter event and seemed like a good way for us to do something all together to help us get out of our... funk.

"The class started on a Friday evening and went all day Saturday, included lodging and meals, and it was very well done. We really learned a lot. One of the first things we learned was to yell FIRE, as opposed to rape, to draw attention to ourselves and to get away, if possible. If we couldn't get away, fight like our life depended on it, since it likely did. This included fighting dirty and doing whatever was necessary. They taught us how to spar in order to practice these techniques, without hurting the other person.

"We continued the sparring at home for a few months, with FIRE being our war call. That really seemed to spur everyone on and acted as a call to arms. As time went on, our practice times diminished. My youngest daughter, Katie, only seven or eight at the time, stuck with it the longest. At her urging, she and I would practice on occasion. One of my older girls, Calley, and I took a second, one-day self-defense course together a couple years back, which resparked my interest. I wanted to follow up with Krav Maga, an Israeli fighting technique, but couldn't find anything near where I live. When I found the Yongmudo classes, it seemed like a good alternative. Now, I'm so glad I did. I really enjoy it."

"Good for you, Mollie. It's nice to see someone of our age learning new things and trying to stay fit. Do you have a black belt or something?"

I laugh heartily. "Not even close. I was recently promoted to a second yellow belt, which is several years of experience away from a black belt. In the fall, I'll test for my next belt. I didn't even realize we could earn belts when I started. It was just something fun to do and good exercise."

"I still think it's great. I like to think of myself as 'sturdy,' but I could do more for my health. I've definitely put on a bit of weight in the last few years. Of course, depending on how things go… well, I suspect many of us will start losing weight as we ration our food."

She must have caught my look, as she quickly says, "But that's a thought for a different day. Tonight, you dine with us as our guest. Besides, I have a few things I've been trying to keep cold using the generator, and it's time to use them up."

The evening was more of a party than a simple dinner. Aideen's husband, Brett, who I'd yet to meet, was a very robust gentleman with an easy laugh. Penny's husband was also a bit of a clown. Peter's wife and young children were a joy. Being with everyone was wonderful and terrible at the same time, reminding me how much I miss my own family.

While everyone tried to keep the evening light and fun, the conversation would sometimes stray to the terrible events of the past several days. The town had implemented its shutdown and was escorting people through as needed. So far, everything was going as well as could be expected. A few town's people were still grumbling about it but agreed it was needed. Aideen said today was a day to celebrate since there were no new terrorism attacks.

I'm back in my motel room before dark, finishing up a few last-minute things for my early morning departure. It occurs to me, I should've stopped and told Harry I was leaving in the morning. But then figure, he's likely already heard via the grapevine. Got to love a small town.

Chapter 41

Wednesday, Day 7

True to his word, Sandy Carmichael is at my door bright and early. I'm pleased to see Stella Jean, in full makeup and dressed to the nines at this early hour, by his side.

"Well, there you are, Mollie, dear. Have you come to your senses and decided to rest another day or two?" she asks, not unkindly.

"Nope. I feel pretty good and am ready to hit the road," I state, choosing not to tell her I really didn't want to get out of bed this morning, and when I did, my stomach revolted, causing me to run to the bathroom. This bang on the head is really starting to annoy me.

"Uh, huh," she says doubtfully, while looking me up and down.

"Let me put your things in the truck," Sandy offers.

As Sandy is putting my bike in the bed of the pickup, Harry walks over and says goodbye and I'm welcome back any time. I suppose we both know pleasure trips are out for the near future.

Sandy and Stella Jean take the front seat of the quad cab pickup while I take the back, along with my small backpack. The rest of my gear is secured to my bike. I tried to do a better job of balancing everything, in hopes of not repeating my crash from Sunday... the beginning of my injury woes.

When we reach the spot Sandy told me he'd drop me off, it's full daylight and a pleasant morning. If I didn't feel so terrible, I'd likely be looking forward to my bike ride... well, not exactly true.

I can't even pretend this is a pleasure ride I'm embarking on. My sole mission is to get home. I have to admit, even though I totally understand Sandy and Stella Jean needing to take me only as far as they are, I'd love to beg them to drive me the rest of the way. I could be home in less than two hours and finish my recovery in the comfort of my own bed.

After a few minutes of unloading and reworking my load slightly, I'm ready to go. Stella Jean envelopes me in a huge hug and says,

"When this whole mess is done, I sure hope you'll come back up for a proper visit. We'd love to see you again. Isn't that right, Sandy?"

"Yes... sure. Please do come up for a visit. Again, I'm so sorry I lost my temper and you ended up in harm's way," he says, with a sad shake of his head.

I say my final goodbyes and take off.

I'm thankful the road is fairly flat so I can get my bike legs. As it is, I have a little too much wobble and am sure I look the fool. There are some serious inclines on this route, and I suspect I'll find myself walking more than riding.

I ride only a short distance before I determine I need to stop for another adjustment—I'm still wobblier than I should be. I take advantage of my stopped time to have a snack and try to send the text I prepared a few days ago. I want to update it slightly to let everyone know I'm on the road. I've had my phone turned off since my first night in Cooke City, so as not to run down the battery. I'm pleased when it starts up and I have almost a full charge.

I make a few slight changes to the text I started before my run-in with Sandy Carmichael: *It's Wednesday morning and I'm on my way home! I'll take the pass home by our wood cutting area. I should be home late Thursday or Friday, if all goes well. I'll camp at night, off the road, so look for me in the daylight. I'll start my ride no later than 7 am each day and be off the road before dark. Jake, if you get this, feel free to come and get me. I'll be ready for a ride. Children, if one of you gets this, please try to reach Jake to let him know where I am. I love you all. See you soon.*"

I don't have a definite cell signal, but also don't have a no service notice. I'm sending this to Jake, my four daughters, and the three spouses, in hopes it will reach someone. At the last minute, I decide to include my neighbor Doris in the delivery, but don't bother to change the content, figuring she'll simply be happy to hear from me, even if I don't address her in the message.

I say a quick prayer and press send. *Please, God, let me have an easy trip home.*

Even so, old habits die hard, and I realize I'm once again trying to handle everything on my own.

I pull out my eReader and queue up the Bible I have on it. I find Psalm 91, sometimes referred to as the Soldiers' Prayer, and read it through. Verse 4 is my favorite part:

"He will cover you with his feathers, and under his wings you will find refuge; his faithfulness will be your shield and rampart."

The vision of being pulled under the feathers, like a mama hen tucks in her chicks to keep them warm and protect them, always settles me. I feel slightly refreshed and ready to get going.

Back on the road, I don't try to win any land speed races. I soon reach the first incline and quickly discover riding uphill is terrible. I soon peter out and end up walking. And so goes my day.

Ride, walk, stop to eat or drink, ride, walk, and so forth. My mind wanders as the day passes, thinking of my life at home; the predicament we, as a nation, are now in; my children and praying for their safety; and so much more.

A few hours into the trip, I realize I've not seen another human. No cars and no sign of life at the scattered houses along this stretch of the road. Are people around but staying hidden? I have seen in excess of two dozen deer, several elk, and a cow and young calf moose.

Thankfully, no bears.

I'm in a designated national forest and wilderness area. While the term national forest conjures up images of wall-to-wall trees as far as the eye can see, this forest contains plenty of open areas.

The trees are clumped together, with the clusters ranging from the size of a football field to hundreds of acres. The pockets of trees alternate with patches of native grass, sagebrush, and low bushes.

Cows lazily graze in the grassy areas. How much longer will ranchers be able to use these highlands without the threat of rustlers? I can imagine hungry people doing whatever is needed to provide sustenance.

Giving extra beauty and ruggedness to the wilderness, and popular with climbers, are the occasional rock outcroppings. Dotting the landscape, like they were shot out of a cannon, are many boulders, ranging in size from a basketball to a Volkswagen Bus or larger. They have no rhyme or reason and may be an individual boulder or several clustered together.

With no logic to the layout of the forest, I never know what will be around the next bend—more trees, open land, or rocks? Even though I've been on this road before, traveling by car, the reduced speed of the bike—combined with walking—really increases the beauty of the area.

If I didn't want to be home so badly, I'd be enjoying the trip even more. And if my head didn't hurt so much and my stomach didn't keep feeling like it was rebelling...

Even so, being on this road brings me hope and spurs me on. I can see this wilderness area, albeit the eastern side, from my home in Bakerville. I'm so, so close.

Late afternoon I stop for a meal. As part of my bear safety plan, I'll eat and then travel a ways up the road before camping. My plan is to reduce food aromas around my campsite.

I haven't traveled as far today as I was hoping to. According to the mile markers, I've gone just over thirteen miles. I could walk this far and wonder if the bike is even helping me any. It's still about fifty miles to home. About an hour before dark, I find a spot to camp, hidden from the road.

I hang a good portion of my food a ways away from camp. I don't have the means to hang all my food, so do what I can. The rest is hidden in a few different areas between boulders—all well away from my campsite.

My thinking is, if a bear is drawn to it, they'll find only one of my caches and not all. Since the food is mostly freeze-dried and dehydrated, it should be fairly low odor, but bears are amazing detectives, so one never knows.

My little one-person tent goes up easy and is plenty roomy. I'm fairly comfortable with my mattress pad and sleeping bag. Even so, I have trouble falling asleep. I try reading but discover concentrating is difficult. I'm reminded Donna encouraged me not to tax my brain with reading. Instead, I lie there listening to the night sounds and working on scaring myself with every snap of a twig and rustle of a tree.

I think of my family. They must be near frantic with worry. It's been days since I spoke with Jake. Saturday was the last time. Today's Wednesday. We've never gone this long without talking.

Even when things were rough between us, we didn't really do the silent treatment. While our conversations weren't always pleasant, often laced with snide comments—mainly from my mouth—we'd still try to put up a good front. For Malcolm, of course.

Oh, I know we weren't fooling him. He could see right through us, and he knew we were having troubles.

Things are different now. We're good, really good.

Was that a grizzly bear? It certainly could've been a bear. I suddenly have visions of being a human version of a pig in a blanket. Then, the howls of a coyote family almost send me over the edge.

Chapter 42

Thursday, Day 8

With sleep coming in short spurts only, I finally give up when the sky is beginning to lighten. I use my super bright LED headlamp and begin to tear down camp. The light helps me feel a little less jumpy. When there's enough daylight to see well, I cautiously start to retrieve my food bags. Whew! Nothing has been disturbed. I take the time to brew water for coffee and scarf down a granola bar before repacking everything and getting all the gear back on my bicycle. If I remember correctly, I'll have a slight incline coming up soon, then a downhill stretch followed by a rather steep uphill for several miles.

While I originally thought I could be home in two or three days max, after only making thirteen miles yesterday, I'm not optimistic. No way I'll get home today, and tomorrow is also unlikely. I'll just do the best I can, knowing I'll make it home within a few days.

I've barely started my trip when I reach a campground with a vault toilet. I wish I would've ridden a little farther yesterday. Maybe staying in the campground would've netted a better night's sleep. I stop for a few minutes to take advantage of the facilities.

I'm not feeling well again this morning. The stench of the vault toilet quickly becomes a bad idea, and I find myself vomiting once again. Vomiting in a vault toilet isn't an experience I ever care to repeat.

I feel so bad, I'm not even up to getting back on the road. Setting up my stove at a picnic table, I heat water for oatmeal and a cup of coffee.

The aroma of the coffee, usually so welcome and comforting, turns my stomach. Ugh. I feel absolutely terrible. I dump the coffee far away from the table and pick at my oatmeal. I end up drifting off while resting my arms on the table.

At least an hour later, I'm back on the road. Too soon, I reach another incline—the first of the day. Still feeling puny, I get off and push the bike. I'm beginning to wonder if I'm ever going to make it home, as much as I have to stop and walk. I'm nearing the crest when I instantly drop into a crouch.

There's shouting coming from the other side of the hill.

Chapter 43

"Get out… get out and move over here," an angry male voice yells.

"Okay, okay. No problem," a second male answers, the fear evident.

"You do exactly what I say and maybe, *maybe*, I'll let you, your wife, and young 'un out of here without a scratch."

"No problem, sir. I'll do exactly what you want," the frightened male stutters.

Then, a whimper from a woman or a child, I can't quite tell. I silently drop my bike on the side of the road, making sure it's somewhat down in the ditch. I start up the hill to see what's happening, when I realize I should take the .22 rifle Ben loaned me.

After taking the loaded rifle off the back of the bike, I then double check the pistol on my hip and check my fanny pack for the pistol's second magazine and the box of ammo for the rifle. With the magazine in the rifle holding twenty-five rounds plus one in the chamber, I shouldn't need more ammo—I pray I won't need more ammo—but want to have it just in case.

Please, Lord, don't let me need ANY ammo.

Walking in a stoop, I begin up the incline. As I near the crest, the angry voices continue, with the one I've decided to call "the bad guy" yelling at the man to put his hands behind his head.

Bad guy laughs and says mockingly, "That gun isn't going to do you any good."

Oh no. Definitely doesn't sound good. I'm off the road in the shallow ditch on the right side, practically on my belly, as I make my way to the top. One of the many boulders along the side of the road looks like a good place to hide behind. I have no idea—*no idea at all*—what I'm going to do.

Once I can see what's going on, maybe I'll be able to tell more about exactly what's happening. From the sounds of it, there's the bad guy, a scared guy, a woman, and possibly a child.

As soon as I get to the rock, still squatting very low, I peer out from the right of the boulder. My assessment isn't completely accurate.

A man and woman plus two guys are on the road behind a beige Toyota pickup. The man and woman are standing slightly off the road, both with their hands raised in the classic surrender stance.

An older, well-dented, brown car is parked in front of the pickup. One of the men has a pistol pointed at the couple. The scared guy is standing in front of the woman in a protective stance, while she's slightly downhill in the ditch area.

Before I can think much more about what's going on, the bad guy with the gun says, "I wish you wouldn't have gone and done that. Now I'm going to have to shoot you. Too bad, I really wanted to wait on this."

He fires one time, and both the man and the woman fall. I stifle a scream and scrunch down as low as I can while still keeping an eye on the situation.

The second guy yells out in exasperation, "Jeez, Dave, why'd you go and do that? You said I could have the woman."

"Oops," Dave, the bad guy, says with a shrug. "I guess I didn't really think the bullet would go through him and on into her. Sorry, but you know, she's still warm. Go ahead and have your way with her anyway."

"Well, jeez. Thanks, Dave. I kind of like it when they put up a little bit of a fight. It's a little more fun for me as opposed to her being dead and all," bad guy number two says, with his voice raising in volume on each word until "and all" is a yell.

There is the wail of a baby. A really young sounding baby.

"Calm down. You can go ahead and do what you're going to do with her, Don," Dave says. "I better go take care of that screaming brat."

"You going to kill the kid, Dave?" Don asks.

"Well, yeah... What else we going to do with it?"

"It's just a baby," Don says. "It's not like it's going to cause any trouble. We can just leave it here on the side of the road.

"Boy howdy, Don. Why didn't I think of that? Yeah, we'll just leave it on the side of the road. 'Cuz, you know, it'll be just fine left on the side of the road. There's no grizzly bears, wolves, or anything around here. It will be just fine taking care of itself."

"Dave, I don't want to kill a baby," Don says forcefully and crosses his arms.

"Don't worry about it, Donnie Boy. I'll go ahead and take care of the kid. You do what you want to do with the woman."

"Fine, take out the kid. I don't care. That's on you not me," Don responds, while gesticulating to make his point.

At this point, I'm pretty much freaking out. There's no way I'm going to let them kill the baby like they killed the mom and the dad.

Okay, Mollie, you know what you have to do. Shoot Dave first— he has a visible weapon. Then shoot Don. My version of a pep-talk. I know I have to do it now before I can think too much about exactly what I'm doing... killing two men.

Breathing deeply to settle my heart rate closer to normal and gather my wits, I creep up slowly to rest across the top of the boulder, using it for support. I take a bead on Dave and then I practice immediately sighting on Don to get a feel for the swing and the weight of the weapon.

The last few years, I started hunting and have done lots of target practice with my hunting rifle, shotgun, and .22 rifle. Since the .22 rifle I have with me was loaned to me by Ben when I left his place in Oregon, I've never shot it before.

It's open sights and, like Ben cautioned, best at less than fifty yards. I'm pretty sure I'm a bit farther from my target, shooting downhill.

Of course, I don't have a range finder on me... sure wish I did. My range finder does this fancy thing where it figures out the true ballistic range for shooting up and down hills. At this distance, and since it's not a super steep angle, I'm not sure it matters much.

I've shot rabbits from a similar distance from atop a hill. And just a few months ago, I went turkey hunting and shot my turkey in a draw, with a shotgun. While I'm wishing for a range finder, I might as well wish for my hunting rifle, which is a .308, instead of this puny .22.

Two quick shots to the head is my plan for Dave, just like I did with my turkey. It goes without saying, I've never shot a man before. But what choice do I have?

None. *No way am I going to let them kill the baby.*

Dave is starting to move toward the cab of the truck. He's in a good spot to avoid anything behind him. I don't want to shoot into the truck and hit the baby by mistake.

I figure it's now or never. Even though he's moving slowly, I have a good bead on him. My heart is beating so loud, I half wonder if they'll hear it.

I take a deep breath and begin my process. Breathe out and take the weapon off safety. Take a deep breath in, and when I let it out, pull up the slack on the trigger...

Then, Don says with alarm, "Hey, Dave, maybe she's not dead. She's twitching a bit."

Dave has stopped moving and is slowly turning toward his buddy, Don. One more nice, deep breathe, in and then out. Next, I inhale and start to exhale, then hold it. As I gently squeeze the trigger, there's a single shot, much louder than the two from my .22 rifle.

Dave is looking at Don as he falls. Did I miss Dave and hit Don by mistake? I don't think so. I think my shot was a complete miss. I squeeze the trigger again. This time Dave goes down.

Don yells out, "Dave, she shot me... she shot me. Dave... what the...? She shot you too. She's quick... she done shot both of us."

I don't really know what's going on. I shoot Dave again. My fourth shot is to his torso and, just for good measure, I place a fifth shot in his neck.

"Dave, she shot you again. She shot you dead," Don says, his voice full of surprise.

I aim my rifle over to Don. I'm slightly surprised he's just lying there on the ground. He would've been smart to move to cover. I shoot him two times in rapid succession to the torso. Don makes a kind of *oomph* noise. I take an additional shot to his head. Miss, aim, and squeeze again. This time, I'm successful.

Chapter 44

I set my rifle down and throw up in the tall, native grass. Once done, I sling my rifle on my back and have my pistol at the ready. While I'm fairly certain Dave and Don are both dead, I'm not 100 percent sure what happened to Don with the first shot.

I think the woman shot him. I certainly don't want her to shoot me. I don't want to shoot her either, but no way am I going in without using caution and lots of it.

I slowly make my way down, using boulders alongside the road as cover, moving from boulder to boulder as needed. When I'm within twenty yards of the carnage, I say, in what I hope is a confident voice, "I can help you. I'm not going to hurt you." I suddenly realize I should've taken the time to refill the rifle magazine. How many shots do I have left?

"Then put your gun down," the woman says. "I still have a gun, and I will use it if I have to."

With a squeak to my voice, I answer, "Sorry. I can't put my weapon down. I can help you and your baby. But I'm not unarming until I make sure those two are dead and there are no other threats. Please, your baby is crying. Let me help you both. My name is Mollie. Mollie Caldwell. I'm just trying to get home and I heard your trouble…" I'm starting to ramble. I shut my mouth.

"I think they're both dead. I can't see them, but I don't hear anything," she says.

"I'm coming near you. I'm armed and not putting my weapon down. I won't hurt you. I'd appreciate the same consideration. You shot the Don guy, right? Well done."

I move to a boulder closer to the woman. From there, I move slightly toward the road, keeping the boulder between us. I have my pistol aimed at Don. I can see him clearly now and am confident he's dead.

I switch my aim to Dave. I walk in a crouch toward him, keeping what I hope is enough distance so I can react if the jerk moves. From the way he's sprawled out and the amount of blood around him, I'm certain he, too, is dead.

I quickly move back behind the rock and wretch once again. As I finish, I realize I'm also crying. I don't have time right now to think about anything more.

When I'm done, the woman asks, "Are you okay?"

"Yeah," I lie.

"I've set my gun down. I'm pretty sure they killed my husband. I'll trust you. Please just take care of my baby," she says and begins to cry.

I peer out from behind the rock and see her gun is on the ground but still within reach. I slowly walk toward her. When I'm near enough, I bend over and pick up her handgun. As I walk, with my weapon drawn toward Don and Dave so I can retrieve their guns, I ask, "What's your name?"

"Madison," she answers.

"Okay, Madison. I'm Mollie."

"You already told me," Madison says.

"Oh, I forgot." I give a nervous little laugh. "I'm not thinking too clearly." Don has a small black revolver in his belt, maybe a .38?

A rather large, scruffy looking semi-automatic is lying next to Dave. In the back of his belt is a second semi-auto in much better condition. Maybe the one he took off of Madison's husband. I set all four pistols off to the side.

"That makes two of us. Can you check my husband, Mollie? I'm pretty sure they killed him, but if you could make sure..." Her voice trails off and is replaced by a sob.

"I will." I keep my gun out as I walk over to her husband. There's no doubt he's dead. "I'm so sorry, Madison."

With a whimper, Madison says, "Yeah, I didn't think there was any hope. My baby—she's okay? I don't think they did anything to her. Can you go check on her? Then I'm going to need you to help me stop this bleeding. He shot me in the shoulder. We've got a good first aid kit in the back of the pickup truck. It's on the far right-hand side at the tailgate. It's a big orange box. Can you grab it?"

"Yes, of course," I answer. I rush to the pickup and open the back door. A rear-facing baby seat holds a sweaty-faced infant. Thankfully, the front driver's window was down, so it's not too hot in the truck, but with all the crying she's done, she's worked herself up pretty well.

"Hey, pretty girl. Let's sit you outside so you can get some air." I hurriedly move the baby, carrier and all, out of the pickup and sit her

175

on the ground. I'd like to position her so she can see her mom, but that'll have to wait until we get Madison's bleeding stopped.

Plus, I want to move the bodies so the baby can't see them.

"Okay, pretty girl. There's a nice breeze, so you'll cool off quickly. Then we'll change your diaper and get you over with your mom in a bit."

I step away from the baby and to the rear of the truck, quickly opening the tailgate and finding the first aid kit. It's a really nice first aid kit. Madison or her husband likely has advanced first aid training. Kit in hand, I hustle over to Madison.

"I have my bandana up against it but it's still bleeding," Madison says. "In the kit are a couple of battle bandages and other things. I don't think the bone was hit too badly but can't really tell. It sure hurts."

I find what I need in the kit. In addition to the battle bandages, I grab an elastic bandage. Following instructions from Madison, I tear open her shirt and put a compression bandage on the front, then gently roll her to look for an exit on her back.

Nothing. I'm not sure if this is good or bad. With the front compression bandage in place, I wrap it with the elastic strip to hold the battle dressing in place. I can't even imagine how much this must hurt. Madison doesn't look too well and starts to shiver.

"Shock," she says. "I need to warm up. There's sleeping bags in the truck."

I find two bags in the back. I open one and cover her with it. At one point, I think she passes out, but then she says, "That's good. Let me warm up a little and rest, then get me in a bag. I think it will be best for me to be zipped in."

The baby is crying again, when Madison says, "It's okay, Emma. Mommy will take care of you real soon. You'll be fine."

I go to Emma and remove her from the carrier. A diaper bag in the back of the pickup has fresh diapers. After I get her taken care of, I check on Madison.

When I step near her, her eyes pop open and she takes a deep breath. "Okay, Mollie. Better. I need to rest a bit, then we'll see what to do next. I need a drink, then I'll take Emma. There's a jug in the back of the truck, plus bottles. We filtered water last night, so it's clean. Help yourself to water also."

I put Emma back in the carrier in order to get the water out. Helping Madison get a drink isn't easy, and she's just about spent afterward. She sighs and says, "Could you bring Emma to me? I'll nurse her... it will probably make both of us feel better. First, can you help me get inside the sleeping bag? I'd like to be off the ground a bit."

We're both exhausted by the time she's in the bag. Emma is crying and bordering on a full-on howl. I find a pillow in the truck to make cradling Emma a little easier. With her on her mom's uninjured side, she quickly settles in. Her crying eases off to the occasional hiccup until she's silent and nursing contently.

I take a long drink of water while thinking about what to do next. I need to cover Madison's husband and figure out what to do with the bodies. I suddenly realize the pickup truck means we can get to help in short order. From here, I can have her into Prospect, and a hospital, in just over an hour.

I find a blanket in the back of the pickup to cover Madison's husband and, as gently as I can, move him off the road. We'll have to come back for his body. There isn't any way I can get him in the truck to take him now.

I'm startled when Madison says, "His name is Scott. My husband is Scott. I suppose we'll have to leave him here. Unless you can get him in your car?"

"I don't have a car. I'm on a bike. I need to go back up the hill for it. Then we'll have to take your truck into Prospect."

"Ah... okay. You know, we were going home today. We went camping before this whole mess started. We figured, with everything happening, we might as well stay camping. Kept abreast of everything by listening to the radio a few times a day.

"Yesterday, when there were no new attacks, we decided to head home. We made it out of the wilderness, and last night we stayed at a campground off the main road—you know, on the side road just before starting up the hill... I can't remember what it's called. Anyway, we thought we'd just get an early start today. I'm not sure where these guys came from. They just flagged us down, and the next thing I knew, they had guns on us." Madison breaks down and is overcome with tears.

Soon, her tears turn to more of a wail. I move over near her but am not sure what to do. Emma starts to fuss, which seems to bring Madison to a stage of alertness.

She croons, "I know, Emma, I know. We're going to miss Daddy, but we'll be fine. Momma will be okay soon. We just need to get to a doctor to fix me up. Mollie, I need to rest for a little while, then maybe we can get loaded up and take off. I just can't do it right now…" Her voice drifts off.

At her side, I check to make sure she seems okay and determine she's sleeping. Her breathing isn't great but doesn't seem in distress. Emma is still nursing but also starting to doze.

I move Dave and Don off the road and into the ditch on the far side—not a small feat and I'm winded by the time I'm done. I dry heave several times in the process. I decide they don't need to be covered and instead can become bird, bear, wolf, and coyote food. There's already crows, waiting. Their *caw, caw, caw* reminding us of their presence. How long will they wait before beginning their feast? I've read they start with the soft tissue first… the wounds, the eyeballs.

I sigh. We can't leave Madison's husband. He'll be scavenger food as soon as we're away from his remains. I'll have to figure out some way to get him in their truck.

I check on Madison and Emma—both are sleeping soundly. I take the opportunity to go up the hill for my bike. It takes only a few minutes for me to return, then I load it into the back of Madison's Toyota. Loading it up takes a lot out of me, and I fight a wave of dizziness and nausea. I sit on the ground and nurse a bottle of water from my pack.

"You okay?" Madison asks, startling me.

"Yes, I'll be fine. I got a little bump on the head a couple days ago and still feel the effects on occasion. It's no problem. Do you feel rested? Can you walk so I can put you in the truck?" I ask.

"I'm not sure. Do you know what time it is?"

"Not certain but I'd guess midafternoon," I say, looking up at the sky.

She starts to respond when we both hear a noise. It's far in the distance, but I'm almost positive it's the sound of an engine.

"Sounds like someone's coming. Friend or foe is my first question," Madison says.

"Let's get you two in the truck and go," I say hurriedly.

"No time. They'll be here before we can make that happen. Help us take cover behind one of the boulders."

Chapter 45

I take Emma, quickly putting her back in the baby seat, and hide her behind the largest boulder. I didn't take time to buckle the seat. I hope she stays put. I try to help Madison up. She almost passes out from the exertion. "I can't do it," she says. "Take Emma and give me both mine and Scott's handguns."

"Maybe I can pull you? I'll grab on to the sleeping bag and move you." I immediately begin to pull on the top of the bag, when she gasps and says, "No. Too painful. Just give me the guns."

I nod, knowing there isn't much else to do. I give her back her pistol and Scott's, grab my rifle, and join Emma behind the boulder. The engine noise is now very loud, and we expect to see the vehicle at any moment. I quickly buckle up Emma into her car seat.

As the front of the vehicle comes into view, it immediately stops. My heart skips a beat. Jake? It looks like his truck.

I quietly say to Madison, "I think it's my husband, but let's just stay where we are for now."

"Your husband?" She says with surprise. I have to admit, I'm surprised too. Either my text went through or he's strayed from our plan and is out looking for me. Or it's not him…

The truck starts to slowly back up. I want to yell, "Stop. Come and help us," but hold my tongue.

"What's he doing?" Madison asks quietly. From her spot on the ground, she can't see much of anything.

"Backing up," I whisper.

"Why?"

"Don't know. Maybe they're concerned it's an ambush or something. You have to admit, two cars stopped is a little suspicious with everything happening."

"Yeah. I guess Scott and I should've been more suspicious."

A few seconds later, a voice I don't recognize calls out, "Everything okay with you folks?" The voice is a whole lot closer than I think it should be, considering the truck backed up out of view.

Right then, Emma lets out a loud, long squeal. Madison quietly says, "It's okay, baby girl," while I make sure I'm at the ready in case we need to react.

"I have no intention of harming you. It sounds like you have a baby. Do you need medical assistance? Ma'am, what about you in the sleeping bag? Are you injured?"

Madison responds, barely above a whisper, "No. Just go and leave us be. We're fine on our own."

"Madison," I whisper. "We're not fine. If he can help, we should let him. I'd like to think he's being truthful and doesn't want to hurt us."

"What if he's lying? My husband is already dead. I don't want my baby killed also," she whispers harshly.

"I don't know..." I admit. "Let me talk to him, maybe we can get more info."

"Fine," she snaps.

I raise my voice and say, as forcefully as I can, "No offense, buddy, but we don't know you and aren't overly inclined to trust a stranger."

"I totally understand. Very smart on your part. We're just trying to find one of our family members. We're not looking to cause trouble for anyone, but the truth is, we need to get by so we can keep looking. Unfortunately, we don't feel safe moving past you... considering these two dead guys in the ditch over here."

I decide to give a little more bravado than I feel. "Yeah... well, those dead guys are dead because they deserved to die. And we're totally prepared to do the same thing to anyone else who threatens us."

"Mollie?" a new voice calls out, from a slightly different location than the first speaker is located. "Mollie, is that you?"

I want to yell, "Yes! Yes, it is!" but I'm not sure who's asking. Of course, most of me knows it has to be someone I know... it's not like I've given my name out.

"Mollie, it's Mike. We're looking for you. Jake is just around the corner." Then he raises his voice and yells, "Jake, it's Mollie. We've found her!"

Mike... *Calley's husband?* Could it be him? That would mean Calley and Mike made their way to my house.

Calley is safe.

"Mike, not that I don't believe you, but I'd feel better if I could see it's you and not just hear you."

"It's okay, Leo," a new person calls out. "That's definitely Mollie. I'd know her voice anywhere."

"Jake!" I yell, while setting the rifle down.

He steps out, no longer hidden by the bend in the road. He's amazing. Tall and muscular, sunlight lighting up his face. Smile wider than I've ever seen, a fringe of silver glistening from the rim of his ball cap.

The next thing I know, I'm in Jake's arms. He's hugging me and kissing me, telling me how glad he is to have me back.

Our reunion is cut short when I say, "Madison is hurt. She needs a doctor." I step out of Jake's arms and turn to Madison.

"Leo, we need you," Jake says.

Mike comes out from his hiding place, and I go to him for a hug. He's a big guy, over six-foot tall and solid. His face is also a mess with a black eye and a Band-Aid across his forehead.

"I'm glad you're okay, Mollie. We got your text a little bit ago and made it here as quick as we could. We weren't quite sure what to think when we saw the vehicles on the road. Leo and I got out and snuck over here while Jake was backing up. When I saw the guys in the ditch... well, we had no idea what happened or who was involved. It was pretty scary."

"Yeah. Let's see about Madison and I'll fill you in. What happened to you?" I ask motioning to his face.

"Oh... I had a run-in at a gas station in Casper. That's why we came up. Casper turned into a nightmare."

"Calley is okay?" I ask.

"She's fine. Back at home and can't wait to see you. Everyone's there."

My heart jumps for joy at the sound of this. I turn toward Madison as Jake starts talking to her.

"Well, except my dad. He's here," Mike looks around, as Jake says, "He stayed with the truck. Why don't you head over and ask him to pull it up?"

"Sure, Jake."

Jake turns to Madison and says, "Hi there. I'm Jake. Mollie is my wife."

"Hello," she says wearily. "Is Emma okay?"

182

"She's in her car seat behind the boulder. I'll get her," I say, thinking how quiet she has been after her screech earlier. When I get to her, she's staring at me wide-eyed while playing with her toes. She gives me a smile, and my heart melts.

"She's just fine, Madison." I leave her in the seat and take her where Madison can see her. A guy I don't know is now kneeling down next to Madison.

"Mollie, this is Leo," Jake says. "He's a paramedic or something. He'll take a look at your friend."

"Pleased to meet you, Mrs. Caldwell. Can you give me a quick rundown of... was it Madison's... injuries?"

"Yes, Madison. She had me put on a pressure bandage. I didn't see an exit wound. We were just getting ready to try to get in her pickup and head for the hospital when we heard the truck."

"Can we take my husband? Can you guys load him? Mollie and I couldn't, so we were going to leave him and come back, but... I don't want to leave him," Madison starts crying.

Jake and Leo look toward Scott's covered body. The breeze has blown the blanket off him slightly, but his face and torso are still covered.

"Yes. We can," Jake says. "What do you think, Leo? Roy, Mike, and I could start getting ready to go? Head to Belinda's mom's place?"

"We need to go to the hospital," I say quickly. "She's lost a lot of blood, and she probably needs surgery."

Jake pulls me aside and quietly says, "The Prospect hospital is out of commission. We don't think we can get to Billings. Belinda Bosco is our best choice right now. In fact..." He pauses and takes a deep breath.

"In fact, what?"

"Angela was injured yesterday. She'll be okay, but Belinda is taking care of her right now. Doris also."

"What? What do you mean Angela is injured and Doris also?" Tears immediately come to my eyes.

Jake's eyes fill with tears, as he softly explains. "They... were attacked. We were out gathering supplies. They were with the truck and trailer when..." he lets out a large sigh and quickly says, "they were both shot. Doris was hit in the side and the ankle. Angela was shot with birdshot, from a distance, so she was only pelleted—it wasn't serious—but the guy tried to... take her. She fought back and shot him. His partner hit her with the butt of his rifle in the head."

"Oh, Heavens, no." I'm full-on crying now. "She'll be okay? You said she'll be okay?"

"Belinda and Kelley have been caring for her, along with help from Leo, Belinda's mom, and Katie. They think she'll be okay, but it's going to take some time. The head injury is pretty severe. They sent someone to Red Lodge today to see if the hospital is operational, with plans to take Angela and Doris there if it is. Belinda didn't want to have them make the trip unless we knew for sure. She's set up a room at Tammy's house—you know, Belinda's mom—and they're doing the best they can right now."

Jake hugs me tight and whispers, "Angela is strong. She's coming around some and asking about Gavin and Tim. She keeps asking them to have you come in the room. I suspect you being there will help. Let's get things done here and get you to Angela."

"Okay. And Doris? She'll be okay?" I ask.

"Her ankle is a mess. They need to operate."

Roy and Mike pull up in the truck.

"Let me talk to Mike and Roy, then we'll get her husband moved." With that, he kisses me and steps away. Leo is talking with Madison while he looks her over. I move near them.

"Mrs. Caldwell, it looks like you did a fine job with the bandage. I'm going to leave it in place until we can get to a better location."

"Leo tells me the hospital in Prospect burned down," Madison says. "They're taking me to your neighbor's house."

"Yes, she's a nurse practitioner. You'll like her," I say.

Leo says to Jake, "Madison says their truck runs and has fuel. How about we have Mike drive it, and we'll put Madison and the baby in the back seat of yours. I'll sit with them in case I'm needed on the drive. Mollie can ride in the front."

"What about Scott?" Madison asks.

"I think we can put him in the bed of the truck," I offer.

She nods, then says, "I'm so tired. Can I rest a minute while you get everything ready?"

"Sure. That's fine," Leo assures her.

I suddenly realize that, like Madison, I'm exhausted. I no more than think it before I find myself sitting on the ground.

"Mollie! Are you okay?" Jake asks me.

184

"I'm okay. Just really tired. I had a bike wreck on Sunday, followed by getting ran over by a very large man in a bar... I'm still feeling the effects."

"Okay..." Jake says warily. "A large man in a bar?"

"I'll explain on the way home. I'm just really ready to go."

Jake walks me to the front passenger's seat of our truck. He helps me buckle my belt, then tells me to relax and we'll leave shortly. I close my eyes for only a minute. The next thing I know, Jake is getting in the truck and turning over the motor.

"Where's Madison?" I ask.

"Leo decided the back seat wouldn't work. We made a bed for her in the back using their camping gear and some of your gear. She and Leo are back there. Emma is asleep in the back seat."

"And Scott?" I ask.

"We rearranged things and he's in the bed of their truck, with Mike and Roy driving it back. We left the... other guys... in the ditch. Madison told us what happened. You did great, Mollie."

I start crying. I don't feel like I did great. I killed two people. Sure, they were terrible guys who had already done awful things with plans to do even more, but... I feel the need to throw up again. I take deep breaths through my mouth to help with the sensation.

Jake reaches for my hand. I settle into the seat and am soon back to sleep.

Chapter 46

I wake to the ring of a cell phone. Jake answers, "Hello? Yep. We're getting close. Your mom? She's tired but seems okay." He smiles at me and gives me a wink. He's talking on the phone. When did the phones start working?

"See you in a few minutes," he says and hangs up.

"The phone works?"

"Somewhat. My old flip phone seems to work better than the smartphones the kids have. That's how we found you. Your text came in while I was on the roof working on the solar system. We were able to call out about Madison before we left, so they're expecting us. That was Katie. She's on the flip phone you gave her for her bug-out bag."

"Ha. Flip phones rule," I say jokingly, while wondering where mine is. In a pocket of my small backpack, I think.

I look around and realize we're in our little town... well, community, since Bakerville isn't an actual town.

I'm suddenly incredibly sad I missed my first look at Prospector Peak, my beacon of home. I'd been on a quest to catch my first glimpse of Prospector Peak since Oregon, and I missed it.

I quickly look toward the southeast, and there she is. The sun is hitting her, making her sparkle like gold. The name of Prospector Peak originated from actual gold found on the mountain.

Prospector County, our county, is named after the peak and the little gold rush that happened here. Prospect, our nearest large town at just under ten thousand souls, and the county seat, is also named after the mountain.

While the vein on the mountain blew out early, there are still many who pan for gold in the local rivers and creeks. We do it ourselves, for fun, and have found a few flakes.

We're close to the driveway to Belinda's mom's house. The clock on the dash reads 2:45. I glance around. Emma is sleeping in the backseat. Leo is sitting on the floor of the truck bed next to Madison— I can't see her but can see her sleeping bag. Mike is behind us, driving Madison's Toyota, with his dad in the passenger's seat.

"Tell me about Leo."

Jake sighs and says, "Yeah, it's what we thought. They're pretty serious... that's what you wanted to know, right?"

"I guess, but also... is he... okay? For our Katie, is he okay?"

"He seems to be. He's smart, a hard worker. When we sent Katie the bug-out bag, he took it upon himself to start researching. He's definitely preparedness-minded." Jake glances my way, and I nod for him to continue. "Between the two of them, they made lots of changes. I'm pretty sure they were living together. If not officially then unofficially. You know... him staying over more often than not."

"And now?" I ask sharply.

"Nope. Katie is in the basement. He bought an RV. That's another thing—he must have had access to a lot of cash. He made several purchases: an RV, a trailer for Art to live in, solar systems, food... lots of stuff to help our family."

"Where'd he get the money? Is he a drug dealer or something?"

"Nah. His folks died a few years ago. He had an inheritance... life insurance or something. And he saved up while in the military. Plus, Katie said he lives cheap, had several roommates and a job back in Manhattan."

"Oh, I guess that makes sense. I'm glad it's not something else."

"Yeah, me too. But you know Katie. You think she'd be with someone who wasn't okay?"

"No, but I wouldn't think she'd... never mind. I do know Katie."

"You should know," Jake says softly, "besides for Angela and Doris being injured, Sarah was nicked... she's fine. It was nothing more than a scratch."

"Nicked? Like with a knife?"

"Bullet."

I gasp, as Jake says, "Morse kidnapped Olivia Hatch. He shot at Sarah in the process, grazing her arm. She's okay, didn't even need a stitch. Belinda cleaned it up and will keep an eye on it."

"Dan Morse kidnapped Olivia? Why would he do that?"

"Don't know. Think maybe he had a thing for her. But that's not all. Katie was attacked—"

"What?"

"She's fine. She got away and, judging from the amount of blood on the ground, hit him good in the process."

"Who? Morse?"

"No, she didn't know the attacker. We didn't find him, but we need to be on alert. Too much is going on."

"So much for our sanctuary," I say under my breath. Jake hears me and nods.

Turning into Tammy's driveway, he slows to a crawl. The rough gravel road is terribly wash boarded. Even though he slows way down, Madison cries out from the truck bed. This isn't an easy trip. We're met at the house by Belinda Bosco and Kelley Hudson.

Kelley and I are very good friends. We moved to Bakerville about the same time and hit it off immediately.

A few years older than me, she's a retired psych nurse and used to work with US Public Health Service and the Department of Defense. Kelley and her husband, Phil, were some of the first people we met after moving up here.

They're also fellow preppers, and while we don't really "swap prepping stories," we're more open with them about what we do than anyone else in our community.

That said, we know there are several other prepping or preparedness-minded families—Doris and Evan Snyder, our good friends and neighbors up the hill from us; Alex and Natalie MacIntyre, who run a homesteading and permaculture school; and a few others.

Shoot, during the winter, the bulk of us are preppers. Most tend to keep well-stocked pantries to prevent needing to drive forty-five minutes to town in a snowstorm to buy a loaf of bread and a gallon of milk. With winter over, I do have to wonder how many people still have full pantries.

My children! Calley and Malcolm are hugging each other while jumping up and down, with Katie standing next to them. Tate has his arm around Sarah. Gavin, in Tim's arms, is waving with excitement. I wonder where Angela is, then remember she was injured. My exhausted brain isn't working as well as it should be.

As soon as we stop the truck, Belinda and Kelley move toward us, as does Malcolm. Katie quickly reaches out to stop Malcolm and says something to him. He nods and gives me a wave. Needing little encouragement, I throw the door open and practically fall out of the cab in my hurry to reach my family.

Our reunion is wonderful with everyone speaking at once. Sarah shows me the scratch on her arm, covered only with a good-sized bandage. She says she didn't even realize it was a gunshot wound until Mike looked at it and saw powder burns.

"Mom," Sarah says, "we think Dan Morse was behind the attack on Angela and Doris. Maybe even the attack on Katie."

Chapter 47

"What? I don't understand. I thought they were out gathering supplies when it happened?"

"Yes, they were. But Doris thought she'd seen Morse earlier in the day. She mentioned it to Evan, but they didn't see him again. Then, when Morse took Olivia, he said something really weird right before he shot at me: 'Now you can go see your sister.' I didn't really understand, but it kind of makes sense if he thought he was going to shoot me and... I don't know. I just hope they find Olivia. Her husband was away for work when... everything happened. He hasn't made it back yet. Their children are at your house. Grandma is the babysitter. In fact, I should call them and let them know you're here. They'll be wondering."

"And Katie?"

"Just seems too strange that someone else would be out attacking people, don't you think?"

There's several more minutes of speculating on the attacks when Calley, with a small laugh, asks, "Did Jake tell you the silly flip phones you got us work but our smartphones are hit and miss?"

I smile and shake my head, thinking how they all teased me about including those in their backpacks.

"Can I see Angela?" I ask her husband, Tim.

"Yes, of course. They said they'll put the lady you found in the room next door. Just trying to make sure she's comfortable enough to move. As soon as they get her in, I'll take you to Angela. She's been asking for you. She's not completely coherent when she wakes up but seems a little better each time. Belinda said it was fortunate the guy only had a .22. It would've been a lot worse if he'd hit her in the head with a heavier weapon." Then, he lowers his voice and says, "I don't know if you know exactly what happened..."

I shake my head and say, "Jake told me very little."

Tim nods, asks Calley if she'll watch Gavin for him, and motions me to the side. Then he fills me in. "We were on a supply run. Doris and Angela were with the truck. The rest of us—Jake, Evan, Tate, and I—were inside a feed store. Seems Doris was shot first, either the guy

190

was a terrible shot or she moved. The bullet caught her in the side, but luckily, the shot didn't do much damage. That was the guy with the .22. Angela was hit with a shotgun blast from far enough away, and he was using a light round. There wasn't much penetration. Before they could get away, the .22 guy shot again and got Doris in the ankle. It's pretty bad. Broke both bones and... well, she needs surgery."

I nod, understanding, as he continues, "We heard the shots, but before we could get out there, they were attacked. The one guy was dragging Angela by the hair. She managed to get her sidearm out and shot him... that's when the other guy hit her with the rifle a couple times. Jake was the first to reach them, and he took out the guy beating Angela."

"What?" I say surprised. Jake hadn't mentioned this part. "Angela and Jake shot them?"

"Yep. Dead."

I'm not sure what to think. Jake, Angela, and I have each killed another person in the span of, what... a day?

I realize Tim is still talking. "Kelley Hudson has talked to Jake about it. Talked to all of us involved. I think he's doing okay. I know he said he'd do it over again if it meant protecting Angela or any of us. Evan says Jake will be fine. When Angela wakes up... well, Kelley will talk with her then. I don't know if she even remembers what happened at the moment. She doesn't really seem to know why she's hurt or even really where she is." Tim clears his throat and steps away, working as he tries to gather his emotions.

Leo and Jake are carrying Madison on a stretcher, with Kelley and Belinda by their sides. Madison gives me something resembling a wave with the lift of her good arm as she disappears into the house. Sarah has taken Emma from the truck and is talking with her. Emma responds with coos and smiles.

"Baby. I want to play with the baby," Gavin says.

"She's too little, Gavin," Sarah says. "She needs to be bigger to play, but you can talk to her like I am."

"Don't want to talk. Want to play," Gavin says with a pout, as he struggles to escape from Calley's grasp. I take the opportunity to gather Gavin into my arms and nuzzle his neck, which elicits a laugh. He puts his hands on my face and looks straight at me, then says, "I'm glad you're home, GrandMo. We missed you. We go to your house to see you and you not there. You not watch me play with the baby goats."

I hug him tight and say, "I'm here now."

Chapter 48

It's only a few minutes until Jake comes out of the house. "Belinda and Kelley are working on Madison. Do you want to go see Angela?"

He doesn't have to ask me twice. Angela and Doris are in a guest room with two twin beds. There's a chair by each bed. Evan is sitting next to Doris while she sleeps. He quietly says, "I'm glad you're home, Mollie. Hear you had a time of it. You doing okay?"

"I'm..." I consider telling him I'm fine but decide just to shake my head. He says he understands. My eyes shift to my daughter. She looks beautiful as she sleeps. There's a bandage across her forehead but no other sign of injury. I move to the chair next to her and reach for her hand. I let her know I'm there, and she stirs slightly but doesn't wake.

"Belinda said she was awake about half an hour ago. Seemed a little better, even, than the time before. She'll come around again." Jake gives my shoulder a squeeze. When I turn my head to look at him, he kisses me, then says, "I'm going to go out with the kids for a bit."

"Mollie? Mollie."

"Yes?" I answer groggily. I must have fallen asleep while sitting with Angela.

Belinda is standing by the door. "You doing okay?"

"Mm–hmm. Tired," I say with a stretch.

"Your friend is resting comfortably. Her baby is in with her now. We sent someone to Red Lodge earlier today to see if the hospital is functioning. I would've expected him back by now... I'm not sure what to think. As soon as we know, then we can make a decision on how to treat Madison and Doris. Angela... well, I think she just needs time. A hospital would be excellent, but we can make do with what we have here for her."

"Who went to Red Lodge?" I ask.

"I'm not sure. Phil Hudson was going to find someone to go. You heard about Dan Morse kidnapping Olivia?"

"I heard," I answer.

"I suppose you also heard about Terry?"

"Terry? Your husband? No... I don't think so."

Grief flashes across her face, followed by anger, before she curbs it. She spats, "He's dead. Murdered."

"Oh. I'm so sorry. I had no idea," I quickly say.

"Yeah. And since it's now common knowledge, I might as well tell you, my dad is the one who killed him."

I don't know what to say to this. I have met Belinda's dad but don't know him well. Jake talks to him sometimes at community events. He used to be a hunting and fishing guide, so they often talk about those things. I don't even know Belinda very well, just enough to say hello when we meet.

"I know everyone thought Terry was this great guy," she continues, "and in some ways, he was. He totally swept me off my feet. But his public persona was very different than the *real* Terry."

She takes a deep breath, then says, "The real Terry was an addict, a cheat, and an abuser."

I start to say something, but she waves me off, saying, "I thought we hid it well, but I could never really keep a secret from my mom, and especially not my dad. He's known for years. The final straw was a few months ago when Terry started abusing our son, TJ.

"Oh... I know I should've left him before it ever got to that point. I should've protected TJ. I didn't. I have no excuses. My dad apparently had a talk with Terry, which I suspect was more than just words. After all of this... stuff... with the world falling apart happened, Terry tried to be the town hero. He tried to put Dan Morse in his place when Morse started causing trouble.

"You know Morse is an oddball, but it turns out Terry had an extra reason not to like Morse—he was... *with* Morse's wife. Cheating on me with her. I knew he had someone he was seeing but didn't know who. Well... my dad caught him leaving her place and sort of... snapped, I guess.

"He killed him. My dad killed Terry. Tried to make it look like an accident but did a terrible job of it. I'd heard talk from people, and even believed it myself. I was sure Morse was the one who did it. The one who killed Terry." She stops talking and stares blankly into space.

I say nothing, and after a few moments, she continues, "But, no. It was my dad, trying to protect me and TJ, I'm sure. Turns out, even though Morse didn't kill Terry, he's more than an oddball. He kidnapped poor Olivia and killed his wife and his dog. Phil Hudson took a group, including my dad because he's such a great tracker, to

194

try and find Olivia. I suppose, after they find her, my dad will be taken in. I don't know. Deputy Fred said the jail is pretty much closed down. They let the nonviolent offenders loose. They sent Fred home. He's a full deputy now and in charge of Bakerville. No more patrols, so he's it. Ha, funny how we always called him Deputy Fred and now he's an actual deputy."

She doesn't laugh but makes some sort of weird noise before continuing, "A couple of guards are living at the jail, keeping the ones who they didn't feel comfortable letting out locked up. When we first found Terry, I went into Prospect. Visited the Sheriff. They wouldn't do any sort of investigation over Terry's death; they said they didn't have the manpower or ability. And we even buried him on our property, since the funeral homes are overloaded." She shakes her head, stands up, and walks out of the room.

The revelations of Terry being an addict and an abuser, combined with Belinda's dad killing him, is shocking. Then, add in Morse killing his wife and kidnapping Olivia—it's a little much along with Angela, Doris, and Madison being shot—I'm overwhelmed.

One of the reasons we chose to move to this small community was the safety factor. We found our land and originally planned to retire here, many years down the road, but quickly realized it was where we wanted to raise our young son and where we could provide a safe place for our family, and select friends, to come if the world fell apart.

We considered it a safe haven.

I guess we always knew bad things could happen, even in a small town, in a life changing situation, but I never expected these things to happen less than a week into a disaster. Angela and Doris were also shot in a small community. Madison was shot and her husband killed on the side of the road in the wilderness. Is there any place truly safe? Bakerville should've been that place.

And Olivia... she's such a sweet girl. She and her husband moved here shortly after we did. She was very pregnant with Lily when we first met. Malcolm and Tony, her son, often play together. Even though Olivia is young enough to be my daughter, we've developed a friendship and often seek each other out at community events.

I pray they find her soon. With her husband gone for work when everything fell apart, her kids must be a mess. Both mom and dad away for the moment; knowing Tony, he's taking his role as big brother very seriously.

My reverie is interrupted by a noise in the main part of the house. I soon hear voices outside the door, followed quickly by a man I don't know entering the room with Belinda on his heels.

Evan stands up abruptly from his place by Doris's bed, his hand resting on his sidearm.

Chapter 49

"Sam... I guess I'm a little confused by what you're telling me," Belinda says.

At the same time, Evan asks, "Is there a problem?"

Belinda looks at Evan and shakes her head. He relaxes slightly but doesn't sit down.

The man Belinda called Sam says to Evan, "I don't think we've been properly introduced. I'm Sam Mitchellini. My family and I moved here last month. We're buying the property next to Phil and Kelley Hudson's place."

"Okay... I'm Evan Snyder. This is my wife Doris. Do you know Mollie Caldwell and her daughter Angela?" He motions in my direction.

"Ma'am," he says to me, looking like he should be wearing a hat to tip.

I'm still wondering what's going on. Leo, Katie, and Jake are standing in the doorway.

"Hello, Lieutenant Mitchell," Leo says.

Sam Mitchellini looks surprised, then visibly collects himself. "It's Lieutenant Commander, son. Have we met? Other than at the community center, that is?"

"Sir, my apologies. You were a Lieutenant when you treated me at MCRD."

"Leo, is it?"

"Yes, sir. Leo Burnett."

"I'm sorry that I don't remember you. Saw quite a few people in the short time I was there."

"I understand, sir."

"You still in the Marines, Leo?"

"No, sir."

"You can stop calling me sir. I'm Sam, or Doc if you prefer."

"Okay, sir."

Dr. Mitchellini or Mitchell... I'm not sure which, shakes his head. Then says to the rest of us, "Sam Mitchell. Dr. Sam Mitchell or, as

Leo pointed out, Lieutenant Commander Sam Mitchell, retired. Recently of Grover, Wyoming."

"Grover, Wyoming…" Evan says slowly.

It all clicks for me. Grover is where the school shooting happened in early May. Dr. Mitchell and his wife stopped the attackers—killing them. Only they insist they only killed two, not three, which is the number of attackers found dead. The school secretary and the gym teacher backed their story. Within a few days, the secretary and teacher were both dead and the Mitchell family disappeared. Jake and I thought the Mitchells' bodies would also be discovered.

"Pleased to meet you," I say.

Leo whispers something to Katie, and she nods her head and says, "Yes, Doctor. Good to meet you… again. Very glad to find out you're a doctor."

Belinda, obviously angry, says, "Wait a minute. You're a doctor, and you're just telling us this now?"

Dr. Mitchell sighs and says, "I was worried about my family. I assume you all know about the… trouble… we had in Grover? We left fearing for our lives after Michael was killed and Rachel, supposedly, committed suicide. Deputy Sandoval helped us get out of town, then he was killed in the line of duty a couple of weeks ago. We have no idea exactly what we stumbled into, but it's nothing good. I had to think of my kids and my wife. We're, I guess you'd say, in hiding. We don't think it was simply some crazies who wanted to kill kids. Things just don't add up." He gives a shake of his head and looks like he wants to say more.

After opening his mouth and closing it several times, reminiscent of a goldfish gasping for air, he says, "After these attacks started, a few radio personalities suggested our Grover shooting was related. Part of a plan to take firearms out of citizens' hands. I don't know, maybe.

"Seems like, if it was, they would've tried again or given the attempt more time to see if there was a gun grab. I've heard all of the conspiracy theories—it's the democrats, it's the president with his own evil agenda, it's the North Koreans, and so on and so on. I can tell you, there's something very fishy about the whole thing. I'm reminded of the quote, attributed to a Yamamoto in World War II, 'You cannot invade America—there would be a rifle behind every blade of grass.' What if the lobby for gun control was part of the plan to eliminate those rifles? Of course, it's widely believed the Yamamoto quote is bogus and the Japanese had no intention of invading the mainland. But it makes me think reducing the number of guns, then reducing and scaring our population, makes for a great start to a ground invasion."

"Doris and I feel the same way," Evan says. "Looking back over things that have happened, it all seems to flow toward where we are now. And we're not in a good place. That said, you should've stepped forward to help when Doris and Angela were first brought in."

The look Evan gives the doctor is anything but kind and understanding.

Sam Mitchell averts his eyes and quietly says, "Honestly, I hated not coming forward when I found out about the injuries. When Phil sent me to Red Lodge today, I thought I could make it right by setting things up at the hospital. But... that's not an option."

"Why not?" Katie asks.

"Someone has taken over the hospital."

"What do you mean?" Evan asks.

"Red Lodge has gone to pot. I heard you were there yesterday, and you reported it was fine?"

Jake nods, while Evan says, "Things were tense, but it was fine."

"Well, today it's like... Syria."

Chapter 50

"Not like a small town in Montana, or anywhere in the United States. The whole town was a disaster, with fires burning, shots being fired, and bodies in the street. I had Kaleb, Alex MacIntyre's son-in-law, with me, and a few times, we wondered if we could even make it to the hospital. When we finally reached the hospital, we were fired upon. We talked to a few people, but no one really had answers as to who it was. The police department had tried to get in and an officer was killed. The person we talked to even thought whoever is in the hospital might have hostages.

"After realizing Red Lodge was a bust, we headed toward Billings, thinking maybe a clinic in Laurel might be an option, if we couldn't get into Billings. Neither worked out. We heard the reports of people being stopped on certain roads, so we tried to work around those places. We were doing okay until we ran into what we quickly determined was an ambush. After that..." he shrugs before saying, "I knew I had to come clean. Probably doesn't matter anyway with things falling apart. Of course, now the phones seem to be working on occasion...

"Look, I can help, but I'd ask you to please keep my true identity to yourselves. I had planned on letting you know I was a doctor but not my real name. I didn't realize there would be someone who would know me." He gives Leo a hard look.

Leo returns the expression, pursing his lips.

Belinda says crisply, "I'm a surgical nurse practitioner. Doris and Madison both need surgery. I can assist, but we need an orthopedic surgeon. I'm pretty sure, from reading about the Grover event, you're a primary care doc. I don't think you're qualified."

Dr. Mitchell straightens up and looks at Belinda. "I'm the only option you have."

Doris, who must have woken up sometime during the exchange, says, "I read about the Grover event also. You were a Navy flight surgeon, originally trained in emergency medicine, correct?"

"For part of my career, yes. Apparently, though, I met Leo here when I was stationed at MCRD San Diego, giving physicals to new Marines. That would've been, what, eight or nine years ago?"

Leo gives a single nod, the hard look still on his face.

"I was promoted shortly after and sent to Camp Lejeune. The media," Dr. Mitchell sneers the word media, "likes to make a big deal about my posting with an airbase. Since it was an airbase attachment, for that deployment, they really played up the flight surgeon part. Most of the time I was just a plain old Navy Doc—a physician. I retired from the Navy and moved my family to Grover three years ago, when I went into private practice. My wife works with me... she's a chiropractor for our office."

"So, if you were a flight surgeon... what's the problem?" I ask.

Doris quickly says, "Flight surgeon is like a general practitioner. They don't necessarily do surgery, it's just what they're called. Kind of like the Surgeon General doesn't have to be a surgeon."

I must look confused because Dr. Mitchell says crisply, "I'm not a surgeon, but I have done surgery in emergency situations. So, Doris, I'd like to examine you and see what we're looking at. And... was it Madison?" he asks, motioning to Angela.

Katie quickly says, "That's Angela. Madison is in the next room. My mom found her and brought her here."

Mitchell looks confused but doesn't ask any questions. Instead, he says, "Show me to the washroom, and we'll get started."

"Listen... Doctor, I need your help, even if you're not a surgeon," Belinda says, "but you need to understand, these are my patients. This is, for lack of a better word, my hospital. This is my community, and I'm in charge. There won't be any pulling rank or dismissing my knowledge because I'm only a nurse. You need to understand—I'm incredibly good at what I do. And I'm dedicated to this community and the people in it. Understood?"

"Got it. Are you conceited or convinced?" he asks with a small smile.

Belinda laughs and says, "Point taken. Let's get you washed up."

After Belinda and Dr. Mitchell leave, Katie turns to Leo and says, "What's wrong?"

All eyes are on him, as he slowly answers, "I knew I recognized him from somewhere... When the whole Grover thing hit the news, I recognized him as the doctor who treated me when I was in training.

Seeing him at the community center, out of uniform and not as a doctor, it didn't click then. And he looks… different. Not just from when he treated me but even from the photos from Grover. Different hair color, glasses… just different. It finally all fell into place when I overheard him telling Belinda he was a doctor. Like he said, he gave me my original exam, and I saw him for a training injury. He seemed like a good guy."

"Sure, I remember you telling me you knew him from somewhere when we met him and his family at the community meeting," Katie says. "And you told me about his treating you in the Marines when we watched the Grover news. I didn't recognize him at all from the Grover news. Why do you seem so angry at him?"

Leo starts to say something, pauses, then lets out a huge exhale before saying, "Honor."

Katie looks confused. I feel confused. Doris, Evan, and Jake all nod.

"What?" Katie asks.

"I think Leo is disappointed Lieutenant Commander Mitchell chose to hide behind the Sam Mitchellini persona," Doris says.

Leo agrees with a nod.

"But it sounds like he was scared for his life and the life of his family," Katie blurts.

"I suppose," Leo says noncommittally.

Katie starts to say something more but is interrupted when Angela says, "Hey, Mom. Can you get me a soda?"

I'm ecstatic she's awake. It's all I can do not to grab her and hug her. Instead, I attempt to calmly say, "I'll see what I can do. How about some water? I have some right here."

She makes a face, which is totally Angela, then says, "I guess so."

After I help with her drink, she glances around, then winces. "Ugh. I have a headache. Where's Gavin? Is he with Tim?"

"He's right outside," Katie says. "I can go get him for you."

"I'll just go outside," Angela says, then starts to move like she's going to sit up. A look of agony crosses her face and she says, "Okay. You can bring him in. What happened to me? I feel terrible." Then she looks over at Doris and says, "What happened to you? You look terrible. Mom, you don't look too great either."

We all, including Doris and Evan, laugh at Angela's honest assessment. Katie steps out to find Gavin and Tim, while Leo says, "Let me get Belinda and the doctor so they can take a look at you."

"Aren't you the doctor?" Angela asks.

"This is Leo," I say, "Katie's boyfriend. Haven't you met?"

"No… I don't think so," Angela says,

I'm confused. Didn't Leo and Katie arrive around the same time as Angela and her family? I look at Leo, who gives a small shake of his head and then steps out, followed by Jake.

Leo returns with Belinda and Dr. Mitchell. They give her a quick exam, determining Angela has some memory gaps. She doesn't remember any of the events after the airplane attacks last Thursday— driving up to my house, meeting Leo, or the attack on her and Doris. When she asks what happened to her, she's given the bare minimum of information for now.

"Mommy. Mommy. Ready for Gavin now?" the sweet little voice of my grandson calls out.

Chapter 51

"Bring Gavin in," Belinda says.

Gavin, holding Jake's hand with Tim right behind them, walks through the door.

Angela's face lights up. "Hey, Gavvy."

"Hey, Mommy. Did you have nice nap? Ready to play with Gavin now?"

Belinda smiles and turns to Doris. "Doris, let's have Dr. Mitchell take a look at you while Gavin talks with his mom."

Evan stays by Doris's bedside, while all of us except Tim and Gavin step out, leaving Belinda and Mitchell to do their thing. Gavin is jubilant over seeing his mom but also concerned she's hurt and keeps asking about her owie... the bandage on her head.

Jake goes outside, while I find a seat in the living room. Both Katie and Leo assure me Angela seems much better this time. Soon we're joined by Tammy, Belinda's mom, and Kelley Hudson.

"The doctor and Belinda are examining Madison now," Kelley says. "Angela is much better."

"Will she remember what happened?" I ask, hoping the answer is no since it was such a traumatic event. I shudder involuntarily, remembering how I killed Dave and Don. I hope Angela never remembers what she had to do.

"We don't know," Kelley says. "Memory loss is normal in instances like this. It could return as her brain heals or maybe not. We'll just have to wait and see."

"Okay, I guess I knew that. Part of me really hopes she doesn't remember all of it."

"I understand. We'll just have to wait and see."

"How are you, Kelley? Are Sylvia and Sabrina here?"

Sylvia and Sabrina are Kelley's girls from her first marriage. They live as roommates in the Phoenix area.

Kelley lets out a huge sigh. "Not here. I don't even know if they're on their way. Things were still okay in Peoria when the phones went out and stopped working. I've tried to call several times since we heard about some phones coming back up, but unfortunately, my calls haven't gone through. I know they had made some provisions so they could leave if needed. Things like filling up the gas tank and packing food and water. Phil and I both talked to them about being ready to go at a moment's notice. But whether they actually left or not... I don't know. At this point, all I can do is hope and pray... and wait."

A short while later, Gavin and Tim come out. With a smile, Tim says, "She's sleeping again, but before she fell asleep, she asked me to remind you she'd love a soda."

"I'll have one for her when she wakes up next time," I say.

I know she loves Dr Pepper, and I'm pretty sure we have a six-pack in the basement.

"I'd like to examine you, Mollie," Kelley says.

"Huh?" I ask.

"Jake and Madison said you had a bike wreck and a slight head injury, plus I heard about... what happened on the road. I'll just give you a quick look over there at the dining room table. Just sit in one of the chairs."

As promised, the exam is quick. Kelley says I seem to be healing okay and should be right as rain in a few days. She also tells me she'd like to see me again tomorrow for a "consultation" to discuss anything I'd like to discuss.

Chapter 52

A short while later, after a long, hot shower and change of clothes, Jake and I are sitting together on the rocket stove bench in our room, holding hands, talking, and occasionally making out like teenagers while he catches me up. The rocket stove bench, really called a rocket mass heater, is a secondary heating system for our bedroom. While we have a whole-house furnace and a woodstove in the great room, adding this to the bedroom was a great idea, if I do say so myself.

The way these heaters work, with the fire burning sideways and capturing the smoke, makes them incredibly clean and efficient. We like them so much we have one in our room, with the two-person sleek cob finished—a mixture of clay, sand, straw, and water—then glazed and tiled at the bottom, giving it a slightly southwestern appearance. The L-shaped design is perfect for the two of us.

During the winter, the fire heats up the bench, making it toasty warm. In the summer, the cob is slick and cool. We have a similar rocket stove to heat our basement recreation room and the bunkhouse. Instead of the sleek cob, we used native rocks for the mass of the stove. The mass is an important piece, capturing the heat and warming people. I snuggle in a little closer to Jake.

"I almost couldn't believe how easy it was to get my parents to agree to come out here. I think they were, I guess, scared. They'd been glued to their television from the plane crashes on up to when the power went out. They saw footage of what was happening in the cities and other towns. I think they half suspected things could turn bad in Prospect."

"And they were right," I say softly. "You haven't been back to Prospect since the day you picked them up?"

"Nope. When Belinda went in about... about Terry's funeral arrangements, she said things were completely crazy. Not as bad as Sam Mitchellini, or whatever his name is, said Red Lodge was, but bad. And that was several days ago. We know the hospital burned since then, but don't know much else. Shoot, Red Lodge wasn't terrible when we were there on... you know, when Angela and Doris..."

"Yes, I know," I say quickly, as I watch a shadow pass over Jake's face. Is he thinking about the killing he had to do?

"Hey, you okay?"

"Sure," he shrugs. "It's a huge relief Mom and Dad were so willing to join us here. And they seem to be settling in fine. The studio is perfect for them. They were pretty funny. Instead of telling me they were nervous about what could happen, they made it like 'we're coming to your place since we can't make coffee here.' It gave them a nice out. And gives me a laugh when I think of it. 'Course, you'd probably be the same way."

"What do you mean? I'd laugh about it also?"

"No, you'd end up making the same decision if you couldn't make coffee at home."

"I guess you're right," I say with a small laugh, as Jake gives me a tight squeeze.

"They're concerned about my brother, his wife, and their girls, of course. They've tried several times to call. I gave them the phone you put in my bug-out bag to use. Those phones were a good idea, even if I did hassle you about having to keep buying time on them so they'd stay active. Did I mention how smart you are?" He kisses me again.

"Thank you, my love. I hope your parents can get ahold of your brother. Talking to him will go a long way toward alleviating some of their fears. I'd like to think they're okay there. Knowing Robert, if things got rough, he'd head up to your old camping spot. You think he'd have fuel to get up there?"

"Maybe. He kept extra fuel for his lawn care business. Enough? I'm not sure. But if they could get up there, they'd do okay—short term anyway. Long term... I don't know. But with the phones coming back on, maybe things will turn around quicker than we think. Or at least maybe the lights will turn on. That would be helpful."

I think we both know, even if the lights come on, it's going to be a long time before things turn around. I choose not to say anything.

After a few moments, he says, "Sarah and Tate buying a camp trailer was good—very helpful considering how many people we have here now... and with Madison and her baby joining us as soon as she's well enough, it was smart on their part."

"I'm impressed. Maybe they're more 'prepperish' than I thought," I say.

"Could be," Jake answers with a nod. "Tate's parents and sister seem happy with the bunkhouse. Karen has told me several times the loft is perfect for her. Like a little tree house. She especially enjoys being able to hear the creek at night. Keith has mentioned he hears her 'rumbling around up there,' but Lois insists it isn't too bad, Keith is just making more of it than it is."

"Oh... I didn't even think about that when we designed the bunkhouse. Just thought it was a great way to add extra sleeping space."

"Yeah, and it is. I don't think it's too big of a deal. And they're happy to be here. Keith did say how glad he is they were up here and not in Tulsa when everything went bad. The other end of the bunkhouse is still empty. I was thinking, maybe Madison could have the downstairs room. You think that'd be okay... you know, a baby in with Keith and Lois?"

"Lois loves children, so I imagine so. Keith tries to act all... crusty, but he's really a sweetheart. Either there or our loft room. Of course, then they'd just be sleeping on the foldouts since we have Tony and Lily in the guest room. We could swap them. We have a few days to decide since Madison will be with Belinda until she's well enough to come here. Maybe, if Keith isn't up to having a baby as a roommate, Katie could move to the bunkhouse and Madison could have the basement room. I'm sure Katie wouldn't mind, and with the kitchenette in the recreation room and a full bath, it might be nice for Madison and the baby."

"True. When we're closer to her being well enough, we'll sort it out. Calley seems to love the cabin. She said it's like living in a cottage at the beach... without the beach, of course. She and Mike took the small room at the front. Mike's parents are in the bedroom at the back with Sheila in the loft above them."

"So the loft above Calley's room is empty, and if we put Madison in the bunkhouse, the loft above her room is empty."

"Yes, what are you thinking?"

"Oh... I was wondering about Olivia and her children. If we could find a space for them in one of the guest houses."

Jake gives me a serious look and says, "Sure, we can see about that, once they find Olivia. For now, it's best for Tony and Lily to be in our house. Maybe we could do a little rearranging—change the loft room from a TV room into a proper bedroom for Tony. And let Lily and Olivia have the guest room. It's not like we need a TV room now."

"For that matter, it's not like I need an office. The office could become the TV room for those times we want to watch movies."

"Sounds like a good idea. Let's give it a few days. Also, Sheila seems to be having a hard time, so I don't think putting anyone else in the cabin is a good idea right now."

"Oh?"

Jake nods, opens his mouth to speak, then shakes his head. I start to ask for more info, when he raises his hand slightly and says, "I don't want to make more of this than it is. All of us are on edge and... concerned. At least, for us, we're in our home. Did I tell you how happy I am you're back?"

He kisses me again, then says, "Sheila, just like our children, their spouses, the other parents... they're here. For the most part, they're happy to be here, but it's still not their own home. I can totally understand feeling... out of sorts and displaced. I'm sure they all feel it, but most hide it and put up a good front. Sheila... she doesn't bother trying to hide it."

"Huh. You know, my first instinct was to say, 'that's surprising,' but truthfully... it's not really. I've noticed a few times over the years where she likes to... I guess, 'be in control' would be the right thing so say. More than once I've questioned the way she's treated Calley or Mike. I asked Calley about it once, and she immediately jumped to Sheila's defense, saying, 'that's just the way she is,' but... really. I don't think just because someone's used to acting a certain way makes it's okay. Especially when there's no regard for other people."

"I'm not sure it's that bad. She jumped on Katie for mentioning God... at least, that's the rumor. Katie hasn't said anything about it. Anyway, let's just give it some time. She'll probably adjust. So... what'd you think about the looks of the little cabin? Oh, I guess Angela and Katie call it the Tiny House."

"Looks good. Blends nicely with the larger cabin, and I really like how you set them up next to each other. It's like mommy cabin and baby cabin."

Jake gives a small courtesy laugh at my amazing wit. "Okay, sure. You know how the bedrooms are in the loft and there's a ladder to climb? Angela isn't going to be able to climb. So I guess talking about where to put Madison... well, we need to talk about where to put

Angela also. Leo mentioned he and Art could share the motorhome if we need the space. Right now, Leo is in it and Art is in the trailer. Art is sure a surprise."

"Oh?"

Thinking of Angela's father-in-law, not much would surprise me about him. A few years ago, he lost his wife, and the next year, his older son. Shortly after, his daughter, two years younger than Tim, took off to parts unknown. Art hasn't handled things well and spends most of his day in bed.

He hasn't worked for well over a year and is currently on temporary disability due to a back injury. Angela says there's a question on how much is a physical injury and how much is depression. It's a sad situation.

"Yep. He's pretty much taken over the chores."

Now this does surprise me. "What do you mean?"

"He started helping me the day after they got here... Monday, I guess. This morning, he shooed me away to check on Angela, and with Malcolm, Tony, and TJ's help, he took care of everything. And he did a great job, even doing extra things I never mentioned. The boys really seem to enjoy Art also. And not just that, Art and Mike's dad took the generator to the meeting at the community center today so they could help with water for people. He's really working to be a part of the community."

"Wow. Amazing. Maybe he just needed... something."

"I think so. Did anyone tell you the story about the Schwan's truck?"

"Schwan's truck? No..."

"Yep, we're the proud, temporary owners of a fairly full Schwan's truck. Tate made a trade with the driver and his manager. His excitement over the assorted ice cream treats, pizzas, potpies, and TV dinners was... what's the word Sarah used? Epic? I think that's what she said. It was pretty funny."

"We have a Schwan's truck? With food in it?"

"Amazing, huh? The truck is in the garage. We'll need to get it emptied out, so expect lots of frozen, processed food over the next few days."

"Sounds... interesting. The solar is doing okay keeping it frozen?"

"It's been fine with the sunshine we've been getting. But it uses a lot more than our regular freezers, so we should think of emptying the truck out sooner rather than later."

"I agree. I can get started on the freezers tomorrow. If I process some of the produce and meat from the main freezer, we can move the packaged food over there."

"Uh... right. About that. I bought a few extra things when shopping. I found a good deal on meat, so... both freezers are full. I was thinking we could put our small, portable freezer into use also. It's pretty efficient."

I stifle a sigh. It was smart of Jake to buy more meat. I won't complain about the extra work of canning and dehydrating. The way things are going, we're going to need every morsel. Should we start rationing?

Chapter 53

"Belinda asked me to bring TJ back to her next time we go over," Jake says. "I'd also like to go by the community center. They were having the meeting at 5:00. It's a little after six o'clock now, but some people may still be around, so we can see if there's anything new worth knowing."

"Okay. Seems like it should be later than 6:00. Was it just three hours ago we pulled into Tammy's yard?" I say, shaking my head. So much has happened in these few hours. "I guess we'd better get going."

Deanne, Calley's mother-in-law, has saved us some pizza from dinner—part of the Schwan's truck score. Jake and I take a couple pieces for the road.

TJ climbs in the backseat of our pickup. We're not even to the bottom of the hill and his head is bowed in sleep. Jake and I quietly discuss the current situation. Red Lodge, one of our favorite towns around, is no more. What could've happened to change it so much in just a day?

"When we were there yesterday, the vibe was slightly off. I didn't think much of it. Figured it was just because of everything happening. But for it to turn into a war zone overnight, I never thought it could happen."

"It's terrible. Doesn't sound like Prospect and Wesley are much better."

"No, it doesn't. When Terry died, Belinda took him to Prospect for burial, and she was turned away. Too many dead to deal with already. And with the Prospect hospital burned to the ground, they're struggling. A couple of people went into Wesley the other day—only one came back. Something happened in town, and they were separated. No idea where he is now."

"Who was that?" I asked, shocked.

"Uh… something Delgado, I think. I don't know him. Phil told me about it."

"Terrible."

"You know, Mollie, I think we've been rather foolish."

212

"In what way?" I ask.

"Thinking Bakerville would be some sort of utopia or sanctuary from the dangers of the world."

I'm not sure what to say to this... he's right. We were so sure our isolated area would be free of trouble.

Jake continues, "We didn't even consider the surrounding areas could be dangerous. It's not like we have any real cities around. Wesley and Red Lodge don't even have five thousand people. How can Red Lodge be such a mess? We thought we'd just hunker down in our own little world and set up trade with the neighboring towns? Fools. We were fools."

Jake's voice has risen with each word, and while not yelling, he's now quite loud and his face is flushed. TJ stirs but doesn't wake up.

"Yes, I guess we were," I answer softly.

What else is there to say?

Even with our tardiness, when we reach the community center, we're surprised to see several people still there, including both Tim and Mike's dads, helping with water and visiting.

People are hanging out there, waiting to hear results of today's search for Olivia and Dan Morse. There's a rumor they'd halt the search before dark and meet up at the community center.

Someone has added a hitching post on the edge of the softball field. There are several horses tied up. While there are still cars and trucks in the parking lot, there are also many ATVs, quads, dirt bikes, motorcycles, and bicycles.

We spend less than five minutes there before Jake says, "Let's go ahead and run TJ home and give Angela her soda."

"That's my grandpa's truck," TJ says, gesturing toward a pickup pulling into the community center.

He starts to go toward the truck, when Jake says, "Wait up, TJ. There's several trucks pulling in. Wait until they stop."

TJ's grandpa's truck parks and several people get out, none of which are his grandpa.

Our friend Phil Hudson, Kelley's husband, is in the second truck. He sees me and gives me a smile and a thumbs up. We've become very good friends with Phil and Kelley over the past few years. Phil is a retired Coastie and somewhat resembles Shaquille O'Neal—a shorter version at six feet tall. He's built very sturdy and sports a shaved head and goatee.

Phil then notices TJ, and his smile turns into a slight frown. *Oh no.*

Chapter 54

Phil walks over to us, offering me a huge bear hug. "Mollie, it's so good to see you. We're sure glad you're back. Kelley will be ecstatic."

"I got back a few hours ago. I saw Kelley at Belinda's place. It's great to be home."

He releases me and turns to TJ. "Hey, TJ, did I see Miss Sally-Ann over by the building?"

"Yes... I think so," TJ says. "Where's my grandpa?"

Phil ignores the question and says, "Can you go over and ask Sally-Ann to take you into the building and bring back a container of those disinfectant wipes from the supply closet?"

TJ gives him a suspicious look before turning and going to find Sally-Ann.

"What's up, Phil?" Jake whispers as soon as he determines TJ is far enough away.

Phil shakes his head and says, "Bad stuff."

The three of us exchange a long look as Phil says, "We found Morse at one of those caves in the wilderness area. We... weren't as cautious as we should've been, I guess. He shot Andy Walsh before we even knew he was there. We all took cover, then Tom went out for Andy and he got hit. Tom didn't stop and pulled Andy to cover. Neither one of them made it," he says sadly.

Jake reaches for my hand, pulling me near him.

"It was a standoff for several hours," Phil continues, "then we heard him yell at us and say something like 'I win,' and start shooting. We returned fire and thought we got him when the shooting abruptly stopped. We went in to bring Olivia out, but... she was gone. He'd killed her at some point. And Morse was nowhere to be found. We have no idea where he went, or exactly how he got away, but he did."

I already had tears running down my face over the loss of Andy and Tom, but at the news of Olivia's death, I gasp.

"TJ is coming out of the building," Jake says. "We'd better take him to Belinda. It's her place to tell him, not ours."

"I agree," Phil says and walks to his truck. He says something to one of the other people, and they quickly get in his truck and pull out, heading in the direction of Tammy and Tom's home.

"Where'd Mr. Hudson go? I found what he needed."

I give TJ a smile and say, "Perfect. We'll meet up with him."

The drive to Tammy's house is quiet. Belinda and TJ live right next door to Tammy and Tom. The driveways are separate, but there's a well-worn walking path between the two homes.

Tammy is fourth or fifth generation Bakerville, with her relatives being one of the original families. At one time, Bakerville was more of a town than a community, sporting a post office, school, small market, and more. Now we get our mail in nearby Wesley, go to school in Wesley or Prospect, shop elsewhere—often Billings where there's no sales tax—but still have the Bakerville community.

Tammy left for several years, which is when she met Tom, while working as a labor and delivery nurse somewhere around Chicago.

They moved back here when she was pregnant with Belinda some thirty-odd years ago. Belinda followed in her mom's footsteps, becoming a nurse, then continuing her education to become a surgical nurse practitioner. She works with a doctor in Prospect. I never thought to ask about him this morning.

I'm guessing it's not good; otherwise, she'd have Doris and Madison at his place for surgery. With Terry's death a few days ago, her doctor partner's absence, and now the death of her dad, I wonder about how Belinda will hold up.

Jake is taking the drive very slowly, no doubt to give Phil time to deliver the news before we show up with TJ. When we do arrive, it's obvious Phil has done the deed.

TJ must have noticed also because he's jumping out of the back seat and running for his mom almost before Jake has the pickup in park.

My heart breaks watching mother, son, and grandma. The three of them walk to a small garden bench, clutching each other tightly.

I touch Jake's arm. "I'm going in to visit Angela and Doris. I'll also check on Madison."

He nods and walks over to Phil, asking if I can send Evan outside if he's here.

Angela is asleep, but Doris is awake and talking with Evan.

"Evan, Jake is outside. He'd like to talk with you."

"What's wrong?" Doris asks immediately.

216

I share the sad story. Evan nods and steps out. Olivia was the same age as my daughter Sarah and Doris's daughter Lindsey. Thinking of this, I suddenly realize Doris must be frantic with worry over her daughters. Her oldest daughter, Jessica, lives in Germany with her husband and two children. Lindsey is a police officer in the Bay Area.

"Have you heard from Jessica or Lindsey?" I ask.

She shakes her head. "Not since the cyberattacks. Katie loaned me her phone earlier today—the flip one she says you put in her bug-out bag—but I couldn't reach either of them. Belinda said some of the smartphones are working, too, but they seem less reliable. Maybe more will come on and I'll be able to reach them soon. I would've at least thought I could reach Jessica. She's in Germany, after all. I don't think they had any of the attacks."

We're both quiet for several minutes, when I look over and see Angela awake.

"Hey there," I say.

"Hi, Mom. You bring me a soda?"

"Yes, I did," I say with a smile, pleased she remembers from earlier today. "Let me put it in a glass and find a straw for you."

"Tammy has straws in the kitchen," Doris says.

It takes me only a minute to return with Angela's drink. I'm surprised to find Angela carrying on a normal sounding conversation with Doris. I'm not even back in my chair before Dr. Mitchell steps in the doorway.

"Hello again. You're the one who brought Madison in earlier?" he asks me.

"My husband brought us, yes," I answer.

"Okay. Belinda and I were getting things set up for operating on Madison and then Doris, but it seems we're going to need to delay for a little bit. Both are stable, so it should be fine. You okay with that Doris?"

"Hey, I'm not really looking forward to going under the knife, so, yep. Just keep the pain at bay and I'm good," she says with a weak smile.

"Why the delay?" Angela asks.

"Hey, Angela, you're looking much better. How's the head?" Dr. Mitchell replies.

"Not great but not as bad as it was. Like Doris, I'd like the pain kept at bay and could use something."

"All right. We can definitely do that."

"Where will you operate?" I ask.

"Excuse me?" he responds.

"You can't go to the hospital. Will you do surgery here? Or at your house?"

"My house at the moment is a travel trailer. Leo and I are working on making a surgical suite, of sorts, in the garage. Belinda's dad had a workshop. We've emptied it out and scrubbed it down. It's not exactly ideal, but it will work. Belinda said there used to be a volunteer ambulance service in Bakerville. We talked about trying to use the ambulance itself as a surgical bay, but she said it isn't operational and didn't think we could get it here. And I don't want to move Doris or Madison more than necessary."

"Yeah," I answer with a nod, "I've heard about the volunteer ambulance. It stopped operations before we moved here. I understand it had been rather robust at one time, but then dwindled down to just one family operating it. A man and his wife, in their fifties, would alternate shifts with their daughter and her husband. They'd get the call and either the older couple or the younger couple, whichever was on call, would respond. They'd take vitals, call in to the hospital for instructions, and load them up.

"Then, one night, a call came in that the parents answered—there had been an accident. A car hit an elk and then slid off into a gulley. Turned out to be the daughter and her husband. Husband died and the daughter was seriously injured. The parents tried to keep the service going, but they eventually moved away. We haven't had a local ambulance since then. Prospect or Red Lodge respond to our emergencies. Of course, now…"

"Yes, now it seems we're on our own," Dr. Mitchell says, looking a little sheepish. I wonder if he's feeling guilty about not coming forward earlier.

"What about surgical tools?" I ask, looking to change the subject.

"Each of us has a medical kit and some supplies. We've combined what we have, and your husband brought over some things to Belinda last night, which we added to our collection."

I'm glad Jake brought some of our supplies over. As part of our preparedness efforts, we've accumulated specific medical kits. Even though our medical knowledge is limited, we thought these kits may come in handy.

I realize Dr. Mitchell is still speaking to me. "In fact, your other daughter told me you have some medical experience and might be willing to help out."

Fresh out of high school I moved to downtown Portland, became roommates with my dear friend Sharri, and went to medical assisting school. The nine-month-long trade school taught me enough so I could work as a front or back office nurse, assist with office procedures, do phlebotomy, and run basic testing equipment. As the saying goes, I learned just enough to be dangerous.

My first job was for a large doctor's practice in downtown Portland. They hired me to be the receptionist. That was where I met my first husband, Jamie. He worked in the same building but on a different floor.

"No. Not really," I answer with a shrug.

"Sure you can, Mom," Angela says quickly.

I shake my head and say, "I haven't done anything medical related since before Calley was born... twenty-four years ago. Before that I was mostly front office. Unless you're looking for someone to answer the phones, I'm probably not the right fit."

"Suit yourself," Dr. Mitchell says, in what I take as a snotty tone, then he turns on his heel and leaves.

"Jeez, Mom. You kind of made him mad."

"Probably isn't used to being told no," Doris adds. "He's military, you know. I'm surprised I didn't peg him as military when I originally met him. I'm usually pretty good at figuring that out."

"I'm going to go and look in on Madison. I'll be back shortly." I kiss Angela on the forehead and give Doris a small wave.

The room next door is dark, but the door is cracked open. Katie is sitting in the chair next to the bed.

"Hi, Mom," she whispers.

"Hi, honey. How's Madison?"

"Sleeping, and the baby too. They were both awake a little bit ago. Dr. Mitchell was in here. Did you hear something happened to Belinda's dad? I didn't get the story, but it sounds like he might be dead. They were close to being ready for Madison's surgery, but are waiting for Belinda and Tammy."

"Yes. I heard. Tom is dead, along with two more members of our community."

"Mom? Olivia? She's okay?"

"No, honey. She's not."

"Oh no," Katie says softly and begins to cry.

I go to her and put my arm around her. I'd forgot she and Olivia met last year at the rodeo. They spent several hours chatting. "I'm so sorry, I forgot you met her last year."

"Not just last year, Mom. We've become friends in the few days I've been here."

"Oh, Katie. I should've realized. With her house burning down and her children at our house... I just didn't put it all together. I'm so sorry."

We spend many minutes talking about how they'd become fast friends and how Olivia was missing her husband and very fearful of Dan Morse due to his obsession with her.

"What will happen with Tony and Lily?" she asks.

"I'm not sure. I haven't spoken to anyone. Sarah told me Jason wasn't home, but I haven't thought much past that. I'm really playing catchup on things."

"They can stay with us until other plans are made?"

"Of course."

"Good. Lily is such a cutie. I think Grandma Dodie is really enjoying having her and Gavin. She seems happy. And Tony is friends with Malcolm."

"Yes, Malcolm and Tony always have a good time together," I agree.

We sit in silence for a few minutes, each lost in our own thoughts, when Katie suddenly announces, "Leo and I were living together."

Chapter 55

I'm not really surprised. Even though Katie had been adamant from the time she was around fourteen that she would not live with someone or do *anything* until she was married, I suspected things had changed.

"I know you're probably disappointed in me. I'm disappointed in myself," Katie says softly. "But I want you to know it's done... uh, not Leo and me, but the physical stuff. We're abstaining until... uh... a future time."

"Disappointed... no, that's not what I'm feeling. Sure, I would've preferred you to not have a sexual relationship until marriage and to save living together until you're married. I think a lot of parents hold that as an ideal, especially since you'd always been so determined your walk with God led you to believe in abstinence before marriage. But disappointed?" I shake my head. "From the sound of your voice, I believe you have remorse. You went to God about this?"

"Yes, absolutely. I just wanted you to know, I... needed you to know how... impure I am now. I let you down. I'm sorry."

"Oh, Katie... you're an adult. The choices you make... made... are yours. The consequences of those choices are also yours. When you first told me you planned to wait until marriage, you had good reasons—diseases, pregnancy, guarding your heart. Those consequences still remain. A failed relationship with someone who you were sexually active with is much more difficult. When you haven't had sex, it's easier to break the bond with the wrong person. Now... you and Leo were sexually active, and you brought him here with you. If you were to end the relationship, it'd be uncomfortable. Jake and I have suspected you two were serious for months. When food started arriving, we knew it was from Leo."

"You knew?"

"Yeah," I say with a shrug, "not for sure at first, but a package arrived a few days before I left for Oregon with his name on it. You'd only told us you two were serious the week before, when you said you were going to visit over the Fourth. We were kind of... we put two and two together."

"Why didn't you say something?"

"Oh, believe me, I wanted to. I wanted to. I wanted to scold and lecture and forbid you to see him. I started to call you many times in those few days before my trip, but... something would always stop me. Jake and I prayed... a lot. We knew, Biblically, we needed to call you out on it. But lovingly. Not out of anger. It's no secret I have a history of overreacting." We both laugh a little at this.

"Yeah, no secret at all." Katie smiles.

I nod and say, "I'm trying to... contain that a little more, to think before I overreact. And to... be more like Christ. It's not always easy for me, but I'm trying."

"I've noticed, Mom. We all have."

"Thanks. So we figured when you were here, live and in person, we could discuss it. Like adults. And..." I let out a large sigh, "I feel partially responsible. I know you probably think I couldn't handle another wedding right now. And a few months ago, when things were so difficult between Jake and me, it would've been true.

"Your sisters' weddings were all wonderful and amazing. But with Sharri and Kenny's deaths, the stress of the weddings, and just... life in general, it was a challenge. Jake and I didn't handle the challenge very well. But we're better now. We talked about the possibility you might announce your engagement over the Fourth and... well, we were kind of excited about it."

"You were? Truly?"

"Yes, truly. Of course, Jake was sure Leo wouldn't be good enough for you, but we wanted to trust your judgement."

"And now you've met him, Mom. Jake knows him pretty well... I guess as well as he can in the few days we've been here. What do you think?"

"My first impressions have been very good. I think Jake likes him also, but we've not had much chance to talk."

"Yeah, I know. I'm sorry to spring this on you when you're just getting home."

"I'm glad you did. I love you, Katie, and always want the best for you."

We visit for a few more minutes, then I excuse myself to go back to Angela. I ask Katie to let Madison know I was here and will be back tomorrow. I'm fading fast and want to say my goodbyes, then go home to sleep.

Angela is still going strong and visiting with Doris. Leo brings her something for her headache, which helps a lot, and then she asks when she can go home. I'm not sure if she means her home, since she doesn't remember the attacks and fleeing to my house, or my home.

She must see the question on my face, as she says, "I mean your place. Doris has been filling me in on what's happened with the terrorist attacks and all of us kids going to your place. I don't really remember it but do get little flashes, which make it almost seem familiar. Doris says you just got home today. I didn't even remember you were missing, Mom. I just remember waking up and you were here. Doris told me I was shot in the butt. Can you believe that?" She laughs a little and shakes her head.

I kiss her on the forehead and tell her I'll be back tomorrow. I give Doris a wave and leave the room, promptly running into Dr. Mitchell.

"Mrs. Caldwell, heading out?"

"Yes. I'll be back tomorrow."

"Belinda is pulling herself together. Sad thing with her losing her husband and now her dad," he says, with a small shake of his head and a more human tone than I'd yet to hear come out of his mouth. "My wife is here also. She was premed in college and will help as needed. Look… I'm sorry about earlier. I think we all got off on the wrong foot. I understand why Leo was upset with me. He's right. I should've stepped forward last night when Phil told me what happened. I wanted to but was worried for my family. We felt like we had to flee Grover or we'd… anyway. I didn't handle his calling me out on my duty well. And to be honest, your declining to help didn't set well with me."

"Why ever for?"

"You did well with Madison. She told me you did exactly what was needed, not only with treating her but with… before and with caring for her husband. You kept your head. We'll need people like you as part of our medical team until things straighten out. Today's deaths are proof we need medical people. Maybe, if I'd went along with them…"

"I did only what Madison told me to do to stop her bleeding, using her supplies. In fact, how'd she know what to do, and why does she have a trauma kit in her pickup?" I can't believe none of this occurred to me until now. Maybe my brain is still wacked.

"You don't know?"

I shake my head.

"She's a veterinarian, and her husband was an EMT."

"Oh, that makes sense. I guess, as a vet, she'd know what to do, and her husband would have a good kit. She'll be a good addition to your medical team."

"She's going to have a long recovery, and she's already talking about going home to Durant. She asked when I thought she'd be able to make the trip. Not any time soon for sure."

After telling Dr. Mitchell goodbye, I make my way to the yard. Phil, Evan, Jake, and another Bakerville guy I know only by sight are talking by the truck. I don't see Belinda, Tammy, or TJ anywhere.

"Angela doing okay?" Jake asks.

"She seems much better."

"She woke up while you guys were gone and was much better than she'd been earlier. Belinda said she thinks she'll start improving quickly now. You might get to take her home in a couple of days," Evan says.

"Let me go and tell her goodbye, then we'll take off." Jake gives me a quick kiss.

"You doing okay, Mollie?" Phil asks.

"I'm tired."

"I can understand that. Jake told me a little about your trip home. You know, Kelley will be around if you need her."

"Yes, thanks. Where is she now?"

"Belinda sent her home. She's taking an overnight shift tonight. Sam's wife is going to help out also. Seems he's some sort of doctor and she was premed back in college before they married. Don't know why he didn't say anything last night," Phil says with a shake of his head. I say nothing.

"So, we all need to stay on alert," Evan says. "With Dan Morse missing, no telling what could happen next."

"True. I'd like to go looking for him again but am not sure where he might be. We checked most of the places we knew about today. Bobby Noland did say he might have another idea. I thought a few of us might go looking tomorrow."

"Phil, I'm not sure it's a good idea," Evan says.

"Yeah. That's what Deputy Fred said also. I guess, after what happened today, it doesn't sound very smart. But I hate the idea of waiting for him to do something more."

"Don't you think he'd take off from here?" I ask. "We know he killed his wife and Olivia, and we suspect he had something to do with Angela and Doris getting shot. Wouldn't he just leave while he can?"

"We're not sure what he'd do," Evan says. "A normal person would probably take off, but a normal person also wouldn't kill his wife, kidnap and kill another person, and have two people attacked. We shouldn't assume anything."

The drive home is only about fifteen minutes, and I fight to keep my eyes open the entire time.

At the house I spend a few minutes with my family. Malcolm, my sweet little boy, barely leaves my side.

"It's good you finally made it home, Mom. I was beginning to think you'd never get here."

"I know what you mean, Malcolm. It was the longest trip of my life," I say, hugging him close.

"So… now that you're home, I guess we have to start school again?"

I can't help but laugh. Malcolm enjoys learning but on his terms. While he'll spend all day reading and researching things he's interested in, knowing we're doing actual "school" is disheartening.

"Maybe we'll wait another day or two. I'm pretty tired and there's lots to do here. We'll start school again soon."

"It's going to be hard to do school without the internet. Lots of the research we do is online."

"True, but we have these amazing things called books," I give him a wink, "and you can use those."

"I guess," he sighs loudly. "But what if I want to know something that we don't have a book about? How will I learn?"

"Just like your mom and I did," Jake says, "in the dark ages, before the information highway."

"Fine. I guess I'll just read books and only learn what you have books to learn."

The disaster of no internet, at least as far as Malcolm is concerned, is allayed for tonight, and we move on to talk about other things.

Malcolm even asks if I want to sit with them while Jake reads. Their nightly reading is something just for the two of them, to the point Malcolm will remind me it's time for me to go to bed so his dad can read. To be asked to stay is quite an honor.

After Jake finishes a chapter, he says, "That's enough for tonight. Let your mom get some rest."

Chapter 56

Friday, Day 9

Friday morning, I awaken when Jake snuggles up next to me. It's still dark out, as he whispers, "I'm so glad you're home." Half an hour later, we make our way to the kitchen for coffee and the official start of our day.

Coffee is a habit and a treat. I can't imagine not having it to start my day. However, at some point, our coffee will run out. While we have a considerable amount in our food storage room, coffee is now finite. Just like citrus fruits, bananas, and several other things, coffee isn't grown in Wyoming. We relied on it being shipped in. With this world we're living in, those days may be over until things can get back to normal. Until the transportation and fuel issues can be dealt with.

We have a loose plan to deal with the loss of coffee, including tapering off so our bodies can adjust to the lack of caffeine. And we have a small patch of chicory growing in the herb garden. Chicory coffee, perceived as a poor's man coffee choice, is preferred in some regions. We started growing it the year after we moved here, more as a novelty and for the greens than the coffee. We've tried it, and it's fine, but it's not coffee. Truly, if running out of coffee was our biggest problem, we'd be fine.

I'm glad I got a little extra sleep but do still feel tired, and my stomach is upset. I know Donna in Cooke City said the concussion effects could remain for a while, so I figure both are related to my bump on the head.

"You make any plans for today?" I ask Jake.

"I'm going to finish hooking up the new solar systems, since I was so rudely interrupted while I was working on it yesterday," he says, while giving me an incredibly robust kiss. Wow.

"Leo and Mike want to work on the greenhouse. There's several other small jobs happening, which my dad and Art have taken charge of. I wish I could've had them here before. It would've really helped me not to feel so overwhelmed. At the very least, I should've discussed my troubles with my dad. I know he would've been more than happy to give us the occasional hand."

I nod in agreement. Jake and I didn't tell anyone about the troubles we were having until they got too big to hide. Then Jake spilled the beans to Calley, and all of our children soon knew. They were all very supportive and encouraging, but it was kind of embarrassing for them to know we were having trouble.

"Did you see Leo last night? Did he happen to say how Madison and Doris are doing?"

"Leo didn't make it home before I went to bed, but Katie did. She said they had just started working on Madison. Sam—or I guess I should call him Dr. Mitchell—Belinda, and Mitchell's wife were all in the makeshift operating room. Leo was monitoring Angela and Doris until midnight when Kelley was scheduled to relieve him. I think they planned on Doris's operation immediately after Madison was finished and stable. Katie also told me about your conversation yesterday. She said she wanted to 'come clean' with both of us."

I nod but say nothing. We both sit quietly, sipping our coffee, when Jake blurts out "Oh, and I forgot to tell you, Katie said her phone worked yesterday. Not only the flip but her regular cell. A friend of hers called. Katie loaned her SUV to someone so they could get home, and they were calling to let her know they made it. Katie said it sounded like things were pretty rough along the way, but they're home in North Dakota or somewhere, hunkered down."

"Hunkered down?"

"Yep, that's the word Katie said they used."

"Has there been anything on the radio about how things are going? Since the phones are working, will the power be back on soon? That'd make a huge difference. Communication helps but power and water will be the big change to getting our country back on track."

"My mom and dad heard the local station's 7:00 pm broadcast. They announced some cell phones working but nothing we didn't already know from our own experiences."

"Well, that's something, I guess. Maybe more stuff will come back on today."

"Yeah, it'd be pretty exciting if it did. It'd go a long way toward raising people's spirits. Uh… you okay about Katie? Part of me wants to have a word or two with Leo. But then, I remember Katie is an adult and can do what she wants."

"Yeah. If she was still a teenager living at home, it'd be different."

Jake agrees and dismisses himself to go do the chores. I announce I'll join him shortly to milk the goats, when he stops and says, "No need. I suspect Malcolm and Art will handle it this morning."

At that exact moment, Malcolm pops out of his bedroom and rushes down the stairs, telling me, "You rest today, Mom. We have it under control." Then he heads to the guest room, I presume to wake Tony.

I'm suddenly alarmed. "Jake, how are Tony and Lily? I can't believe I didn't even think to check on them last night."

"As well as to be expected. Lois and Karen took care of telling them about their mom and stayed with them. They brought them in and put them to bed shortly after you went down last night. I thought we'd probably want to keep them here until Jason comes home... provided he's able to. They have really bonded well with everyone here and, as far as I know, have no other family around."

"Right. I think she said their family is in California, where they moved from. Katie asked if they could stay also. I didn't realize she and Olivia had become friends over the past several days."

"Yes, they did. Sarah was friendly with Olivia also. I know she's pretty upset about everything, especially since she was with Olivia when she was taken." Jake shakes his head, then adds, "I'm going to head on out. Like Malcolm said, we have it under control. You rest today."

"How about Tony? Do you think he needs to be helping with chores after just losing his mom?"

"Good point. I'll take care of it."

"Take care of what, Dad?" Malcolm asks, walking into the kitchen with Tony on his heels. His face is drawn and his eyes tired.

"Good morning, Tony," Jake says. "Did you sleep much?"

"Not much. Lily was crying a lot. She's sleeping now."

"Why don't you head on back to bed? We'll take care of the chores this morning," Jake says, resting his shoulder on Tony's shoulder.

Tony nods as his eyes fill with tears. Malcolm looks at Tony and says, "Sorry. I forgot... I should've let you sleep."

229

"It's okay, Malcolm. I like helping with the milking, but I think sleep would be good. Glad you made it home, Mrs. Caldwell." Tony turns and scurries back to his room.

"Will he be okay?" Malcolm asks quietly.

"He'll miss his mom for a long time," I say. "We'll need to remember and help both Tony and Lily while they grieve."

"Ready to go, Buddy?" Jake asks as they head toward the door.

Jake's suggestion of my resting sounds wonderful, but several things need to be done. Specifically, emptying out the basement freezer and fridge, plus moving the Schwan's truck goodies to a small, portable freezer we have, which will run better on the garage solar system. There's also a full laundry basket in our bedroom, and I suspect Malcolm's is in the same condition. I wonder if anyone else needs to do laundry.

On a sunny day, our solar system can easily run our washing machine. Heat takes too much energy to produce, so we'll line dry the clothes.

The solar systems in both the bunkhouse and the cabin are much smaller—each being a twelve-volt system—and a regular machine isn't suitable. Of course, Jake is changing to the new systems he and Leo purchased.

Even so, I have these small little RV-style machines which work well. The size of them makes them portable, so they're stowed in a closet until needed. The loads are small, and the process is slightly labor-intensive, but nothing like washing by hand would be. I'll be sure to check on everyone in the group and see if they've been washing or if we need to have a laundry day to catch everything up.

I decide to make a list of the things I want to accomplish today. Top of the list is making my way over to Tammy's house to check on Angela and visit with Doris and Madison. I want to start processing the items in the basement freezer. I have no idea what's in there since this freezer was empty when I left home and has been filled with Jake's purchases over the last few days.

I need another cup of coffee before heading to the basement. As I'm pouring, there's a slight knock on the door before Sarah opens it and comes in. She gives me a big hug, then starts to cry.

"I feel so bad about Olivia. I should've done more to keep that terrible man from taking her," she gulps out between sobs.

"Oh, Sarah, from what I've heard, there wasn't anything you could've done."

"I could've shot him. If I would've had a gun, like we're supposed to have, I could've taken care of him and not let him take Olivia."

"What do you mean, 'like we're supposed to have,'" I ask, not quite understanding.

"A few days ago, we all talked about how dangerous things are getting. We went up to Doris and Evan's and all had lessons on shooting handguns. I'd shot Tate's before, but this was a very in-depth class. We were supposed to start having daily lessons and practice, but with Angela and Doris getting hurt, those were put on hold. I should've had a gun on me, then this wouldn't have happened," she says, breaking down again.

"You don't know that," I say. "Just carrying a gun doesn't automatically provide protection. And if you aren't comfortable with getting it out of your holster and shooting it, that could be even more dangerous."

"You carry a gun. You had to shoot those guys to save Madison and her baby. You're a hero, Mom. And Angela, she killed the guy trying to take her away. Jake killed the other guy. And what do I do? Nothing. I let Olivia be kidnapped and killed."

I choose to simply hold Sarah and say nothing. I don't suppose it will do any good to tell her how terrible I feel for not being able to keep Dave and Don, the monsters I encountered, from killing Madison's husband, or how I threw up several times after killing them. Killing a person is a terrible thing, even when it has to be done.

We spend several minutes holding each other before Sarah says, "I suppose you're right. I've never even tried to take a gun out of a holster. And I don't have one anyway—a gun or holster."

While we've been focused on preparedness for a decade, arming myself wasn't something I thought about until the last few years and then it was a slow journey.

Jake has hunted since he was a child and was very comfortable with both rifles and shotguns, but he also didn't carry a handgun until we moved up here and realized we'd be hunting and hiking in bear and cat territory.

At that point, we each took a handgun course, through firearm instructors Evan and Doris, and started practicing. My first gun, a .357 revolver, wasn't great for me. The trigger on it made firing it difficult.

231

I could do it but would end up with an achy hand after shooting only a few rounds. I blame breaking my hand several years ago. I then purchased a .40 caliber subcompact semi-auto from Springfield Armory. Wow, what a difference.

Shooting still uses several different muscles I'm not used to engaging in my daily life, so I take my range time in small doses. My hand will still ache after thirty or so rounds, but my back usually starts to tell me it's time to quit before then.

Jake and I have a small hundred-yard range at the top of our property, with a dugout area making a safe backdrop. We aim for a "range date" at least one time per week.

While Jake prefers not to carry in his daily life, I conceal carry pretty much each time I leave the house. When I'm home, my Springfield is locked in a case underneath a table in the front room. The .357 is in a similar case next to my bed. I have a .40 caliber compact Glock, my newest purchase made only a week before I left on my Oregon trip, in the main gun cabinet along with my little Ruger .380, which I use when my clothing doesn't quite work for one of my full-size guns.

The little "pocket pistol" gives me a measure of comfort when hidden in my bra or strapped to my leg. With the addition of the Taurus 9-millimeter I brought back with me from Oregon, I definitely have the option to share a handgun with Sarah, and I have a nice selection of holsters.

Will Calley and Katie need pistols also? From the story told about Angela, I know she was carrying a sidearm when she was attacked. After using it, I wonder if she'll be up to carrying again. Of course, at this point, she doesn't even remember she had to use it...

Sarah composes herself. "I'm going back out to my trailer to see if Tate's awake. We've all been having breakfast on our own, then a couple of people are in charge of lunch and supper each day. Today, Lois and Karen are in charge of meals. We've been using your kitchen. Is it okay to continue in here? The bunkhouse kitchen is great but not when cooking for twenty or so people."

"Yes, of course. I found out last night Deanne is in charge of the schedule for cooking. I've asked her to add me into the rotation."

Sarah gives me a hug and takes her leave. My stomach is suddenly not well, and I make a rush for the bathroom. Ugh. When will I feel better?

Chapter 57

I'm back in the kitchen when Lily comes out of the bedroom asking for her mom. She sees me, must suddenly remember the events from yesterday, and begins to wail.

Katie comes up from her basement bedroom a few minutes later, presumably awoken by poor Lily. Lily goes to Katie, who takes over comforting her while I get breakfast going.

The wonderful aroma of coffee is suddenly not so wonderful. I dump out the remains of my cup in hopes of preventing my stomach from rebelling.

"Katie, Sarah said everyone's on their own for breakfast. Have you been eating with Jake?"

"Not really. Leo and I brought some food along," she has a bit of a sheepish look about her as she says this. "The easy stuff, cold cereal, is gone now. And I think we finished the last of the instant oatmeal yesterday."

"What about Tim and Gavin? What are they doing for breakfast?"

"Same, I suppose," she says with a shrug. "Cold cereal and such. Pretty sure they still had a few days' worth, so they should be okay right now."

"Do you mind running over and seeing if they've already eaten? If not, ask Tim if they'll come over for breakfast. Art also. Stop and invite Leo too."

"You do know Jake wanted you to take it easy today, right? He told all of us last night to make sure you did."

"Believe me, this will be easy. I noticed the fridge is full of eggs, so I'm making German pancakes."

"Yum. I'll be right back and can help you. Lily, want to go for a walk with me?"

Lily says nothing but lifts her arms up to be carried. Soon, everyone's back from chores and gathered around for breakfast. Over the meal, I find out more about what has been going on the last few days, and even find out we have been posting a sentry.

Apparently, Evan and Phil stopped by last night after I went to bed and suggested we beef up our security measures. One of the special projects my father-in-law, Alvin, plans to work on today.

Alvin is currently on sentry duty. He started at 4:00 am, his normal waking time, replacing Tate's dad. Jake will replace Alvin at 8:00 am. Then Tim is on at noon. Tim says he wants to go visit Angela before his shift and asks if I want to ride along. Leo catches us up on Madison's and Doris's conditions.

"Madison came through the surgery fine. They had to remove several pieces of bone from the shoulder but both Belinda and Dr. Mitchell said it could've been worse. They got the slug out."

"That's great. She'll have full use?" I ask.

"Probably not. One of your neighbors—I can't remember her name, but her husband is the former detective who helped when we found Terry Bosco—she used to be a physical therapist or something. They're going to see if she'll work with her. In fact, they're going to try to get her on the medical team. The way the bullet went through Madison's husband first… well, it probably saved her life. Still did some damage, though."

"It was point blank," I say blandly. "The guy was only a few feet away. And you saw the gun… what was it a .45?" I ask.

"Ten-millimeter, in terrible condition. Don't think the guy had ever cleaned it," Leo says.

"Is the doctor worried about infection?"

"Yeah, but it seems antibiotics are something Belinda and Kelley both have in stock," Leo says.

"Not the fish kind we have either but the real ones," Jake adds. "Sam has a few meds and supplies too. Pain meds are a different story, though. Belinda wouldn't keep those because of Terry's addiction issues. Kelley has some they're using for medicating Madison. Evan found some old meds they're using for Doris. Thankfully, Kelley stored anesthesia, both local and general. I gave them a bit of stuff from our stock also."

"And did they operate on Doris?" I ask.

"They were working on her when I left," Leo says. "I'm not sure they'll be able to do everything needed. Yesterday, Belinda said they really needed some hardware to put the bones back together—pins, or screws, or something. The bullet didn't provide a clean break and there are pieces of bone missing."

I shudder thinking about it.

"I think the plan was to set it and hope the bones will fuse back together."

"Well, it's a good thing we found a doctor in our little community."

"Yes, but Dr. Mitchell gave Belinda all of the credit after Madison's surgery. Said she was amazing in the operating room and he was really the one assisting her."

"I'd imagine so, considering the number of surgeries she's done," Jake says. "Tom used to brag about her quite a bit and how the doc she worked for couldn't have done nearly as well without her."

"Belinda told me to come back at 4:00 this afternoon. You think she'll need me sooner?" Katie asks.

"Doubtful," Leo says, "I think the plan was for both Belinda and Dr. Mitchell to be there today, sleeping when they could but available if needed. Kelley relieved me at midnight, Tammy is relieving Kelley at 8:00 am, then you'll relieve her at 4:00. I'm on at midnight."

"Sounds good. I'll do stuff around here, then. Mom, I saw you made a to-do list, so I know what to start on while you're visiting Angela. I'll start with cleaning up from breakfast and taking care of Gavin while you guys are gone."

"So, we have a patrol at Tammy's," Leo says. "After what happened to Katie, and with Morse being on the loose, it just seemed smart. I'm not sure who's there right now, but they know to expect you. They'll let you inside."

Chapter 58

People disperse, with Tim asking if I can be ready in fifteen minutes. Katie and Leo linger until they're the only ones besides Jake and me left in the house.

"Sir, uh, Jake. Can we talk with you and Mrs. Caldwell for a minute?"

Jake and I exchange a quick look, then I say, "Please, call me Mollie."

"Yes, ma'am," Leo nods, while Katie gives a slight laugh.

"I know Katie spoke with both of you about our relationship. Katie… it wasn't her fault."

"Are you trying to tell me you forced yourself on my little girl?" Jake bristles.

"No, Jake. He didn't. That's not what happened. Leo is trying to… I guess, be a gentleman, but it was me too. Just as much." She reaches over and takes his hand.

"So, you're not pregnant or something? You lived together, but that was all?" Jake asks warily.

"I'm not pregnant. We lived together. We're not… uh… living together any longer. We're just—" she gives a funny smile, "I guess we're just boyfriend and girlfriend now, huh?"

Leo laughs and says, "I suppose so."

Jake shrugs, I shake my head, and Katie says, "So we just wanted to make sure you both knew that we both knew that you both knew."

"What?" I ask, while Jake says, "That makes zero sense."

"What Katie means is, we want you to know we're serious about each other, committed. But we're not going to have a physical relationship until after we're married. I'm not asking for your permission to marry her today. That time will come. We just wanted to… come clean. We're starting fresh. We've committed to each other and to God to abstain until we're married. We're committing to you also."

Jake shakes Leo's hand while I hug Katie. Then Katie goes to Jake. Leo and I have an awkward moment where he offers me his hand and I go in for a hug. We finally work it out. I admire them for coming forward. It would've been easy for them to say nothing about living together. Oh, I'm sure I would've brought it up at an opportune time. But their maturity in bringing it to us and coming clean impresses me. Sure, there's lots worse things than living together.

For me, the sneakiness of not telling is a bigger problem. I can handle a lot of things but not that. I'm suddenly reminded of an issue between Jake and me. We had a time where honesty was not at the forefront of our marriage.

Jake has a tobacco habit, chewing tobacco. He said he'd quit but was still sneaking it. I busted him one day, and it was not pretty. I didn't really have a problem with him chewing, but the sneaking and lying about it was terrible. Now that it's out in the open, things are much better.

But he wasn't the only one not honest in our marriage. I've had plenty of lies of omission. From the simple things of when he'd ask what was wrong—my answer "fine" meant anything but fine—to larger things. We worked through a lot of this in marriage counseling.

There are still things Jake doesn't know about. Before I left for Oregon, before the planes crashed and our world fell apart, it seemed I'd have no choice but to tell him. When Brad called the last time, he made it clear he wouldn't let it rest. He'd be showing up *at my house*. At my house! Brad was pushing me into a corner, and all of my secrets would come out.

But now… maybe this disaster has brought me a reprieve. Maybe I won't need to tell Jake about Brad. Because if I tell Jake, I'll have to tell others. I'm not ready. I don't know if I'll ever be ready.

Chapter 59

Angela is awake and seems fully alert, lying on her side, chatting quietly with Tammy when we arrive. On the other hand, Doris is completely out with Evan sleeping in the chair by her side.

"Hey," Angela says, while reaching for Tim. He greets her with a big kiss, then she says, "Tammy said they might let me walk around today. That sounds pretty good. I've been in pretty much this same position since I got here. Roll from one side to the other, that's all I do. And I'm pretty sure there's still some BBs in me. There's a couple of spots I really feel when I move."

"Maybe we can run a magnet over you and get them out," Tim teases.

"Would that work?" Angela asks excitedly.

"I was only kidding, Angel. I don't think it'd work. It'd have to be a really strong magnet to pull them out. Besides, I don't think it was steel shot but rather lead. And I know Tammy removed everything she could get to."

Tammy nods and says, "Some may fester up, then we can see about taking them out. We did take out 102. Evan thinks it was #4 bird, so there could be more. He said a shell holds 135 pellets, but with the pattern, we're sure some didn't hit you, Angela."

"So, if there's lead inside of me, am I going to get lead poisoning?"

"Lead toxicity is something Belinda and I discussed," Tammy answers. "We're hopeful enough of the pellets were removed, or will come up so we can remove them, so this won't be an issue. We're not overly concerned right now."

"Well, I'm just excited to walk around today," Angela says with a smile.

Even though we were speaking quietly, Evan stirs. "Hey, Mollie. You look like you got some rest."

"I did. I'm much better today. How'd Doris do last night?"

Sadness crosses Evan's face before he recovers and says, "It went pretty well. She needed a lot more done than Belinda and Sam had the ability to do. They talked about raiding a toolbox to see what they could find in place of the proper hardware, but decided the risk was

238

too great. They said they really needed some kind of plates but don't have them. So they set the bones as best they could, cleaned things up a little more, and put her back in the air cast. They'll do a hard cast once the swelling is down. She'll be completely off the leg for several months. We can only hope… no, pray, she'll be able to bear weight on it again."

"I'll do it," Doris says weakly. "I'll walk again."

Evan drops a kiss on her forehead and says something too quiet for the rest of us to hear. We avert our eyes to give them a modicum of privacy, not easy in a small room.

After a minute or two, Doris says with more conviction, "As soon as they determine I'm not going to keel over from last night's operation, they're going to let me go home. For once, I'm glad we went with a single-level home, planning for our old age, instead of the two-story I really wanted. At least I'll be able to get around okay."

I nod, thinking of the wide doors and hallways in their house. Doris has told me many times it wasn't the house she really wanted, but they planned to live there as long as possible, so it made sense to have it somewhat accessible.

As part of our preps, we have crutches in a few different sizes, a couple walking boots, and a folding wheelchair, which belonged to my dad. The wheelchair, while nothing fancy, will work well for Doris.

"They're letting me get up and walk around today," Angela tells Doris. "I think I'll be able to go home in a day or two also."

Tammy excuses herself to check on Madison, while the conversation continues and moves on to more cellular phones working. Evan was even able to connect with Doris's daughter Lindsey, a police officer in the Bay Area, briefly—just enough to find out things weren't going well there.

She and her husband, Logan, are planning to leave, but for the time being, are sheltering in place, waiting for the craziness to calm down. She tried to stay on the job, but it became too dangerous. She said she'd call when they were ready to leave and head this way. He tried calling Jessica, Doris's older girl living in Germany, but hasn't been able to connect.

Doris seems very relieved just with the report of Lindsey being okay at the moment. We all think Germany is probably safe and not affected by what's happening here, so there isn't much concern for Jessica, her husband, and their children's safety. As a mom, I know there's always worry—even when the world isn't falling apart. It's a natural instinct to want to protect our children, no matter how old they are.

I briefly think of my own mom. Last time I heard from her, she was living in Spain. Is she doing okay?

Chapter 60

Tammy pokes her head in and says, "Madison is asking for you, Mollie. You want to pop in and see her?"

"I do. I wasn't sure if she was awake."

"I'm awake!" Madison declares from the other room, making everyone laugh.

I'm surprised at how good Madison looks, lying in the bed with Emma asleep at her side. Her color is back, and her hair is combed. "You look great," I tell her.

"Thanks, I'm feeling better. You getting the bleeding stopped so quickly made a huge difference. I have no doubt the outcome would've been different if you wouldn't have acted when you did, not to mention stepping in and taking care of those two guys."

"One guy," I say. "You had the first one on the ground with what was likely a fatal wound. I just ended things for him a little quicker."

"Yeah, well... How are you doing? You okay with it all?"

I shrug as my eyes well with tears. "I hated having to do it, but I'd do it again. I just wish... I wish... your husband. I'm so sorry I wasn't there just a minute sooner. Maybe..."

"No, Mollie. Don't do that to yourself. Scott dying wasn't your fault. You saved my baby," she says, while planting a kiss on Emma's sleeping head. "You saved me so I can take care of Emma. I can tell her about Scott, and while it won't be the same, it will have to be enough."

Madison and I visit for a few minutes more, as Emma stirs awake. Whoever is on duty helps with Emma as needed. Madison has still been nursing her but changing her diaper and meeting her other needs are a challenge.

I take my turn at changing her and playing with her for a few minutes before Emma declares it time to eat.

Shortly after, it's time for Tim and me to head back home for his sentry duty. Angela, awake since before we arrived, is ready for a nap and then will try walking.

Evan says he's going to head out when we do; he and Phil Hudson made plans to meet up with Jake when his sentry shift ends to go over plans for the community's defenses.

I realize it's likely sentries are stationed at many of the houses in our area. All wondering when, or if, Dan Morse will strike again. Instinctively, I touch my side where my holster sits. I'm no longer carrying the Taurus and, once again, have my trusty Springfield nestled where it belongs.

After lunch a few of us are still sitting around visiting when Leo says, "Katie, Calley, you two want to spend some time shooting? How about you, Sarah?"

"Yes," all three responded in sync, then give a slight laugh.

"All right, good. I spent some time this morning with the guys, working in groups of three. I think they're all feeling more confident. The training with the Snyders the other day was great. Now they just need range and dry fire time. I'd also like to run some drills, practicing drawing—you know, the usual stuff."

"The usual stuff," Katie says with a nod. "Sure, Leo. I don't even understand most of what you said, but why not? All part of the plan to make us fighting machines?"

Leo gives her a small smile, while I ask, "What's that mean? Fighting machines?"

"Oh... you know, Mom. Kind of like our own little army."

"Okay... are we starting our own army? Oh, you mean the sentries?"

Jake looks slightly uncomfortable as he says, "We're going to probably do a little more than just have sentries, but yes, the sentries are part of it. We're also putting a few other measures in place."

The silence is palpable as we all consider what this means. Finally, Jake's mom is the one to break it by saying, "Seems the only smart thing to do. We've already had troubles and the power has only been out a few days."

"Yeah, Mom. I don't think we have much of a choice."

"Your friend Evan was smart to have you and your dad buy those extra rifles. I pray we won't need them, but if we do..." Dodie's voice fades off. Then, stronger, she says, "I didn't take the shooting training the other day. You know, I hunted with your dad when I was younger. Even killed a deer, just one. I felt bad afterward and never hunted again. But now, this? To know our Angela was injured, Sarah

242

too, and Olivia killed. I don't think there's a choice but for all of us to learn to defend ourselves, to defend our children."

In a rare display of affection, Alvin stands up and walks over to Dodie, kissing her full on the lips—something I've never seen between them—then says, "Dodie, my love, as much as I hate to agree with you, I agree with you."

"Go on, Alvin. Don't be making a spectacle in front of our family."

While her voice holds a reprimand, the smile on her face and blush to her cheeks indicates she enjoyed the sentiment.

Jake clears his throat slightly and says, "So, Leo, how about those weapons we brought home from... I mean, with Mollie?"

"Boy, those were a mess for sure," Leo says with a nod. "I cleaned up the handguns. One was a Ruger .38 Special five-round revolver, wasn't in too bad of shape."

"Don's," I say, "that one belonged to the guy Madison shot... well, I shot him, too, but Madison shot him first."

Calley looks at me with wide eyes, even though they generally know what happened, I haven't given details.

"Yeah, okay. The other one..."

"Dave," I offer.

"Okay, a 10-millimeter semi-auto, and it was a mess. Took it apart, cleaned it all up, then put it back together again," Leo says. "I fired it and it seems to be fine. Would've been a great gun if he'd bothered to take care of it. I also cleaned Madison and her husband's weapons. Neither were dirty but it was the right thing to do. Jake had me put them in your main gun case for safekeeping. Be a while before Madison is able to shoot. I have no idea how she even managed to get the one shot off."

"Yeah, she was pretty amazing," I agree. "What about Don and Dave's guns? Can we use them?"

"For sure. I'm not sure if you know, but we checked their car and removed items we thought could be useful, including a .243 rifle and a 12-gauge shotgun, both in about the same condition as their pistols. Cleaned them also and we've added those to our arsenal. Jake told Phil and Evan we'd be keeping them to help arm some of our people."

"Good," I say. "So do we have enough firearms to go around? If we're going to have our own... army, then we need weapons."

"I think what we're looking at is more of a security force, or even a militia, than an army," Jake offers.

"Fine, then. Whatever you want to call it. About the weapons?"

"Yeah, we're pretty good," Leo says. "People brought things with them, and with what you have here, there's a decent assortment of handguns, rifles, and shotguns."

"Welcome to Wyoming," Jake and I say in unison, causing both of us to laugh and most everyone else to roll their eyes.

"I guess so," Leo shrugs and nods. "Evan and Jake were able to get a few more things the other day from a friend of Evan's in Red Lodge, which should fill in any missing pieces so everyone can be well armed."

"Jake, have you spoken to everyone living here?" I ask. "Is everyone okay with this, or are you planning for them and hoping they'll go along?"

"I think everyone's on board. Didn't I tell you about the lessons Doris and Evan gave us?"

"Did you? I don't think so... Oh, Dodie, you did just mention shooting training."

"Mom, we talked about it this morning, remember?" Sarah says. Did we? My rattled brain, when will it work like it should?

"Oh... yes, I guess we did."

Jake nods. "The other day—"

"The day before Angela was shot," Calley says.

"Yeah, that day. Everyone went through training based on what we already knew."

"Not everyone," Alvin interrupts, "Dodie skipped it. She'll need to play catchup."

"Okay, everyone but my mom had training. So, yeah, I think they're all on board. Even more so after the latest events."

"Umm..." Calley says, running a hand through her hair. "I don't think Sheila is on board now. Mike?"

"Don't know," he shrugs. "She's not talking to me. You could ask my mom or dad... but I'm not sure she's talking to them either."

"Okay... well, let's count her in the numbers so we have her covered, just in case," Jake says with a small frown.

"My sister, she's even learning," Tate interjects quickly, to help change the subject, "she wasn't... well, she wasn't a fan. She thought only people who were in the military or police and maybe ranchers to protect their livestock should even own guns. She often gave our dad a hard time about owning guns. Since they lived in the city, she felt there was no need. She's definitely singing a different tune now. The shot across the bow changed her mind."

"Shot across the bow?" I'm confused.

"Uh, yeah. I showed you the scrape on the hood of the car?" Jake says reluctantly, while Tate looks like he wants to crawl under the table.

"No, I don't think you did. Is this something we should talk about later?" I ask, as kindly as I can muster.

"Uh... right. Let's talk about it later. Now, where was I? So we're working on training and arming our..."

"Militia?" Calley offers, Mike gives her a slight jab in the arm.

"I was going to say family unit," Jake says.

"Okay, so we'll probably be good," Leo says. "Well, ladies, let's go shoot. After you three, I'll take three more. Mrs. Caldwell—Dodie, would you like to shoot this afternoon?"

"I suppose I should," she reluctantly agrees.

"Great. I'll have you with Tate and Mike's mom. You'll be next, so in about an hour. Then I'll finish up with Karen plus see if Tim would like to practice since he didn't get to this morning. And, Mollie, if you'd like to join us, you're welcome."

"Mmm. I don't think so. I'm still a little... off from my trip. Maybe tomorrow I'll have my balance back."

A look of worry crosses Jake's face. I quickly add, "I'm fine. Just a little sick to my stomach still. I think my equilibrium is messed up."

"You're sure?" Jake asks.

I nod and ask, "You need handguns? Sarah you want to use one of mine? Dodie?"

"I have your .357 already. You mind if we take your Taurus and your Glock?" Leo asks.

"No problem. I'll get them."

"I'll get them," Jake offers with a smile.

Chapter 61

Once Leo has what he needs, the group breaks up to go about their tasks. Sarah and Calley promise they'll be in to help me after they finish shooting practice. I make my way to the basement freezer to decide where to start with preserving. I have no idea what to expect since these were purchases Jake made while I was gone.

The basement freezer is surprisingly full: beef roasts, pork roasts, whole chickens, steaks, pork chops, hamburger, sausage, cut fryers, chicken hindquarters, and assorted other packages of meat along with frozen vegetables, TV dinners, ice cream, and treats.

There isn't much I can do about the TV dinners, ice cream, and treats, but I can easily make the meats and veggies shelf-stable. I'll quick-thaw the veggies and get them going today. The meat will need to be fully thawed before I can start processing it.

I move several packages of frozen meat to the basement fridge to begin the thawing. The fridge is half full of many packages of cheese, hot dogs, and bacon plus a few other longer-term items. We can wax the cheese and move it to the root cellar. It's a perfect group project, so I'll wait until I can find a few helpers.

An hour later, I have one of my pressure canners with a load of previously frozen green beans and a water bath load of pickled cauliflower. Canning from frozen, while safe, will give different results, so instead of crunchy pickled cauliflower, it will be slightly soft. Ditto for the green beans. While not ideal, it will be fine.

After frantically searching for my other two pressure canners, I discover Jake loaned them to Doris so she could can some of their freezer. I'll check with Evan on how far she got with this and finish up as needed.

I'm working on putting a batch of mixed veggies in the solar food dehydrator when Jake announces Evan and Phil are pulling in the driveway.

"You mind if I invite them in for something to drink while we discuss? That way you can be included. I think Kelley is also with them."

"Sure, perfect. I'll set this aside and work on it afterward. I didn't realize they were here. Penny and Scooter didn't sound their usual alarm."

"My mom has taken a liking to them and has them in the apartment visiting Butterball. Gavin and Lily are in there too. I imagine it's quite the zoo."

Butterball is Alvin and Dodie's ten-year-old Yorkie. Scooter is my fourteen-year-old Chihuahua, and he doesn't play. He may be watching the festivities, but I can't imagine he's participating. Penny is a six- or seven-year-old rescue dog who looks like a dachshund and is full of energy. She's likely giving Gavin and Lily plenty of licks, one of her favorite things.

As Jake ushers everyone in, a cloud of exhaustion hangs over our guests. Both Evan and Phil are looking pretty scruffy—Evan with several days' growth of beard and Phil with his usual Mr. Clean head sporting a five o'clock shadow.

Kelley, a natural beauty with her dark eyes and flawless complexion, wears her fatigue like a lead cloak, seeming to be weighed down and depleted.

"Sorry we're later getting here than planned. We've had another death. Andy's wife, Helen."

"Helen?" I say with alarm.

Kelley gives a slight nod as her eyes fill with tears. She quietly says, "She killed herself. She even left a note. Did you know she was sick?"

I shake my head. While I know Helen enough to say hello, we don't have much of a relationship.

"Her note said Andy pretty much did everything for her, and with him gone, she didn't want to be a burden on anyone else," Phil says. "She asked any resources found in her house and on their property be put toward the good of the community, especially her church members."

"I wish she would've reached out to someone. I'm sure many of us would've been happy to help," I say. "Does Pastor Ralph know?"

"Ralph was there when we left. So was Isaiah Avery and Jonathan Dawson along with Deputy Fred."

"The retired judge and retired lawyer?" Jake asks.

"Yes, since what she left behind was, essentially, a last will and testament, Fred thought it'd be best to bring them in on it."

"What does Fred say about the situation with Morse?"

"He was able to reach the sheriff by radio last night," Evan answers. "They want to find Morse. The problem is, everyone's up in arms over Dan Morse. If we thought we had a posse yesterday going after him, today it's a lynch mob. And I totally get it. I'm right along with the group wanting to see justice done.

"Fred made it clear he's an official deputy now and we won't stray from what the law allows. Of course, we don't have any sort of jail if we do find Morse. The sheriff told Fred the road between us and Wesley isn't good. Several people have been killed along it. Some kind of bandits."

"I wouldn't have thought we'd have that here," Kelley says sadly. I agree. Jake was right. We were foolish to think we had found a place which would be untouched by violence.

"So what's Deputy Fred thinking? Go looking for him again, and if he's found, lock him up somewhere until the cavalry arrives?" Jake asks.

"Yeah, something like that," Phil answers with a nod.

"Any idea where he's gone?" I ask.

"Not a clue. Andy Walsh knew about the caves he was using before. He said there was one more spot, but he wasn't sure he could find it. Bobby Noland thought he might know of another spot, but Fred decided against going there. Thinks it's too dangerous."

"If Morse is smart, he's taken off and we'll never see him again," Kelley says.

"He's plenty smart, but I think he's the type who likes to get the last word. I can't imagine he'd scamper away with his tale between his legs," Jake says. "I think he'll be back but on his terms. I don't trust him at all, and truthfully, I worry for the safety of my family. We have a sentry posted now, up on the hillside where Evan suggested, and have started some of the other security measures, but I think we need to do more. You have other ideas for us? Evan? Phil?"

"Well… you had a few things already in place. The fence, ditch, and bushes along the front are good. You can lock the gate and add a second sentry there, which will really help stop access along the front. I saw your dad has a crew up the hillside digging out a foxhole to become the new sentry area."

Foxhole? First I've heard of this.

"From there, it's a full view to the front of the property," Evan continues. "Good the trees you've planted are still young, helps with being able to see the bad guys.

"Behind the foxhole is a concern. You have barbed wire fence along the backside but no secondary deterrents. I think the most likely entry point would be the front of the hillside coming up from the Georgia people's shop. There's even a nice little two-track going up the hill there. Be easy pickings to walk up the hill and sneak in past the foxhole."

"Or, even worse, sneak up on the foxhole," Phil says.

"Right," Evan nods, "we don't want that. I think you should put a second foxhole beyond your property line—not quite at the top of the hill but pretty close, facing the river—and have a third sentry there. In fact, I think it'd make a whole lot of sense for protecting our entire neighborhood to add another foxhole and get everyone in on manning it."

"Can't do it, Evan. That property doesn't belong to us. Like you already said, it belongs to the Georgia people. It's Austin and Carmen Snipes' place."

"True," Phil says, nodding. "And you know we totally respect property ownership. Right now, though, things are different. The lines are slightly blurred, and it's important to think about your family. I met Austin last time he was here. He was a nice guy, seems like the kind of guy who'll make a good neighbor. If he was here, you think he'd have a problem with it?"

"Don't know, he's not here to ask," Jake says briskly.

"Where do they live?" Kelley asks quietly.

Jake looks at me for the answer. While he knows they're from Georgia, that's the extent of his knowledge. "Somewhere outside of Atlanta," I answer.

Jake gives a big sigh and says, "Atlanta. When the national news was still coming in, wasn't it one of the places... not looking too good?"

Everyone nods but says nothing. I suspect we're all thinking the same thing. After a minute or so, Jake says, "Mollie, don't you have their phone number? Maybe, with the phones coming back up, you can reach them and ask. How about it? Mollie tries to reach them. If she can't reach them within, say, twenty-four hours, then we'll go ahead with adding the foxhole on their property. Once this is all over, we'll fill it in. I'm sure we can find something nice to do for them as a thank you."

"Sure, I'll try to call them. I have to say, I hope within twenty-four hours the problem with Dan is no more. I'd hate to think we'll have to be watching over our shoulders for who knows how long."

Jake gives me a look, and I instantly realize what I've said. "Huh. I guess I'm still thinking we're in a normal situation. I guess, until things return to normal and we know law and order is restored, there's likely to be more than just Dan Morse to worry about."

"Sad, but true," Kelley declares, while patting my arm. "Don't worry, sweetie, we're all having a hard time remembering things are different. I still turn on the light switch each time I enter a room."

Everyone gives a dull courtesy laugh.

"There's something else we want to mention," Phil says. "A few people are starting to run low on food. Or, more accurately, components to make a complete meal."

"Already?" Jake asks. "It's only been just over a week since the planes went down. And the power's only been out since Saturday. I know the saying most people only keep three days' worth of food on hand, but I wouldn't have expected that here."

"True, and if it were winter, they'd have more. Plus, I don't think people's cabinets are completely empty. It's more like the easy stuff is gone and many people are limited with their cooking options. Sally-Ann is one of them. Her house is completely electric. She has a propane grill, but is almost out of fuel, and all the easy heat-and-eat food she could cook on the grill is gone."

Jake nods and says, "Ah… makes sense. What are you thinking?"

"That's the hard thing. Phil and I have talked about it, but we can't really come up with a solution we're fully comfortable with," Kelley sighs.

"Same here," Evan says, "Doris and I chatted about it also. You know there are a few of us who do more than keep things on hand for a winter storm. I know we all don't really talk about it, but we've made a point of stocking up on meat, as evidenced by the multitude of chest freezers we own, which I'm trying to keep frozen as we speak."

So there's my answer to their processed meat question. Not completed.

"How many people are we talking about?" I ask.

"Just a few so far, mostly single people, like Sally-Ann, and one family we know of. Of course, *know of* is the operative phrase. The Bakerville community is pretty spread out, don't really know what's happening with the people who haven't been coming into the community center or staying in contact with someone. I suppose we ought to check on them," Phil says wearily.

Kelley gently admonishes, "Phil, honey, I know you don't like hearing this, but there's only so much you… we… can do. How many people live under the umbrella of the Bakerville community? Three hundred seventy-five? Four hundred? We've talked about this. You can't take care of all of them."

"What does Fred say about this?" I ask.

"Good question," Phil says. "We talked with him, Judge Avery, and Jon earlier about the food situation. Helen and Andy's supplies will be put toward the community use, but *how* is the question. Right now, Fred has posted a guard at the house. The judge suggested, once word gets around, people might start helping themselves."

Jake and I both nod. Unfortunately, if people are starting to get hungry, they might do things they'd never have thought about doing before the world fell apart, such as stealing from their neighbor.

"We talked about setting up something like neighborhood watch people," Evan says. "Maybe have one person in charge of each area or section. They check on their group and report back to… I don't know, a committee or something. With the phones on the mend, something like this would work and become easier.

"Fred likes the idea but says he isn't the one to head it up. Judge Avery suggested Phil and Kelley be in charge because of what they started at the community meetings. I think it's a great idea. We know neighborhoods tend to do things together during normal times. Shoot, our group over here is always having get-togethers of some sort. Doris mentioned it at one of our meetings, remember, Jake?"

"I think I do. She was stressing how we usually act like neighbors, so we need to continue. I really like the idea of having a main contact in each neighborhood. With the phones working, you could set up a phone-tree of sorts. We used to have something like that at a church Mollie and I attended. It'd be a good way to find out who needs what and how the community, as a whole, can help."

"I don't mean to sound… uncaring, and maybe the bump I got to the head is adding to my thoughts, but shouldn't people also be

251

expected to take responsibility for themselves? Jake and I have spent a lot of time, and money, to try and have a safe place for Jake's parents, our children, their spouses, and our grandchild. We've even somewhat planned for the in-laws. And we'll be caring for Madison and her daughter since I found her and she's here now, plus we have Olivia's children.

"Kelley, I know you're counting on your daughter's getting here and have made provisions for them. And Evan, aren't Lindsey and Logan heading here as soon as they're able to? I love this community and most of the people in it... but I don't want to help others to the point of taking something away from my loved ones. I like the idea of the neighborhood watch or whatever you want to call it, but I'm not sure I want to help much beyond my own family, close friends, and immediate neighbors."

I'm rather surprised I've said this; I sound incredibly selfish. Jake and I have stored things specifically for the community, but not as a handout—as options for trading.

We know we'd be very generous with our trade goods but what I think I'm hearing sounds more like handouts. Plus, what we do have stored is nothing more than a Band-Aid. Things are looking bleak, and our food storage is likely to run out before the grocery stores come back online.

We've always known the one-years' worth of food stored would only be to carry us through while we learned to rely on the garden and livestock and had some sort of local barter system in place. And why am I so uptight about digging a hole on the hillside? We can, and will, refill it when things return to normal.

Jake is giving me an odd look. Phil and Evan just look uncomfortable. Kelley is nodding, as if she agrees, then she says, "I understand what you're saying, Mollie. And I don't think we're asking you to take food and supplies away from your family. I know you haven't been here for our meetings, but we're not making it like a... I don't know... welfare situation. The help that's been given so far has been more of an exchange. Jake set up the water and provides the generator and gas, but other than having someone monitoring it, people are filling their own containers. And, Jake, correct me if I'm wrong, but haven't people even been offering you things in trade?"

Jake looks me directly in the eyes, nods, and then kisses me on the nose. I suddenly feel like a heel.

Kelley's not done with me yet. "We probably didn't make it very clear what we were thinking of for people like Sally-Ann. She still has food stuff, and we were thinking we could trade the things she has— flour, rice, and other things she can't cook—for things she can cook. Or maybe we should start some sort of soup kitchen at the community center and people can do something to earn meals. I don't know, but I can't sit by and let our friends and neighbors go hungry. Mick Michaelson has offered to butcher one of his cull cows, and he'll be agreeable to more as time goes on. Without refrigeration in most homes, we'll need to cook it up quick or can it or something. That will be a help. And, Mollie, dear, I know you can't let people go hungry either. I do think your bump on the head and the trauma of recent days is coming out."

Her tone carries no reprimand, simply matter of fact assessment. I've heard this tone from her before and think of it as her "shrink voice," which is likely what I need. She's absolutely right, I wouldn't even think of letting someone go hungry if there's something I can do about it. I nod solemnly.

"Another thing we talked with Fred and the judge about—and I'm not sure you all will care for this much, but it needs to be considered— is the empty homes," Kelley says. "There are many from our community who were away when things fell apart. Not just like Mollie on a business trip alone, but entire families on vacation—the Styles, Pedersen family, Hamiltons, and a few more."

"The Batemans, just down the road, left to visit their children," Evan says.

I didn't know that. Their house is one we can see from our place.

"Right. Them also. We know Olivia spoke to the Styles about an hour before the phones went down," Kelley continues. "They were in Florida with no prospects for heading home. They'd flown down and hadn't rented a car since they were staying at a resort. By the time they realized what was going on, they couldn't find a rental car. They even tried buying a car but couldn't make it work. There's little chance they'll be able to get home until things change with the power and fuel situation."

"Wait a minute," Jake interrupts. "Kelley, are you suggesting we raid their house and steal their stuff?"

"Yeah… I guess we are. It sounds terrible when you put it that way. But, yes, that is what we're suggesting."

253

"No. No way. I can't believe the judge would think this is okay. Evan, what do you think of this? You were a police officer. Are you okay with the idea of taking things from people?"

Chapter 62

All eyes turn to Evan. He doesn't say anything for several long beats, then he shakes his head and says, "Jake, in normal times, nope. But these aren't normal times. We're all very hopeful the phones coming back on is a good sign... and it is, for sure. But we also know the grocery stores around here have been stripped to the walls. With the fuel problem after the refineries were hit, how long until we start getting deliveries? Shoot, we don't even know what's up with the food producers and manufacturers. Is Chef Boyardee even still in business?

"We can hunt and fish, but right now isn't the time for hunting, too many calves and fawns. If we go killing their moms before they're old enough to survive on their own, we'll have shortages. Of course, taking a few bucks might not be a problem."

"What about testing for Chronic Wasting?" I interrupt.

Evan and Phil look at me like I have two heads, Kelley looks confused, while Jake gives a small nod. I hurry on, "Our area is testing positive way too much. We were fortunate to come up negative with last year's deer and elk. But how many of your friends tested positive last year, Jake... ones hunting in units with check stations?"

"Several. Many hunt units have been hard hit. I heard a rumor, I don't know if it's accurate, but almost 50 percent of the deer tested in some of the units came back positive. Our unit didn't have any... but we don't have a check station. We're responsible for sending our own test kits in. Mollie's right. It's something to think about."

"Zombie Deer? How can that be a threat?" Phil sounds dismayed.

Jake shrugs and then motions to me. "Ask her. She's done a lot of research on it over the past couple of years."

"Okay, Mollie. Go ahead," Phil says with a sigh.

"It might not be a threat. The thing is, we don't really know. Deer or elk infected with Chronic Wasting Disease—CWD or Zombie Deer, as Phil called them—have a prion disease similar to Mad Cow disease in cattle or scrapies in sheep and goats. Squirrels and other mammals can also get their own type of prion disease... I can't remember what it's called. Humans too. One of the most infamous prion diseases in humans is kuru, it affected... hmmm, a tribe

255

somewhere… New Guinea, maybe? Anyway, they were cannibals and ate the brains of dead people as part of a funeral ritual."

"Ewww," Evan says, while Phil makes a face. Jake doesn't react. He's heard my rhetoric before. Kelley nods and says, "I remember reading about them. Go on, Mollie."

"Yeah, so, anyway, the prions are abnormal proteins which spread and create additional abnormal proteins. This leads to brain damage and affects the nervous system… which is how the term Zombie Deer was coined; they stumble around like zombies. Prion diseases are always fatal. In humans, the demise tends to be pretty fast but in deer, elk, moose—oh, not antelope. They're a different species and aren't currently affected—but the cervids, they can all be affected, and it can take eighteen months to five years before they show any symptoms."

"Wait. You're suggesting a healthy-looking deer could have CWD? I thought we just had to look out for the sick ones and not shoot those," Phil asks in a worried voice, which matches Evan's face.

"It's possible," I shrug. "That's the thing, we don't know. Without a test, we can only guess. And we don't have a home test. It's something I tried to find, but I guess it doesn't exist. I did read they were working on a field test kit that would look for a specific bacteria—which is one theory of CWD, that it's a by-product of a bacteria and not a prion—but as far as I know, it wasn't yet available. Besides, the guy saying it's a bacteria is in the minority. Pretty much everyone else says the science proves it's a prion. Before, we got a test performed at Game and Fish and they sent us the results. There's a couple of over-the-counter test kits, which work the same and the results come from a lab, but now, of course, we have no way to send in for the results."

"Can we do an autopsy?" Kelley asks.

"I don't know. I've saved quite a bit about CWD to flash drives. There's some diagrams and things that might make sense to you."

"Even if a deer or elk was infected," Phil says, "we could still eat it, right?"

"That, Phil, is the million-dollar question. Tell 'em, Mollie," Jake says.

"The CDC had some guidelines. Things like don't shoot animals that look sick."

"Yep. Knew that one," Phil says with a nod.

"Right, seems like common sense anyway. And the next one, wear gloves when field dressing or handling the meat."

"We do that," Evan nods. "Doris insists on it."

I give him a smile, so he knows I know. "Don't handle the organs, specifically the brain and spinal cord tissues. They, of course, recommend testing all meat in areas known to have CWD... which Wyoming is. In fact, I think it has been reported in every Wyoming county and many of the counties in Montana... especially the ones that are our nearby neighbors."

"Well, that makes sense," Evan says. "We all know the herd doesn't recognize state lines and goes back and forth."

"Sure. So we're back to the fact the CDC says we should test since it's here... and by here, we don't really know how many deer or elk are infected. Elk... it's not thought to be many, and last year, none tested positive in our area, so that's good. We have the occasional moose stroll through Bakerville, and there are some up in the wilderness, but CWD is still pretty rare in moose, so I wouldn't worry about them. But deer, they're not so good. Official estimates are 10 to 25 percent of the deer population could be infected.

"Unofficially, there's talk of as many as 50 percent. Game and Fish makes a point of saying something like, 'CWD is likely under or overrepresented because of small sample sizes in some areas,' so... we don't know. They were supposed to start some sort of task force to come up with a management plan. I don't know what became of it... not that it matters now."

"How can it be managed?" Kelley asks.

"I don't know. There isn't a treatment for it, even though there were rumors one was being developed... and it's always fatal. It's passed by saliva and bodily fluids, and prions can even live in the ground. Scrapies, the prions affecting sheep and goats, survives in the soil for years. They believe it's the same with CWD but are continuing to test this theory. The scary thing to me is, they don't know if it can jump to humans by eating infected meat."

"How about we just cook the meat extra well? Even though it will taste terrible, it should solve the problem, right?" Evan, always a fan of rare meat, asks.

Kelley, shaking her head, says, "Prions are forever. At least in humans, I know they're forever. They've done experiments on affected brains. Heat, cold, chemicals... nothing killed the prions.

257

Even time. One experiment, I can't remember all of the details, but they preserved the affected tissues for years. They liquefied and diluted it and injected it into mice. Several of the mice got the disease."

"Exactly. It's believed the same in cervids—the prions are forever. That's the trouble with it and why the CDC recommended not eating meat with confirmed CWD."

We sit quietly for several minutes, all of us considering this new wrinkle in our survival. Wyoming has been hit very hard by Chronic Wasting Disease, if we lived somewhere not so severely affected, things might be different.

"So… I guess we should keep this in mind," Phil says slowly. "We don't really have a choice but to harvest game. Mick Michaelson is willing to donate cull cattle, but he made it clear he won't wipe out his herd."

"Only makes sense. Can't kill everything or else there will be nothing to reproduce for future years. Plus, when this is over, he still has a business to run," Evan says with a nod. "Even if a deer or elk is infected, as long as we avoid the brain and nervous system… uh… I guess the spinal column, too, we should be fine, right?"

"I think we could do that fancy quartering you do, Evan," Kelley says. "The one you tried to teach Phil last year."

"Yeah, gutless field dressing. We take the front and hind quarters, backstrap, and tenderloin and leave everything else in the field. It's great for deer and antelope, but for elk, we lose the neck meat. I guess we shouldn't be cooking the meat on the neck bone with the Wasting Disease threat."

"Yes, would be a good compromise. And take the meat off the quarters. Don't save the bones for cooking," I say. "Again, they can't prove it can jump to humans, but they did do an experiment with some kind of monkey, feeding them infected deer, and several became infected. But another species of primate, which more closely resembles humans, wasn't infected. The guy who thinks CWD may be caused by a bacteria also believes a certain percentage of Alzheimer's patients may have been misdiagnosed. Instead of Alzheimer's, they may have… umm, Kelley, what's it called? The most common human prion disease?"

"Creutzfeldt-Jakob disease?"

"Yes, I think that's it."

"Hmmm. Don't know about that," Kelley says. "The symptoms are similar, but CJD progresses much more rapidly than Alzheimer's."

With wide eyes, Evan asks, "And they got this from deer?"

Chapter 63

"No... sorry," I shake my head. "I strayed a little from our original conversation just to make a point that prions might be more common than we think. So far, there's no concrete evidence it can jump from deer to humans. Still, we should take precautions and avoid contact with the brain and spinal column plus not eat the bones."

"And definitely don't eat the brains," Kelley says with a shudder. "I think that should be for all mammals. I remember reading about the guy who ate squirrel brains, and he did get a variant of Creutzfeldt-Jakob disease, thought to be from the brains. It's a horrible death—we don't want that."

"So we also have fishing... there's no problems with fish, right?" Evan says with a wise-cracking smile.

"Well, now that you mention it," Kelley says with her own equal smile, "there are toxins and things like mercury in fish. We wouldn't want to make fish the staple of our diet."

Jake, Evan, and Phil all shake their heads. Personally, I'm not nearly as worried about fish as I am about Chronic Wasting Disease.

"Be hard to exist on fish. Especially as hit or miss catching them in our river is. Jake, you and Malcolm went fishing a few times before all this started. How many did you catch? Two each time? And you were there a couple hours?"

"Maybe an hour. But, yes, I agree with you. They stopped stocking the river, and if everyone's fishing, we'll fish it dry for sure. Of course, they did just stock the BLM reservoirs the first of May."

"Lobb and Hogg? Those are usually good fishing. We'd use some gas to get to them. What are they, ten miles?"

"About that," Jake nods.

I notice Jake doesn't mention we also stocked our three ponds in May with a few varieties of trout.

"Would have to make it worth the trip, but it could be an option. The river, though—we'll have the same problem as with the deer, elk, and few antelope we have here," Evan says, while Phil nods. "We'll wipe them out and be wanting for more. And if we can't eat the entire deer and have to quarter them out, we'll be leaving nutrition behind. Oh... what about the liver and heart? Can we eat those?"

"I think the recommendation is to discard all organs, and fat too," I answer. CWD could be an extreme hindrance to our survival. Head to tail eating and consuming as much fat as necessary makes sense in a survival situation. But here we are, talking about leaving more than half of the animal behind. Not good. Oh, I know it's necessary. My research has convinced me of it.

"Makes sense," Evan says. "Talking about this fully convinces me commandeering the available food is a good idea. And likely we're not the only ones who have thought of it. I'd hazard a guess Morse's place has already been pilfered. Phil? What do you think?"

"Possibly. Especially considering one of the first things we noticed was an abundance of electronics and other items. We think there's a good chance Dan was involved in the rash of burglaries our area has been experiencing."

Over the past few months, the neighboring towns, and even our quiet community of Bakerville, have been experiencing break-ins. The burglaries all happened when the homeowners were away and hadn't resulted in any injuries. The usual stuff—TVs, stereos, computers, jewelry—was being stolen. The pawn shops in the area were all on high alert but nothing had shown up.

"Why is that?" Jake asks.

"They had several TVs and other electronics in one of the bedrooms. Not hooked up or anything, just in there like they were in storage. Plus a drawer full of jewelry and other things. Seemed pretty suspicious. I suppose we should clear it out, if one of the others from that day hasn't already done so. Johnston was with me. You know, his house was one of the ones burglarized. I wouldn't fault him for going back and seeing if any of his stuff was there."

"Maybe he should help?" I ask.

"Not a good idea," Evan jumps in. "We don't want people knowing about what we're doing. Too much potential for issues. We'll have enough of an issue with Andy and Helen's house. We only spoke with the judge and Fred about this. They agree we'll get plenty of people angry if we do this, but... well, it needs to be done or else we could have people going hungry soon. So if we're thinking we can take the food from the unoccupied houses and use it for the community, we'd best get on it. I'd suggest we inventory everything, and if the family were to return, we can make amends. Somehow."

"Where will we keep it all?" Phil asks.

"Jake? You have room here to store things?"

"Shoot, Evan. Why would you want to store it here?"

"You have the best setup," Kelley says.

"Not true," I quickly add. "You and Phil are set up as well as we are. And what about the church? They'll already be taking Helen's stuff."

"Not the church. We need to keep this quiet, and there are too many people in and out of there. I think it should go to Phil's and your place," Evan says. "If a place is closer to Jake and Mollie's, bring it here. Kelley and Phil get stuff from near them. Both of you are well set up on your own, and there are no worries of you keeping the food for your use."

"How about the community center?" I ask. "Wouldn't that be better? Especially if you want to run a soup kitchen out of there?"

"No security there," Phil says. "People find out about the food and they'd try to steal it."

"You think they won't try to steal from us?" I ask haughtily.

"Probably will, if they get desperate. We need to help ensure they don't become too desperate," Phil says, nodding.

"What are your security plans, Phil? With just you and Kelley, you think you can handle it?" Jake asks.

"Nope. We had talked with a few friends about joining us if the time came. No one has shown up yet. If they do, it will be helpful. Right now, we plan to ask a few people to move over to our place. Dr. Sam and his family will be pulling their trailer over today. We're also thinking the people running out of food might be good ones to add. We like them all and each has skills we can use in addition to taking a turn at security. There's a few more we've thought of also."

"Sounds like a good plan. Plus, with the MacIntyres' place bordering yours, you could join forces," I say.

"Yes, we've talked with them also. They did remind us they consider themselves pacifists and aren't comfortable carrying guns."

"Huh. I guess I never realized that. It's not really a conversation that ever came up," I say. "Of course, in some ways, I consider myself a pacifist also. While I completely support our military men and women, I don't find most wars to be justified. But we're not talking a war in some far away land, which may or may not be justified. We're talking about preserving our lives, literally and completely. Not in a theoretical 'war is bad' sense, but in a 'holy cow, we might be attacked' sense. Yesterday, I shot and killed two men. Jake shot and killed a man the day before to save our daughter. That same sweet daughter, without a mean bone in her body, killed a man to preserve her life. This has now become a case of survival, not idealism."

"You're right, Mollie. But they'll need to come to that conclusion on their own. Kaleb, their new son-in-law, and his family who's stuck here after arriving for the wedding, made it clear they'll do whatever is needed. And the rest did offer to act as lookouts, but will not be armed while doing so," Phil clarifies.

Our conversation wraps up with the men deciding to go and loot the Styles' house right away. I'll finish up what I'm working on and then be ready to receive the booty. I have plenty of mixed feelings about this but do agree feeding those hungry now is important. When the Styles come home, we can make amends.

I did briefly consider, since Phil and Kelley are going to invite the people who run out of food to their place, raising an objection again. But then, I realized the food will likely still be needed. If it wasn't, Kelley and Phil wouldn't have suggested we use it.

Evan says he'll bring my canners back down. I thank him and let him know I'd be happy to work on canning their meat while I do ours and he should move some to the fridge to thaw.

"I have some in a cooler to make into jerky. I just haven't had the time to get it going. Doris took it out the morning we went scavenging."

"Bring it down with the canners, and I'll do it first. With the outdoor canning setup plus being able to can inside, I can have up to five pressure canners going at one time. Bring Doris's canner also."

"Thanks, Mollie. I appreciate it. Are you making jerky also?"

"Yes, I'm going to have Jake get the smoker going, but probably not until tomorrow. I'll just can what you have thawed out since I'm ready for that."

Evan gives me a nod, and Kelley hugs me tight as they leave, saying, "Try to rest. The events of the past several days have taken a toll on you. Let's try to chat tomorrow."

"Sure, sounds fine," I say with a wobbly smile.

Chapter 64

I spend several minutes having a good cry, suddenly feeling completely overwhelmed, before returning to my preservation tasks. The addition of Doris's pressure canner will help to move things along, with the range in my house and our outdoor kitchen set up for pressure or water bath canning.

Also set up near the outdoor kitchen is our solar food dehydrator: a simple box with a screen on the bottom and a removable screen door on top. It's as low-tech as it gets. With a bit of wind, common in Wyoming, and the heat from the sun, I expect to have the veggies dehydrated in two or three days. At night, I'll move the contraption within the outdoor kitchen and cover it with a cloth to prevent dew from adding moisture.

Back in my kitchen, I marvel at being home. Our main entrance opens up to a small foyer. The living room—or great room, as many call it—is directly ahead. Our masonry-surrounded woodstove is on the left, with my office beyond, sharing the woodstove wall and providing cozy warmth to the room. A door from the office leads to the master bed and bath.

Back in the great room is a small hallway connecting the guest bath, guest room, and staircase to the second floor, where Malcolm's bedroom, bathroom, and a TV room, or as we call it, the loft room, are located.

There truly is no place like home, and there's definitely no place like my kitchen. We designed it to be the heart of the home.

The great room opens up to the kitchen, with a raised breakfast bar providing a barrier and hiding any dishes left in the sink. The decent-sized, U-shaped kitchen has plenty of countertops and cabinets plus an island in the middle.

The large refrigerator is quite spacious, a welcome addition during harvest season. A second dorm-size fridge houses beverages and is for minor overflow when entertaining. Of course, the second fridge in the basement can also come into play when needed.

The dining area part of the kitchen has large windows, bringing in the morning sun and providing a view of the treetops on the nearby creek and mountains in the distance.

The large table seats a dozen. The size of the space allows us to add additional tables and chairs as needed. Combined with the six stools at the breakfast bar, we've served thirty people before without feeling too cramped. The open space allows for setting up eating areas in the great room to feed even more.

Lois and Deanne join me to help with the food processing. Neither have pressure canned before, but they're willing to learn. It's fairly easy, and my canning books give us the detailed information we need to know, how long and at what weight the processing needs to occur.

We soon have the processing completed for the day with the jars at rest, then today's dinner crew takes over my kitchen. Hopefully, tomorrow, I'll have more things thawed to be able to move forward with getting it all done.

The community meeting is at 7:00 tonight, and I want to visit Angela beforehand. I decide to get a quick bite, skipping the group meal, and head over to Belinda's. Katie starts her shift at 4:00. I offer to drive, but Mike insists on taking us. He even offers to drive back and pick Katie up at the end of her shift.

Once there, I'm amazed. "Angela, you look great!" I exclaim, noticing her hair has not only been combed but put in a braid, a look I've never seen on her before, and her complexion is rosy. At first, I think she's wearing makeup but decide she's just healing.

"Thanks, Mom. I feel better. My head still hurts, and I'm dizzy when I move too fast, but for the most part, I'm not bad. I still don't remember the... shooting... or anything from that day. But I do remember all of the terrorist attacks and meeting Leo. It was weird how that sort of just came back to me. Doris and Tim were talking about the terrorist attacks and I overheard them. As they were discussing it, I suddenly remembered it. The planes going down, the bridges, the food poisonings, the cyberattacks and everything else. Jeez, what a disaster. I almost wish I didn't know just how bad it really is."

Angela gives a shudder, then continues, "I guess you and Jake are going to be stuck with us for a while. It's amazing you two set things up so well. I have to admit, sometimes I thought... well, I thought you were a little looney doing all of the things you've done. I mean, really, who does that stuff? You spent a crazy amount of money and time building something 'just in case' the stuff hit the fan? Not normal, Mom."

I'm a little dumbfounded by her admission. Sure, I agree, it's not normal, but of all of the children, Angela has always been the most supportive. To the point we've had in-depth discussions about preparedness and she even does her own food storage. I glance at Katie. She is also shocked Angela is saying these things.

Before I can give any sort of response, Angela forges on, "But now, it's obvious I was wrong. I'm terribly sorry for making fun of you and Jake."

"Making fun? I don't remember you making fun of us," I say.

"Oh... oops. It probably wasn't to your face."

"Jeez, Angela," Katie says, "way to go."

The whole thing strikes me as amazingly funny and reminds me of the way I was with Kelley, Phil, and Tim earlier. I bust out laughing. The more I try to get myself under control, the more I laugh. I soon have tears running down my face and can barely breathe. Angela is laughing along with me, while Katie and Doris look at each of us like we're nuts. I blame our head injuries.

We finally have ourselves under control and enjoy a nice visit. Dr. Mitchell and Belinda are letting Angela go home tomorrow. Doris and Madison will likely be released the day after.

"Mom, Tim said we'll probably have to move to the bunkhouse since I shouldn't climb the stairs up to the loft. But I'd rather stay in the Tiny House. I can sleep on the futon until it's okay for me to do the stairs. I think it'd be much better for us to have our own space. You think that would be okay?"

"I'm sure it would, as long as Dr. Mitchell and Belinda agree."

"Good. I asked them, and they said no problem. So make sure no one moves our things, okay?"

While there, I check in on Madison. She seems to be holding up okay, considering everything. She's had a couple visits with Kelley. She also says, while she'd very much like to go home to Durant, she realizes it can't happen any time soon.

The stories she's heard of the dangers on the road, and what she experienced firsthand resulting in Scott's death, are enough to convince her to stay in Bakerville for now. And Dr. Mitchell wants her to join the medical team as soon as she's well enough.

"You'll be joining us also, Mollie?" she asks.

I sigh in response.

"What's wrong?"

"I don't really think I'd be a good fit. I took a nine-month medical assisting course. I worked mostly as a receptionist for a doctor's office, and I don't really have the medical skills and training needed..."

"Neither does Katie," Madison interjects.

"True, but she does have recent training. Just in the past few months she's taken classes, and she's read Leo's manuals. I've not done anything but research herbal and alternative medicines for over twenty years. Shoot, I don't even visit a doctor unless I've broken a bone or something similar," I say with a smile.

She finishes with, "We need you, Mollie."

And with that, I know I'll help if called upon.

Chapter 65

Saturday, Day 10

Saturday morning dawns crisp and clear. I awaken with Jake's dual 4:30 alarms. Even though the time and alarm features never stopped working on our phones, he's setting a backup, a small battery-operated travel alarm, to make sure he wakes up. That's my Jake.

Our bedroom captures the first rays of dawn. A band of orange in the distance hints at the rising sun. Overnight we had a light rainstorm. It didn't sound like much, but every little bit helps. Today will be a busy day, and while I'd love to snuggle back under the covers with Jake, we both need to get going.

As I think about our day, my dream from last night suddenly hits me. It was one of those really confusing dreams where it starts one way and then goes in different directions, but none of it makes much sense.

The overall impression from the dream I'm left with this morning is a feeling of conviction. Jake and I need to have a serious talk. My past is coming back, things I thought I could leave buried and not deal with. Things that fill me with shame and remorse. Things that could not only change my marriage but other relationships. Even though Brad won't be showing up on my doorstep, my own internal condemnation is beginning to be a problem.

But not today. Today, Angela is coming home.

Last night's seven o'clock news update was short and sweet, sharing nothing new. No reports of the lights coming back on, phone service is still hit or miss, and—best news of all—no new attacks.

At the community meeting following the news, Olivia's, Tom's, Andy's, and Helen's burial services were announced for today. The burials will be at 5:30 for Andy and Helen, at their home, and 6:15 for Tom and Olivia.

Dan Morse's wife, Traci, will also be buried at Andy and Helen's. Andy and Dan had been friends at one time before some sort of falling out. Traci and Helen were also somewhat friendly. Dan and Traci rented a small place from an owner living somewhere in Montana, so burying her at Andy and Helen's seems smart. And an easier option, allowing for a service for all three at one time.

Tom and Olivia will be buried in the new family plot at Belinda's place, where Terry was buried just a few days ago. Scott, Madison's husband, is also going to be buried at Belinda's place at the same time.

Belinda offered the spots for Olivia and Scott. Olivia, since they rent a house in the community instead of owning land, and Scott, since there's no way Madison can take Scott home. Belinda suggested they could always move him after things return to normal.

Normal... it's hard to think of when we can once again have the lives we knew before the attacks. We're still holding on to hope the return of phone service, even if it's unreliable, is a sign things will be fine.

There will be a community meal at 7:00, after we listen to the news broadcast. When Terry, Belinda's husband, died, they had a group meal also—a potluck with everyone bringing what they could.

Now, several more days have passed since the beginning of the national disaster, and a potluck is no longer the best option. Instead, Kelley Hudson, Natalie MacIntyre, another community lady, and me will provide the meal. It will be a simple fare consisting of salads of garden greens, soup, and sandwiches.

We were pleased to find two sixty-quart stock pots in the community center kitchen. Kelley will make one pot, and I'll make the other. How to carry the full stock pot is my biggest concern this morning. I'm expecting it to weigh in the neighborhood of a hundred pounds.

That much hot soup sounds like a recipe for disaster. I'm also making many loaves of bread for sandwiches using our outdoor bread oven. The oven will allow me to cook six loaves at one time. I'm figuring on a dozen slices per homemade loaf, and plan to have a dozen loaves.

I started the sourdough bread last night before bed and need to get it in the oven soon so it will be cool enough to cut without falling apart. Jake will start the fire in the oven before beginning chores, the reason for our 4:30 alarm.

I can also use the oven in the house and in the bunkhouse since both operate without electricity—a nice feature not found on a standard oven but part of the specialty ovens we purchased. Jake went

269

around to the neighbors last night to borrow bread pans. I think I'm set.

Evan is providing several game roasts for the sandwich filling. There were several people who donated ingredients for the soups, salads, and sandwiches last night. I guess it was something Evan and Phil had suggested when they met with people yesterday.

The donations are mostly fresh produce, which have seen better days, also a suggestion from Evan and Phil, and includes carrots, celery, onions, potatoes, and more. There were a few canned goods given, and we'll use things found at the Styles' house as needed. My family's contributing anything necessary to finish off the soup, along with most of the bread ingredients and a few bottles of salad dressing. We've been steadily eating our own garden greens so don't have anything to offer for the salad fixings.

Sarah is in charge of providing daycare at the community center while the adults attend the funeral services. She did this for Terry's service also, the same day Angela and Doris were shot. Katie, Calley, and Karen will assist.

Sheila… I'm really starting to worry about her. I speak with Deanne, her mom, and find out Sheila is only stepping out of her cabin to have a smoke. When she's in the cabin, she stays up in her sleeping loft.

"Ah… that's not good," I say to Deanne, as she fills me in on Sheila. "You think it's some sort of depression? Maybe we should see if she'll talk with Kelley Hudson?"

"I wish she would. But… I don't know." Deanne's normally raspy Jessica Rabbit voice has a slight squeak to it. "She's so upset. She'll barely eat. I just don't know what to do about it. She seems angry over everything… stuff that wasn't really an issue before is now… extreme. I say the smallest thing to her, and she rants over it. Roy and I were sitting on the futon, praying, and she heard us and started freaking out. Saying we were 'pushing our worthless religion' on her. I just…" With each word, the squeak in her voice increased, and now she completely breaks down, dissolving into tears.

I hold her but say nothing.

After several minutes, she squeaks, "I'm sorry about this, Mollie. I know she should, we all should, just be grateful to be here. And we are… Roy and I are so thankful you and Jake were willing to let us join you. I know…"

270

I interrupt her and say, "You know it was partially selfishness on our part, on my part, right? I couldn't bear the thought of Calley not being with me if... if things went bad in our world."

"Oh... well, of course. But that doesn't really matter, does it? Even if you think it was selfish, we're grateful to be here."

I nod but say nothing. Deanne takes a deep breath. She shakes her strawberry-blond hair, almost like she's clearing out the disturbing thoughts. "Anyway, we really are thankful you opened your home to us. I'm sure Sheila will be fine in a few days." The tone and timbre of her voice has returned to its wonderful, husky quality. "I'm going back to the cabin for a bit. I'll return to help shortly."

While Sheila's mental health is concerning, I know there isn't much I can do about it at the moment. There are so many things going on, Sheila is just one piece of the rather large puzzle.

Chapter 66

The clean out of the Styles' place went well yesterday. I was amazed at the amount of food and other useable goods brought back. I have yet to start the organizing and inventory. Jake told me about some of the finds, which will be very useful.

We made a cache of some of the personal things we found, knowing they'd want to keep them. The general consensus is, anything left at the house could meet an undesirable end. I'm pleased they thought to pull out the potatoes found in the pantry, just starting to grow eyes, to use in the soup. Of course, the items left in the fridge and freezer weren't salvageable for humans. Some is fine for livestock; some just needs to be burned. They brought those things back in garbage bags.

Today they plan to go to the Hamiltons' house and repeat the procedure. Those goods will go to Kelley so I have time to deal with the mess I already have.

Jake also made a few more caches for us. We'd already set up a few in various spots on our land, the adjacent public land, and up in the national forest. When I asked him why, he had no good answer. Just a feeling.

I'm one who operates by my gut a lot, so I can understand this answer. He drew rudimentary maps of the new caches and stashed them in our gun room, along with the maps of our original caches.

At ten o'clock, Sarah, Calley, Katie, and I are going to pick up Angela. Originally, Tim was going to go, but it was decided his time is best spent helping get the security measures in place.

Calley and Sarah, who helped with those tasks yesterday, were also planning to stay home and continue their work, but I felt like the five of us needed a little time together. Even if it's just driving a few miles down the road, loading Angela into the car, and driving home. I know it sounds silly, and Jake even pointed that out to me, but I just want a little time with my children.

Malcolm will be staying here. I asked him if he wanted to go along, but he wanted no part of our "girl time," as he called it.

I start my day with a detailed to-do list so I can have everything I'd like to accomplish today on paper. Well, that's not entirely true. My day started with a rush to the bathroom to alleviate my upset stomach. Ugh. When will this stop?

I'll make bread for tonight's dinner once the sun is up, move the dehydrating items out and give them a stir, move more things from the basement freezer to thaw, empty the Schwan's truck, prep the soup ingredients, pick up Angela, process the thawed meat from yesterday—including page numbers from my recipe book so I don't have to search later—and before bed, start more bread for tomorrow.

Most of these items will likely be on my daily to-do list for the near future. I'm already beginning to feel like a pioneer.

While the bread is cooking, I work on the freezers. We've made a good dent in the Schwan's truck food, and with what I emptied out of the basement freezer yesterday for canning, along with our little portable hunting freezer, we're able to fully empty the truck.

The rest, minus what will be today's lunch, is in the basement freezer. When I return from picking up Angela, I'll fill all four pressure canners. Each will hold seven quart-sized jars, and each jar holds about two pounds of meat, making a fifty-pound dent in the meat. Woot-woot. Getting the meat shelf-stable as quickly as possible will be a huge relief.

When the bread is made and as much prep as possible for the soup has been completed, I decide to spend a few minutes getting ready to go. While I'm feeling better today, I'm still not completely myself. I'm tired and notice dark circles under my eyes. My head is slightly achy and my stomach… ugh, my stomach.

I reserve makeup for special occasions but decide I'm in need of it today. A little concealer, foundation, and blush along with a whisk of mascara seems to help.

I dress in my favorite pair of leggings, which sport small bubbles in a variety of colors, a long flowy dress in turquoise—to pick up the turquoise bubbles in the leggings—with a black tank underneath and short cowboy-style boots in black with silver accents.

Between the tank and the turquoise shirt, I'm wearing a corset holster, with my Springfield nestled on my right hip and an extra magazine on my left. While I do carry every day in my normal life, today I've decided I'm going to double carry. My black tank top isn't an ordinary tank. It's a concealment tank, with my little .380 tucked under my left armpit and a second magazine under my right.

Ridiculous? Absolutely.

Chapter 67

Last night, after the community meeting, we had a family meeting. We continued our earlier afternoon chat of providing arms for everyone. Evan and Jake took a few minutes to sort through the items from Red Lodge. Jake also did an inventory of our ammo.

Even though we don't know how to reload, as part of our preps, we have the supplies and equipment to do so. Many in our community, including Evan, do reload their ammo, so our hope is one of the neighbors who are already adept at it will be willing to teach us.

Truthfully, we should've learned this already, but it was one of the things we put on hold while we've been rebuilding our marriage and family life. Because of Doris's injuries, we don't want to bother Evan with this, so Jake is going to talk with another neighbor, Pete Fairbanks, to see if he'll train us.

It's not urgent, since we have plenty of ammo, but he doesn't want to put it off. Several in our family unit indicate a desire to learn the process.

When discussing the new security team, Sarah spoke up, "I was thinking about earlier today. Jake, you said we aren't forming an army but rather a militia. I don't think we should call ourselves a militia. Can we just stick with security team?"

"I don't suppose it really matters," Jake agrees. "But out of curiosity, why?"

"Militias are antigovernment," Sarah states matter-of-factly. "For all we know, it could be a militia behind these attacks. I don't want to be associated with that."

All eyes are on Sarah as Leo and Jake both clear their throats.

It's Alvin who says, "The history of the militia goes back to the beginning of our country, before that even. How do you think we defeated the British? They teach you about the Minutemen in that college you went to? Or even in high school?"

"Sure, Sarah," Malcolm chimes in, "didn't Mom do a unit study with you on George Washington? Minutemen fought alongside his army guys."

Sarah shakes her head. "Mom didn't homeschool us. You're the only one, Buddy. The rest of us went to public school."

Eyes wide, Malcolm looks at me and asks, "That true, Mom?"

"Yes, it's true. I always worked away from home when your sisters were in school… well, not when Calley and Katie were in junior high. But by then, they were older, and I wasn't sure I could teach them well. So they stayed in public school. Now, I would've liked to have taught them at home."

Malcolm quietly huffs, "Then maybe they'd know about Minutemen."

This garners small chuckles from the group.

Tate, very diplomatically, says, "Militia does seem to be a dirty word lately. Likely perpetuated by the mainstream media. But a well-regulated militia is an important part of our Constitution, in the Second Amendment. Officially, our militia now is the National Guard and Air National Guard. But with the way things are, it only makes sense we need to have our own protection, whatever we call it. Personally, I like militia. It sounds more… uh, I guess, organized than security force or sentries. Army doesn't sound right, especially since Leo is a Marine and I was an Airman—a Crew Dog to be exact—'course, my dad was in the Army, so it works for him."

"All right," Sarah says with a shake of her head. "I guess I see your point. And it's not like CNN is going to be here interviewing us about our militia, so… it probably doesn't matter."

Gently changing the subject, Leo begins talking about the day's shooting lessons. He praises everyone on how well they did with target practice and makes a point of complimenting each person by name and mentioning progress or a strength, while gently encouraging additional improvement. We were able to sort it out so every adult wanting a handgun now has one and is learning how to use it.

Sarah chose to keep my revolver. She said she liked it over anything else she tried. I gave her a simple belt holster and my "garter" holsters with a belt, along with two speedloaders.

Calley and Katie are pretty well set up from their shopping excursion on the way here. Malcolm, much to his dismay, won't yet be carrying a handgun but will have a few lessons to become comfortable. For now, a .22 will be his weapon of choice—a new one Jake bought a few days ago, as opposed to the single-shot youth model he's had since his eighth birthday.

He won't be on patrol or a sentry, and the .22 will only come out when needed. Likewise, Tony will learn to handle one of our other .22s.

This morning, Leo arrived home from his overnight shift at Belinda's and immediately started handgun training, with Sarah, Calley, and Katie as his first students. The plan is to become comfortable with carrying and drawing their weapons and begin carrying full time. We're well on our way to starting our own militia.

Chapter 68

A few minutes before ten o'clock, all three girls meet me in the kitchen. Calley and Katie are dressed in jeans, T-shirts, and athletic shoes with their sidearms visible. When they were very young, people would ask if they were twins.

Calley was always on the small side, so starting when Katie was around three, they were very close in stature and looks. Both have wild, curly hair, thanks to my wavy hair and my first husband's grandmother, a descendent of the Miskito of Central America and an African slave. Jamie's own soft brown hair and pale skin didn't provide any hint to his ancestry unless he spent a little time in the sun, then he'd easily tan. And when his hair would get a little long, the natural spirals would appear.

Calley and Katie both keep their hair long, so it's curly all of the time. Katie sports highlights from a bottle, but Calley has her hair in its natural medium brown color. The same color mine used to be before the gray strands took over and I turned to a bottle to even things out.

As adults, Katie is four inches taller than Calley's height of five foot even. When Angela is standing next them, the resemblance between the three is amazing. Angela is the tallest of the three, at five foot six. All share full lips and a perfect nose, compliments of their dad, and my green eyes.

Sarah, who always prefers to wear a skirt or dress, is in a very graceful vintage fifties-style halter sundress and ballerina slippers. Her dark brown hair is styled in an old-fashioned pageboy, akin to Rosemary Clooney's in *White Christmas*. I'm always amazed how she can get her hair to smooth out so nicely. She inherited very little of my wave. Sadly, she did get my aquiline nose with its prominent bridge and lips on the thin side. Sarah knows all of the right makeup tricks to make her less than desirable features fade into the background and bring out her natural beauty.

All three are wearing light makeup and look ready to go on a shopping excursion, followed by lunch at a top restaurant, rather than to pick up their sister from a pseudo-hospital in the country.

After telling Jake and Malcolm goodbye and confirming "we'll be careful out there," we're off. We take my little car—the one with the crease in the hood from a rogue gunshot while Jake and Karen were in Prospect.

When he finally shared the story of how he drove up on some guy taking pot shots from his house while the neighbors watched on, I was so thankful it was just the hood of the car. A few more feet... I shudder to think of it.

I'm driving with Sarah in the passenger's seat and Calley and Katie in the back. On the return trip, Angela will get the passenger's seat and the other three will cram in the back seat. Even though it's a five-passenger car, it's not really roomy enough for three in the back.

The two miles of gravel leading to the pavement is always a slow trip. Driving too fast tears up the car and the road, so I try to keep it around twenty miles per hour. They share snippets from this morning's shooting lesson with me. Leo showed Sarah how to use the speedloader to make reloading the five-shooter quicker.

"I had no idea something like that existed," Sarah gushes. "It made it so easy to fill it back up. I can see how it'd be important in a self-defense situation to get the cartridges back in as soon as possible. Definitely helped. I'm carrying a speedloader in the extra pocket on the garter. Speaking of the garter, I expected it to be more comfortable. I can feel the strap running from the garter belt to the thigh holster—you know, to help keep the holster in place—rubbing my skin. Next time, I'll put those tight bike-style shorts on underneath to provide a barrier."

"Oh, yes. I should've mentioned that. I usually wear Spanx or something with it. When I wear the thigh holster for my .380 without the garter belt and strap, it stays in place pretty well, but the larger gun might not. Do you want to turn around and go back to change?"

"Nah. I'll be fine for this short trip. I'll remember for next time."

We finally get off the bumpy gravel and onto the pavement. I think our road gets worse every day. We're talking about nothing when suddenly...

"Mom! What's going on? You're going to go off the road," Sarah shrieks.

"I don't know. I'm not sure what's wrong. I just... it won't stay straight."

I have my foot off the gas and we're coasting. "I have no control, so I don't want to use the brake… there, we're slowing enough, and we'll be fine."

I glance in the rearview at Katie and Calley. There's slight fear on their faces, but they seem okay.

"You've got a flat," Calley says.

"At the very least, I have a flat," I answer, trying to keep the alarm out of my voice while guiding the car to a full stop. Once the car is no longer moving, Sarah opens her door.

"No," I say forcefully. "You three stay in the car. I want you to watch in all directions. I'm not sure what's going on, but this doesn't feel like any flat tire I've ever experienced."

"Mom," Sarah says quietly, "it's him."

Chapter 69

And there he is.

Dan Morse walks out from behind a hill alongside the road.

Dan's a big guy—a couple inches taller than Jake's six-foot height and bulky. He wears his hair cropped so he looks almost bald. His left arm sports a tattoo sleeve.

He's outfitted in his usual armament: a sidearm on his right hip, a large Bowie knife on the left hip, and a rifle attached to a sling, allowing it to hang crosswise on his back. He isn't holding any of his weapons in a threatening manner.

I watch his right hand move to his holster. He rubs the butt of his gun, caressing it a few times before lifting his hand toward me, almost in a Hitler-style salute. Weird.

"We're okay. We'll be fine," I say, trying to reassure my daughters and myself.

Suddenly, two more people, men I don't recognize, come out from behind a hill. My stomach drops. I feel slightly dizzy, and my mouth goes dry. They each have their weapons drawn and aimed in our general direction.

"It's him," Katie gasps, "the guy from the river."

"Which?" I ask.

"The big one."

He's about the same size as Dan but has a heinous sneer on his face, which makes me think he knows something I don't, and it's not anything good.

The other one reminds me of what my dad would've called "a dirty hippy," with stringy blond hair, a ratty beard, and baggy clothes. He looks like he's in need of a shower.

"Well, well, well. Mollie Caldwell. Surprised to see you here. I heard you were stuck on the Left Coast somewhere. Figured you'd just stay there and dissolve into the horde. That's where you're from, isn't it? The Left Coast?" Dan says with a guttural laugh, as his minions join in the merriment like it's the funniest thing they've ever heard.

I say nothing. I look in my rearview mirror and catch Katie's eyes, wet with unshed tears. A sniff from Calley, as Sarah says in a whisper, "What do we do?"

"We fight," Katie answers softly.

"Yes," Sarah says, while Calley says, "I love you all."

Dan Morse tells us to get out of the car. I briefly consider telling the girls to open fire so we can take them by surprise.

Instead, I whisper, "Stay calm, do as they say. Keep your eyes open for a chance…"

The doors fly open and the minions order us to get out and keep our hands visible, or else.

Calley and Katie's guns are confiscated, as Dan says, "What do we have here? Your girls have some guts on them and carry guns? I'm surprised by this, Mollie, knowing your aversion to handguns."

I have no idea what he's talking about. The look on my face must have shared my confusion.

"Oh, you think I don't remember one of the first times we met, when I asked you if you and Jake carry?" he says. "You both looked at me like I had two heads. You sneered 'we haven't found a need for it,' like some hoity–toity sorority girl. It was obvious then, you thought I was some lowlife thug simply for exercising my God–given right to defend myself."

Now I'm extra confused. I'm a huge supporter of the Second Amendment and have never questioned anyone's right to bear arms. Sure, I didn't choose to exercise the right myself until a few years ago, but I never considered him a "lowlife thug" because he did. I thought him a lowlife liar because of the stories he told, but that's a different thing.

"Dan, I've never had a problem with you carrying a gun. If I gave you that impression, I apologize. I may have indicated I wasn't comfortable carrying a gun, but that was my thing, not anything about you."

"Yeah. Whatever. Lots of good those guns are going to do your daughters. My friends here had zero trouble taking them away from them."

As he talks, he again rubs his gun, then his holster. I've noticed this about him before. I used to find it intimidating, but then decided it's some sort of nervous habit. Even so, I don't like it.

282

"Dan, how about you guys keep those and just let us be on our way?"

"Sure, Mollie. That's a great idea. Not that you can be easily on your way with four flat tires. No… you see here, I figure the only person who actually saw me with Olivia is that girl there," he says, while pointing at Sarah "And, well… that's a problem."

Sarah opens her mouth to say something. I give her a look I hope she interprets as *stay quiet*. She must because she closes her mouth and looks at her feet. I'm grasping at straws now. I'm pretty sure Morse and his goons have no intention of letting us go.

"Dan, that's not true. Sarah may have seen you with Olivia, but there were other… indications of your involvement with Olivia and Traci."

"You leave my wife out of this. It wasn't supposed to happen the way it did. She just… never you mind. I loved Traci, and we'll just leave it at that."

"Dan, just disappear. We all know you're an amazing outdoorsman and you could take off in the wilderness and no one could find you. You should just go, start a new life somewhere else."

"Oh, I plan to. Once I tie up this little loose end. We'll be taking you ladies along with us… for a spell, anyway. My friend Bo here has been keeping an eye on your place and noticed your daughters. Of course, it's too bad about the other one… her getting shot and all."

I maintain eye contact with Morse but say nothing.

"Ha. You know, don't you? Who figured it out? Doesn't matter. My guys were supposed to take care of that nosey Snyder chick. Your girl just happened to be there at the time. 'Course, I didn't expect my guys to be the ones to end up dead," he says with a shake of his head.

So it's true. Doris thought she'd seen him earlier in the day, and while there was suspicion he was behind the attack on Doris and Angela, we didn't know for sure.

Why in the world is Dan doing any of this?

Maybe I get his fascination with Olivia. Several months ago, she mentioned to me he kept stopping by her place when her husband was out of town. She was beautiful and very kind. She said she wanted to discourage his visits but wasn't sure how to do that without being mean. I told her she should be very point blank with him and say he was not welcome to visit when her husband was not around and to not answer the door for him, ever.

But all of this… it makes no sense. Even if he is behind the burglaries, why target my family? Why target Doris?

I shake my head and ask, "Why? I don't understand any of this."

He looks at me with a grin I can only describe as evil. "Because I can. There are no longer any rules or anyone who can stop me from taking what I want. Oh, sure, we've got that useless Deputy Fred," he sneers, "for all the good he is. A jailer. Ha. He's going to protect you all? He doesn't know his head from a hole in the ground. People like you are a dying breed, no way for you to survive in this new world. Deputy Fred is just going to get you killed quicker. Bo, Sanders, and I are the future. We have what it takes to not only survive but to thrive. I've been waiting for this day.

"I planned on leading Bakerville into the new world, but your husband and the others think they know better than I do. I almost danced a jig when loudmouth Terry was found dead. What a surprise to find out it was his father-in-law who did it. I sure got a good laugh out of that one. 'Course, after I found out Terry was banging my wife, I wish it would've been me who killed him. Her infidelity cost her… boy, did it cost her. And Olivia, she was supposed to be Traci's replacement, but the tart wouldn't stop whining about her husband and kids. Can't have that.

"I already told you why I'm here, for your daughter. We've been keeping an eye on your place, waiting for a chance. Bo was watching this morning… oh, yes, we've been noticing you people digging holes like you're in the Army or something. You know the public land bordering your house? Makes a nice place to watch all you losers. We even know your little girls have been trying to learn how to use their big, bad guns we so easily took from them. That Army man living at your place set up a shooting range? Doesn't seem like something gun-grabbers like you and Jake would have."

I'm seriously confused now. We added the range three years ago. All I can figure is Dan hadn't been over near our place since then and he thinks it's a new addition, added since the attacks. From the public land, they'd have a good view of the house and surrounding buildings, but the range would be obscured. They'd be able to hear the shooting but nothing else. And gun-grabbers? Wow. He doesn't know me at all, I hope I can use this to my advantage.

The crazy nut is still talking. "When Bo saw her come out of the trailer house all dressed up, well, we thought she might be going out on the town or something. But since town has gone to pot, our second thought was she was going to Belinda's place to check on your girl. Imagine my surprise to get all four of you in one vehicle. Woo-wee.

"Sadly, you and the others are what they call collateral damage. Of course, now that I think about it, I'm okay with it. I suspect poor Jake will be brokenhearted over losing you all, and it seems pretty fitting. He deserves to suffer. And maybe, after I'm done here, I'll go to Belinda's and finish up the job on your other girl and the Snyder woman. Her ex-jack-booted thug husband deserves to suffer too.

"You know, that's what's wrong with this place. Too many old cops and too many old military people. This was a nice community to live in before all of those thugs moved in."

Before all of those thugs moved in? Dan hasn't lived here too much longer than us. Yes, several retired military and police moved in around the same time we did, but many, many more were already living here. I can think of at least a dozen who've lived here a decade or longer.

"Jack-booted thugs?" I say cautiously, thinking if I keep him talking, maybe we'll figure out a way out of this.

"Of course! You know, all those cop friends of yours? You think they're something special? Well, they're not. Who do you think enforces the stupid anticonstitutional laws the psychopaths in congress dream up?"

I'm not really sure if he expects me to answer or if it's a rhetorical question. I give a slight shrug.

"All those unjust laws are enforced by your jack-booted thug friends. Lousy cops choose their jobs and pensions over doing what's right."

Keep him talking, I think to myself, as I say, "Okay, sure. I see what you're saying. And I agree, there have been plenty of things supporting your view. I remember reading about a no-knock drug raid on a house... in Texas maybe... where they went in without announcing themselves, killed the dog, and when the husband and wife tried to defend themselves—from what they might have believed where criminals—they were killed. Turned out the drugs expected to be found at the house, weren't there."

"Exactly! That's what I'm talking about. And everyone's like, 'Oh, those poor cops,' when the cops were the criminals. And that's not the

285

only time. ATF, FBI, locals—they all do it. You think the ones we have living around here are any different? Nope."

"So what are you thinking, Dan? The retired LEOs here are going to go door to door and take people's weapons?"

"You'd like that, wouldn't you? Commies like you think only the thugs should have guns. Well, not going to happen. They're going to have to pry my gun out of my cold, dead hands. Enough of this. Let's get moving. Bo, you have those zip ties?"

I guess that's it. Keeping Dan talking went full circle back to me somehow being the bad guy here.

"Sure do, boss," Bo answers, as he holsters his weapon and reaches for his backpack.

This leaves the other guy, Sanders, with his weapon on all of us and Dan's handgun in the holster with his rifle within easy reach on his back. If we're getting zip tied, we're done for, our window of escape will rapidly diminish. Dan has made it abundantly clear they'll be taking us along for now—to do who knows what to my beautiful daughters—and then we'll be "collateral damage." No doubt they'll kill us.

Even though Sarah and I are still armed—since they never searched us—I'm under no illusions we can take on these guys and come out ahead. But what choice do we have? Katie said it in the car.

"We fight."

Chapter 70

If we don't fight, we'll surely die. I think Calley knew this when she said, "I love you all." I wish I would've answered, told them each how much I love them, how they have made my life complete, how proud I am of each of them... and Angela and Malcolm also.

Poor Malcolm. If this goes badly, he'll lose not only me but three of his four sisters. If we don't stop Dan, he might even go after Angela. And my sweet little grandson, Gavin; he needs his mom. How I long to hug Gavin tight and smell his sweet baby hair.

Jake will understand. He'll hate it, but he'll understand and know we fought. He'll be brokenhearted and proud at the same time.

With feelings of love for my daughters and family, I catch Katie's eye. She and I are the only ones with anything resembling current training, and that's limited. She's been taking Krav Maga for a couple months. I've been learning Yongmudo for less than a year. Calley and I took a daylong course a couple years ago. I don't think Sarah has done anything since the workshop we all attended years ago. I can only hope she remembers the training and sparring we did some twelve years back.

Katie glances at Sanders. He's within arm's reach of her, with his gun out but not necessarily aimed at any of us. My heart drops when she gives me a barely perceptible nod and glances his way again. I briefly close my eyes. I can feel the tears welling up.

This is no time for tears.

Katie, Sarah, Calley, and I are in somewhat of a semicircle, with Katie on the opposite end as me. The three bandits are facing us, with Sanders on Katie's end and Morse on my end. Bo, the dirty hippy, is in the middle.

Sanders is the most immediate threat since he has his weapon drawn. He hasn't done a very good job of keeping us covered with it, and he doesn't practice any sort of muzzle control. The gun seems to simply be an extension of his hand, and he'll move it at random.

I'm not sure if it's because he hasn't had any training or if he's just reckless. Either way, he's a wildcard. And my Katie has indicated she's taking him. It's only logical, with her being closest to him, but it hurts my heart.

Bo seemed to have more discipline when his weapon was drawn. He was careful with how he held it and paid attention to covering us. He even reprimanded Sanders a time or two to watch where he was pointing his gun. I'm glad he has his weapon holstered but suspect he knows how to draw.

Out of the corner of my eye, I see Calley make a motion. I think she's in on the plan, such as it is. I hope between her and Sarah, they can remove the threat of Bo.

Morse. I'm not sure what to think of him. I've never seen him unarmed and can only assume he'll be quick on the draw. The way he's always touching and rubbing the butt of his gun or his holster could be part of his draw practice. I have a small hope he just likes to carry his weapons around. I have to assume, though, he's proficient. Catching him off guard will be my only hope.

I signal Katie in the same manner to indicate I'll take Morse. Again, the slight nod and a wink.

My sassy little girl, her way of saying all in one, "I love you and let's do this." All those years ago when we used to practice our self-defense moves learned in that weekend retreat, she and I stuck with it the longest.

She'd often wink at me right before she attacked. My gaze runs past Calley and Sarah, both seem fearful to the point of trembling. Not good, but no choice but to go ahead.

I briefly think through my plan, can I draw on Morse and shoot before he has a chance? Unlikely. Quick draw isn't something I've practiced. A glance at his holster tells me his gun isn't strapped in. He's already unsnapped it, and he's ready to easily pull it from the holster.

Can I take him down while preventing him from removing his gun from the holster? I remember a sequence of moves Master Shane, my Yongmudo instructor, taught us.

Time seems to slow down completely while I envision the sequence. Jake and I practice this move, and many others, at home.

Jake is close to the same size as Morse, but not as soft and weighs slightly less. I've been taught techniques to overcome the size difference, and my momentum and adrenalin will play in my favor.

Even so, I know it's going to take divine intervention for the girls and me to get out of this. My girls... maybe they'll at least have a chance to get away.

A flash of indecision hits me, maybe this isn't the right thing to do. Maybe we should submit and look for a chance later.

Then I remember Psalm 91, The Soldiers Prayer.

"He will cover you with his feathers, and under his wings you will find refuge; his faithfulness will be your shield and rampart."

Oh, I know God hasn't promised we won't fail, we won't get hurt, or even we'll all make it out of this with our lives. But he does promise he'll be by my side, carrying me through any rough patches. And he's promised I'll never have to fight alone. I'm taking the completely literal interpretation of this and trust he'll be by my side in this. He'll cover us with his feathers.

Then another verse, which I can't remember the address of, pops into my head.

"Fear not, for I am with you; be not dismayed, for I am your God."

Let's do this. With Bo distracted retrieving zip ties from his backpack, and Morse and Sanders eyeballing him instead of us, I yell, "FIRE!"

Chapter 71

I'm moving before the word is out of my mouth. I'm on Morse like white on rice. A palm heel upward thrust to his jaw connects before he even has time to process what's happening. I immediately swivel and deliver an elbow strike to his sternum, putting the power of my entire body into it. An *oomph* escapes from him.

As he folds forward slightly, I move in for his right arm, sweeping up the inside while turning the elbow pit and forcing him to his knees. I'm going all out as I feel the elbow snap and he lets out a howl.

My knee, positioned under his chin, lifts up, throwing him to the ground. He hits the ground hard, moaning like a zombie, as the wind is knocked out of him. His rifle, still slung on his back, is pinned beneath him. His broken right arm isn't looking too good for drawing his sidearm.

There are two shots in rapid succession then... maybe a third.

Who shot?

No time to think. I keep going.

Dan's manhood is in a prime position for my boot-clad foot to land hard—and it does. Unfortunately, while on the ground, he's unsheathed his knife, and it's now sticking out of my boot.

Ignoring the pain, I've bought myself enough time to pull my Springfield. As soon as it's released from the holster, I aim and squeeze. One, two, three shots center mass.

Morse isn't moving. I take a final shot to his forehead. I've left a grisly sight with blood and tissue everywhere. I'm sure he's dead but remove the handgun from the holster and toss it aside. "Cold, dead hands," I whisper.

I crouch and swivel at the sound of another shot.

Katie is lying on the ground, curled in a fetal position. Calley is sitting on her butt, holding a large handgun aimed at Sanders. He's on the ground and not moving.

Sarah has her gun out and is pointing it at Bo, the dirty hippy. I move toward Bo and tell Sarah, "Shoot him in the head."

"No need, Mom."

"Do it anyway," I order, then turn to Sanders. The top of his head is already gone. Calley is holding Sanders gun. She still has it aimed at his dead body. Shot with his own gun. Seems rather fitting.

Sarah's gun barks as I go to Katie. Her blood covered hands are holding her side.

Chapter 72

"Calley! Go get the first aid kit out of the back of the car."

Calley looks at me blankly. "Calley. NOW."

She shakes her head, sits the gun on the ground, and runs toward the car. Sarah is at my side.

"He had a second gun, Mom. I didn't know," Katie whispers. "You should've seen me. I was like Trinity in the movie you like. I got the first gun away from him and had him down, then he pulled something from his leg, and... he shot me. But Calley, she took care of him. She was pretty amazing grabbing his gun. They're dead? Morse and the other one?"

"They're dead," I answer, as Calley runs up with my first aid kit. While it's better than a standard car kit, I'm not sure how much good it will do. I start opening it up, as I say to Sarah, "We need help. We're closer to home than Belinda's. Take the car and go."

"Shouldn't Morse have a car? They wanted to take us somewhere. Let me look really quick and see if I can find it; it'd be better than trying to drive with four flats," Sarah answers through tears.

I nod and pull out a zipper bag with tampons and feminine napkins. Oh, how I wish I had a compression bandage in this kit, like the ones Madison had. We do have a few in our gunshot kit, but it's at home.

Stupid not to have it in the car, but we packed this thinking it'd be used if we came upon a car wreck. The feminine napkins were even kind of an afterthought. Considering I'm supposed to be a prepper, I'm not feeling very well prepared as my youngest daughter lies on the ground bleeding.

"Lift your hands, Katie."

She looks at me, pale faced, and says, "You're going to use a tampon in my gunshot wound? Oh... I guess that would absorb some blood. Better hurry, I'm not feeling very well."

The hole is smaller than I expect. I decide against the tampon, at least on the entrance wound, and quickly press a pad in place.

"Calley, hold this here. Katie, I need to roll you over to check the back. I think the shot went through." I don't mention there's an insane amount of blood, and I'm not sure what all it hit on the way through.

She was hit on the right side. I try to think what all is there… liver, intestines… not good.

"Fear not, for I am with you; be not dismayed, for I am your God."
The words again.

I glance up to see Prospector Peak shining in the distance. The morning sun doesn't produce the light show the setting sun does, but it's still an amazing sight.

My mountain, my quest for home, my safe place. I stifle a sob and continue to evaluate Katie.

There's a hole on the backside, almost directly in line. It's slightly larger but not significantly. I decide to stick with a second pad.

The sound of an engine. A few seconds later, there's a truck on the road. The horn beeps and Sarah sticks her arm out the window.

"Can we move her, Mom? Take her right to Belinda?"

"Yes!"

"I'm cold, Mom. You have a blanket?"

"Can we get you to the truck and I'll get you covered up?" I ask, thinking how hard it'd be to keep the blanket on while we try to move her. I'm glad we're only thirty feet or so from the road.

"Katie, this isn't going to feel very good. We'll be as gentle as we can, but we need to get you into the truck and to Belinda's for help."

"I know, Mom," she says softly. "I'm okay. I'm not afraid. Let's go. It will be okay."

"Sarah, can you help us carry her?"

"Wait," she answers, as I hear the gears on the truck grind. The truck begins to crawl off the road making its way toward us. Sarah pulls the truck to a stop just a few feet away.

She hops out of the truck and pops open the tailgate. Then the three of us carefully lift Katie, with me at her head and the girls at her feet. I stumble with my first step, forgetting there's a knife in my foot. I do my best to recover without dropping Katie. The pain is beyond excruciating.

"Mom! Your foot," Calley says aghast.

"We'll take care of it in a bit," I answer.

After we get her in the truck, Calley grabs the first aid kit. She climbs up in the bed and is barely inside before Sarah is driving across the rough field, then on the road heading toward Belinda's. Katie has her eyes closed but her lips are moving.

"Katie, let me get you covered up. You doing okay?"

"I'm not afraid…" is her only answer.

I get Katie covered with an emergency blanket from the kit and then notice she's bleeding through the pad on the back. I take off my over shirt, wad it up, and press it hard on the wound. She winces but says nothing, then softly, "*Matrix*. I was like Trinity in the *Matrix*, Mom."

I nod and say, "You were wonderful. I knew when you winked at me you'd do it."

"Mom, your foot? And your face?" Calley asks.

I run my forearm across my cheek. I'm bleeding but not too badly. Morse must have caught me with an elbow or something. I never even felt it.

"My face is okay. Leave the knife for now. Call Jake. Put it on speaker."

Her smartphone won't connect, so she pulls out the flip phone I gave her as part of her bug-out bag. We hear it ring, and just as I think it's going to voicemail, Jake answers.

"Hello?"

"It's me. Katie's been shot."

"What? How?"

"Morse. We're heading to Belinda's. You'll see the car on the way. Best find Deputy Fred. He'll want to clean up… what we left behind."

"Okay. How's Katie?"

"She's here. You're on speaker."

"Katie?"

"Jake, I'm cold and tired. Bring Leo with you to Belinda's, okay?"

"We're almost there. We're turning on the drive now," Calley says.

Just then, Sarah lays on the horn, making a full racket.

"Jake, see you soon," I yell over the horn and nod to Calley to disconnect.

There's Phil Hudson, weapon drawn, using his truck as a shield.

Chapter 73

I start yelling, "Phil, Phil, it's Mollie Caldwell. Put away your weapon. Mollie Caldwell. My daughter has been shot. Phil Hudson, put away your weapon."

A wave of recognition crosses his face as Sarah slides the truck to a stop.

I yell again to capture everyone's attention. "I'm Mollie Caldwell! My daughter Katie has been shot. We need help NOW."

The reaction is immediate. Belinda, Kelley, and Phil swarm the truck. Dr. Mitchell and his wife are right behind them with a stretcher. Seconds later they have removed Katie from the truck and are gone.

Sarah, Calley, and I collapse into each other. We're sitting on the ground wrapped in a three-way embrace when Sarah turns her head and vomits, barely missing Calley. It's so close, and the smell is so strong, I almost follow suit.

"Sorry about that," she says. "It was just... so much blood. And the smell..." She pukes again.

We carefully stand up, the knife still in my boot, and begin to move to the bench near the front door. Along the way I step a few feet from my girls to alleviate my own upset stomach.

Jake's truck is turning in the drive, followed by Leo in his truck. How fast did they drive to get here so quickly?

The truck is still rolling when Tate jumps out of the passenger's side of Jake's truck. Sarah runs to him, as Mike emerges from Leo's vehicle. I'm in Jake's arms when Leo asks, "How bad?"

"I don't know. She was shot in the stomach. Not right in the center, about three inches to the right of her belly button."

His already ashen face pales considerably more.

"Through and through?"

"Yes, entrance and exit wound. Lots of blood. You should go in. They may need you, but first, can you help me with my foot?"

I gesture to my boot with the visible knife.

"Mollie!" Jake cries out.

"It's okay, doesn't hurt much but my boot is feeling a little sloshy, so I know there's blood. I remember impaled objects can provide

295

something resembling their own first aid, so... it's still there. And with Katie hurt, I didn't really think much about it."

"Okay, let me get my first aid kit, then we'll take a look. We'll fix your face too," Leo says stoically. I know he'd rather be in with Katie—so would I.

He quickly returns, opens his kit and grabs out a few items, then says, "This is going to hurt."

It does. Bile fills my throat and blackness swarms my eyes as he pulls out the knife. My boot is off seconds later. The metallic smell of blood fills my nostrils.

I swoon for a second, then relax. I'm not sure if I'm awake or asleep. Jake's voice, sounding far away, soothing, loving, telling me it doesn't look too bad and I'll be fine. The next thing I know, my foot is encompassed in gauze and things are starting to come back into focus. Leo cleans the cut on my face and applies a butterfly bandage.

"Dr. Mitchell will need to look at your foot as soon as... he can," Leo says haltingly. I know the focus now is on Katie, and I'd have it no other way.

"Thank you, Leo. It's fine for now. Go see Katie. See if they need your help."

He nods and turns to leave. He stops and says, "I'll be out as soon as I know more."

Chapter 74

Time seems to stand still as we wait. What the clock on my phone says is five minutes feels like five hours. After another five minutes, Tim pulls in the driveway. Evan Snyder steps out of the passenger side.

Evan walks up and envelopes me in a hug. "You okay?"

"No."

He nods and then says, "Saw your handy work. Your idea for the coup de grâce?"

I nod but add, "No need for the one they called Sanders. Calley took care of him with her single-shot."

He turns to Calley and says, "I'm very sorry you had to do that."

Fresh tears come to Calley's eyes and she says, "Sarah too. She shot the skinny one."

"The dirty hippy," I say without thinking.

For some reason, this strikes Sarah and Calley as funny. Both say, "Mom!" in a shocked voice and then bust out laughing. I join them, knowing we really don't find it funny. It's a response to the stress, worry... and killing.

Our men give us odd looks and shrug. Like a switch, Calley's laughter stops and she's racked with sobs. Sarah is trying to hold herself together, as am I. We fail, as our husbands do their best to comfort us.

Tim says he's going to go in and see if he can visit Angela. As he reaches for the door, it opens. Phil Hudson is there. His face telling a story.

I feel my eyes fill with tears again, as he says, "They took her right into the makeshift surgery suite. I wish I could give you some good news, but... at the moment, I'm not sure," he shakes his head.

Jake pulls me tight against him, his hot tears dripping on my shoulder, and I feel his body shudder.

Katie, though not of his blood, is his little girl. She was younger than Malcolm when Jake and I married. I know he loves all of the girls, but Katie and him have always had a special bond.

Dan Morse, this is what he wanted, for Jake to hurt. I'm suddenly so angry. I'd like to go back and shoot his dead body again—after I kick him in his privates again.

There's nothing for us to do but wait, cry, and wait some more. Tim is in visiting Angela, and we all squeeze in her room so we're together.

I'm startled by the ring of my phone. It's Alvin.

"Mollie? What's going on?"

"Nothing good, Alvin. We were attacked, and Katie was shot. We're waiting to hear. Is Malcolm okay?"

"Nope. Bawling his eyes out. He was with Jake when the call came in, so he knows and he's nearly frantic. I have to admit, most of us here aren't much better. With Angela hurt the other day and now Katie, this is a little much for us old folks to handle. Thought it'd be safe up here in Bakerville..." His voice fades off, likely realizing he's saying more than he should at the moment.

Truthfully, I fully agree with him. This *is* supposed to be someplace safe. We thought we were building a haven for our children, our grandchild, and our family.

"I know, Alvin. It should've been. They've been watching us—Morse and his guys. They were over on the BLM land. They saw us leave and ambushed us."

"I'll kill them," he says without hesitation. It's so out of the norm of his usual character that it takes me completely off guard.

"No need," I respond.

He says nothing for a few beats, then, "Ah... I understand now why Jake had Tim get Evan and follow behind. We'll take care of Malcolm and the other kids. Let us know when you have information on Katie."

"We will, Alvin," I say, as I click off.

Jake pulls me tight again and asks, "Malcolm?"

"Not good. Maybe we should go get him so he can be with us while we wait?"

"Yes," Jake responds instantly. "Phil, can I impose on you to get our son?"

Half an hour later, in Angela and Doris's room, we still have no updates on Katie. Angela had been waiting for us to take her home. She was dressed and out of the bed, even helping to put fresh sheets on it. We're sitting on the made bed and have brought in several chairs. Doris is still in her bed. The room is almost to capacity.

I'm surprised to see Madison in the doorway.

"Mollie. I heard what's happening. I wanted to check on you."

"Madison, should you be out of bed?" I ask.

She shrugs and says, "Tammy had me walking earlier."

Tim quickly offers Madison a chair while Sarah asks about Emma.

"Asleep. I can't carry her yet while I'm walking. You can get her if you want," she says with a knowing smile.

Sarah doesn't need to be told twice and soon has the sleeping Emma in her arms. They both look very content.

Chapter 75

Phil returns with Malcolm. Phil must have advised him to be quiet, and he's doing his best to accommodate. As soon as he sees Jake and me, he falls apart.

"First Angela and now Katie. Why are they hurting us?"

"Shhh, shhh," I say, trying to soothe him.

"What happened to your foot? And your face?" Malcolm asks.

"I'm fine. Just... small cuts. That's all. Leo patched me up, and Dr. Mitchell will check my foot after he's done with Katie."

A rustle at the door. Kelley Hudson. Her face is grave. She gives a slight smile, and I know Katie is still with us.

"It's not good," she says. "She needs more blood. Tammy gave a donation and Leo is hooked up to her now—we're doing it combat style. Thankfully, Katie is AB positive and considered a universal receiver, so she can receive blood from anyone."

I briefly wonder how they know Katie's blood type. We have EldonCards, self-testing kits we ordered online, as part of our trauma kits.

Of course, like the combat bandages, they're at home. I really need to rethink our kits.

Maybe Leo knew Katie's blood type. I certainly don't remember it, if I ever knew it.

"Will Katie be okay?" Malcolm asks.

"We pray so," Kelley answers. "Her blood pressure is dangerously low. In addition to the blood, she's on an IV for fluids. There was some internal damage, which Dr. Mitchell and Belinda tended to, then they stitched her up. She'll need antibiotics. We're fortunate Belinda did such a wonderful job of stocking up on emergency equipment.

"She says she always made a point of having things on hand since we're so far from the nearest hospital and you never know what can happen with farmers and hunters. Even keeping blood typing kits on hand was smart. Knowing she's a universal recipient means we don't need to use the kits to find a match for her. Who wants to be the next blood donor?"

Before anyone can respond, Malcolm says, "Me. I'll give Katie my blood."

Kelley smiles warmly at Malcolm and says, "You're the best brother ever. But until you're a little bit older, you need to keep all of your blood. You don't have enough to share. Maybe one of your sisters' husbands?"

Kelley looks around. Tate quickly volunteers. Sarah, gently rocking Emma, says, "I won't be able to donate. I'm pregnant."

My heart swells, I'm a grandma again. "Oh, sweetie! I'm so happy for you," I exclaim.

She nods and says, "This isn't how I envisioned telling you. I'd been thinking it was possible for a few days. I finally took a test this morning. I planned to tell everyone once we got Angela home."

Tate hugs Sarah and says, "We'll celebrate later, with Katie."

"Congratulations, Sarah. When things settle down, you should meet Dr. Mitchell. I'm going to take Tate back. Then, when I return, we're going to check out your foot, Mollie. Leo briefed me on it. You want something for the pain?"

I think about this. The pain isn't horrible, more like a throb and ache combined. "Tylenol or Advil. Nothing stronger," I answer.

Sometime later, with my foot looked at again and Tylenol on board, we're still waiting. Madison is now laying in the twin bed formerly occupied by Angela so she can rest a bit. Emma is in her arms.

Everyone else is either in chairs or sitting on the floor. Angela is propped up against the wall in the corner. Even though she's much improved, the day is taking its toll on her. She offered her bed to Madison, but I now wish she was in it resting.

I consider saying something, then Dr. Mitchell, Belinda, and Tate are entering the doorway and the thought leaves my head.

"She's critical," Dr. Mitchell says without preamble. "As you know, she lost quite a bit of blood. There was some internal damage we were able to repair. Her blood pressure is still low, but we think it will come up as her fluid levels increase. Tate's donation went well. We'll hold off on any additional for now. We'd like someone who hasn't been recently injured and isn't pregnant," he gives Sarah a nod, "to be here at all times for the next twenty-four hours in case we need to tap someone else."

"Critical? Like she'd be in the Intensive Care Unit if this was a hospital?" Jake asks.

"Yes, she'd definitely be in the ICU."

"Will she be okay?"

We're hoping for the best," Dr. Mitchell answers without commitment.

"Does that mean yes or no?" Jake asks abruptly.

"It means maybe, Jake. She lost a lot of blood. Mollie and your girls did right by applying pressure so quickly, but she was still bleeding internally. A few more minutes, and, well.... There's also concern of infection. Thankfully, antibiotics are something we have... for now. We just have to wait and see. We'll know more tomorrow or the next day. Your girl is healthy, and from what I know of her, she's a fighter."

"You have no idea," Calley says. "She had already disarmed the guy and taken him down. He pulled a little tiny gun from his ankle."

"It's a good thing it was a small caliber," Dr. Mitchell says with a nod. "It still did damage but not as much as something larger would've done."

We're all quiet and then Doris says, "I put off asking while we were waiting to find out about Katie, but I'd be interested to hear what happened."

Chapter 76

Sarah, Calley, and I all shake our heads. None of us want to relive it by telling the story. But at the same time, I'm so proud of all three of them. The story has to be told.

Tate, looking a little woozy, steps in and sits on the floor by Sarah. Leo, in the doorway, catches my eye and gives me a small smile and a nod. He needs to hear also.

The trouble is, I was so focused on Dan Morse, I have no idea what the girls were doing, only the end result.

I start with how we suddenly found ourselves with a car that wouldn't go due to flat tires and how Morse and his goons were on us. I mention how we probably should've open fired while we were still in the car.

Evan quickly says that wouldn't have been a good idea since we were sitting ducks in the car and we couldn't use it for a quick escape. He's right, but I hadn't realized it at the time.

"When we were in the car, Katie said we needed to fight. They got us out of the car, and seeing Calley and Katie were armed, took their guns. Sarah and I had our weapons concealed. I do have to say, I'm going to rethink how I carry. I couldn't figure out a way to get my dress up and my gun out before those… kidnappers… could react.

"Anyway, the girls and I took a self-defense class years ago. After the class we'd sometimes practice what we learned. *Fire* was our battle cry. I prayed the girls remembered. When Katie caught my eye, then moved her eyes toward Sanders and back to me, she gave me a wink. Something she used to do when we'd practice. I knew then she'd react. I hoped Calley and Sarah would also.

"Sanders was haphazardly holding his weapon on us. Dan Morse had his handgun in his holster and his rifle slung on his back. He never did have them out. A few times I thought he was going to withdraw his handgun, but he'd just rub the butt or the holster in his weird way."

"Yeah, he does… uh, did… seem overly affectionate with his sidearm," Evan says with a nod.

"Mm-hmm, for sure," I say. "Anyway, Bo, the dirty hippy, had his weapon on us. He was actually the most attentive, but then Morse had him get zip ties to restrain us. While he was messing in the backpack. I yelled 'FIRE' and went after Morse. I got his gun away and him down on the ground, he stabbed me in the foot, then I shot him. I could hear other shots but didn't know what was happening until after I was sure he was... uh... neutralized."

"Neutralized," Jake says dazedly.

I give him a look, but he just shakes his head and pulls me closer.

"I saw the looks you and Katie shared," Calley says. "Sarah touched my arm, and I knew she knew also. I don't know how I knew, but I did, Sarah was going to shoot Bo. I would help Katie. As soon as you yelled out, Katie pounced. She was fast. So were you, Mom.

"I barely had time to register what was happening when Katie and you were on them. I'm pretty sure Katie broke Sanders' arm when she hit him, knocking the gun away. Sarah drew and shot Bo, I think he was looking around for an actual fire and had no idea what was happening. I went after Sanders's gun. Katie hit him a few more times, then he shot her. I had his gun. It was close enough to the gun I bought the other day, so I figured it out pretty quickly. I guess my aim wasn't too good, though. I was aiming for his chest not his head." She shudders, then tears run down her face. Mike puts his arm around her and kisses her on the head.

"I was scared to fight. I was worried about my baby. Tate and I have been wanting a baby for so long." Sarah's voice fades off. She straightens her shoulders and says, "With the dirty hippy," this garners a small laugh, "occupied digging in the backpack, I figured I'd have time to draw and shoot. I'm so glad drawing was something Leo worked with us on this morning. I knew exactly what to do. I didn't realize it at the time, but I shot him four times. When Mom had me shoot him in the head, that emptied my weapon."

"You shot him four times?" I ask, surprised.

"Yes, I think we all may have shot more than we think. I'm pretty sure Calley fired Sanders's gun twice. You shot Morse six times, I think."

"No, three times, then a final shot to make sure," I say with conviction.

Sarah shrugs and Calley says, "I have no idea. It was so crazy. Sarah could be right about me shooting Sanders twice."

"Check your weapon, Mollie," Evan says. "It holds ten rounds? How many you have left?"

I stand up and safely clear my weapon. I'm shocked to see only three rounds. "What happened here?" I say with surprise.

"It's common," Evan says. "Your training took over. You neutralized the threat. Memory distortion is normal. I've heard stories of officer-involved shootings where the officer has no recollection of even firing. Calley, you probably shot at least twice. He had a wound on his neck also. I'd suggest all of you spend some time talking with Kelley. You're going to be okay, but she can help you through this."

I look at Calley and Sarah, both are crying. I realized I am also. A glance over at Angela shows me she's also crying. Then she says, "I'd better talk to Kelley too. I'm starting to remember."

Chapter 77

Several hours later, after a quick peek at our Katie sleeping in the freshly scrubbed second guest room, the one Madison had occupied, we head home. Belinda and Dr. Mitchell promise they'll call if we're needed.

Phil Hudson and Evan both offer to remain and be a blood donor if needed. We assure them we'll send someone back shortly. Angela goes home with us. Leo stays behind. My heart is torn. I don't want to leave but am exhausted. I need to rest and then I'll return to be by my baby girl's side.

Back at our homestead, we find Lois and Deanne have taken charge of finishing the soup and have even processed the meat I planned to do today—crediting my to-do list for giving them the information they needed.

Ha. I knew there was a reason why I've stuck with paper and pen for my lists instead of switching to a digital system. Lois even took care of retrieving the meat from the Snyder house for sandwiches, with Evan's permission.

Everything is ready, and they'll leave shortly to go to the community center. Roy, Keith, and Alvin went to the burials, wanting to be there if help was needed and to pay their respects. Karen and Art are handling the daycare at the community center. Tony and Lily are with Dodie, ready for a ride to their mom's funeral service. Malcolm quickly changes clothes, with plans to go along and support his good friend.

We had called Alvin earlier, so everyone knew Katie was stable. They also knew the situation was still serious, but we're all hopeful.

"You're just in time to help us get this big pot in the car," Lois says to Tate.

Tate, looking slightly pale, possibly from his blood donation, nods. Jake and Mike step in and offer to help, suggesting Tate have an orange or something and a glass of water.

I hadn't given much thought to the burials or the dinner tonight. All I want is to crawl in my bed. I can't believe Belinda, working on my daughter, didn't say anything about the fact they're burying her father today.

I guess that does explain why she wasn't around the last hour or so. I decide to pull myself together and go to the service for Tom, Olivia, and Madison's husband.

I check my watch, 5:45. I can make it. Jake tries to dissuade me but finally agrees. Dodie, as always, will watch Gavin. Sarah also hustles to get ready, wanting to pay her respects to her new friend Olivia. Angela and Calley beg off. Tim and Tate will stay behind as sentries.

Mike offers to go to our pseudo-hospital to be Katie's on-call blood donor. He'll stay there overnight to be available as needed. Sheila is still holed up in her loft bedroom and didn't even answer when Deanne asked her if she wanted to go along.

My foot, which hurts like the dickens and I was told to keep weight off of, is terribly swollen. Jake finds my old crutches, from a sprained ankle, in the basement. I wash my face, put on a touch of makeup, pop some Advil, and change my clothes. We're back in the truck, heading toward Belinda's house by five minutes before 6:00. I plan to see my daughter again after the service. I've yet to decide if I'll go to the community meal.

The turnout at the service is impressive. As expected, it's very solemn. Even more so with the knowledge Tom killed his son-in-law.

Tammy, Belinda, and TJ do well at holding their emotions together. Afterward, they thank everyone for coming and say they'll see everyone at the dinner.

Tony and Lily, Olivia's only family in the community, are well comforted. Tony is very stoic throughout the short service. Lily, age four, doesn't really grasp what's happening. She does say many times, "Mommy won't be home," with a sad shake of her head.

No one from our community knew Madison's husband, Scott. Pastor Ralph met with Madison for a few minutes to learn what he could. He does a fine job with eulogizing Scott.

Madison, under orders from Belinda to remain in her chair during the service, takes a few minutes to share a little more about what a wonderful husband and father Scott was. I don't believe there's a dry eye when she finished.

After the service, Jake and I pop inside to check on Katie. Dr. Mitchell, the wife, is in with her.

I knock softly on the partially open door and say, "Hello, I don't think we've met. I'm Mollie Caldwell, Katie and Angela's mom."

She's a very attractive woman. Of course, I've seen video and photos of her when the Grover shooting happened. With shoulder-length hair, a slightly round face, and high cheek bones, she reminded me of the singer Adele.

Today, her lovely face is covered with a surgical mask and her hair enveloped in a scrub hat. A small strand of hair has escaped. Very dark, black hair. Not the auburn color I remember from the news reports. She stands as we enter the room. She's short, almost as short as I am. She looks very fit, like a runner, but not skinny. I suspect, as a chiropractor, she's plenty strong. She'd have to be.

She steps to the doorway and says, "Mrs. Caldwell, so nice to meet you. Jake, good to see you again." She gives him a nod.

"June, or do you want to be called Dr. Mitchell?" Jake asks.

"My name first name is Georgia. June's my middle name."

"Georgia June," I say with a smile.

"Yeah, there's a story behind it. I'll tell you sometime. For now, please let's stick with June. Sam told me a few of you know, but we're still trying to keep things quiet... you know, about who we really are."

"Of course," I answer, "but with everything going on, it would seem you'd be safe now."

"Perhaps," she shrugs. "Sam's resting so I'm sitting with Katie. She's doing well. We're keeping her sedated for now. We'll likely start bringing her around in the morning. We don't really have the medicine we need to go much beyond then. Her vitals look much better, with her blood pressure still low but holding in a safe range. We're optimistic at the moment," she says with a smile.

"Wonderful! Can we sit with her for a minute? We're going to go to the community dinner but wanted to see her."

"You can. We're trying to be super careful of infection, so you'll need to scrub first and use a mask and gown. Do you know where the hallway bathroom is? Everything is in there, including instructions on how to proceed."

After scrubbing and donning our disposable masks, open-backed paper gowns, shoe covers, and a paper surgeon's hats, we return to the room.

"Good. You put it all on. With our makeshift quarters, it's important," June says. "I'll give you some privacy. Please avoid touching her for now."

Our visit lasts only a couple minutes before Jake says we should pay our respects at the supper and then get me home to bed.

I agree. Not only does my foot hurt, but now my arms hurt from the crutches and my cheek is stinging.

The turnout at the community center is very large. Everyone from Tom's funeral and then some are here. I suspect many people who went to Andy and Helen's funeral didn't attend Tom's and vice versa.

Jake and I barely knew Andy and Helen, so likely would not have attended—even without today's events. Tom, we had talked with many times over the years. At first I was surprised about Tom killing Terry, but the more I think on it, it starts to make sense. He always called Belinda "Pumpkin." She was definitely his little girl, and he'd do anything to protect her.

Everyone quiets for the seven o'clock news, which is more of the same. At one point I actually wonder if it was a recording from the night before. The good news, again, is no new attacks.

The topic of conversation isn't the news we heard on the radio, but rather the news regarding my family. The Bakerville telegram system is alive and well, and everyone knows we killed Morse, Bo, and Sanders. They know Katie is fighting for her life.

People don't really know how to act around me. I'm a killer.

Not only Morse but the two guys on the highway after they killed Madison's husband. Some people are uncomfortable, while others seem to be in awe. Killing the guys from the highway isn't quite the same as killing Morse.

Morse was a local. He lived in our community for seven or eight years—even longer than Jake and I have lived here. While most people thought him odd, I'm sure many liked him. Even though he's behind the burglaries, killed his wife, kidnapped and killed Olivia, and planned to kill me and my children, I think there are some hard feelings.

I eat a little soup and part of a sandwich, then ask Jake to take me home.

Jake and I sit outside on our patio sharing a cold drink. It's still too early for sunset, but the lightshow from Prospector Peak and the wasteland has started. Right now, everything is showing in pink tones.

I know, as the setting of the sun progresses, the pink will intensify, then turn a golden hue followed by a deep coppery tone full of fire. It will sparkle and shine. Even surrounded by the beauty, my heart is heavy.

I cry myself to sleep.

Chapter 78

Sunday, Day 11

I stay in bed when Jake's alarm sounds. My sleep was terrible. I dreamed of the attack, but in the dreams, things go badly. Not just Katie is shot but Sarah and Calley too. In my dream Angela is also there. She keeps saying, "I remember, I remember."

And the real kicker and weirdness to the dream, Morse isn't Morse. He's someone else, someone I've tried to forget. Brad. Who found me several weeks ago and has insisted on setting the record straight. He's seen the photos. He is certain he knows the truth.

I awaken with a start and have trouble returning to sleep. I had just nodded off when the alarm sounded.

Instead of trying to immediately go back to sleep, I take my Bible off my nightstand. It's been so long since I've opened it, there's a fine layer of dust on it.

We try to read the Bible together as a family each day, but that's from a Bible we keep in the great room, and we haven't opened it since I've returned home.

This Bible is for my own personal Bible reading. I often use the eReader Bible more than the paper version, but it's still sad to see the dust.

I read Psalm 91 and then try to find, "*Fear not, for I am with you; be not dismayed, for I am your God.*"

I end up needing to switch to the eReader so I can use the search feature. I finally find it in Isaiah. I've read Isaiah before, and I've tried to do some memorization but tend to give up before really committing the words to memory. I'm actually surprised I remembered it at all. Maybe I had stored up the words in my heart; part of another Psalm, if I remember correctly.

I read different sections of the Bible, and after several minutes, finally feel I can sleep.

A few minutes after eight o'clock, Jake quietly enters the bedroom. "You awake, honey?"

"I'm awake, just resting."

"Leo came back a few minutes ago. Katie is doing well. They've upgraded her to 'serious' and decreased the sedation. She asked about you when she woke up. You want to go visit?"

"Absolutely."

"The girls and Malcolm want to go also. Leo says we shouldn't all go in at once, but we can each spend a couple of minutes with her, you know, like in a regular hospital."

"Give me just a couple of minutes. Can you grab the crutches for me?"

"You need some Tylenol or something?"

"Just took some." I motion to the bottle of ibuprofen on my nightstand.

Jake is very attentive and helps me get ready. The pain in my foot is ratcheted up several notches from yesterday. A look in the mirror shows my entire cheek is swollen and bruised, making the small bandage on it look almost silly. The cut above my eye, from my bike wreck in Yellowstone, really adds to the affect. I resemble a prize fighter—who didn't win the prize. My head aches and I'm slightly sick to my stomach. The last week or so has been such a rollercoaster for my body and my emotions.

We take only Jake's truck, cramming Sarah, Angela, Calley, Alvin, and me in the cab while Tate, Tim, Leo, and Malcolm ride in the bed. Mike spent the night at the makeshift hospital in case Katie needed blood. Alvin will be the next on-call donor, spending the day there. Dodie decides to stay behind with the other children, as usual. She does ask if she can visit later in the day. The rest of the extended family also stays behind to work on projects or act as sentries.

Driving over, I think about last night's dream. About how convoluted it was and how, right before I killed Morse, he turned into Brad.

I know what I have to do.

Chapter 79

At Belinda's, the back seat and truck bed quickly empty. Sarah and I stay in place as Jake walks around to help me out—due to space, the crutches rode in the truck bed, leaving me slightly stranded.

"Here's your sticks, Mollie," Jake says, holding them up for me.

"Thanks, honey."

Sarah scoots out and walks over to her husband. I put my arm out to stop Jake.

"What's wrong, Mollie?" His eyes search my face.

"Um... Jake, I was hoping I could talk with you. There's something I've been wanting to tell you."

"Sure. Of course. Now?"

"Let's visit with Katie and then get back home. It might take some time, okay?"

"Everything all right, Mollie?" Jake asks, concern lacing his voice.

"Yes, sure. I mean... nothing urgent, other than the things you already know about," I give a small smile.

Jake gives me a curious look and says, "Let's go see our girl."

Dr. Sam Mitchell greets us at the door and shows us to the living room.

"The news is much better than it could be. We're not completely out of the woods, as there's still risk of infection or a new bleed. Overall, I'm pleased."

There's a collective sigh of relief.

"She's going to be okay?" Jake asks.

"Maybe... but my maybe is more optimistic than yesterday's maybe. I'll be honest, I didn't think she'd do as well as she has been doing. Her vitals are much better. We've lessened the sedation, but we're still heavily managing her pain."

"You have enough pain medication?" Jake asks.

"We have what was collected when Doris and Angela were first injured. Plus Georgia and I, along with Kelley, had a few things in our supplies. We'll be okay to keep her comfortable, but if you have narcotics, please let us know."

"Sorry, Doc. That wasn't something we were able to store," I say. "We have a few topical anesthetics."

"Might come in handy later," he nods. "Katie should be waking up again. You can go in two at a time but only for a few minutes each. I don't want more than twenty minutes total for visiting. As you know, the risk of infection is high. We scoured the room, after moving Madison out and changing the bedding. You'll each need to wash thoroughly before going in, wear a mask, and don't touch her."

"The gown, booties, and hat also?" Jake asks.

"Just booties. We have enough of those to continue to use them, but we're going to have to ration the gowns and hats. We need to remember we're not in a real hospital and just how precarious our situation is. Going forward, infection control will likely be our standard for all injuries and sickness. We have only a finite amount of antibiotics, and we'll need to start thinking about preservation and alternatives."

We worked out payment for Angela's care by trading some of our medical supplies and washing laundry—since we have a washing machine still in operation.

Belinda and Tammy are getting six chickens and a pig. The Mitchells asked for canned mean and winter gear along with fresh meat when we butcher a pig or goat. Kelley Hudson asked for an IOU—they have nothing specific they need now but want to be sure we can team up on things in the future, and she wants me to help on the medical team.

We have disposable gowns and hats in our supply, not a lot but a few. We also have a decent amount of cloth gowns, hats, and masks. Maybe we should contribute some of these things to the hospital.

Now is as good a time as any to start making trade arrangements for Katie. Jake must be thinking the same thing because he says, "Doc, you all want to start thinking about trade items for Katie's care? Maybe some of the anesthetics and—"

"We'll work something out," Dr. Mitchell interrupts. "Now, you and Mollie want to see Katie first?"

We scrub, don our masks and booties, and quietly step in her room. Katie is sleeping. Tammy is sitting at her side, reading a paperback. She rises and says, "I'll be in the hall if you need me."

Katie's still pale, but she looks considerably better than last night. I sit in the chair next to the bed, and Jake stands next to me. Katie must realize we're there because she opens her eyes and looks over.

"What's with the masks? You look silly," she whispers.

I smile, which she can't see behind my mask, and say, "Dr. Mitchell wants to make sure we don't give you our cooties."

"Good thing. I don't think I need to get anything else. Leo said I'm going to be okay. I feel pretty terrible today, so it's hard to believe him, but I want to."

"You'll be fine," Jake says with conviction. "You're doing great."

"We can only stay a few minutes. Your sisters and Malcolm also want to see you. Dr. Mitchell doesn't want us to tire you out. We brought a robe and some slippers for you. Can we bring you anything else?"

"I'm looking forward to a burger and one of those Schwan's treats. Make sure I'm saved something. I think it will be a few days before I can have solid food, but maybe ice cream will be allowed sooner."

"You got it," I say. "I'd kiss you goodbye, but we're not supposed to touch you."

"More cooties?"

"Exactly. I love you. We'll come back as often as we're allowed."

"Mom, I had the strangest dream earlier. I dreamed I was on your farm and a chicken kept trying to pull me under its wings. Sometimes I was a chick, but most of the time, I was me and the chicken was really big. With this chicken all over me, I should've been scared. I mean, it sounds like a nightmare, right? But it wasn't. I felt... safe."

Tears instantly hit my eyes. *Psalm 91.*

I know this kind of thing sounds, well, crazy. But it's what I felt, too, during the battle. Then, when my Katie was hurt, I was immediately fearful, and even angry.

These last hours, not knowing if Katie would live or die, have been terrible. Even so, I've still felt God's presence and his love. I knew if she died, I'd be devastated and even blame myself, but he'd be there to help me through it.

I've tried grieving on my own before, when I lost my first husband and then when Jake and I lost our dear friends Sharri and Kenny. Learning to lean on him, instead of my own abilities, is still hard for me. I have no doubt I'll continue to struggle with this.

315

Before I can say anything, Katie, with tears in her own eyes, says, "It was God. It reminded me of the verse you and I used to read after my dad died. The one about not fearing the terror at night or the arrow during the day."

Not trusting my voice, I nod in response and pantomime blowing her a kiss.

"He hasn't left me, even though I haven't been living the life I know I should. He's still with me. I asked for forgiveness, but I still wasn't sure... was I forgiven? I know the Bible says, 'Ask and it shall be given,' but what if..." She lets out a big sigh and smiles. "He did. He forgave me."

With my eyes full of tears, I once again nod.

"I love you, Mom. You too, Jake."

"We love you too. See you later, Katie," Jake says with a wave as we leave the room.

As agreed, the entirety of our visit takes less than twenty minutes for all of us to let her know we were there and we love her. It's not yet 9:30, and we're getting ready to head home.

Dr. Mitchell reappears and addresses Sarah. "In the next few days, I'll want to meet with you. We'll get your history and start a prenatal file."

"Sure," Sarah says with a smile.

"And, Mollie, I notice you're getting around pretty well. How about you let me take a quick look at that foot before you head out?"

I start to shake my head, but Jake says, "Great idea, Doc. It's hurting her quite a bit today."

"To be expected. Kelley briefed me on the wound."

"Okay, I suppose..."

Beeeep. Beeeep. Beeeep

"What is that?" Jake asks.

Sarah and Tate both say, "My phone." Calley, Mike, Tim, and Angela are also pulling out phones. I'm surprised all their smartphones are working since it's been so hit or miss. I reach for my flip phone, but nothing is happening on it.

"Please, God. No," Doris yells from her sick room.

Kelley and Phil Hudson along with Evan Snyder all come running from the back.

Evan, frantic, says, "Did you get the alert? Did you read what's happening?"

316

"No. Not this," Sarah wails.
Thrusting her phone toward me, she begins to cry.

BALLISTIC MISSILE THREAT INBOUND TO UNITED
STATES. MULTIPLE INBOUND MISSILES DETECTED. SEEK
IMMEDIATE SHELTER. THIS IS NOT A DRILL.

Thank you for spending your time with the people of Bakerville, Wyoming.

If you liked this book, please take a moment to leave a review.

I appreciate you!

Join my reader's club!

Receive a complimentary copy of *Wyoming Refuge: A Havoc in Wyoming Prequel.* As part of my reader's club, you'll be the first to know about new releases and specials. I also share info on books I'm reading, preparedness tips, and more.

Please sign up on my website:

MillieCopper.com

Now Available

Havoc in Wyoming

Part 1: Caldwell's Homestead

Jake and Mollie Caldwell started their small farm and homestead to be able to provide for an uncertain future for their family, friends, and community. They have tried to plan for everything, but they never imagined this would happen.

Part 2: Katie's Journey

Katie loves living on her own while finishing up her college degree, working her part-time jobs, and building a relationship with her boyfriend, Leo. When disaster strikes, being away from family isn't quite so nice, and home is over a thousand miles away. Will she make it home before the United States falls apart?

Part 4: Shields and Ramparts

The United States, and the community of Bakerville, face a new threat… a threat that could change America forever. As the neighbors band together, all worry about friends and family members. Have they found safety from this latest danger?

Find these titles on Amazon:
www.amazon.com/author/milliecopper

Coming Soon

Havoc in Wyoming

Part 5: Fowler's Snare

Welcome to Bakerville, the sleepy Wyoming community Mollie and Jake Caldwell have chosen as their family retreat. At the edge of the wilderness, far away from the big city, they were so sure nothing bad could ever happen in such a protected place. They were wrong. Now, with the entire nation in peril, coming together as a community is the only way they can survive. But not everyone in the community has the people of Bakerville's best interest at heart.

Acknowledgments

Thanks to:

Ameryn Tucker my editor, beta reader, and daughter wrapped in one. I had a story I wanted to tell, and Ameryn encouraged me and helped me bring it to life.

My youngest daughter, Kes, graphic artist extraordinaire, who pulled out the vision in my head and brought it to life to create an amazing cover.

My husband who gave me the time and space I needed to complete this dream and was very patient as I'd tell him the same plot ideas over and over and over.

Two more daughters and a young son who willingly listened to me drone on and on about story lines and ideas while encouraging me to "keep going."

Wayne Stinnett, author (WayneStinnett.com). A few years ago, I was looking for tips on moving my nonfiction PDF books to a new platform. I read Mr. Stinnett's book *Blue Collar to No Collar*, and while there were useful tips for nonfiction, what I really discovered was, I had a story I wanted to tell. As long as I can remember, I'd start creating narratives in my head and, occasionally, move them to paper. *Blue Collar to No Collar*, and specifically Wayne's story, inspired me to move forward. Imagine my thrill and surprise when an email to him received a response and tips on how to proceed in my own publishing. Thank you, Mr. Stinnett! I'm also a fan of his fiction works, *Jesse McDermitt Caribbean Adventure Series* and *Charity Styles Novel Caribbean Thriller Series*—very fun reads!

My amazing Beta Readers! An extra special thanks to Tim M. for his expertise in firearms and all things that go boom, Joe I. for reminding me to keep it simple, and Judy S. for always saying, "I can't wait to find out what happens next!"

And to you, my readers, for spending your time with the people of Bakerville, Wyoming. If you liked this book, please take a moment to leave a review. I appreciate you!

Notes on Mollie's Quest

For the fictional Caldwells, preparedness is a lifestyle. Many times, a book like this will result in a wake up to the need to become prepared. Or for those who are already preparedness-minded, the need to move on to the next level.

To help you with your "prepper" research, I've developed a Pinterest page full of information shared in Mollie's Quest. Go to: https://www.pinterest.com/MillieCopper33/havoc-in-wyoming-part-3-mollies-quest/

About the Author

Millie Copper was born in Nebraska but never lived there. Her parents fully embraced wanderlust and moved around a lot, giving her an advantage of being from nowhere and everywhere. As an adult, Millie is fully rooted in a solar-powered home in the wilds of Wyoming with her husband and young son, while four adult daughters are grown and living on their own. Since 2009, Millie has written articles on traditional foods, alternative health, and preparedness—many times all within the same piece.

Millie has penned three nonfiction, traditional food focused books, sharing how, with a little creativity, anyone can transition to a real foods diet without overwhelming their food budget. Her food storage book, *Stock the Real Food Pantry*, was the number one new Amazon Kindle release in its genre when it debuted in January of 2019. The *Havoc in Wyoming* series is her first foray into fiction, using her homesteading, off-the-grid, and preparedness lifestyle as a guide. While this is her first time putting a story into print, the stories have been rattling around in her head for years. What a relief to finally let the stories out!

Find Millie at www.MillieCopper.com
Facebook: www.facebook.com/MillieCopperAuthor/
Amazon: www.amazon.com/author/milliecopper
BookBub: https://www.bookbub.com/authors/millie-copper

Made in the USA
Coppell, TX
17 July 2020